Her Dark Lies

J.T. ELLISON

mira

Recycling programs for this product may not exist in your area.

ISBN-13: 978-0-7783-8830-2

Her Dark Lies

This edition published by arrangement with Harlequin Books S.A.

For questions and comments about the quality of this book, please contact us at CustomerService@Harlequin.com.

Mira
22 Adelaide St. West, 40th Floor
Toronto, Ontario M5H 4E3, Canada
BookClubbish.com

Printed in U.S.A.

Praise for the novels of J.T. Ellison

"[A] high-tension thriller... Alternating points of view raise the suspense, blurring the lines between what's true and false."
—*Publishers Weekly*, starred review, on *Good Girls Lie*

"An entertainingly twisted coming-of-age tale."
—*BookPage* on *Good Girls Lie*

"Outstanding... Ellison is at the top of her game."
—*Publishers Weekly*, starred review, on *Tear Me Apart*

"A compelling story with a moving message."
—*Booklist* on *Tear Me Apart*

"Well-paced and creative... An inventive thriller with a horrifying reveal and a happy ending."
—*Kirkus Reviews* on *Tear Me Apart*

"Exceptional... Ellison's best work to date."
—*Publishers Weekly*, starred review, on *Lie to Me*

"Comparisons to *Gone Girl* due to the initial story structure are expected, but Ellison has crafted a much better story that will still echo long after the final page is turned."
—*Associated Press* on *Lie to Me*

"Fans of Paula Hawkins, A.S.A. Harrison, Mary Kubica, and Karin Slaughter will want to add this to their reading list."
—*Library Journal* on *Lie to Me*

"The domestic noir subgenre focuses on the truly horrible things people sometimes do to those they love, and J.T. Ellison's latest, *Lie to Me*, is one of the best...an absolute must-read."
—*Mystery Scene* magazine

"Wonderful... A one-more-chapter, don't-eat-dinner, stay-up-late sensation."
—Lee Child, #1 *New York Times* bestselling author, on *Lie to Me*

Also by J.T. Ellison

Look for J.T. Ellison's next novel
available soon from MIRA.

For Ariel Lawhon, who helped me find those damn dogs.
And, as always, for Randy.

Her Dark Lies

Mr. and Mrs. Brian Reed and
the late Dr. Dylan Hunter
and
Mr. and Mrs. William Brice Compton

Invite you to join in the
Celebration

of the marriage of their children
Claire Elizabeth Hunter
and
William Jackson Compton

Saturday, June 12
Two Thousand Twenty-One
at half past six in the evening
Isle Isola, Italy

Adult dinner and reception to follow at 7:30 p.m.

This is a private event.
Please do not share the time, date, or location.

1

Beginnings and Endings

She is going to die tonight.

The white dress, long and filmy, hampers her effort to run. The hem catches on a branch; a large rend in the fabric slashes open, exposing her leg. A deep cut blooms red along her thigh, and the blood runs down her calf. Her hair has come loose from its braid, flies unbound behind her like gossamer wings.

In her panic, she barely notices the pain.

The path ahead is marked by towering cypress and laurel, verdant and lush. A gray stone waist-high wall is all that stands between her and the cliffside. It is cool inside this miniature forest; the sky is blotted out by the purple-throated wisteria that drapes across and between the trees. Someone, years ago, built an archway along the arbor. The arch's skeleton has long since rotted away and the flowers droop into the path, clinging trails and vines that brush against her head and shoulders. It should be beautiful; instead it feels oppressive, as if the vines might animate, twist and curl around her neck and strangle her to death.

She tries not to look down to the frothing water roiling against the rocks at the cliff's base. She thinks the ruins are to her right. From what she remembers, they are between the church and the artists' colony, the four cottages cowering on the hillside, empty and waiting.

A horn shrieks, and she realizes the ferry is pulling away. A crack of lightning, and she sees the silhouette of the captain in the pilothouse, looking out to the turbulent seas ahead. A gamble that he makes it before the storm is upon them.

Don't panic. Don't panic.

Where is the church?

There it is, a flash of white through the trees. The stuccoed walls loom, the bell tower hidden behind the overgrown foliage. Now the path is moving upward, the grade increasing. She feels it in her calves and hopes again she is going the right way. The Villa is on the hill, on the northwest promontory of the island. If she can reach its doors, she will be safe.

It is too quiet. There are no birds, no creatures, no buzzing or cries, just her ragged, heavy breath and the scree shuffling underfoot as she climbs. The furious roar of the water smashing its frustration against the rocks rises from her left, echoing against the cliffside.

The dogs begin to howl.

Climb. Climb. Keep going.

She must get to the Villa. There she can call for help. Lock herself inside. Maybe find a weapon.

A branch snaps and she halts, breathless.

Someone is coming.

She startles like a deer, now heedless of the noise she's making. Fighting back a whimper of fear, she breaks free of the cloistered path to see an old decrepit staircase cut into the stone. Careful, she must be cautious, there are gaps where some steps are missing, and the rest are mossy with disuse, but hurry, hurry. Get away.

She winds up the steps, clinging to the rock face, until she bursts free into a sea of scrubby pines. Two sculptures, Janus twins, flank a slate-dark path into a labyrinth of rhododendron and azalea.

This isn't right. Where is she?

A hard breeze disrupts the trees around her, and a rumble of thunder like a thousand drums rolls across her body. Lightning flashes and she sees the Villa in the distance. So far away. On the other side of the labyrinth. The other side of the hill.

She's gone the wrong way.

A droplet of water hits her arm, then her forehead. Dread bubbles through her.

She is too late. The storm is upon her.

The howls of the dogs draw closer. The wind whistles hard and sharp, buffeting her against the stone wall. She can't move, deep fear cementing her feet. Rain makes the gauzy dress cling to the curves of her body, and the blood on her thigh washes to the ground. None of it matters. She cannot escape.

When he comes, at last, sauntering through the storm, the barking beasts leaping and growling beside him, she is crying, clinging to the wall, the lightning illuminating the ruins; the ancient stones and stark, headless statues the only witness to her death.

She goes over the wall with a thunder-drowned scream, the jagged rocks below her final companions.

MONDAY

Insecurity is the worst sense that lovers feel; sometimes
the most humdrum desireless marriage seems better.
Insecurity twists meanings and poisons trust.

—Graham Greene, *The End of the Affair*

2

The Party

Nashville, Tennessee

The last few days before a wedding are the most stressful of a bride's life.

I repeat this mantra to justify accepting a fourth glass of champagne from the slim, silent, white-gloved server. The champagne is delightful, cool and fizzy against my throat.

I am well past tipsy, and thankfully, it seems the evening is winding down. The quartet is looking decidedly tired, and the servers have been circling with the macarons for over half an hour. All I want to do at this point is sneak off to a corner to discreetly rub the bottoms of my feet; I'm wearing my five-hour heels but I'm pushing hour six and feeling it. I am smiled, chatted, and air-kissed out.

I take a second sip, then cast a glance across the crowded ballroom to my bridegroom. Jack doesn't seem stressed at all. Quite the opposite; he is as relaxed and calm as I've seen him in weeks. He is in his element, surrounded by benefactors and businessmen, people of standing and stature. His dark blond hair is mussed, his eyes a bit glassy from all the toasting. The quintessential quarterback—impossibly handsome, easy smile, thick hair, oozing sex appeal. The kind of guy who doesn't flame out after college, but goes the whole way, becomes a brand, gets endorsement deals, marries a supermodel and has two perfect kids and an architecturally interesting home.

Though Jack is not a quarterback, and I am hardly a supermodel. I am tall, and I do have an awful lot of blond hair, but that's where the resemblance ends. I'm an artist, a painter. My talent is large canvas abstracts, modern oils. And even that has been enhanced by Jack's influence.

These assets don't seem enough, and yet, William Jackson Compton has chosen to spend his life with me.

Yes, that Jackson Compton, eldest son of the illustrious computer magnate William Brice Compton III, and his brilliant wife, Ana Catalano Compton.

This party is our last obligation before hopping a flight to Italy. To have our wedding on Isle Isola, in the Comptons' private centuries-old villa, packed with modern art and old secrets. It's belonged to the family for generations.

Personally, I would have been fine with the courthouse, but there will be nothing but the best for Jack.

At my request, the ceremony itself will be for our closest family and friends only, but because so many people wanted to celebrate with us, the powers that be—Ana, and our wedding planner, Henna Shaikh—decided a precursor event would be fitting. A reception before the wedding, complete with a tanker truck of champagne, heavy hors d'oeuvres, five hundred well-heeled strangers, enough staff to circulate food and wine for the masses, one gregarious groom, and one extremely shy bride.

And twinkle lights. One must never forget the twinkle lights.

This prewedding extravaganza is why I'm now standing in

an outrageously expensive Elie Saab column of the palest ivory satin and sky-high Jimmy Choo heels in the ballroom of Cheekwood mansion quaffing champagne as if my life depends on it. One wall of the ballroom has been lit up all evening with tasteful black-and-white photographs from our courtship, interspersed with photos of Jack on-site in foreign countries, holding babies during their inoculations and drilling water wells, part of his duties with the Compton Foundation, a hugely successful and popular philanthropic endeavor. There are even a few shots of me in my studio and my paintings. They look so fascinating in monochrome, it has me itching to sneak away to my studio tonight, though this isn't going to happen. A—I don't often like the results when I paint drunk. B—We leave tomorrow for Isola, ergo, there is no more painting time for me until after the wedding.

Jack senses me watching him. His smile grows wider, into a grin that is pure, sheer delight. *You are mine, and I am yours, and we are so very lucky*, it says. He tips his glass my direction, and I tip mine in return, then take a sip, promptly spilling a teensy bit onto the front of my dress. Shit. I have definitely been overserved.

I set the glass down on the nearest table and discreetly dab at my collarbones with my cocktail napkin, feeling the scratchy embossing of our conjoined initials in golden scroll against my bare skin.

Jack must have seen my faux pas because he crosses the room like a torpedo. He's not upset, he's highly amused, judging by the rumbles of laughter coming from his broad chest. His arms encircle my waist and he sweeps me up into a hug that takes my feet off the ground. He whirls me in a circle.

"Darling, darling, my beautiful, lovely, wet darling."

"Oh good, you're tipsy, too. Set me down, you silly man."

But there is a tinkling noise, metal chiming against the champagne flutes, which is how I've gotten so merry to start with. So. Many. Toasts.

Jack kisses me, still twirling. The crowd cheers uproariously, and my head spins in all the right ways. Nothing matters but this—this man, me in his arms, our lips touching. Forever. He's mine forever.

"Want to get out of here?" he whispers, stopping finally. I slide down his body like a ballerina until my toes touch the hardwood.

"God, yes. Now?"

"Now."

"Excellent. Can we just sneak out? Irish goodbye in three, two, one…"

"Darling, we can do whatever we want. It's our party. But let's say goodbye, just to be polite." He turns to the crowd and puts up a hand, and silence descends on the room.

His power over people is magnetic. If he ever wanted to take over his father's company, the world would bend over backward to pave his way. Lucky for me, Jack is content with the Foundation.

"Thank you, all, for a lovely evening. So glad you've been able to celebrate with us. We'll see you on the other side."

Quick as a magician, Jack has us out of the room and on the slate path to the black Suburban waiting outside before the applause and calls of best wishes and congratulations fully dies down. His personal security guards, Gideon and Malcolm, materialize like well-armed ghosts and fall in silently behind us. I call them the Crows because they are practically identical, with their buzz cuts and beefy arms, dressed in unrelenting black from head to toe, and hover, continuously, over their prize. How his people know when and where to be ready for him is still anyone's guess. I suppose I'll learn. Though Jack moved into my house in 12th South several months ago, he still travels constantly, and I've rarely accompanied him on business.

So far, I've managed to escape the Crows' scrutiny. It is only at my insistence that they don't flank Jack and me twenty-four/seven. Once we're married, that will change. The Crows will be at my side, too, and I don't have a choice in the matter. There have already been too many security briefings for my taste.

I collapse into the back of the Suburban and kick off my heels, sighing in relief.

Jack leans over and nuzzles my neck. "You smell like Möet & Chandon."

"I suppose there are worse things. The party was fun. I'm sorry your mom had to miss it."

"No, you're not. But that's fine. She and Henna are going wild at the Villa, running the servants ragged getting everything prepared. All we have to do is show up and smile."

"I love your mom. She's just a bit…intimidating."

"She will *love* hearing that. Speaking of, did you speak to yours tonight?"

"For a moment. She called when they arrived in Rome. Said Brian and Harper are making noises about never coming home. She said they'll meet us on Isola Thursday. At least we'll have a day to decompress before my family descends."

An inadvertent sigh slips from my lips. I love my family, but we aren't terribly close. Everyone is pursuing their own agendas, their own lives. My sister has been acting especially weird lately, and that's saying something.

Truth be told… I think there's a little jealousy going on. Things have been more strained than usual since Jack and I announced our engagement.

"Good. The majority of the guests should be arriving Thursday morning as well. The rehearsal is Friday, and Saturday, you, my darling, will officially be Mrs. Compton."

"I like the sound of that."

He kisses me lightly. "I do, too."

Jack's hand is wandering up my thigh, but I bat it away. "If you're looking for postprandial treats, you'll have to wait until later, cowboy."

"They don't care," he murmurs into my ear, but I shake my head.

"I care. Wait until we're alone, and then you can have your dessert. I noticed you passed on the macarons."

He flops back into the seat. "They were stale. Mom will be livid."

"They were? I thought they were yummy."

"You'll learn. Once you've had one fresh out of the ovens on the Champs-Élysées, you'll see what I mean."

"You, my darling, are a snob."

"And you love me."

He kisses me sweetly, and the Suburban pulls to the curb in front of our house. We spill out, both loose and uncoordinated, under the watchful eyes of the Crows. Gideon stays with us while Malcolm sweeps the house. He gives us the all clear. Once we're inside, they disappear into whatever crevice they live in overnight.

I carry my heels in one hand, grateful for the lack of stress on my arches. Jack tosses his jacket over the bar stool at the eat-in counter, tugs at his tie and unbuttons his collar, rolls up his sleeves, the motions so quick, so practiced and fluid, it's hypnotizing. He sees me watching and makes it into a tease, stepping closer with each turn of the fabric.

"You should try that with the buttons," I say, running my tongue over my lips.

He grins, lazy and confident. "Naw. I'll let you have the honor."

A step closer, another. My hand lands on his chest. My mouth tips up to his.

I smell something odd, something acrid and primordial, and step back.

"What the hell is that?" he says, pulling away.

"I don't know. It smells terrible. Like burning hair. Is something on fire?"

"Shh," he says, straining, listening. All I hear is the air-conditioner. But no, there it is. A thump. A creak. The unmistakable sound of footsteps.

Someone is in the house. Someone is upstairs in our house.

Jack bolts from my side, takes the stairs two at a time. I follow, just in time to see the door to the attic is open.

"Get Gideon and Malcolm," Jack shouts over his shoulder, throwing himself headlong into the darkness. But I am frozen. My mind can't process what's happening. I am cold with terror, the adrenaline rush forcing away my reason. I can't think. I can't move.

A masked man bursts from the darkness above and launches himself down the stairs. I am in his way, and he knocks me to the ground in his haste. I smash backward into the wall, banging my head hard against the chair rail. Jack is there a heartbeat later, calling for the Crows as he throws himself at the intruder, arms out, a perfect flying tackle. They go down hard on the landing, scuffling, locked in a deadly battle. Jack is the bigger man, he has the leverage he needs to get an arm on the man's windpipe, but the intruder is quick, kicking out at Jack's stomach until he connects and Jack is knocked off.

This gives the intruder the upper hand. He flips Jack onto his back, punching wildly while reaching behind to his waistband. My mind registers the gun, and the peril Jack is in, and without another thought, I kick the man's arm just as his fingers close around the gun's grip. It spins away, clattering against the baseboards. We lunge for it at the same time. I am closer. I get there first.

The shot is deafening.

The intruder falls to the floor at my feet, moaning, squirming. Blood pours from his side. So much blood. The man bleeds and bleeds and bleeds until he is still. I watch, fascinated, as a small trickle of crimson runs toward my bare foot.

Then Malcolm and Gideon are hoisting me to my feet, and the roaring in my head overwhelms me.

3

The Long Night

When I look back on that night, I still can't be entirely sure of the sequence.

Everything happened at once, with a blurred intensity so strong that, under the influence of alcohol and terror and a blinding concussion, all I know for sure is that my life was irrevocably changed. A split second, a reaction, a protective urge, and my entire axis shifted. If it weren't for Jack, I don't know what might have happened to me. What if I had come home alone to this monster in my house? The tables would be turned, I'm sure.

It would be me who was dead.

I remember shouting.

Muffled curses.

A yelp of pain.

The crash of the front door.

The pounding of feet on stairs.

The acrid scent of burning wire.

The adrenaline rush of stark fear.

The vision of a hand wrapped around the grip of a gun—is it mine? Is it Jack's? Gideon's? Malcolm's?

The gunshot.

The hard finality of the crash when the body of the intruder landed at my feet, knocking me backward into the wall with such force I sustain a concussion.

A Crow ripping off the intruder's mask, but I can't look. I can't look.

Jack screaming at them.

The haziness begins there.

There are flashes, moments that feel like dreams, like movies. It doesn't feel like it's happening to me. It doesn't feel like something I've done.

Who is he? Who is this man who's broken into my home and tried to kill me?

When the police ask me later what I saw, what I knew, what happened, and why, I reply with the truth I've been given.

Malcolm shot the intruder.

Malcolm shot the intruder.

Jack had me repeat it, again, and again, and again, before the police and EMTs arrived. There needed to be a consensus among us. It was the only safe way to proceed.

Me: Malcolm shot the intruder.

Jack: Malcolm stepped to the landing and shot the intruder.

Malcolm: Yes, sir, I shot the intruder.

I don't remember.

Three words, so simple, yet so duplicitous.

What is memory, anyway?

Echoes of reality twisted and molded into what we want to believe. What we want to remember. What we want to remember. Our brains allow us grace to cope with trauma. They give us space to heal, to come to terms with our actions, our fears.

Couple extreme trauma with alcohol and the events blur.

How can I remember with exact precision my lassitude at the party, the stale macarons, the hard crystal flute against my lips, the floral tang of the champagne, getting into the car and divesting myself of my shoes, Jack's kisses, light along my jaw-line, the gaping maw of the attic's blackness, and not remember the exact moment I killed a man?

WEDNESDAY

"If adventures will not befall a young lady in her own Village, she must seek them abroad."

—Jane Austen, *Northanger Abbey*

Welcome to Italy! We are so honored you could join us for our getaway wedding! We have scheduled plenty of downtime so you can get a little vacation while you're here. You'll find a book we chose just for you in your welcome package, something to inspire you to find a hammock and chill.

The Villa has a boat launch for you to catch the hydrofoil back to the mainland if you want to visit some of the other small cities in the area. But stick around! The island's occupation dates to Roman times, which you will be able to see on guided tours of the Villa, the towns, and the incredible ruins. It was also once a famous artists' colony. Both Hemingway and Picasso spent time here.

Conservation of the island is ongoing, so we ask that you keep to the paths and follow all the signs. There are some dangerous areas that are totally off-limits, but they are well marked. Irony alert: the internet signal isn't the strongest, but we hope you find the break restful instead of infuriating.

And now for fun, some spooky history... The island is haunted! Legend has it there is a Gray Lady who appears to only the purest of heart. Which means we will absolutely see her this weekend!

Lots of love,
C & J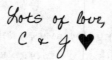

4

Our First Glimpse

Isle Isola, Italy

The prow of the boat powers through the stormy waters, the spindrift lacing the air. Misting water gathers on my cheeks and hair. I'm grateful for Jack's bulk behind me. His hands are warm on my shoulders, his mouth almost touching the tender skin of my neck.

"That's it, darling. There's the island. What do you think?"

It's a good thing he's standing behind me—it gives me time to school my face into a somewhat neutral expression. My pulse betrays me, though, rioting blood through my body, singing through my veins, making me feel more alive than ever before.

What do I think?

Oh. My. God.

The island is stunning. It shoots straight up from the water, the sheer rock face stark and unforgiving. We're approaching from the southwest, this I know from eavesdropping on Jack's conversation with the captain. From this vantage point, Isola seems to drift on top of the water, though I know it is an illusion.

The cliff is adorned with tiny shoots of bougainvillea desperate for purchase and a steep stone edge that makes my heart go into my throat. I'm not afraid of heights, but the idea of standing up there, looking out over the water, and stepping wrongly, makes me suddenly terrified, even as I long to set the colors of the cliffside on a canvas.

The formula begins brewing in my head. *Two parts ultramarine, two parts raw umber, a dab of titanium white to brighten up the edges, tone the middle with Payne's—*

"Claire?"

"Incredible," I manage, brought back to earth, voice breaking on the words.

Jack squeezes me closer. "I know. I love that cliff. We used to scare Mom and Dad, promising one day we'd try diving off the edge. There's no way—it's much too high, but it was so fun to watch them panic."

"Cruel children."

"All children are cruel, aren't they?" Jack says absently. "They don't know any better. Look, there's the Villa."

I can't see it, not yet, not until the boat rounds the promontory. The shoreline appears, a rocky beach with lines for a few small boats stretching into the channel. To the left, a smattering of pastel-colored houses built one atop the other stagger drunkenly up the cliffside. Gunmetal stone walls bisect the hills to the west, the terraced olive groves and vineyards that produce for the family's bespoke line verdant with promise. And then the edges of the Villa appear, copper and rust and molded stone, and I fight back a gasp.

Truly, it is misnamed; not a villa, it is a castle. A modern fortress, down to its gated entry, state-of-the-art security system, and helicopter landing pad.

An island castle, beautiful and forbidding, and soon to be

mine. No, ours. This vivid, lush, foreboding Italian paradise where I am going to marry the man of my dreams belongs to his family, to whom I am about to pledge my life.

I glance down at the teak deck of the boat carrying us to the island like Odysseus home from the wars. *The Hebrides*, it's called, named for another set of isolated islands popular amongst the Compton clan.

A boat. Who am I kidding? This is a full-blown mega-yacht.

"It's perfect," I say. I turn in his arms and kiss him full on the mouth. Jack isn't fooled.

"What's the matter, darling?" He lifts my chin and searches my face, his cobalt eyes full of concern—*they are the color of the sea, where the waves meet the rocks.* "You look a little green. Is your head hurting?"

I fight the flashback as it happens—the searing pain, the confusion, the rough edge of the EMT's blanket. My hand travels to the lump on the back of my skull. It is tender, and the stitches itch. I tap the scopolamine patch behind my ear, just to make sure it's still there. Check.

Despite my precautions, I am feeling a little peaked. The waves have been surging on the trip over from the mainland, and the yacht moves in time.

"I'm fine. I just love you. For making all of this happen, for… everything." I rest my forehead against his collarbone. He smells good, of cedar and sunshine and home.

As if he can discern my thoughts, Jack gives me a tight squeeze, then turns me around and starts pointing out landmarks. "See that white building, halfway up the hill? That's the entrance to the artists' colony. I can't wait for you to see all the sculpture. With luck, we'll have enough time for you to set up a canvas and capture some of the cliffs. The labyrinth is just there, follow my finger, look straight. See the dark spot in between the trees? And above that is part of the original fortress, built by Julius Caesar. Dad says it will be fully restored in another couple of years, enough for people to visit safely. It takes forever because of all the permits and conservation rules they must follow. But we'll take a walk through it, naturally. And ahead, on the right, by the old houses? On the second floor of Villa la Scogliera? See the terrace?"

I do. It has the same cheery patina as the Villa's coral stucco walls. A lemon grove pours over the wall, meeting the gaily striped ochre-and-tan umbrellas by the infinity pool below. On the terrace itself, on either side of the French doors, petunias spill from terra-cotta pots in bursts of aubergine and gold. It's like a *Condé Nast* photo shoot for the perfect Italian retreat.

It *had* been in a *Condé Nast* spread, but that was years ago. I read the piece when Jack first suggested we have the wedding here. I'd cut it out and used it as the basis for a painting I'd called *Scylla*, it inspired me so. It sold for $40,000 to a couple in Nashville with an obsession with mythology.

Hidden away on the western edge of Italy in the southwest of the Tyrrhenian Sea, out of sight from the mainland and the more popular islands of Capri and Anicapri to its north, lies the isolated Isle Isola. Originally a remote, hard-to-reach private armory of Julius Caesar, it is sometimes thought to be the island from which Homer's Scylla perched in the cliffs, waiting for unsuspecting questing sailors like Odysseus, who had to choose between sailing closer to the six-headed beast or sinking into the gaping maw of Charybdis's whirlpool. It is also said the island houses an oracle, but no documentation has been found to prove this claim. There have been a disturbing number of shipwrecks in the waters of the bay, surprise waves driving ships against the rocks at the base of the cliffs, and storms are known to arise without warning.

A more speculative fiction surrounds it; like any remote area, rumors abound about the island's many hauntings over the years, including a famed Gray Lady who lingers about the fortress, supposedly the ghost of the daughter of one of the island's many generals, who was sacrificed, given to an enemy who brought a mighty navy to attack the island. When he came ashore to parlay, the young woman was given to the man in good faith and disappeared that very night in a terrible storm. The storm raged for weeks, and the invading navy was driven away.

Sea monsters and unverifiable history aside, Isola's occupation dates to Roman times, and is home to the stunning Villa la Scogliera, the house on the cliff, currently home to famed cinematographer Will Compton. The Villa, a former monastery, perches on the hillside and ties into the abandoned Roman fortress. While the Villa itself is of this century, and has been modernized with electricity and water, the fortress, abandoned for centuries, is undergoing a full renovation, sponsored in part by the Italian antiquities committee and the Compton Foundation.

In addition to grapes and olives, the island is known for its lemon groves. It also houses a natural rookery, home to the many birds who fly off course, find themselves lost in the straights and unable to return to land.

How romantic, how very Gothic and creepy, and how very Compton to choose an island in the middle of nowhere surrounded by sea monsters and exhausted birds to call their own.

"I see it. It's lovely. Say the name again?"

"Villa la Scogliera."

I try to mimic the way the *R* rolls off his tongue and bungle it massively, which makes Jack laugh.

"I've been studying the tapes and everything. I swear it."

"Say it slowly, like this. Sko-lee-AIR-a. It means cliffside."

"Skola-air-a."

"Close. Emphasis on the third syllable, and roll your *R*," he says, planting a soft kiss on my cheek. "Chef Boy-ARRR-dee. Sko-lee-AIRRR-a. You can just call it the Villa, you know. No one will mind."

"I need to learn Italian properly."

"And you will. But let's focus on one thing at a time, shall we? We have our whole lives ahead for me to teach you."

Our whole lives. Lives that can be changed in an instant.

Stop it, Claire.

"The terrace is lovely. Is it special? Historically important? Did Medusa stand there or something?"

He rolls his eyes. "Not Medusa. Venus, maybe. The whole island is loaded with odes to Venus. No, my dear, it's special because that's where you will spend your first night as Mrs. Compton. Just you, and me—"

"And thirty of our nearest and dearest."

He laughs. "Well, they won't be watching what we get up to in there. Besides, I've been told the bed is magic."

There is something…wistful on his face. I run my hand from his cheek to his temple, smoothing back his too-long hair. There is the lightest sprinkling of silver in his part, just a few hairs here and there, lending him a serious, studious air.

"A magic bed? What, does it fly?" I tease.

"In a way. Rumor has it ladies tend to get knocked up on their wedding nights. My grandmother and my mother swear by it."

"Ah." A deep sense of foreboding seizes me, and I instinctually scan my body for any signs of pregnancy. It's a reflex, something I've done regularly since we first became intimate. An accidental pregnancy terrifies me. I can only imagine the headlines, how I'd be portrayed. Prevailing wisdom: a woman like me can only land a man like Jackson Compton if I get pregnant and he is forced to do the right thing.

I run my mind over our sexual escapades from the past month. I had my implant taken out; it was making me feel terrible. I have been taking my pills on time, haven't I? We've been careful, yes?

Stop it. You're being paranoid.

Yes, of course we've been careful. The dull ache deep in my stomach is certainly my impending monthly, just in time to ruin our wedding night. The malaise I've been feeling for the past couple of days is stress and travel related. I've never flown well, even short hops leave me with a headache, clammy and uncomfortable. Add in a mild concussion and a boat on slightly stormy seas? I'd gone to the doctor for a preventative motion sickness patch before we left; it is helping tamp down some of the nausea from the bump on my head, too.

The long night coupled with the long journey from Nashville to Naples is catching up to me. We'd been forced—*quelle horreur*—to fly first class on Delta instead of being chauffeured across the sea in the family jet. Jack's father is flying in from Africa, where he's been on business with Jack's brother Elliot. As heads of the company, their travel needs take precedence.

Yes, it was a terrible burden for me to be waited upon by the dark-eyed flight attendants with their prettily accented Italian and sly smiles for Jack. The wine was plentiful, the carbonara and crusty bread delicious, the lay-down beds surprisingly comfortable. I'd only disliked being separated from Jack. He was in the cozy suite behind me, and I felt all alone, watching the flight attendants' faces light up with pleasure as they walked past me to tend to Jack's needs.

The breeze picks up, and I realize Jack is looking at me curiously. "Everything okay?"

"Yes, but good grief, don't wish a baby on us just yet. I want to be married for a while, first."

"No promises, darling. My parents will explode with happiness at the idea of another heir."

There is a certain hopefulness in his voice. Jack is a decade older than me. A widower. His first life was stolen from him. He is ready to start a family. I understand. He's already experienced so much. I'm only getting started. I'm not ready for a child. I might not ever be ready. I need to tell him that, before the wedding. In case it's a deal breaker.

I take a deep breath. "Jack?"

"Yes, darling?"

But we are interrupted by a call from the upper deck. Gideon, beckoning. "We need you for a moment, Jack."

Jack squeezes my shoulder. "Be right back."

I watch Jack stride away and wrestle my urge to confess back into place. What purpose will it serve? He'll just get upset, and who knows, maybe I'll change my mind.

You know what they say about digging your own grave.

I turn back to the island.

Unlike the smoky gray open waters of the bay, the water in the shallower edges of the channel is cerulean and almost clear; schools of dark fish race away. What are they running from? The boat? A predator?

The breeze cools, the azure Mediterranean early summer sky turning hazy. Bad weather is coming. Italy is under a Red warning this long weekend, a severe weather alert, expecting the worst storms in a decade.

I hope everyone gets here in time. The channel crossing to Isle Isola is too dicey to manage anything smaller than the yacht or the hydrofoil ferry in bad weather, and the hydrofoil normally runs to Isola only once a week, though it's running three days in a row for us to get all the guests on the island. And obviously, the choppers can't fly if the storm is too bad.

The Hebrides is approaching the cliff's edge now. The imposing granite face is sheer and unforgiving. We're so close I can see the striations of the stone, the moss growing in the cracks. At the top, there is a flash of white. What is that?

A scarf, my mind fills in. *A woman's scarf.*

And then it is gone.

Someone is watching for us.

5

Old Bones

The crew begins to shout, and Jack appears back at my side. "We're putting in. The radar looks nasty, the first of the storms is coming in faster than they were expecting. I hope the hydrofoil is right behind us. They might have some trouble if they haven't launched yet."

"What did the Crows want?"

"Malcolm and Gideon," he corrects automatically. "You have to stop calling them that, darling. Especially now. They were just running me through the new schedule. Mom called, she thought it might be wise to move everything up a day. The storm will blow through during the night and day tomorrow, then there will be a break in the weather. So, the rehearsal dinner will be Thursday night instead of Friday, and the wedding Friday instead of Saturday. Is that okay?"

I fight back the urge to snap—*Are you kidding me? We've had this schedule laid out for months. What if the guests don't get here on time?*

But the girl who's marrying Jack isn't the type to get fussed over something so insignificant as a schedule change. No bridezillas here. Ana and Brice are funding most everything for the wedding anyway, and with Henna planning everything, I'm just along for the ride. My only goal is Jack's—our—eternal happiness.

"No problem. With everyone here I suppose it doesn't really matter when things happen. If Henna's cool with it, so am I."

"Good. Thanks for being so understanding. Now the only issue is getting the ferry here before the worst of the storm hits." He looks over his shoulder to the open waters as if he can conjure the hydrofoil. I run a hand along his arm, for once reassuring him.

"I'm sure they will. I have faith in the Compton magic. Everyone will be here safe and sound before the heavens start to squall."

"I love how you talk."

"I love you. By the way, someone was watching for us on the cliff. I saw a flash of white, a scarf, I think. Your family must be expecting us."

Jack's brows furrow. "No one should be up there now. It's blocked off for the renovations."

"Someone cheated then."

"You're sure you saw someone?"

Am I? The flash of white, the sense that a woman had turned and walked away...

"Yes. Of course, I am."

"All right. I'll mention it. We don't want anyone getting hurt."

The engines reverse, growling their displeasure. The teak deck shifts beneath our feet, and I grab onto the railing for extra balance. The island looms ahead, its lush, forested hills gleaming, the massive cliffside disappearing from view as the boat comes around. The sun catches my ring, making it flash and sparkle.

I breathe in the sea air, taking a moment to revel in the warm sun, the shrieks of the gulls, the calls of the crew, the strong arms folded across the rail next to mine. The incessant whapping of a helicopter's rotors bleeds through the bucolic seascape. Jack's father and brother, beating the storm.

"It's all going to be fine," Jack says again, sensing my need for reassurance. The past forty-eight hours have been off the charts nerve-racking.

"I know. I'm not worried."

Many marriages are made on such little lies. It's so much easier to reassure than laying oneself bare. Saying I am terrified is unthinkable. All of this—the break-in, the trip, the island, the wedding, the storms—it is too much for me to bear. And yet, I smile winningly at my fiancé, squeeze his hand. He mustn't know I'm second-guessing everything. He would take it the wrong way.

I look toward the pier. A knot of people comes into focus, and there is the small strobing of a blue light. Alarm seizes my stomach.

Malcolm shot the intruder.

"Jack, what's going on? I can see blue lights flashing. Is that the island's police?"

His attention snaps to the pier. "Our local island *polizia*, yes. The Italians have both local police and military police, but here on the island, it's just a couple of local guys. There's no crime on Isola."

Unspoken—*Our security sees to that. You're safe with me, Claire. Always.*

Safety is something Jack offers in spades. After Monday's escapades, I've been shown that in person.

"What do you think's happened?" I ask. "They aren't here about Monday night, are they?"

"I don't know. I suppose we'll find out. They're blocking our way up to the Villa."

It's another ten minutes before we can disembark. Jack is silent and watchful the whole time. He holds my hand and plays absently with my ring. I see the muscle in his jaw tick, tick, tick as he grinds his teeth.

When the gangplank finally settles against the ground, he says quietly, "Just follow my lead." He steers me down the pier toward the flashing lights. We're fifteen feet away when he sucks in a breath and says, "Wait here."

"But—"

"Wait here, Claire."

Jack doesn't normally command me. I'm so shocked I halt immediately, and he surges ahead, disappearing into the crowd. I stand awkwardly alone, shivering in the salty breeze. I can hear Italian, spoken very quickly, much too fast for me to follow even the few words I've picked up, then Jack's baritone, all overlaid with a cacophony of seagulls—the island's rookery for wayward birds must be nearby. I'm just grateful for the solid ground. Maybe I *was* getting a little seasick.

Jack reemerges moments later, his face pale.

"The timing is impeccable," he grumbles.

"Are they here for us?"

"No. The restoration people dug up a body."

"A body? Whose?"

"No idea. Sorry, technically it's not a body, it's a skeleton. Remains. This happens frequently in historical restoration."

"Remains?" I've had just about enough death for a lifetime. Two bodies in two days?

Jack smiles. "Don't freak out. You know this island dates back. Sometimes there are little mudslides that expose ruins, or the restoration people my dad hired will dig into the ground and find a tomb, or tunnel under a building and uncover disarticulated bones."

"So it—they—aren't recent?"

"Goodness, no. I'm sure they're not. My parents will have to meet with the people from the historical society, just to be certain, but it's all going to be fine. It's just one more thing to handle."

He sounds annoyed but supremely unconcerned, so I relax, too. I have learned to take my cues from Jack. This is a whole new world I'm stepping into, and camouflage is my only weapon.

"Let's get up to the Villa. I'm sure my parents will want to see you. And I'd love to show you around, if you're not too jet-lagged. Plus, we have the meeting with the lawyers this after-noon."

Ah, the lawyers. I've almost forgotten about the prenup sign-ing. Almost…

What, you thought it was going to be different? You missed the part of the story where Prince Charming sat Cinderella down with an annuity payout schedule because the glass slip-per earned interest at 4.8 percent a year? This is the Comptons we're talking about.

Jack might love me beyond all reason, but his family will protect him at all cost.

"I'm not too bad actually. Awake enough for greetings and explorations, at least."

"Then let's go."

6

The Benighted Path

I try not to gawk as we walk past the remains. Whoever the poor soul is—was—they're now wrapped up in a blue tarp. It's creepy, knowing that fifteen feet away lie the dusty, mud-streaked bones of a person who walked this island, who stared at the same beautiful views, who experienced joy and sadness and pain and love. A hundred years or a thousand, it's still a person. A dead person.

I shake myself from this reverie before Jack notices. I never know when it will hit, this protective retreat. Death of any kind can do it to me. I never go to funerals, or viewings, mainly because of the horrible tradition of leaving the casket open that happens so often in the South. For years, I even had to be careful with movies and television and books, reading the online synopses and reviews first to make sure I wouldn't be caught unawares, because a shock death of characters I cared about threw me off my stride for days. I've spent an inordinate amount of time making sure nothing bad will happen to the people around me so I won't be forced to witness them in their final resting state, and if their recklessness can't be managed, I've cut them loose.

And now I get to mark my wedding weekend with dead intruders and skeletal remains? Lovely.

I try to put the lump under the tarp out of my mind. Jack takes my hand, and we follow the crushed shell path that meanders up the hill to the Villa.

"If we're going to see your parents, can I change first?"

"Why? You look great. We're fine as is."

This is decidedly not true.

Looking at Jack's preferred daily garb, you'd never know he was from one of the wealthiest families in America. Granted, the security muscle is a giveaway, at least marking him as someone important, but he likes to keep things casual. I look him over from head to toe: his favorite pair of striped canvas shoes desperately need a run through the washing machine, the worn Nirvana T-shirt that belonged to his favorite, now deceased uncle, has a rip under the left arm, and his button-fly Levi's are so frayed around the edges it looks like he's rolled down several hills in them. It is a state that can only be achieved from extensive, loving wear and benign neglect, nothing manufactured about it. How he can go from tuxedo to vagabond is stunning.

But I've shed my shimmering chrysalis, too.

I'm currently wearing dark skinny jeans in slightly better repair than Jack's with an artistic rip in the knee—purchased, not worn in—a white linen button-down, a thin black leather jacket with the sleeves pushed up, and Converse high-tops. My hair is screwed up in a bun on top of my head, but I can feel tendrils floating around my face, escaping the clip. My nails are short and painted black.

This is my summer uniform. In winter, the Converse are swapped out for a pair of luscious buttery brown leather Frye boots I inherited after a roommate decided she didn't like them anymore, or my disreputable Doc Martens, and I cover my white tops with a heavier leather jacket or sweater, depending on the function. Simplicity. I like simplicity beyond all measure. I no longer use my body as a canvas—I leave that to my art.

"We look like we've been traveling. Your mom—"

"Loves you just the way you are, as I do."

If she had met me when Jack did, I wonder what she would have thought. It was bad enough he brought home an artist whose biggest sale was the result of Jack's own checkbook. One pierced and tattooed—I didn't exactly fit the wholesome family image the Comptons were shooting for. I've worked hard on that image. I didn't want to give them any reason to dissuade Jack from my side.

But they seem to like me. I've never gotten any weird vibes off his mother. She's not clinging to her baby boy and pushing me away. Actually, she has been quite the opposite—loving, engaged but not overbearing, respectful of our time and desires for privacy, and interested in my art for its own sake. If this continues, she will be the perfect mother-in-law. And his father is relatively absent from our relationship. Though he and Jack work together and I've seen some fraught moments, he's never been anything but kind to me.

The walk from the dock up the hill to the Villa gives me a chance to calm myself. The island has seen a wet spring and the path is fragrant with the heady aroma of the blooms. The florals are nearly overwhelmed by the warm scent of fresh lemon. No wonder, the lemon groves along the path sport monstrous fruits; I've never seen such a thing. They are everywhere, like mutant, aromatic tennis balls hanging on the hills, perfuming the air.

I hear barks, deep throated and sharp. Jack smiles. "Here they come. Okay, remember what I told you. The wolf dogs are highly trained but the first time you meet them—"

Two massive silver-and-black dogs burst around the corner, braying at our intrusion. I have never seen such gorgeous creatures. Jack told me all about his family's dogs, all descended from an original brother and sister, bred specifically for protection and companionship. Lupo Italiano—Italian wolf dogs—a supposed cross between a wolf and a German shepherd.

These two look more like wolves to me. Sleek and huge, they look like they eat elk for dinner. One elk to one dog. Good grief.

I stand still. They reach Jack first, but only give him a cursory glance—it is me they're interested in. I wait, allowing them to come to me. They do, snuffling delightedly at my sneakers, rubbing against my jeans. The slightly bigger of the two puts his nose into my hand.

The second dog is yipping in excitement. Jack gets down on one knee, grabs the beast by the ears, and starts talking to him like he's a baby. "You're a good boy, aren't you? Who's a good boy?"

The bigger dog is still nosing my hand. I move slowly—he could take it off with one bite should he want to—but when I scratch his ear, he closes his eyes in bliss and leans against my leg.

"He likes you." Jack is grinning, looking at me in admiration. "That's Romulus. This is Remus. They're my grandfather's, but we get along fine, don't we, boys?"

Jack picks up a small branch and launches it up the path, and the dogs tear off after it.

"I'll teach you their training words, but you aren't going to have any issues with them, I can tell. Romulus isn't a people person, he fell in love the moment he saw you. Just like I did."

"Awww. He's a beauty. His fur is so soft."

Jack gives me a small kiss, and the dogs come back, dancing merrily around him. He heaves the branch again and off they go.

I glance back down the path, but my view of the pier—and the body—is obscured. I can see the circular top deck of *The Hebrides*, the helicopter landing pad like a spaceship rising over the trees. The clouds gathering in the distance are ominous, but for the moment, the sun is out, and the birds sing in the trees. Idyllic as a postcard. Except for the old bones.

Jack seems consumed by nervous excitement, hurrying ahead to pick a bright red flower to tuck behind my ear, running back to retrieve the dropped hairclip he knocks loose, throwing the branch for the dogs again and again. I laugh obediently at his antics, but my heart isn't in it. He is trying to distract me. He's always been so good at creating distractions.

Or maybe he is distracting himself?

Don't ascribe your emotions to him, Claire.

I run my hands through my now-freed hair, which has taken on a life of its own in the salt air. I twist it back up in a chignon and secure it with the clip he hands over. A rock has somehow found its way into my shoe. I stand on one foot, balancing with a hand against his shoulder, dump it out and slide back into my Converse.

Every motion feels like a delay. Jack finally stops goofing around and squeezes my hand.

"Darling, what's wrong? You're a million miles away."

"No, I'm not. I'm right here, on this gorgeous, lovely island."

He pulls me close. "You might be here physically, but you're distracted. You aren't worried about the wedding, are you? Getting cold feet?" He's joking, but I can see the tiny furrow between his brows.

"No cold feet. I guess I'm just a little bothered by the body down at the pier. On top of the break-in. It's a lot."

Not exactly true. Not exactly a lie, either.

The horn of the hydrofoil ferry floats up from the base of the path. I'm relieved to hear it. I'd like some of my people around to buffer the Compton grandeur.

"Ah. Good. Some of our guests are arriving," Jack says.

"So it seems. Should we wait for them?"

"No. Let's hurry ahead so we can get a few more minutes alone. I want to talk to you for a second."

He sounds grave and it makes me nervous.

"We're alone now. Talk."

"Come on. I'll race you." He grins and starts jogging backward, gesturing with both hands for me to follow. I rise to the challenge. I'm pretty quick; I ran track in school and getting out of the blocks fast was my biggest strength. I'm not much of a runner now, I prefer yoga and my bike, but back then, I was a cheetah, built for blisteringly fast but short sprints. I burst into motion and beat Jack to the top of the hill by two whole seconds.

"Take that, Compton."

He reaches me a heartbeat later, barely out of breath, and kisses me on the nose.

"Look," he says, and spins me 180 degrees to see the Villa.

7

Villas and Pearls

Up close, the Villa is even more magnificent than I expected. Five stories of imposing wind-worn stone crouch on the side of the hill, holding on to the cliffside for dear life. It wraps around out of my sight. From the water's view, I know that hidden edge is where it meets up with the walls of the ancient fortress. Plenty of room for us, our guests, Jack's family, and of course, the staff.

Staff. Something else I'll have to get accustomed to.

Like the terrace above, overflowing pots of petunias flank the front doors, two massive slabs of weathered wood thrown open in welcome. A wide grass-and-slate courtyard with iron tables shaded by jaunty striped umbrellas waits to our right. Ahead are stairs down to a second courtyard that looks out over the water. The only thing that feels off are the cameras, mounted on every corner. An elaborate, state-of-the-art security system enhances the feeling that we're standing in front of a fortress.

It is impossible to take it all in, the sheer size and beauty of it.

I wander toward the patio, drawn to the water. The gray stone is warming in the sun and two cats—one calico, one tuxedo—nap on the ancient stacked stone wall overlooking the sea. The dogs bark at them, but I can tell it's a game—the cats ignore them.

The view. The *view*. Roman kings and explorers and ancient witches had killed to possess this spot, to gaze at the sea, at the jutting knees of volcanic rock ringing the island. These conquerors would stand in this very spot and think themselves safe. They could see their enemies approaching, have days to make preparations. They thought they could never be overthrown.

All things, all people, can be conquered. I'm not silly enough to believe otherwise.

The beach below is raked clear of rocks and seaweed; there are chaise longues and umbrellas, though currently being stacked and lashed to the rocks in preparation for the storms to come. Two stone jetties abut each side of the beach, creating a natural cove. *The Hebrides*, looking even more imposing and elegant from afar, is back in full view, being serviced by the crew at the pier. The hydrofoil has put in at the other pier and people are wandering off, taking pictures or simply staring up at the Villa, then getting in line for the funicular that will bring those less inclined for a hike to the top of the hill.

It's such a shame that everyone's taken a week off to be with us and it's going to rain most of the time. About as fair as getting your period for the wedding night. Ah, well. Life is cruel.

I scan the people disembarking for familiar faces. Most of our guests are friends Jack has collected over the years, and the Compton family. I'm expecting only my mother and stepfather, my sister Harper, and my best friend Katie. I don't see any of them.

I'm not the type to surround myself with acquaintances. The curse of the introvert, Jack calls it. I don't see it as a curse at all. I just don't play well with others.

"It's quite grand, isn't it?" Jack asks.

"What? Oh, the Villa? It's absolutely beautiful. But what did you want to tell me, Jack?"

He walks me to the stone wall. The calico blinks and yawns, and I run a hand down her silky back. The cat's eyes slit with pleasure and she stretches two long front legs contentedly, claws unsheathed, purring like an outboard motor.

"That's Rosa and the tuxedo is Nina. They're my mother's cats."

"They're beautiful."

Jack takes my hand, gently kisses my knuckles.

"Oh, Claire. It's so good to have you here. I love you, and I am so happy to be marrying you."

"Me, too." I watch him, eyes searching his, sensing there is more. He's being so formal, so unlike the Jack I know. He looks away.

"Maybe now isn't exactly the time."

My heart stutters. *Oh, no. He's changed his mind. He doesn't want to marry me. He's figured me out. I'm being jilted.* I tense, fighting my instincts. *Run, Claire. Run. Get away, now!*

"Not the time for what?"

"For this." With a sly grin, he pulls a long flat box from his pocket and hands it to me. The black velvet is warm from where it was nestled against his body.

I hold my breath as I pry it open.

The pearls are so luminous they shine up from the velvet as if lit from within. They are graduated, smaller near the clasp, growing in size to the center pearl, which has to be the size of my thumbnail.

"Oh, Jack. They're gorgeous."

He looks very young in that moment. Though he is ten years my senior, he sometimes looks as vulnerable as a teen. His words are soft.

"They were my great-grandmother's originally. Eliza wore them every day, and when she...died, they passed to my grandmother, May, who also wore them until her death. I want you to have them. To wear them, always, like my grandmother and great-grandmother did."

"I don't know what to say." I truly didn't. I'd never owned anything fancy or beautiful before Jack. Now, thanks to a chance meeting a year ago, I'm being bedecked in bright diamonds and a dead woman's pearls. *You've come a long way, Claire.*

"They can be your something old. If you like them."

I swallow back the tears. "Jack, I love them. Thank you. I'm...so touched."

He snakes the pearls around my neck. I feel them settle at the base of my throat like they were made for me, specifically measured to fit into the sharp, hollowed notch between my collarbones. Jack steps back and looks at me approvingly.

"They are perfect on you. I knew they would be."

I touch them self-consciously. "I never thought I was a pearls kind of girl."

"All women are made for pearls. And you most of all."

He settles his mouth on mine, warm and soft, and in our rising passion, the intense connection I feel to him whenever we touch, I am able to push away my traitorous thought.

Did Jack give his great-grandmother's pearls to his first wife, too?

8

Dead Wives

I didn't know, when I met Jack, the details of his life before me. I didn't press him, and he didn't offer. Maybe I was naive. Maybe I was just a girl in love. We existed that first month of our courtship in a kind of bubble, with eyes only for one another. And when he finally shared his story, I wasn't deterred.

A month into our courtship, Jack took me to his brother Elliot's wedding, where I met his family for the first time. They were as intriguing, smart, and lovely as he was. I guess my own prejudices about wealth and privilege made me assume the worst, but I found the Comptons as intensely fascinating and philanthropic as their son. Brice hadn't exactly started Compton Computers in his garage—his money was inherited—but he'd grown it into a rival to Microsoft and Apple. Ana was editor emeritus of *Endless Journey*, the travel magazine started by Jack's grandmother. Elliot worked with Brice on the day-to-day running of the business. Jack, of course, was in charge of the Foundation, and the youngest, Tyler, was a doctor. The family's most recent project of note was working with Bill Gates on getting universal sanitation to some of the poorer African nations, for heaven's sake.

The Comptons were doing real work to make the world a better, safer place. They were warm, funny, and kind.

I was enchanted.

It didn't hurt that Jack's elegant mother, Ana, talked nonstop about my painting, the one Jack bought the night we met. She was having it hung in the lobby of their Manhattan office, where everyone would see it. She admired my talent. She wondered if I would be willing to discuss a series of pieces for their private collection.

Um…yes?

After Elliot's wedding, I started getting commissions. Magazine features. I was painting like crazy, and people liked my work. It was surreal. I think anytime an artist has a modicum of success, you distrust it, as do the people around you. Too good to be true. What did you do to get it? Who did you blow?

In my case… I was blowing Jack Compton, and my career was on fire.

I had love. Success. And yes, for the first time, money. These are the elements of many dreams come true.

When he asked me to marry him, I couldn't say yes quickly enough.

Jack completed me in ways no one had ever before. Not family. Not lovers. Not friends. He was the other half of my heart. He drove away all of my insecurities with his love.

There was only one thing, one tiny, bothersome issue that cast a shadow on my happiness.

Jack did not talk about his dead wife. Nor did anyone in his family.

It struck me as strange, in the beginning. There were no reminiscences, no regrets. Certainly, no comparisons. He sat me down one night after dinner, three weeks after Elliot's wedding, said, "I have something to tell you," and recited the facts.

He'd been married before, the marriage was a short one, and had happened a decade earlier. She died only a few weeks in. He didn't like to discuss it, but felt I should know, considering the path we were clearly on.

Then he kissed me, and as we joined together, I realized what he was actually telling me. I didn't see then the lack of intimacy of the admission, nor feel any sort of fear or warning. What I took away from the conversation was this: He'd just declared his intent. He was planning a future with me.

I overlooked the fact that he didn't tell me how she'd died, nor did I ask. Not then, at least. It was all very mysterious and speaking about it was completely off-limits. It felt...dangerously romantic in a way. There was so much about him I did not know, and I clung to those mysteries like a child. I'd been disappointed by people so often in my life that I suppose I was just hoping he wouldn't let me down.

No, in the beginning, none of it mattered to me. I'm a practical woman, logical to a fault sometimes. I was only eighteen when Jack was so briefly married, in the throes of my own cataclysmic life earthquakes that I had no desire to revisit. I didn't see the story in the news. Even if I had somehow come across it, why would I care about some gazillionaire's missing wife?

I've learned not to look back. Never. That way lies madness.

Jack and I had a long life ahead of us. He'd talk about Morgan if he wanted.

If I was that curious, there was always the internet. The Comptons were a very public family, after all.

Katie thought I was crazy not to press Jack for every little detail. When I refused, she dug up everything she could, invited me out for coffee under the pretense of a catch-up, sat me down at the Frothy Monkey, and forced me to listen. This is what I learned:

Jackson Compton met Morgan Fraser at a cocktail party in Tiburon, California, at the house of a famed literary agent, a stunning arts and crafts renovation across the bay from San Francisco. Their courtship was brief and glamorous. Jack was a party boy then, on the circuit, dating models and actresses, in the gossip columns all the time. Most eligible bachelor, all that. Feckless. Wealthy. Fun.

Morgan, a well-educated former foster child who studied computer science on scholarship at Stanford, was the exact opposite of the kind of woman Jackson Compton was attracted to, according to the salacious stories. There was nothing simple or easy about her. Her background was murky, her business interests bordered on the unethical, and she was clearly not interested in settling down.

But she was a stunner. Breathtakingly gorgeous. Beautiful, and brilliant. The night they met, she was out celebrating. She had secured the first round of venture capital for an eponymous IT company that was making waves with a nanotech microcamera that would eventually change the way the security industry handled smart home technology. Heady stuff. The Comptons bought out her company and made her a small fortune.

"See? He has a pattern of seducing women away from their passions," Katie cried, getting even angrier when I laughed and told her I'd heard enough. She refused to stop, plowed ahead as if anything, anything, could change my mind.

I learned that after only a few months of dating, Jack and Morgan eloped. The move angered his parents, who felt he was too young to settle, and caused all the gossip magazines to launch covers with a grainy, out-of-focus telephoto shot of Morgan from behind in a slinky white dress that clung to her curves. It could have been anyone.

Three weeks later, on the last day of their honeymoon, she went missing.

There weren't a lot of details. They were sailing off the coast of Monterey, having a last afternoon on the water, nothing risky. A storm blew up unexpectedly. Jack wrestled with the boat, but the boom sprang free and Morgan was swept overboard.

He circled, called the Coast Guard, but they couldn't get to him for over an hour. By then, she was well and truly gone.

Her body wasn't found right away. Eventually, a piece floated ashore. A hand, with a bent pinkie finger, wrapped in black cloth, the same color of sarong she was wearing when she went missing from the boat.

The hand was identified through DNA as belonging to Morgan Fraser. There was nothing else left of her. Sharks were blamed.

After a period of solitude ascribed to overwhelming grief, Jackson Compton threw himself into the family business, took over running the Foundation, traveled the world doing good for all mankind, and by all accounts, hadn't been on the dating scene until that evening in Nashville, when I caught his eye.

Katie was not at all happy this story didn't move me. What does it matter, I asked, heatedly at last? It was a decade ago, and he's clearly over her. He wouldn't be dating me, we wouldn't be getting serious, otherwise.

She insisted I needed to be careful. I disagreed. We didn't speak for a month.

Jack didn't talk about his dead wife. So what? It was a matter of respect between the two of us. I didn't ask. He didn't tell.

Though sometimes, when he got quiet or short, I wondered if he was thinking of her. Mostly, though, I didn't let it bother me. Not at the beginning. Not while I still thought Jack and I were destined for happiness.

9

Yes, Dahh-ling

A shrill scream comes from our left, and we jump apart like naughty children.

"Claire Elizabeth Hunter–soon-to-be-Compton, you are the luckiest girl in the world. Look at this place! It's insane!"

"Katie! I'm so glad to see you." I glance at Jack, expecting him to be grimacing—Katie Elderfield isn't his favorite person, nor, obviously, Jack hers—but he is smiling broadly.

"Welcome to Italy, Katie," he says, opening his arms for a hug. Good thing, because Katie crashes straight into us, tackle hugging, knocking me back a few feet. Romulus takes a step toward me, but Jack calls out something guttural and the two dogs sit immediately, quivering, five feet away.

"I am so excited to be here. My gawd, look at this place. Are those wolves? Jeez, Compton. And you—" She spins me in a circle, then raises both of my arms out to the side, staring at my neck. "Aren't *you* the radiant bride. Are those pearls you're wearing?"

I feel the blush creep up my neck, probably making the pearls stand out even more. "A wedding gift from Jack. You like?"

Katie runs a finger along the necklace. "Yeah. They've gotta be worth a fortune."

Ah, there it is, that embarrassing twinge I have anytime anyone mentions the obscene wealth of the Comptons. I have to get over it. I might have started off with nothing, but I will never be in that state again, thanks to Jack.

Katie, her sleeveless top showing off the edge of a new and not-so-discreet tattoo, stamps up and down the length of the courtyard in her floral Doc Martens, staring at the Villa. The last of the prestorm sun glimmers off the diamond stud in her nose.

"Nice shack, Compton."

"I'll let my father know you approve."

The tension between them is back, damn it. "Any chance my parents and Harper were on the boat? I know they were planning to come from Rome tomorrow, but with the weather…"

"I didn't see them. If Harper were on it, I'd have noticed. She'd have been taking pictures nonstop."

I look to the billowing storm clouds.

"Jack, should we reach out to them? The hydrofoil won't be able to manage the return trip with the storm, will it?"

"Don't worry, darling. It will run until the storms arrive. We might get lucky and they hold off. Worse comes to worst, we'll send the helicopter for them when the weather breaks."

Katie can't resist a teensy eye roll. "Yes, *dahh-ling*, don't worry. They'll find their way. I want to see inside this place, and then I want to sleep for a week. God, I hate jet lag. Compton, are you offering tours or are we supposed to stand out here in the courtyard?"

"Katie," I start to scold, but Jack has other ideas.

"Actually, if you don't mind getting yourself settled in, Katie,

Claire and I need to sit down with my parents for a bit. And the lawyers."

"Lawyers?" Katie asks, gathering her bags. "What did you do that you need lawyers?"

My heart kicks up a notch and I glance at Jack. I feel an answering squeeze—a warning.

Malcolm shot the intruder.

"It's just wedding stuff. There are a number of hoops we have to jump through for the marriage to be legal here in Italy."

Katie gives me a salacious wink. "Oh. Of course. Go sign your prenup. I'm going to drop my stuff, grab a bite and crash, so I'll find you when I wake up. Don't do anything I wouldn't do."

I notice a tall, gray-haired, dark-eyed woman in a black silk top and slim black pants standing unobtrusively by the front door. Has she been waiting there all along, hidden in the shadows? Her voice is gently accented, calm and sweet. "I'd be happy to show Signorina Elderfield to her room, Signore Jack."

"Thank you, Fatima. This is Claire, by the way."

Fatima inclines her head graciously. "A pleasure to meet you, Signorina Claire. I have looked forward to this moment for many weeks."

"The pleasure is mine, Fatima. And Claire is fine."

"Let's get a move on, ladies," Jack says, overly cheerful. "Lots to do."

Katie gives me a knowing look, clearly feeling dismissed. She steps carefully around the dogs and follows Fatima into the house. I hear her start chattering, asking about the Villa. I want to call after her, apologize for Jack's brusqueness, reassure her, but stop myself. I love them both, but they must figure out their relationship; power struggles aren't my thing.

Jack snaps his fingers and the dogs melt away around the side of the courtyard.

"Follow me, soon-to-be Mrs. Compton."

It must be my imagination, but I swear his eyes linger on my throat, at the pearls draped there, before he offers me his arm.

The interior of Villa la Scogliera is as surprising as the exterior. I've seen pictures, of course, and the spreads in *Condé Nast* and *Architectural Digest* are well thumbed. Jack has shown me some from his childhood. We've lain in bed, his iPad between us, looking at the photos, historical and current.

I try to act cool, like I belong here, but nothing has properly prepared me for the actual splendor of the Villa.

The entry, through two massive olive wood doors, as wide as it is deep, has whitewashed limestone walls offset by a warm terracotta tile floor. Modern art stretches the length of the interior, elemental and striking. I itch to break free of Jack's hand and step back, taking them in one by one. I spy a Pollock, a Mondrian. Joan Miró.

"Is that a Matisse?" I blurt.

Jack glances over his shoulder at the blue on white canvas we've just passed. "I think so. You're the expert, darling. I know the painting in our bedroom is a de Kooning—I've heard mother talk about it with guests before. And there's a Picasso somewhere around here, from when he and my grandfather were catting around. He painted it here, in the colony, and left it behind as thanks. Don't worry, you have the rest of your life to take inventory of our family's artwork."

Our family.

I feel a bit faint. I've been in galleries worldwide. I've seen great art. I've met great artists. I've even made some great work of my own. But the knowledge that all of this will essentially belong to me one day is overwhelming.

I can't help but wonder when I'm going to wake up from this dream of the handsome prince and his faraway castle, but for now, I satisfy myself with one last glance at the Matisse and keep walking.

At the far end of the house, at least thirty yards away, three sets of tall wooden French doors give the illusion of a wall of glass, and beyond, the lush emerald of the garden and aquamarine of the sea. I want to run to those doors, fling them open and scurry outside, capturing the colors on a canvas. I can see myself standing there already, grinding my pigments and blending, blending, blending, until my palette is ready, and I can capture the scene forever. I'm not much for plein air work, but this view might sway me out of my studio. My fingers actually twitch into the form I use when holding a paintbrush. It is so fresh and open, so welcoming. I shake my head in wonder.

"What?" Jack asks, looking at me curiously.

"Oh, you know. You can take the girl out of the country…"

"My little country mouse. Just you wait."

"Seriously, it's so much…happier than I expected. Especially since the outside is so old."

"Oh, Claire. What were you expecting, cobwebs and a hunchback to greet us?"

"Well, maybe just the hunchback. Elliot could audition for the role. He'd be a shoe-in."

He laughs, his head tipped back and throat moving with the effort, and I join in. There is nothing more joyous in my life than watching Jack laugh.

He finally gathers himself. "I told you my grandfather stayed in some Hollywood starlet's Villa in Tuscany and came home full of ideas. He and my grandmother renovated the place back in the seventies. They wanted it to be open and airy, welcoming, a good place for kids to run and scream. We took advantage, trust me. The entire Villa was redone, but this is the most modern area and yes, I can see what you mean, the happiest space."

"It has great energy. I can't wait to explore every corner."

"We will explore it all, darling, I promise. But for now, let me show you our room."

10

Venus Calling

We start for the stairs—this place is a rabbit warren, a maze of corridors and hallways. It's going to take me weeks to learn my way around. Jack points out rooms—dining room, breakfast room, parlor, billiards, the path down to the kitchens, another to the gardens—but he's in a hurry, and my mind is spinning too much to comprehend anything except the massive grand staircase that winds up and up and up to the residential floors of the Villa.

The staircase: thick semicircles of marble with a dove gray runner up the center. Columned on both sides, it sweeps up seventeen steps before the landing diverges into two formal curves, one left and one right. The banisters are made of dark polished wood and iron spindles. A balustrade runs the length of the hall above, the parapet giving a magnificent view of the foyer below. I halt, craning my neck backward to take it all in.

"Oh, wow."

"You like?" Jack asks, smiling.

"I do."

They make such a statement; I feel drawn to them. I can see a painting forming in my mind, swirls of gray, roiling in fury, limned in spectral white on the edges. There is a sense of the uncanny to this, of ghostly presences scurrying in our wake. A metaphorical ascent to the unknown. A foreboding journey. I'll call the painting *Cassandra*.

We begin our own ascent. The six-feet-tall windows on the first landing show the sea. The thunderhead still crouches possessively over the mainland. In the distance, I see a bright fork of lightning. The labyrinth path leads away beneath us, and further still are the cottages.

I catch something out of the corner of my eye. A flash of white. The scarf I saw earlier? Is the mysterious cliff greeter now in the cottages?

"Jack?"

But it's gone before he can say, "What, darling?"

"I thought I saw something—someone—in the cottages. The same white scarf from the cliff."

He stares out the window, but there is nothing more to see. The scarf, and its wearer, are gone.

I laugh lightly.

"It must have been my imagination. I think the jet lag is setting in. Or my head is playing tricks on me. I thought I'd done so well resetting my body clock by getting up at 4:00 a.m. for the past week, but maybe I was wrong."

"Oh, my poor girl. I've tired you out." He kisses my forehead, and I try to shake off the eerie sense of lingering otherness that hangs about the landing.

"I'm sorry, Jack. The break-in—"

"Shh. It's okay. I promise we'll get everything sorted out." He grins, trying to set me at ease, as always. "Come on. The sooner we get this meeting out of the way, the sooner you can crash."

I'm not sure how he can just forget everything that happened.

He's a good compartmentalizer; I'm the opposite, I worry things to death, running them through my mind over and over.

"Stop. Please. I want to know who broke into our house. I want to know why."

Jack tugs me up the staircase to the right. The hallway is tastefully lit, slate floors covered with a silk geometrical-patterned runner, marble tables that house a few elegant pieces, a few wooden armoires, and more art.

"We'll know more soon. Karmen is handling things. She'll be in touch as soon as she has answers. Trust me, darling. You're safe. Nothing bad is going to happen."

Karmen Harris is the head of Compton Security. Wherever Brice is, she is close by. And technically, the Crows work for her. That's why she's looking into the shooting, dealing with the police. It is her charge who shot the intruder.

I haven't met her yet, but I know Jack thinks she's smart and tough. I suppose this makes me feel better, but still, Karmen wasn't the one staring down at the masked face of an intruder in her house.

"Okay?" he asks, smoothing my curls back from my face.

Be patient. Listen. Follow Jack's lead.

I nod.

"Good. This takes us to the west wing, where our rooms are. Many of the pieces here are ancestral, from the Comptons who lived in England. I know you'll enjoy familiarizing yourself with everything. There's a catalog in the library, too, if you want to check it out."

An austere white-haired man with a dark Mona Lisa smile and Jack's eyes hangs in a lit niche of honor. Jack stops in front of it. "That's my great-grandfather William. Lucian Freud painted that of him."

Normally I would be examining every brushstroke—Freud is a favorite of mine—but I'm too tired. Everything feels so wrong.

Strange. I am uncomfortable, and feel a wellspring of anxiety hovering, ready to pounce.

Maybe it's the concussion. Or the scopolamine patch. They said that might make me dizzy. That must be it.

We wind down another hall, and Jack finally stops in front of a tall wooden door. It would look like any sixteenth-century castle door except for the biometric keypad to the right of the heavy iron handle.

Jack puts his fingers on the black screen, and there is an almost instantaneous click. He flings open the door to our bridal suite with a grin. "Welcome to our rooms, my darling."

Staggeringly lovely, spacious, and decorated to perfection, "our rooms" is more of an apartment, consisting of three connected spaces—an expansive sitting area with couches, an office with a huge, battered wooden desk, and a master bedroom the size of our living room back home. We wander through and I see there is a half-naked statue in front of a long tapestry opposite the sumptuous bed. When will I ever stop being surprised by the Comptons' earthiness?

He interrupts my thoughts with a gentle squeeze of my hand. "Darling? Do you like it?"

"I do, Jack. It's perfect."

"Legend has it one of the emperors had his lovers brought to this chamber. There used to be some sort of passageway down to the grotto. They would bring in the women by boat, then into the Villa through the tunnels. But the passageways have been walled off for centuries, now."

I stop in front of the sculpture, similar in nature to *Venus de Milo*. "Is this Venus?"

"It is. Venus Genetrix. Goddess of love, sex, beauty, and fertility." He grins at that last, pats the sculpture on her truncated shoulder. "Isn't she a beauty?"

The statue is missing a head, and arms, but yes, she is quite beautiful. The carving is impressive, you can tell how diaphanous her robes are, how they cling to her curves. Seduction. She is seduction personified.

"A replica, I hope?"

Jack glances at me oddly. "Goodness, no. My great-grandfather was friends with Paul Getty, he gave this to him in appreciation of some good deed. I would assume the Getty Museum has the replica, or whatever museum she's currently been loaned to. Come see the view."

Oh, great. Just what we need, a centuries-old sculpture in our bedroom. I'll probably knock her over in the middle of the night on my way to the bathroom and shatter her into a million pieces.

I step around the statue cautiously and obediently follow him to the French doors leading to the terrace, which stretches around the corner to the living room access.

The terrace is remarkable; slate and wrought iron, it stretches across the width of the suite and curves around to the living room. A pergola provides shade and shelter to one quarter of the space. It even has a dining table and a stone fireplace on the western edge. The chairs and longues have deep cushions with gaily striped pillows. It's meant for sunning, for reading, for loving. For us.

The vista is impressive. The steeple of the church rises to my left, and to my right…water, water everywhere. The sun peeking over the edge of the cliff casts gloriously long shadows across the beach, as if someone's hand is perched above the island, open-fisted, fingers outstretched. The storm still lingers over the mainland as if it hasn't made up its mind to advance across the water to the island yet.

I feel suddenly claustrophobic, isolated. All this water, the land too far away to reach.

I am still alone, despite Jack's presence beside me. I still am not sure about what happened. Who broke in? Why? Who did we kill?

There are things happening that are out of my control, and the thought sends a tight shiver through my body. I pretend to stifle a yawn as cover for lurching away from Jack's hand, but if he notices, he laughs it off.

"Do you want to take a nap before the meeting?"

"It's tempting. You need to rest, too."

"No, I'm fine. I was in Europe all last week, remember? My body clock is already adjusted. Seriously, if you want to lie down, I can go check in with my parents and let you rest."

My silence worries him, because Jack folds me into his arms again. "I'm sorry this has been such a strange couple of days."

"Yes," I murmur, pushing away my concerns, letting myself be comforted. Now that we've stopped moving, the adrenaline rush of our arrival is fading fast. I am suddenly so tired. I just want to crawl into the bed and sleep for a year.

"If you're up to it, once we finish with the lawyers, and you've had a chance to catch your breath, I'd love to introduce you to my grandfather. Though if you're not in the mood, I can push it off."

Get it together, Hunter. Be strong. I tuck a stray hair behind my ear, straighten my spine.

"I'm fine, I promise. Would you rather we go talk to him now, before we go to the library?"

"We'll do it after," Jack says lightly. "I think he's taking a walk. He usually does this time of day."

As he says this, there is a ruckus from the hall. A woman's voice, speaking in gentle Italian-accented English, cajoling. "Signore Compton, no, Signore Compton, not that way. They're in the bridal suite."

"Oh," Jack stands straighter, brightening. "He's back. Apparently, you do get to meet him now."

I look to the sea again, to the billowing, blackening clouds, take a huge, deep breath through my nose, the salty air tinged with the heady scent of the spring flowers and lemon, then blow it out and go to Jack's side to face my soon to be grandfather-in-law.

11

Make Way for the Great Man

I'm not sure what I was expecting from my first meeting with the world-renowned Will Compton, but the robust, tanned, bull-chested man in front of me isn't it. I've seen pictures, of course; Will Compton is a legend in his own right, not only the father of a genius. His work is all over the internet, as are his well-documented exploits. He got his start shooting military footage in Vietnam, then pivoted into the entertainment industry in the late seventies. The movies he worked on are classics, shot in foreign locales with beautiful actresses and brooding actors. Worldly, cosmopolitan Will Compton, the great cinematographer.

But in person, he is something more. I'm not at all prepared for his presence, his stature. His thick, steel-gray hair sweeps back from his forehead, hanging to his shoulders like a well-aged surfer. He is exceedingly handsome still; I can see echoes of Jack's face in cheekbone and chin. This is what Jack will look like when he is seventy-five. Not like his father, with his nervous rabbit demeanor and shifty eyes, or his severe great-grandfather, but like his compelling grandfather.

I put out my hand. "Nice to meet you, Mr. Compton."

That's when I realize as physically imposing as Will Compton is, something is off. When he locks eyes on me, he seems frail. Damaged. Sad, and frightened. He searches my face, wariness creeping over his craggy features.

"Who is this?" he demands in a deep, rusty, ancient voice. He looks from me to Jack, who says, "Hey, Grandpa. This is my fiancée, the painter, Claire Hunter. You remember, I told you we were going to be here for the wedding? I sent you one of her paintings. You loved it."

We sent him *Silvia*, a small oil I'd painted in school, layered grays and whites and blacks that Jack said reminded him of the waters on Isola during a storm.

Will stares at us, standing there side by side with hopeful smiles, then surges into the room, eyes suddenly wild, an angry snarl on his face.

"No, it is not. Who do you think you are, bringing that girl here? You get away from her." He heads for Jack, and throws a punch, connecting solidly with Jack's cheek. Jack stumbles back in surprise, hands up to ward off the attack.

"Gran, stop. I'm Jack. Your grandson."

"You know what's going to happen. It happens every time. You get away from her, right now. You don't touch my girl." The old man grabs my bicep, his grip like steel, and Jack pulls me away, putting himself between us.

"Hey, now. Lay off, old man."

"Signore Compton!" The nurse is yanking at her charge's arm. "*Basta!* Stop that, right now."

"He killed her. He killed her. You know that he killed her." Will is jabbing a thick finger at Jack, shrieking, while the nurse tries to manhandle him away, toward the door. Her voice is gentle again, soothing.

"*Va bene*, Signore Compton, *va bene, va bene*. That's your grandson Jack, he's here to get married to that sweet girl with the blond hair. Nobody killed anyone."

The nurse speaks over her shoulder, whispering, "He's just confused. He has good days and bad days. Ignore him." She tugs at his arm, hard. "Signore Compton, let's get you back to your room."

Will Compton is having nothing of it. He whirls toward us again and rages on. "I am not confused. He killed her. I saw it with my own eyes. We must see justice done. I can't let it happen again. It will happen again if I don't stop him now." And to me, "Stay away from him. He's dangerous." He starts back into the room, lasering in on Jack, who steps toward him, ready now, fists clenched. I am reminded of two lions squaring off. One will hurt the other, badly, before this is through, whether physical or emotional, I don't know.

The nurse finally gets a solid grip on Will's arm and hauls him back toward the hall.

"I know, Signore. Let's go back to your room, and we'll call the *polizia*." To Jack, she says, "*Mi dispiace*. So sorry. He gets like this sometimes. Let me get him to his rooms and you can come see him in a little while. Sometimes he gets upset when we change his schedule. There's been quite a bit of disruption these past few days."

The old man finally settles, muttering to himself as he is led away.

The nurse calls back over her shoulder, "*Allora*, I nearly forgot. Signore Jackson, your mother is looking for you. She says it's important she speak with you immediately."

"*Grazie*, Petra," he replies.

Shaken, I reach for Jack's hand, surprised to see tears in his eyes. He is horrified. Or is he terrified?

"Oh, honey, are you okay? He really clocked you."

Jack clears his throat, swipes a hand across his face. "I didn't know he'd gotten so bad. I knew about the dementia, but I didn't realize how much it had progressed. My parents didn't tell me. I'm so sorry, darling. I didn't want you to meet him like that."

I smooth his ruffled hair, the widow's peak so reminiscent of his grandfather's, and kiss the spot where Will punched him. "It's not your fault, Jack. How old is he?"

"Seventy-eight. God, that was…unsettling. Do I have a bruise? He hit me pretty hard."

I examine his face. "It's a little red, but I don't think it's going to mar your beauty. Why don't we get you some ice? That will help so it doesn't swell."

"Good idea." He doesn't move, though, is staring at the empty doorway like he's worried his grandfather is lying in wait in the hallway.

I hesitate only a moment. "Jack? Do you know who he was talking about? Who was killed?"

"I have no idea what he's talking about, Claire," Jack says flatly. "Why don't you rest for a few minutes. I'll grab some ice and go see what my mom needs. Love you."

And with that, he disappears into the hall, leaving me in our suite, alone.

I sit down on the edge of the bed, kick off my Chucks, and lie back, staring at the wood-beamed ceiling.

What, exactly, was that about?

And what, exactly, am I getting myself into?

12

Bad, Bad News

Jack hurries down the main stairs, swings through the kitchen for some ice, and makes his way to the library. Ana is waiting for him in the hall outside the double doors. Something is wrong, he can see it in his mother's stance. Her hip is cocked, she is smoking a cigarette. She and Fatima are talking, but at Jack's appearance, Fatima nods to him and hurries away. He can hear her giving instructions to someone down the hall, her voice fading as she moves toward the kitchens. Jack waits until he's sure they are alone. He runs a knuckle along his jaw, feeling the rasp of his beard and the lingering soreness of his grandfather's knotty fist.

"Where's Claire?" Ana asks.

"I left her to freshen up. I had a feeling you wanted to see me alone."

"You were right." She touches his jawline. "What happened to you?"

"I got slugged. Gran attacked me. Accused me of killing someone, in front of Claire, no less."

"Will attacked you? Whatever for? What did you say to him?"

"It was totally unprovoked. He took one look at Claire standing next to me and tried to pull her from my side, shouting I'd killed someone. Then he lunged in and punched me. Claire was terrified. You said he was in decline, you didn't say he'd gotten violent. Why didn't you warn me?"

His mother presses a hand to her forehead. "Oh, Jack. I'm so sorry. I know that must have been very difficult for you. For Claire, too. Will is…challenging right now."

"If he's attacking me, what happens when he comes across someone he isn't familiar with? We have to do something."

"I'll speak to your father."

Jack has heard those words from his mother at least a thousand times over the years. It is the foundation of their family dynamic. Their catchphrase. He and his brothers would come to Ana with their grievances; she'd say calmly, "I'll speak to your father." And the grievances would be resolved.

As he's grown older, he understands the dynamic behind it better. Jack doubts Ana ever actually said anything to Brice unless it was impossible to avoid. Ana didn't need Brice's permission or attention to resolve matters with her boys. His dad was constantly consumed by his work, by the company, by his legacy. He was rarely present in their childhood lives in any meaningful way. Oh, Brice was there physically, most of the time, just not emotionally. Who could be present when they were constantly hooked into the office? Granted, he'd been more involved with their lives as they entered their twenties, looping all three boys into the company in various areas, one after another. But could you ever get past that initial sense of abandonment? At least Ana had been there. Always, even though she was running the magazine and traveling, she'd somehow managed to be at nearly everything important in the boys' lives.

It is hard on her, Jack thinks, having them so distant. Ana is happiest when all her chicks are in the nest.

She doesn't look happy now, though. Watching her smoke, he is struck for a moment at just how much she's aged in the past year. At fifty-nine she is far from old, but new lines crease the skin of her forehead and bracket her mouth, and in the right light, sparkles of platinum dust her hair. She's had extremely discreet work, done, nothing invasive, and, for the most part, looks as graceful and elegant as she had at forty. But there is something else now, a haunted depth to her eyes that ensures that despite age or intervention, she will never be considered a young girl again.

"Anyway, Gran's nurse said you needed to speak to me?"

Ana smiles, but it's tremulous at best. "Yes."

"What is it?"

"I thought you should be made aware of something."

"What's that?"

"The body they found? The bones draped at the pier? We believe... It's her. It's Morgan."

Jack is too stunned to speak. Horror sparks, deep in his gut. Now? Of all times, now the bitch washes up?

This is insanity. This is impossible.

This is dangerous.

This is very, very dangerous.

There was a narrative. A well-planned, well-thought-out, well-executed narrative. It had taken extensive effort to make it work. For the media. For the police. For those few outside the small circle of family who knew the truth.

My wife died when she fell off the boat.

My wife died when she fell off the boat.

My wife died when she fell off the boat.

He'd even identified the partial remains of the body months later, for God's sake.

And now, with the events in Nashville, they have another narrative to keep track of.

Jack finally gathers himself. "How do you know? What makes them think that it's her, after all this time?"

His voice sounds remote, lost, even to himself.

"The bones of the hands have the deformity she was born with, that bend in her pinkie finger."

"Fuck." He ignores his mother's wince—she hates vulgar language—paces a few steps away, then back, then away again. "There's nothing that can be done. I have to tell Claire. I can't keep this from her."

Ana lights another cigarette, blows blue smoke toward the ceiling. "Let's not get hasty. I know this comes as a shock, Jackson. It was a surprise to us, too. No one ever expected her to actually surface. But we have a plan, we always have had one, just in case."

"Another plan, Mother? The last one nearly took us all down."

"And who's fault is that, Jackson?"

"I'm not like you, Mother. Lying isn't my strong suit."

Ana's lips tighten but she continues on. "If you stick to the plan, there won't be any problems. We're going to share that the DNA tests have shown this is Elevana, Fatima's mother. It's been so many years since she went missing, without exceptional scrutiny of the body by outsiders, the identification will hold. The documents are being fixed as we speak. Karmen has already taken care of things."

Of course, she has. Karmen is beholden to the family too deeply. There is nothing she won't do to keep them safe. She'd offered to take the blame for Morgan's death herself when the accident happened. Jack wouldn't hear of it.

He runs a hand through his hair. "How do you know this is really her, Mom? How do you know this is Morgan? Clinodactyly is not that uncommon a malformation. These remains could be from anyone. The hand could have been broken at the time of death, from a fall, just as easily. There's no way to know for sure."

Ana's eyes grow distant. "You'll just have to trust me, Jack."

"This is unbelievable." He feels rage brewing in him, knows he must shut it down until he can figure out the right way through this.

Ana, too, is struggling to keep it together. She's not used to arguing with her son. Her word has always been the last, and the law. Since Morgan's death, they've clashed too often.

"I know this is hard for you. It's hard for us all. But we need to stick together, like always, and we'll get through it. We'll get you married to your pretty little artist and your life can start again, unsullied by this mess. Honestly, knowing it's her makes things better, doesn't it? This is real closure, Jackson."

"I want to see the body."

Alarm flashes in his mother's eyes. "No."

"I insist."

"What good will that do? It's been a decade, there's nothing to see but the bones."

He starts to speak again but she puts a finger across his lips. Moments later a servant rushes past, head down, red hair streaming. Jack can't help it, his heart stutters for a moment. Any time he sees a woman with long, loose red hair, it's the same, a sudden rush of adrenaline and then the endorphin release that feels like panic, leaving him out of breath as if he'd just run a mile at top speed. Morgan affected him that deeply. Still does.

Yes, it makes him feel better to know her remains have been recovered. As sick and awful as it sounds, there is a certain sense of closure. Not that the lies can be reversed, not that their lives won't be affected, not that the specter of Morgan won't hang over the wedding, and his new life, forever.

Putting her bones in the ground and knowing there is six feet of earth on top of them will allow him to at least try and close this chapter. He can go into his marriage to Claire with an open heart and open mind.

Still.

"I want to see the body, and I refuse to take no for an answer."

"Fine," his mother snaps at him, finished. "She's been taken to the crypt. I trust you can manage to say your goodbyes without alerting Claire to this story? There's no need for her to know Morgan died here. Let her, like the rest of the world, think she went missing in California. I refuse to have you implicated, Jackson. That tramp wasn't worth it."

"Mother—"

"If you won't do it for yourself, do it for Claire. Do you think she'd really understand if she knew the whole truth?"

"Yes, I do. You underestimate her, Mom. Trust me, she is stronger than you know."

"Perhaps I do." She delicately grinds out the butt of her cigarette in a crystal ashtray on the marble table to their right. "But there's no sense cluing her in on the whole story before the wedding. Let this be. We have an answer now, and we can finally, truly put the chapter behind us. I must go—your father needs me. I'll see you later."

She presents her cheek for a kiss, which he dutifully provides, then sweeps off down the hall, leaving Jack with the lingering scent of cigarettes and the still smoking butt in the ashtray. The ash is the color of bones.

Her bones.

Her bones.

Morgan's bones.

He refuses to think about that night.

That awful, terrible, unforgettable, inevitable night.

The night Morgan died.

13

A Watcher in the Night

I was there the night he met her, you know. He wasn't hard to track at all. A few keystrokes and his weekend itinerary appeared on my screen. Alfred Hotel. Nashville, Tennessee. Penthouse and three rooms under the name Jack William. A bachelor weekend for Elliot, the scum.

Drunk, Jack had wandered into the studio, spied that gaudy painting, signaled to the owner. A blonde in the corner, slightly tipsy from the cheap champagne, was summoned. She strolled over, the excitement on her face clear. She looked a mess, like she hadn't brushed her hair in weeks. It twisted and twined around her face and all I could see were snakes, snakes, everywhere.

He bought the painting and took her back to the hotel bar to celebrate. The room was quiet and elegant, and in the darkness, she had something transcendent about her, some ineffable quality that drew all the eyes in the room. When she laughed, he acted like it was cashmere against chilly skin. When she picked up her champagne glass, he watched every move as if imagining her hand gripping something other than the flute's stem. Her hair glowed like a halo; her lips were the color of rubies. The slender ring through her septum sparkled despite the bar's dim light, as did the diamond stud in her nose and the parade of silver up the edges of her left ear.

She wasn't his type. Not in the least. Jack had never shown the slightest interest in the bohemian. But here was this ethereal, artsy, snaky blonde with her piercings and her well-worn leather jacket and her Doc Martens and her cashmere laugh and her glowing emerald eyes and her questionable talent with a canvas, and Jackson Compton was lost.

The moment he dipped his wick, she had him by the balls. Fucking predictable.

He bought her a studio, launched her career, pushed a reconciliation with her mother and sister, controlled, controlled, controlled. I watched him wine her, dine her, and sixty-nine her—they fucked like bunnies; Jackson's hip, hot Goth girl had bedroom eyes.

I could see exactly what was happening. He was shaping her into the woman he thought he'd always wanted. When he met her, she was unmolded clay with a modicum of talent. With Jackson pulling the strings, Claire Hunter became the marionette of his dreams.

On nights I grew bored, I replayed their greatest hits, hitting Rewind when something particularly special came up. I sat in the dark with a glass of wine by my side and a hand down my pants, alone, so damn alone, the night bleeding around me like a storm. I listened to their secrets. Their hopes for the future. Their dreams. Their plans.

They were *destined* for one another.

Destiny. Bullshit. There is no destiny.

Life is a series of chance encounters that arrange themselves into meaningful moments on a sliding scale between happiness and sadness, and then you die. We all die. Deal with it.

14

The Blood Fitting

I am cold, so cold, icy and shaking, but the chill comes from inside of me, deep in my chest, spreading out through my limbs.

Eyes closed, I sense the remnants of a dream: a woman with red hair and pale skin, her white gown in tatters, rain streaming down her body, her mouth open in a scream. So frightened. Is she calling out a warning? Or crying for help? She is choking, choking, a hand to her throat. Blood-red tears begin to stream down her face.

There is the slightest pressure, almost a whisper, against my forehead, as if someone is checking me for a fever.

My eyes shoot open and I jerk fully awake, sitting up with a cry. I swipe my hand frantically across my forehead, wiping away the strange lingering feeling, the horrible sense that I've stepped through an invisible cobweb and the silk has enveloped me, sticking to my skin like a shroud. I can't catch my breath, I can't swallow. I'm choking…

The pearls. The pearls around my neck, so tight, so unfamiliar. They've gotten twisted around the collar of my shirt and are pressing against my windpipe.

I yank them away from my skin, drag in an unrestricted breath. The clasp gives, but the strand doesn't break, the hand-knotted silk strong even after all these years.

I pant for a few moments, until my mind catches up with my body.

You fell asleep. It was a dream. Only a dream. You're fine. You're okay.

Gingerly, I remove the necklace and look at the clasp. It's bent a bit, but the safety catch held. I breathe a sigh of relief. I hardly want to tell Jack I've ruined his great-grandmother's pearls the first day I've worn them. Careful not to break the ancient clasp, I squeeze the metal back into place and return them to my throat. They feel warm against my skin, alive.

My God, what a dream. I'm relieved to be awake. I glance at the clock; it's nearly four. I slept for almost an hour. Wow. I need to get moving. Make myself presentable.

I resist the urge to curtsey in front of Venus as I cross the room. I settle for a simple "Hey, V. Do me a favor. Don't let me get knocked up just yet, okay?"

It would be so much easier if she only had a head.

The French doors to the terrace stand open, and I close them for some privacy. I don't know why I bother, it's not like anyone can see me from here.

The bathroom is combined with a closet and dressing room. Marble vanities, thick, fluffy white towels. A huge double slipper claw-foot tub begs for me to sink into the water; when I glance up, I realize the ceiling is bisected with white rafters and painted lavender. It is an utterly romantic room. Our bags have been fully unpacked. Fatima's doing, probably. There are expectations to be met for the new Mrs. Compton. I'm mildly uncomfortable with this. But again, I must get used to how the Comptons work.

I glance at the trashcan, sitting empty. How long will it be before the Comptons' servants know everything about me? There is remarkable intimacy in the service of people who live in your home. They know all of your most private details. The things you choose to keep to yourself, and your physical state, simply through your daily detritus. I try to remember they are caretakers, have been in their positions for years, attending to the family's needs, and they will take care of me now, too.

I step on something sharp and curse aloud. What the hell? I fall into the chair and draw my foot up onto my left knee. A shard of glass is sticking out of the ball of my foot. Wincing, I maneuver it out, press a tissue to the cut. Damn, that hurts.

The floor itself is travertine but the throw rug glitters in the light. It is covered in broken glass.

Carefully, I gather up the edges and tip the rug over the trashcan. The glass tinkles into the decorative metal. Well, there's no way to get all of that out and put the rug back down. I roll it and set it to the side of the trashcan. I'll tell Fatima, or Jack, that someone broke a glass and the rug needs to be washed.

The bleeding has stopped but the cut is deep enough that I don't want to go sticking my bare foot in my shoes without some protection. Looking for a Band-Aid, I pull open the top drawer on the left side of the double vanity, quickly realize this is Jack's side. His comb peeks out from beneath a piece of notepaper, folded in quarters. Suffused with curiosity, I unfold the paper.

Don't you miss me, darling?

It is not Jack's handwriting. I don't recognize it at all. What in the world?

I eye the paper warily, read the note again and again. Surely this is a lover's note from my betrothed; Jack calls me darling, has from the beginning. Instead, in strange handwriting, it feels implicitly like a threat.

Was this meant for Jack, not me? It was in his drawer, after all.

I feel anger bloom inside me. Who would send such a thing to an almost-married man? Who should my fiancé be missing?

It's a mistake. Or a joke. Whatever. I crumple the paper and toss it in the trashcan with the broken glass, use the restroom, wash up, run my fingers through my curls to fluff them, and tear off the scopolamine patch, carefully disposing it wrapped in a tissue, as the instructions demanded. I won't be needing it anymore.

I look at the pearls in the mirror, encircling my throat like a dog's collar. I've never been one for necklaces, but these are quite beautiful. They set off my collarbones, making them look less bony and more elegant.

The French doors are open again. There must be a problem with the latch. Another thing to mention to Fatima. I pull the doors closed again, this time making sure they are secure. I mustn't have closed them all the way before.

In the living room, in addition to amber bottles of whisky, the wet bar has an automated espresso maker, teapot, and a small fridge full of Orangina and Evian and snacks. I make an espresso and pour sugar into it. It is rich and delicious, and so strong I feel life pouring back into me. A banana and a bag of almonds later, I'm feeling more like myself.

There is a gentle knocking on the door, and a woman's quiet voice.

"Signorina?"

"Who is it?" I call.

"The seamstress, and me, obviously," Henna Shaikh says brusquely.

I throw open the door and Henna hurries inside, followed by the seamstress, a young-dark-haired girl, who is carrying my wedding dress in an extralong garment bag folded twice over her arm like a limp mink. It is bigger that she is. She waits patiently while Henna bustles around, setting things to rights that weren't out of place to begin with.

Henna finally stops moving and eyes me critically. "Claire? Are you all right? You're pale. You aren't coming down with something, are you?"

"No, I'm fine. I promise. I sat down for two seconds while Jack went to talk to his mom and fell asleep."

"Good, you need your rest. So? What do you think? Isn't the island gorgeous? I told you."

Her enthusiasm is, as always, contagious, and I feel myself start to relax. "It is. It's a shame it's going to rain all weekend."

"With any luck, the storms won't be too terrible. They come in waves, anyway, so there should be breaks in the rain. If not, that's why we have umbrellas. I laid in extra, just in case, rain boots and jackets, too."

"You think of everything. Talk to me. What's on my plate?"

Henna flips open her omnipresent planner. "We need to get this last fitting out of the way. I need to run you both through the rehearsal, and of course, there's the bruncheon tomorrow morning." Her eyes drift to my throat. "The pearls look divine on you. I knew they would."

"You knew Jack was gifting me his great-grandmother's pearls?"

"They're a family heirloom. Passed from Eliza to May to Ana and now you. Ana wore them for a time, but they're not really her style. Jack asked Ana's permission, and she consulted me, of course."

Of course, she had. There is nothing Henna doesn't participate in when it comes to Ana Compton. She plans everything for the woman. They are attached at the hip. I should be honored to have Henna loaned to me. Scratch that, I am honored. Henna has planned the wedding for us with ease. I've only had to say yes, or no, though I've said yes much more. She has exquisite taste, and the Compton checkbook to match.

Henna is wearing a stunning gray wrap dress with tall black boots, her black hair gleaming. She always looks so professional, so damn stylish and put together. I think of my Converse under the bed, wondering. Should I do a wardrobe update once Jack and I are official? I bet Henna would die of happiness if I asked. I've upgraded almost everything else about myself. I've taken out most of my piercings and had my ill-advised teenage tattoos removed. Why do I resist this last bit of polish? The part that is temporary, changeable, hell, seasonal? I glance down at my torn jeans and decide, yes, I should put in a bit more effort. Jack would like it.

"Claire? Everything okay?"

"Yes, completely. Sorry. Zoned out there for a moment. I hadn't realized Ana wore them, too. Wow. Four generations of Compton women."

"Take good care of them. You need to wear pearls regularly. Your skin's oils will keep them lustrous. They will look lovely with your dress, for starters."

I'm a little squicked out about the idea of four generations of DNA hanging around my neck, but I smile and nod agreeably.

The seamstress pulls the dress out of the storage bag. My beautiful dress. At the sight of it, a confection of ivory, satin, and tulle, as romantic as any fairy tale, my heart soars.

In it, I feel like Cinderella at the ball. The top is simple ivory, the front and back attaching at my collarbones. I'm not the type for a strapless dress. The skirt is the palest pink, like the blushing inside of a shell. The layers look like petals of a rose, layering one on top of the other, with so much tulle it's almost stiff and holds me upright. It is demure and elegant, the dress of a fairy-tale princess, the most beautiful thing I have ever seen.

I've been sketching versions of my wedding dress since I was a child, the drawings getting more sophisticated and precise the older I got. After Jack proposed, I dug out those old drawings from the trunk of precious things that lived in my attic. I lost an entire afternoon leafing through the sketchbooks. So many happy memories were tied up in those dreams. Happy memories, and tragic ones. My father won't be here to walk me down the aisle, and that stings deeply.

I started work right away on designing my more modern, adult version of the gown, the one I'm going to wear for the ceremony. My sister, Harper, found a woman to make it to my specs, and it's utterly perfect. I can't wait to see Jack's face when he sees the dress. I know he'll love it. I've managed to keep everything about it secret from him.

The seamstress holds the dress open and I duck into it, head and shoulders first. She slides the satin down my body, settles it over my hips, then begins in on the tiny buttons that line the back.

I look at myself in the mirror, the transformation from girl to woman, bride to wife, hitting me. I finger the pearls around my neck, so happy I chose the bateau neckline for the dress. The pearls, nestled against my throat, complete it perfectly. The next time I put on this dress, it will be to walk down the aisle to marry Jack.

Tickled with how I look, I twist and swirl, and as the skirt moves, I hear twin gasps from behind me.

"What is that?" Henna says, and there is horror in her voice.

"What's what?" I look over my shoulder, trying to see, but by the look on Henna's face, I know it's bad.

"Hold still," Henna commands, and I freeze in place. I feel them pulling at the layers of satin and tulle, the seamstress letting out little mewling gasps like a blind kitten removed from her mother's side for the first time.

"What is it, Henna?" I twist my neck around and catch a glimpse of something red. *That's not right*, my mind helpfully provides. *There isn't anything red in my dress.*

"Oh no, my foot must still be bleeding. I stepped on some glass. Is it ruined? Can we get it out?"

"Take it off," Henna demands. The seamstress unbuttons the few she's finished, and I step out of the dress.

Henna has a hand to her mouth. She has gone quite pale. "Oh, Claire. No, this isn't from your foot. I am so sorry. I don't know what happened. Maybe something leaked in the storage bag?"

She finally lets me see.

There is a wide slash of what looks like dark crimson paint across the back interior fold of my dress.

My heart is hammering, trying to burst from my chest. We lay the dress on the bed reverently, the three of us gentling the fabric like it's a spooked horse. Pieces of the red fall off onto my hand.

The stain is not paint. It's putting off a disgusting, musty odor, and bits flake off onto the floor.

It is blood.

And it spells out a ragged, blurry word.

WHORE

15

Panic at the Disco

The cry I let out must sound quite pained because Henna grabs me, pulls me into a tight embrace. "Shh, shh, shh. We'll figure something out. Perhaps we can sew the panels together—"

She's smothering me, and I fight to get loose. She lets me go so suddenly I stumble into a small marble-topped table, causing all the incidental items to fall on the floor. The seamstress dives for them, clearly grateful for something to do.

When I right myself, I can barely look at my dress. "I can't get married in a dress that has that nasty bloody word on it, Henna. No."

"Then we'll cut the damage free, create some sort of bustle. It will change the line of the dress, yes, but—"

"Stop. No. The dress is ruined. Throw it away."

I want to ask her who had access to it, how she could let this happen, *why why why why why,* but I bite my tongue. As far as I know, the dress has been in three places until now—my house, the salon of the seamstress in Nashville, and here, but trust me, when I gave over the dress to Henna, it hadn't been defiled. Henna had come to collect it in Nashville last week, and she's been in charge of it since. But accusing her of letting this happen isn't going to solve the problem.

You're being awfully logical, Claire. It's okay to have feelings about this.

I don't particularly like having feelings. It's not that I avoid them, it's only that strong emotion makes me feel weak, and that kick-starts my panic.

Breathe, Claire.

I breathe.

Henna paces.

The seamstress, pale and shaking, having retrieved the table's baubles from the floor, rebags the dress. She disappears into the hall with a whisper of fabric before she can be blamed for this fiasco.

When we are alone, Henna practically growls the words "Who would do such a thing?" Her voice is quaking with anger and that sets me off.

"Someone who clearly hates me. And it must be someone close. How else could they get to the dress?"

That's it. The tears pour down my face unchecked. The shock has passed, and reality is setting in, and I can't dance away from it any longer.

Someone broke into my house, and died there. My wedding dress is ruined. A storm is bearing down on the island, Jack's grandfather is addled, there's a dead body down by the pier, and I don't even want to think about what else might go wrong.

I don't have panic attacks anymore. It's something I left behind when I met Jack. He makes me feel so protected, so safe, that my lifelong anxiety has faded away. With Jack by my side, I feel in control again, strong, capable. I'm not that destabilized little girl who blamed herself for everyone's bad moods and sharp words. I felt no need to pop pills or smoke joints to help me re-treat from the world into a tiny cocoon of safety and warmth. His loved healed me, smoothed all my broken edges.

So I thought.

All of that progress, gone in a moment.

When I come back to myself, legs drawn into my chest, the slate floor hard beneath me, I realize Henna has put some sort of cold cloth on my neck and is stroking my back.

"Oh, Claire. Poor girl. I'm sorry. We'll figure something out. It's just a dress. It's the vows that really matter."

Just a dress. This from the woman who insisted on Louboutin bags for our hostess gifts. I am filled with a sudden desire to slap her hand away. Another vestige from my past, my anger, my impulse to lash out, to hurt, rearing its ugly head.

I struggle to my feet, pushing away her proffered hand, dragging in deep breaths.

"I'm okay. I'm fine."

"You are not fine."

"I am. It was a shock. I'm fine now. I'd like to be alone. Please."

Henna frowns but takes the hint. "I'll see what can be done for your dress. I still think it can be saved. We'll get to the bottom of this, Claire. We'll find out who did it. It's a terrible, nasty prank, and we'll find the culprit, I promise you."

It is a good speech. I almost believe her.

With one last appraising glance, Henna strides out, heels clicking on the slate. I lock the door and make myself a cup of tea, go back to the bedroom, sink onto the heavenly soft bed, losing myself in the fluffy cream duvet. The scent of overripe lemons and dank vegetation and wet concrete drift through the room. I need to talk to Jack. There is no longer any doubt—we are under attack. The question is, from whom? And even more importantly, why?

I pull my phone from my pocket and send him a text—
I need you.

I get nothing in reply. My phone has only one bar inside the
room. I drag myself from the bed. I feel achy and sore, like I'm
coming down with the flu. My throat is scratchy, my eyes burn.

I go out onto the terrace, into the salty, ozone-laden air.

The text still doesn't go through.

I should go find him. But I don't know where he is.

I feel another keening building inside, a desperate fear that
something has happened to him, that I'll never see him again.
What would my life look like without Jack? Empty. Desolate.
Over.

*Grow up. Stop being such a spastic little girl. Why do you always
act like such a child?*

I leave the doors ajar so the air circulates and lie back down
on the bed.

I haven't felt this helpless and alone since my dad died.

And I can't go *there* now, or I will fall apart completely.

I hear a scraping noise and let out a startled cry when the cal-
ico I was petting outside earlier leaps onto the foot of the bed.
"My mother's cats," Jack had said, and it makes sense that the cat
had sought out her spot, considering this room had long been
Brice and Ana's space, was just given over to us as the newest
Compton bride and groom.

But the door is locked. I locked it myself when Henna left.
How did the cat get in?

*Off the terrace, perhaps. Or she could have been hiding under the
bed. Stop being so spooky, Claire.*

I reach down and stroke a finger lightly between the cat's ears.
"Hello, Rosa. Is this your normal home? I'm sorry I locked you
inside." The cat purrs in answer and snuggles into my hand. She
doesn't seem upset at all to be stuck with me instead of Ana.

I hear a keening wail, high-pitched and eerie. Like a woman
crying, but it's just the wind, gusting, rushing along the cliff-

side. The terrace doors blow open, the curtains flapping into the room, flinging splashes of water onto the Aubusson carpets. I hurry to the doors, slamming them shut before the rain ruins the drapery and rugs. A massive flash of lightning breaks the darkened sky, disappearing behind the edge of the cliff. Thunder rumbles on the strike's heels, so close I can feel it in my bones. I don't even have time to count it off. The cat, tail fluffed, dives under the bed with a sharp *chirp*.

What I wouldn't give for the freedom to hide under the bed, cowering in the face of a threat. I have to face this, face everything, with or without Jack by my side.

Jack, Jack, Jack.

The center of my universe. The yin to my yang.

Our new life together is getting off to a rocky start.

Jack sticks his head back inside the suite a little before five. "Darling? Are you up? They're expecting us in the library. We shouldn't keep them waiting."

"Finally. I've been texting you. Where have you been?"

He glances at his Patek Philippe, the only outward trapping of wealth he allows himself. It is sleek and unobtrusive, water-resistant, a college graduation gift from his parents. Jack, and his brothers, went to Yale, where Brice studied. Another huge difference between us. I'm a Nashville Watkins School of Art alum. There was no reason for me to go to a traditional college—I wanted to be in the arts. But Jack, he's Skull and Bones all the way.

I have a regular Apple Watch like the rest of the world, though Jack hates it. "I don't know why you want to be so connected. Anyone could track you down. They aren't secure."

But I insist. I like it. I may have changed myself from the skin out for Jack, but I can't give up everything that gives me joy.

"Sorry, darling. Henna said you were doing a fitting, so I stayed out of the way so I wouldn't see the dress."

"Did she tell you?"

"Tell me what? Are you okay? You look upset."

"Someone ruined my dress. Someone painted the word *WHORE* on it in blood."

Jack goes utterly still, his face a blank mask, but I can feel the rage roiling inside of him. I fight back threatening tears. I can't fall apart again.

"Who would do such a thing?" Jack asks quietly, so quietly I wonder if he's talking to me or himself.

"I don't know."

"It's an awful, terrible trick. Can Henna fix it?"

"No, I don't think so. I have the dress I was going to wear to the rehearsal. I can try that instead."

"I don't care if you wear your jeans and Converse, my love. It's not what you're wearing that matters. But I know you loved the dress. I don't know what to say. If I had any idea who did it… I am so, so sorry."

He wraps me in his arms and I sigh in relief. I can handle anything with him by my side.

"Darling. I'll make it up to you, I swear it."

"We'll figure it out. I'm sure Henna has told Ana by now, and the whole place will be in a kerfuffle soon enough. I take it it's time to sign the prenup?" I ask, trying to keep my tone light.

"The lawyers have been very patient this afternoon. Shall we?"

"Let's go. Take my mind off things. I don't want to be cooped up with my thoughts anymore."

I follow Jack back down the hallway to the grand staircase, this time trying to memorize the path. I don't want to get lost if I'm on my own.

When we got engaged, everyone warned me I'd have to sign an iron-clad prenup if I wanted to go through with it. No problem on my end, I have no intention of needing it. Leaving Jack is unthinkable; he feels the same, I know. We are meant for each other. We balance each other. We complete each other.

And now that we've been to death's door together, nothing will tear us apart. I mean, he could be implicated, right? Hiding the truth about a crime?

No, we're in this together, for better or worse.

16

The Compton library is done up in old-world style. The room is expansive, two stories of bookshelves, floor to rafters, and the rest dark, well-oiled oak wainscoting. The scent of lemon and ancient paper permeates the air. This is my room; I realize it immediately. I feel utterly at home. Yes, I love painting, but reading is a close second. There are so many books that my mouth goes dry with anticipation.

Not only collectors of important works of art, Jack's family possess some rare and exciting texts in their many homes. This is the library of an investor, yes, but also of a reader—paperbacks with bright covers peek out from the staid gold and gilt, a human touch in the midst of the opulence.

Despite how much is crammed in, the room doesn't feel crowded, rather elegantly stuffed. There are some well-lit oils here and there—warships a-sail, hunting scenes—more traditional as befit the library's purpose. They don't excite me as much as the modern art, but they are impressive pieces.

There is a stone fireplace that a five-year-old could stand in comfortably, the wood stacked and ready for the match. To my right is the second-story balcony accessed by a massive curved staircase with wrought-iron spindles. The dark oak handrail is wide enough children could slide down it. Jack and his brothers slid down it.

Our children will slide down it. There will be shouts and cries and games in this room.

It hits me—this is happening. It is really happening. I'm going to pledge my life to Jack, to be his wife, the mother of his children. I do a giddy spin, taking in the rest of the room.

Toward the nave is a stunning stained-glass window, the detail remarkable. It depicts two men, one wearing a horned devil's mask, one holding paper and pen. Faust. A man caught in the act of selling his soul to the devil for all eternity.

A shiver passes through me. What a strange scene to have in your library. Then again, the idea of all the knowledge in the world bringing ultimate power was a cornerstone of the Compton computer software system. *Putting power in the hands of the people, for the greater good,* that is Brice Compton's mantra. It's fitting; the Comptons do so much for the greater good.

Under the stained-glass window is a long, wide table littered with vases of peonies, stacks of books, and a tower of papers. Behind it, two blue-suited lawyers sit side by side, one man, one woman, both in their fifties. The man is salty haired and round as a blueberry, the woman has a curly blond shag, light eyes, and a cadaverously thin frame. They look up in unison and jump to their feet, and the man waves us into the room.

"Jackson. So good to see you. Felicitations on your joyous day. This must be your beautiful bride."

Jack smiles. "It is. I'm pleased to introduce Claire Hunter. Claire, this is Henry Stephens and Margaret Haynes. They are our personal family attorneys."

"Call me Maggie." Her smile is warm and welcoming, much

less formal than her partner. Her eyes are the queerest color, not blue, as I thought earlier, but a celadon green. "We're so pleased to meet you at last, Claire. So pleased you've stolen our Jacky's heart."

"Maggie, for heaven's sake. I'm thirty-eight, not ten," Jack says, shaking his head in mock embarrassment. "Obviously, Henry and Maggie have been with the family for a very long time, Claire."

"We both started with the Comptons right out of law school," Henry says. "We've watched the boys grow up. We're normally based in Palo Alto, but Brice flew us in last night."

"We wouldn't miss it," Maggie says. She has a kind smile.

"I'm very pleased to meet you. Sorry we've taken so long to show up. Thanks for waiting."

I'm getting intimidated in the face of this continued opulence and generosity. Generational pearls and family lawyers and Faustian bargains and private Italian villas packed with priceless art—what's next? A royal entourage? Will Jack's mother sit me down and teach me the finer points of the princess wave?

"Not a problem at all," Henry says, waving a hand around the room. "We've had plenty to entertain us. Now, Claire, I'm sure Jack explained to you about the structure of your prenuptial agreement? Oh, sit, sit." He gestures to the empty chairs opposite. We settle in, the four of us as cozy as can be. I need to get used to these intimate enclaves, the odd sense of intrusion into our private life from the ancillary members of the Compton clan. First Henna and Fatima, now Maggie and Henry.

"We haven't discussed it in detail, no. But I'm not in this for the money, so I'm not concerned. I'm sure whatever you've drafted will be fine."

Maggie gives me a sharp glance. "If we handed you paperwork right now that explicitly stated you would forgo any settlements upon the marriage's demise, you'd sign with no qualms?"

"Of course. Hand me a pen. All I want is Jack."

And a dream dress, a swank destination wedding, and a castle on an island, but who's counting?

Jack beams at me, and the lawyers share a private look. Henry opens a folder and pulls out a pale blue–backed legal document.

"Happily, Claire, we do things a little differently here. We have no intention of asking you to forgo anything should your marriage to Jackson end in divorce, or death. A settlement of 30 percent of Jack's estate, including all fixed assets, confers to you regardless, right now."

I can't help sputtering. "Thirty percent? What? That's…that's too much."

"It's yours. The accounts are in your name, and your name only. As soon as you've legally changed your name to Claire Compton, that is. We've done all the necessary paperwork for the religious ceremony to be legal in the eyes of the Italian government, and as such, the Americans as well. You'll be issued a marriage certificate here after the ceremony, and as soon as you're back on US soil from your honeymoon, you will have a new social security card so you can get your new driver's license, and then you'll head to the bank. All will be waiting for you."

This is more than a shock. Thirty percent of his estate? Regardless?

"That seems…overly generous."

"We take care of our own," Maggie says, teeth flashing again. Her grin is now predatory.

"You're going to be my wife," Jack says, taking my hand. "The mother of my children. A full-fledged member of this family. That means you'll have your own money, to do with what you will. We won't be getting divorced, though, will we, Claire?"

"Of course not," I reply, touching the warm pearls around my neck. "I wouldn't bother marrying you in the first place if I had any intention of leaving. That would be counterproductive."

We all laugh, and Maggie slides over the papers. "Just for the record, Claire, the money and assets will revert back to Jackson's estate if you pass away before an heir comes along." They pause, as if to let this morbid idea sink in a bit.

"Naturally. I wouldn't need it if I were dead. I understand."

Cross my heart and hope to die.

And there it is again, that overwhelming curiosity—did Jack's dead wife go through all of this? Or is this new, something they've cooked up just for me?

Maggie gives me another sweetly predatory smile, like an adorable but feral barn cat.

"Excellent. What you're signing here, Claire, in addition to the prenuptial agreement, is basically a nondisclosure agreement. Everything we've discussed today must stay between us. If you tell anyone outside of the people in this room anything about the Comptons' financial arrangements with you, you will forfeit it all. Do you understand?"

Interesting. "I do."

Jack squeezes my knee, recognizing the echo of the words to come.

"There's more. You are precluded from discussing any personal information you might learn about the family through your marriage and subsequent time spent with them, their history as a family, anything to do with the Villa and all their other properties. If you do, you will forfeit your 30 percent, and there will be other legal ramifications. Is that clear as well?"

"Crystal. I would never divulge family secrets. I take that vow very seriously."

"Read this over, then," Maggie says, relaxing into the chair, "and here's a pen."

I read through the paper in front of me. The language is quite clear, but I read it carefully. Halfway down the page is the stipulation that everything depends on me legally changing my name to Compton and agreeing to raise my children under the Compton surname. I have no choice there.

And if I disclose anything personal about the family without express approval, the family can come after me legally. It should probably strike me as strange, and looking back, I can see that of course this was completely out of the ordinary. But in the moment, with Jack smiling at me and the lawyers waiting expectantly, their requests for secrecy and silence seem to be the most perfectly reasonable request I've ever heard. This is a family everyone wants a piece of. They are internationally known, famous, wealthy, targeted, and as such, understandably private.

An all or nothing setup. I understand it just fine. I will erase Claire Hunter completely, morph into Claire Compton, Mrs. Jackson Compton, and forevermore leave that damaged, empty part of myself behind that attaches to my maiden name.

And I want that. I want it so much. It's not the money, though. I swear it. I want Jack. I want his oblivion.

Without another thought or glance, I sign my name above the line where *Claire Elizabeth Hunter* is printed, and date it.

Soon enough, everything I sign will say Claire Compton. It is astounding to think of. I always thought when and if I got married, I'd keep my maiden name. I intended to be Claire Hunter forever. Call it karmic debt, a nod to my dead father permanently etched on me, legally and ancestrally.

When I told Jack I wouldn't be taking his name, early in our engagement, he'd been so stricken I walked it back immediately. "I'm open to discussing it, of course," I said, but he'd shaken his head. "You don't understand. If you aren't a Compton, legally, I can't protect you. I'm afraid you won't have a choice in this, darling. I'll make it up to you though, I swear it."

"We could hyphenate our children's names."

"Out of the question. My children will be Comptons. It's how our lives are set up. It's a legal thing, darling. You know how it is with these big ancestral estates. Draconian rules."

The Hunter name isn't without its own melodrama. Perhaps

leaving it behind in service of marriage and children would clear my karmic debt and I'd be a whole new woman.

I eventually realized that by claiming the title and becoming the new Mrs. Compton, I would not only make Jack happy, which, at the time, was paramount, I could also banish the ghost of his first wife.

And he *is* happy right now, watching me closely as I initial each section and sign my name with a flourish, page after page after page. One last signature, one last initial, and it's done. I hand the papers back to Maggie.

"Wonderful, wonderful," she says, signing her own name as witness, embossing the page with a notary's seal, adding the date, then tapping the papers together smartly so their pale blue edges are perfectly aligned. Amazing to think of the power in her hands. The money these family lawyers control.

I start to rise, but Jack puts a hand on my arm. "Hold on, darling."

Now what?

Maggie sends a quick text on her phone and moments later a hidden door to our right opens. I jump. It's as if the wall itself stretched and yawned, and people walked through its mouth. I shouldn't be surprised, a house this large must have access corridors, but I am.

Jack's parents step into the library, alongside a younger version of Brice with a deep tan and cold sable eyes. Poor Elliot looks tired. There is a man with them that I don't recognize. He stays unobtrusively by the door.

"Elliot." Jack jumps to his feet and shakes his little brother's hand. "Good to see you."

"You too, you too. Hey, Claire. How goes the great painting?"

There is always something so louche in Elliot's tone when he speaks to me. It annoys Jack to no end; I can feel the tension running through him when Elliot drawls at me. I haven't bothered to tell him Elliot hit on me at his wedding. He was drunk off his ass, and it was relatively harmless, but I've been on my guard with him since. He's never acknowledged the event. Maybe he was so drunk he doesn't remember. Maybe he's not stupid enough to risk Jack's wrath. I vote for the former.

"Hey, yourself. It goes, on and on and on." Appreciative laughs, the piece I'm working on is another monstrosity. "Where's Amelia?"

Ana Compton answers before Elliot has a chance. "She's resting."

Jack looks at Elliot curiously, but simply nods and smiles. It's how the family dynamic goes, lots of nods and smiles and inside looks that are impenetrable to outsiders.

"We'll see her later, I hope," I say. I like Amelia. She's the best part of Elliot, in my opinion.

Elliot coughs out a little laugh that sounds like "Yeah, right." Uh-oh. Something has happened.

Ana though, glides over this with equanimity. She is dressed in a flowing Ted Baker silk dress and soft leather sandals, expensive gladiators in saddle and gold. Her sable hair is tied back, styled in an incongruously bouncy ponytail. I don't think I've ever seen Ana without a French twist screwed into place. The ponytail looks good on her. Takes five years off. Okay, ten.

Beside her, I feel disheveled, but Ana takes us in with nothing but delight on her beautiful, austere face.

She draws me in, smelling of Chanel No. 5 and Camel Lights. Ana's thick hair swings around her neck and tickles my nose.

"Claire. My dear. Welcome to Villa la Scogliera."

17

The Biometrics

Ana's voice is a warm contralto, with the hint of an indefinable accent from her Continental upbringing. She looks and sounds like a young Sofia Loren. "Your trip in, it was good?"

"Very much so. The island, the Villa, they're quite stunning. Thank you for letting us use *The Hebrides*, too. You've done too much, as always."

"Oh, of course. They'll be yours, too, soon enough." Brice shoots Ana a look, somewhere between amusement and exasperation. She runs him a merry race, that's for sure.

Jack is now enfolded into his mother's arms, and Brice Compton holds out his arms for me. I step into them dutifully. It's not that I don't like Brice, I do. He's just very intense. He has a new beard, the pale edges of it still stiff and tipped in palest strawberry blond, and the same strange scent he wears clings to him like a shroud.

"Money," Katie said, when I told her about it. "He reeks of *eau de* money."

As amusing as that quip was at the time, it's not money Brice smells of. The scent is more earthy, as if he's just stepped in from digging in the garden. Not entirely unpleasant, but strange. It strikes me, the earthy scent could very well be something organic in nature, though I've never smelled weed that reminds me of an open grave before.

"Welcome to the Villa, Claire," Brice says. He squeezes my shoulders. "We are delighted to have you. You're sure the trip over was okay?"

"Yes, sir."

"Good Lord, none of that. It's high time you start calling me Brice. Or Dad."

He doesn't notice me wince. I can't call anyone but my father *Dad*.

"Brice. Thank you. *The Hebrides* is gorgeous. And the Villa… I have no words."

Elliot gives me a subtle thumbs-up. Brice appreciates understatement.

"Speaking of, Claire saw someone up on the cliff as we came in." Jack says this casually, but there is a note in his voice that makes my spine straighten.

"You did?" Ana crosses her arms on her chest, her face suddenly strained. She peers at me, an eyebrow raised. "Are you certain?"

"Yes, I saw a white scarf fluttering in the breeze. I figured it was someone from the house, looking out for us to arrive. I'd forgotten—I was distracted by the bones."

Ana looks at Brice, the glance so quick I almost miss it. What's that about?

Jack doesn't seem to notice. He massages my shoulder. "What an introduction to the island, right? I told Claire that we do come across remains from time to time—it's the nature of the beast with an island that's been populated for so long, especially one under a historical restoration."

Ana starts to answer but Brice talks right over her. "Come, come, we can deal with that all later," Brice says heartily. "Why don't we finish up the legalities so we can get to the fun."

Brice snaps his fingers and the stranger steps forward. I've forgotten him entirely. His accent pegs him as Italian, but his English is perfect.

"Signorina, for the Italian religious marriage to be legal we must do a blood test. If you wouldn't mind showing me your arm?"

"Ugh. We didn't have to do this in Nashville for our marriage license." But I roll up my sleeve compliantly, only wincing a little at the pinch. Jack rubs my shoulder compassionately.

"Formalities, darling. Ah, it's my turn."

The Italian is very fast. He takes a vial from Jack, then places them both in a padded box. *"Grazie,"* he says with a teensy bow, and leaves as quietly as he entered.

Brice says, "Good. Good. The hard part's over. Now for the rest. We'll need a photograph, Claire, for the Villa's facial recognition system, as well as an iris scan and fingerprints. All our homes are biometric. Once you have all of this in the system, you won't ever need a key. Everything will be coded to you, and you alone, so you'll be completely secure and able to access anything you need."

"Do you want to swab me for DNA, too?"

Brice laughs. "Not necessary, we'll have all that in your blood-work."

Well, that's not unnerving at all.

Elliot has all the tech in his bag. He takes a digital photo, unsmiling, does the iris scan, and holds up a small gray screen that I press each finger to, watching the loops and whorls appear as if by magic.

"Oh, and sign this for me, would you?" He pulls out another small reader. "We like to have the family signatures on file. In case anyone ever tries to forge a signature. This machine takes such minute measurements, the pressure you use, the angle you hold the pen, it all but guarantees no one can ever forge your name."

I sign my name with its usual flourish on the *R* at the end of Hunter and watch it load into the system. "Cool."

"Totally cool. But you need to sign it Claire Compton. Claire H. Compton, if you'd like."

"Oh. Oops." They laugh politely, and I do it again, smooth and elegant. It's not like I haven't written my name with Jack's before, like a teenager with her first crush covering her notebook in hearts and flowery cursive.

"I'm going to get you uploaded right now," Elliot says, opening his laptop. "Welcome to the family, sis."

The lawyers bundle together their papers and briefcases. They shake our hands and disappear out the door.

Finally, we're alone, just me and the Comptons. Once the door clicks closed, all eyes fall on me.

Brice clears his throat. "Jack told us what happened in Nashville, Claire. I'm so glad you're all right. Jack said you were hurt when you…fell?"

"I'm fine, really. Just a bump on the head." And dissolvable stitches, but that's no biggie.

"And Malcolm shot the intruder?" Brice asks.

I nod. "Yes, that's right. It was all such a blur. Thank goodness he was able to respond so quickly."

"Yes, indeed," Ana says. "We are so very lucky Malcolm was able to get to you both in time."

Jack threads his fingers through mine. "Do we know what the man was after? Has he been identified? We haven't heard from anyone yet."

"They'll be in touch soon, I'm sure," Brice says. "Karmen has been fully briefed. She's running point with the Nashville police. In the meantime, let's try to enjoy ourselves this weekend. The storms are going to put a damper on the outdoor activities, but there's plenty to keep us occupied. Shall we have some champagne? And perhaps a bite to eat? I'm sure you're hungry."

Brice gestures and we follow like obedient little lemmings, through the library door, down the hall, and into the majestic dining room. The inlaid parquet floors show a sunburst pattern; the walls are the lightest robin's egg blue plaster, with extensive millwork. The ceiling is vaulted, with frescos painted the length, and ribbed buttresses offset in dove gray. Naturally, the table has room for a good thirty or so, ready for intimate entertaining. As you do.

I stifle a giggle at the idea of Jack and me at opposite ends of this monstrosity, calling to one another to pass the salt.

I'm relieved to see that despite the grandeur of the room, this is an informal family dinner, rather than something more organized. The table is laden with platters, cheeses and meats and fruit and bread. Champagne cools in silver buckets, water in carafes are set on the sideboards.

Brice pours champagne for Ana, then for me. Elliot is tapping on his phone, and a few minutes later, Amelia shows up. She's been working out; she's got on yoga shorts and a sleeveless top, her hair piled carelessly on top of her head, the roots dark with sweat. Always too thin for my taste, she now looks downright unhealthy. She's all bones and sinew, dark circles under her pale eyes as if she hasn't slept in weeks. I watch as she takes some grapes and a sliver of prosciutto and retreats to the opposite side of the table.

"It's good to see you," I say as warmly as I can, biting back my concern.

"You, too, Claire. You're certainly blooming. The sea air agrees with you."

She's going through the motions; her voice is flat, empty. Something is definitely wrong. Is she sick?

The rest of the family ignore this exchange and start talking about the details of the weekend, and I'm amazed at how calm and collected they are.

Jack plops down next to me, his plate full.

"Should I call Katie? I hate that she's missing dinner."

Jack shakes his head. "She's crashed in her room. Fatima checked on her."

Fatima. I look up to see her watching me intently. I hadn't even noticed her standing in the corner of the room, hovering like a benevolent spider. I smile, and she smiles back.

"That was kind of her."

Jack feeds me a piece of parmesan. "This is the best cheese you will ever have. They make it north of here and we bring it in by the boatload."

It is amazing. I follow it with a strawberry, then some champagne. I am feeling the surreality of the moment bleed away, and realize I'm starting to enjoy myself. I am a part of this family now. With a few words and the stroke of a pen, I am one of them. I know it's not official until we wed, but this feels…right.

Until Elliot explodes.

"Shit!"

"Language," Ana says automatically.

But Elliot's face has gone from white to livid red.

"What is it? What's up?" Jack asks.

"Um…we have a problem. The fucking servers have been hacked."

"What do you mean, hacked?"

"I mean someone's gotten into our private servers and wiped them clean. I don't know who, but everything's gone." There is something sharp and frightened in his tone.

Brice shakes his head. "You mustn't have logged in properly. That's impossible."

Jack nods. "With as many firewalls and redundancies as we have, surely there are backups."

Elliot, still tapping hard on his laptop, shoves a hand through his hair. "When I say it's all gone, I mean, it's all gone. I've been searching every server. There's nothing left, anywhere. Even the backups are gone. Jesus, we're screwed."

Brice's phone rings on his son's final syllable, and he glances at the screen, staring as if the caller ID is in hieroglyphics.

"It's the SOC in New York." The SOC, I know, is the Security Operations Center, which houses the company's exceptionally advanced cybersecurity team. Jack told me how their company works last month.

Brice clears his throat and puts the phone to his ear. He listens for a moment then explodes.

"That's impossible. How could you let this happen?"

Ana lays a hand on his arm, but he shakes her off, starts issuing instructions rapid-fire.

"Get Karmen, right now."

"Is it a DDoS attack?" Jack asks Elliot, who is white-faced.

"I don't know what the fuck is happening. If some little shit thinks he can try to ransom the servers…" He punches numbers into his phone and the deadly calm in his voice chills me to the bone. "Get me into the SOC call with Brice, right now."

I do not want to cross Elliot. He's someone to keep on my side, for sure. When he's angry, I sense he is no longer in control. That could make him very dangerous. Amelia is watching him as well. She gets up and sets her plate on the sideboard, leaves without a backward glance. She's done her duty for the night.

"Wait, I'm getting a message." Elliot taps on the screen. "Oh, son of a bitch."

"What does it say?"

Elliot turns the phone around. "It says, *'You have twenty-four hours to tell them what you've done, or I will.'*"

18

Into the Labyrinth We Go

I'll tell you this. Ana Compton is a seriously cool customer.

The dining room feels like a battleground. Elliot is freaking out, pacing back and forth, Brice is speaking urgently into his phone, Jack is holding on to my hand so tightly the blood supply is cut off and the bones crunch painfully.

But Ana simply takes a long, deep breath and smiles, sanguine and calm, and holds out a hand to me. "Claire, why don't we take a walk."

I glance at Jack, who looks as shocked as I feel at this display. He releases my hand immediately and nods.

Okay. I'll bite.

I set down my champagne and accept Ana's outstretched hand. She draws me from the dining room into the hall. We walk in silence back to the main stairs, then past them to the French doors that lead to the main floor courtyard. The first of the promised breaks in the rain is upon us, so that's a bonus, but the air is scented with brine, thick and oppressive.

She shuts the doors behind us and falls into step beside me.

"You've had quite an eventful few days. Henna told me about your dress. I am very sorry. She's going to do what she can to make it presentable again. Still... What can I do to help? Shall we have another flown in? Your family is still in Rome, I believe. If you give me your size, perhaps Henna can coordinate a replacement."

This is such a kind offer I find myself fighting back tears. "I honestly don't know what to do, Ana. I'm starting to worry..." I trail off, but she urges me on. We're at the edge of the labyrinth now. The boxwoods rise at least eight feet—it's impossible to discern the path through by sight. The hedges didn't seem so high from the landing window. There are marbles statues everywhere. They must be the signposts for how to navigate the maze.

Ana knows what she's doing, though. She strides right into the opening, past two ancient statuary, so I follow. She chats as we take the turns.

"What are you worried about, my dear?"

I can't take this level of solicitude. When I'm upset, compassion always sets me off. I choke back the sob.

"I think someone's trying to stop the wedding. First someone breaks into our house. Then my dress is ruined. Now the servers are hacked?"

"It has been a difficult couple of days."

We turn left, right, left again. Ana walks purposefully, but slow enough that I wonder, for a moment, if we're lingering on purpose.

But another few turns and we're out the other side, and on the path to the artists' colony. We're close to the edge of the cliff, and I don't dare look down. I can hear the sea crashing against the rocks.

Ana stops, and we stand together, staring out over the water.

The air is sultry with the oncoming flow of another round of storms, the humidity rising again. It looks like it's raining hard on the mainland; the horizon is opaque, and I can't see the mountains in the distance anymore. A low-lying fog is creeping up the path, covering the ground so the cottages look like they're floating. It makes me uneasy, and I shiver.

Romulus and Remus appear at our sides. They've made a stealthy approach. Romulus sits on my foot, and I scratch him behind the ears.

I realize Ana is staring at me.

"That dog likes you."

I smile. "I know. He was all over me when we arrived. He's a sweetheart."

We stand a moment, the four of us, the dogs' tongues lolling. It is surprisingly comfortable.

"I always wanted a daughter," Ana says quietly. "After three boys, we stopped trying, but I so wanted a girl. I figured, my boys will marry, they'll bring home their partners, and out of the three I'll probably get at least one girl to bond with. When Elliot met Amelia, I had such hopes. But Amelia and I have never seen eye to eye."

"She doesn't look so good."

"No. She's quite unhappy. She's asked Elliot for a divorce, which we're granting. We've tried to keep it quiet. We didn't want to ruin your weekend. They've put their animus aside for now—we won't have any drama. But I thought you should know. After this weekend, Amelia will no longer be a part of the family."

"Does she get thirty percent of Elliot's estate as well?" *Oh my God, Claire. Rude much?* I put my hand over my mouth. "I'm so sorry, that was tacky of me."

But Ana laughs. "Hardly. She'll receive a nice payoff, and will live comfortably. But she and Elliot don't have what you and Jack do, so we didn't take the same…precautions. It's a shame.

I think Elliot truly thought he loved her, but it wasn't born of any sort of passion, only lust. A mother can sense these things. I never expected Amelia to be a long-term part of the family. Not like you."

She looks over at me, assessing. I am struck again by how silly I must look to her, my ripped jeans and wild hair. Thank God she'd never seen the art that covered my body. I can't imagine she would have appreciated my choice of canvas.

"My son loves you very much."

"I love him, too."

"I know you do. That's why we agreed to the terms of the prenup when Jackson approached us. That, and...you know he was married before. It didn't turn out the way he'd hoped, but that marriage, too, was doomed. Morgan wasn't right for Jackson. I worried from the moment he brought her home, hoped it wouldn't get serious."

"I don't know much about her."

Lies. Such dark little lies.

"Romulus doesn't like many people. He despised Morgan. When Jack brought her home, the dogs made such a fuss, growling and circling her. She was scared of them. They were young then, just pups, not fully trained, but in my experience, animals are good judges of character."

I go very still, enough that Romulus looks up at me with a tiny whine of concern. I'm now on full alert, because this is the most I've heard about Morgan from a Compton.

"She was such a beauty. She had that energy around her that many overtly sexual women have. She was bright, too, almost too bright for her own good. You know we invested in her company, don't you? Her talent was clear from the beginning. Brice and I immediately knew the value of her work. Scientific innovation is commonplace now, with so many people looking for new, better ways to communicate, but most of the young thinkers we came across, though brilliant, were only looking for ways to cash out. They didn't want to build a long-standing business. They wanted the quick and easy path, develop an app or idea good enough to be bought out by a bigger company, so they could move on to their next moment of genius.

"Morgan wasn't different. She created something useful, something she could grow, and she knew her work's value. We did as well. We took full advantage. Maybe she didn't like that. We gave her more than market value for her company, did everything we could to make sure she was given credit, too. Instead of being grateful and excited, she resented us. She tried to pull Jackson away from us. Even before the wedding, she was very busy driving a wedge into our family. She wanted him all for herself, didn't want to share him with us, with the world. She was obsessive, controlling, destructive. Jackson was so unhappy. I've never seen him like that before. Cowed. Beaten. He knew he'd made a mistake from the beginning. No, their marriage was never going to have a happy ending."

She pushes a few stray strands of hair that are caught in the wind off her face, then bestows a small smile upon me.

"You're different. You're an artist. You're making something that can nourish the soul. Your talent isn't ephemeral. Computers are obsolete almost the moment they come out of the box. Phones, tablets, cameras, software. The science changes as quickly and often as the weather. Art is enduring. You aren't taking from him, you're adding. He appreciates that. As do his father and I."

The compliment is a kind one, but it strikes me—Katie was right. They invested in Morgan like they invested in me. Ana saw talent, and wanted to nurture it, in both of us.

Her voice is soft. "Jackson told me what happened on Monday. I know everything. I need to ask. Did you shoot the intruder in Nashville, Claire?"

I don't hesitate. "Malcolm shot the intruder."

I feel her relax.

"Such a terrible thing to have happen on your wedding weekend. I admire your strength, Claire. You are a true match for my son. And for this family. One day, this will all be yours. Yours and Jackson's. It will be your responsibility to protect this family, protect our legacy, just as it is mine, now. You must be willing to do whatever it takes. Do you understand?"

"Yes. Of course."

"Good. I hope you know you can have anything you want from this world now that you're a Compton. Anything. Let's get back to the house. I'm sure Jackson is missing you, and I want to talk to Henna. We'll see what we can do to find you a dress that isn't ruined."

She whistles, and the dogs disappear.

And with that, our audience is over.

19

Wee Obsessions

It's embarrassing to admit, but I didn't start looking into Morgan's death until after my blowup with Katie. I'd made such a big deal out of not caring that I felt like a hypocrite. And I know myself. Once I latch on to something, it's hard to let go. "Like a dog with a bone," my dad used to say, but he meant it kindly. My obsessions were amusing to him. A way for me to get smart. It meant late nights with a book in my lap, and then a computer, looking things up. It's why my reports for school came back with extra points for my exhaustive research. When I found painting, realized I was attracted to the modernists, I became a walking encyclopedia on the movement. I was eight.

I think it's why I'm a decent painter. For me, painting is simply storytelling. Throwing a mental obsession onto a canvas. To have an idea in your head, a vision, to layer it day after day after day until it becomes a visual narrative, something a stranger can look at and comprehend, that's the key to a successful project.

Though interpretations vary. Beauty is in the eye of the be-holder, isn't that right?

My obsession problem is also how I ended up getting so many tattoos during my teen years.

"Doesn't it hurt?" Harper would ask, tongue stiff through her freshly tightened braces, and I'd nod and try to explain that it's the kind of pain that feels good. It gives a serotonin rush, and you seek it out again and again. Some people become ad-dicts, some use their bodies as canvases or pin cushions. Some bite their nails. Some starve themselves. Some cut. Some over-eat. Some find succor in hours of exercise. Some gamble. Some drink. Some fuck. It's a thing. Everyone has their thing, right?

Katie knew I'd fall down the rabbit hole if she gave me the right push. She left a window open on my computer with a be-guiling shot of Morgan in profile at a cocktail party. Within days, searching the internet for pictures of Morgan became a thing for me. Even as I erased the mistakes of my youth, be-coming the woman I thought Jackson wanted, which became its own torturous pleasure—trust me, it hurts a hell of a lot more to remove a tattoo than to get one in the first place—Morgan became my idée fixe. She was heroin, and the internet my fa-vorite pusher.

I tried so hard to keep it private. To look only when he wasn't around. But it got out of control, as all obsessions do.

It got to the point that even when Jack was lying in bed next to me asleep, when I was most at risk of discovery, I would have my phone out, screen fully dimmed, sound down, searching. Honestly, I would feel less guilty if I was looking at porn and satisfying myself rather than waking Jack to tend to my desires.

I can see why he was attracted to her. She is a dynamic pres-ence on the screen. Flaming red hair. Heart-shaped face. Pillowy lips. A sharp jaw. Elegantly arched brows, exactly the right thick-ness, two shades darker than her hair. I go back time and again to a shot of her laughing, mouth open wide enough that I can

see her bottom teeth aren't perfectly straight. Such a tiny flaw.
Was she self-conscious about it? She doesn't seem self-conscious
about anything. She seems like the kind of woman I always
wanted to be—confident as hell and disdainful of those mere
mortals who gave a damn about the way others perceive them.

And the way Jack looks at her...

I have a private Pinterest board where I save all her photos,
capturing all of her many moods, her looks, her style. Every
single thing I was able to find of the two of them, or her alone.
From her pictures in high school, the vague gaze off to the side
of the camera, to the one with the smudge of dirt on her chin,
to the one from Stanford, with her in some electrical suit, a
gadget with wires and lenses on the table in front of her. I have
shots of her smiling shyly. Giving Jack coquettish glances. Staring frankly into the camera as if to say *Yes? What do you want?*

Their wedding photos—most from magazines, taken by drone
paparazzi. From above, she looks so austere and elegant in her
gown, but I can't see her face, or the details. Just Jack's arm
around her waist.

Don't get me wrong. Jack loves me. I don't doubt his affec-
tion for a moment. He loves me in a way that is impossible to
fake. He's *in love* with me. He does look at me like he looked at
her; I'm sure others can see it in our photos.

But does he touch me like he touched her?

When we make love, and he does the things he knows I like,
things I didn't know I liked until he taught them to me, I can't
help but wonder, did he teach them to her, too? Did she teach
him?

The idea of her writhing in pleasure in his arms drives me
mad.

It would stand to reason that I'd start painting her.

Even in abstract, she became a part of my work. Her hair, a
swirl of cinnabar in the center of the canvas. Her eyes, the base

of my sky. Any flash of creamy skin or strawberry hair or a cardinal in a branch reminds me of her.

But I can't share this with anyone. Morgan is my darkest secret. My enduring obsession.

It would be so much easier if he'd just talk about her every once in a while. I mean, it's natural, right? When someone was a part of your life, weird little things remind you of them, and it's perfectly normal to remark on these things.

Oh, Morgan liked apples.

Oh, Morgan enjoyed foreign films.

Oh, Morgan was great at trivia.

Oh, Morgan struggled with split ends.

Anything, anything, to give me a better sense of why he loved her enough to marry her. Why he chose her to spend his life with.

I know my fiancé. He's not a shallow man. He wouldn't marry someone just because she was smart, or beautiful. There was something about her that he connected with on a visceral level, something that made him tingle with desire at the thought of her. Despite what Ana has just shared, I know it wasn't just a business transaction—yes, I already knew that Compton bought Morgan's burgeoning company soon after she and Jack met.

I know it was something more.

I know she had something more.

If she hadn't died, would he still be with her?

He won't speak of her. It's as if she never existed. As if there aren't a thousand photos of them together on my computer, hidden away, a humiliating treasure trove that I revisit night after night, day after day, adding to it whenever something I haven't run across before captures my attention.

Was that what Ana was trying to do? As I follow her back to the Villa, I wonder if she was trying to set me at ease, trying to make me think the ghost of Morgan doesn't live in the small, liminal space between Jackson and myself. Though I feel her there, as distinct as a plate of glass.

Does Ana know he holds that part of himself separate from me? From our life together?

Jack can never find out about this. It makes me look weak, and childish, to spend so much time on a dead woman. But the truth has kept me up at night for months. Despite Ana's strange reassurances, I know the truth about my soon-to-be husband.

I am his second choice.

20

Women Become

The week after Claire met Jack, she made an appointment to start laser surgery to remove the ill-advised tattoos on her ankle, shoulders, and lower back—especially focused on the tramp stamp she'd gotten to defy her mother and cover her surgery scars. That tattoo wasn't the best artwork money could buy anyway.

A month after they began dating, Claire took out all her extra piercings—her nose, her septum, her belly button, her left nipple—leaving just the two main earring holes and a double piercing on the left.

Three months in, she dyed her didn't-pay-for-it ombré hair back to her normal dusky blond and had it properly highlighted, with sun-kissed bits bright around her face. The money piece, the hairdresser called it. How very appropriate. The woman also trimmed Claire's shaggy Medusa mop into a sleek bob that she straightened to swing below her chin. The keratin treatment cost a fortune, but it was worth it, for the time it lasted.

Jack came home from an exceptionally long trip to Africa and she was changed. Altered. He was traveling a lot those first several months, so whenever he made it home, and she was a slightly fresher, sterilized version of her old self, he simply kissed her and told her she was beautiful no matter what and took her to bed.

He pretended not to mind her transformation, but I could tell he hated it. The way his jaw tightened when he saw her as a regular girl was a dead giveaway. I never thought he'd go for that kind of thing—the external evidence of internal pain and punishment—but with her, he lapped it up. She was his little artist girl, his artiste, his dark and broody girl, spending her days with the oils and adulations and her nights with his cock in her mouth. And here she was, his dirty little girl, scrubbing herself clean for him.

Claire's mother, Trisha, enjoyed the changes. She came for tea, nodding approvingly at the state of the house's renovation, *love love loving* the paint colors, the exposed beams, the gray kitchen cabinets, the Carrara marble single-sheet backsplash and the champagne brass finishes. She approved of the woman Claire was turning into, becoming such a grown-up. She approved of Jack. Approved of his family, especially. Who doesn't want their kid marrying into wealth and privilege?

Katie, though, questioned every step vociferously. Oh, the fights they had. She accused Claire of trying to fake her way into his family. *Why don't you let them judge you for who you are? Why do you have to conform to some ideal you think they're looking for? And what happens when he dumps you for the real deal?*

Do you blame her? Claire spent years layering on a disguise and Katie understood her like that, understood her motivations. Katie couldn't fathom why Claire would want to fling back the curtains and let the world see everything. It was the ultimate betrayal. Conformity was a sick disease in her mind. Katie was a free spirit, a daredevil. She resisted the idea that Claire wanted a different kind of normalcy.

Jack was Claire's salvation, and she was wise enough to leap on the opportunity.

By the time Jack took Claire to New York to deliver the promised canvases to Ana and Brice, she had completely reverted to her preteen self, the one who existed before her father died. Blond hair, green eyes, creamy skin and subtle gold hoops in her ears. She was demure. Feminine. Adoring.

They loved her transformation.

They had no idea she felt like a fraud.

Claire wanted to change for this man. She wanted him to see her as she was meant to be, not how she'd changed, altered, punished herself. She wanted him to think she was a typical, normal woman, not understanding there is no such thing as normal. And there was no way to erase the slices to her soul that drove her to the artistic path in the first place. She was doomed to repeat them.

But that's what true love does, right? It opens you to the possibility of who you were meant to be. Like raindrops in a thirsty garden, you open, you flower, you become.

Some women become more than others.

Some don't.

21

Server Down, Server Down

Jack no longer thinks there is any sort of coincidence in the past few days' events. Someone is after the family. After him, and after Claire. The only questions that still lingers—who, and why now?

Though the latter is easy enough to answer. With the entire family on the island, they are vulnerable. They are stuck here, being lashed by the storms, soon to be without recourse to leave, to defend themselves. He needs to get Claire by herself, now, tell her everything, and find a way to keep her safe.

"We need to coordinate," Jack says. "We need to make sure everyone's safe. Whoever is after us, they have an ax to grind."

Elliot throws his phone on the table, though Brice is still talking. "Why is someone after us, Jack? What's going on?"

"How the hell am I supposed to know?"

"Well, I haven't done anything wrong. I have nothing to confess. Fuck, man. Our personal servers are gone. Deleted.

The corporation's systems are untouched, it is only the private servers."

"How is that even possible?" Jack asks. "Who even knows about our servers? They're only for the family."

"And yet, someone very talented has managed to slip inside our family's wards, Jackson. Someone with the means, and the desire, to bring us down. Why do you think that is?"

Jack leans forward, fingers curling on both hands. He is lit with white-hot rage at his brother's tone.

"Elliot, what the hell are you saying?"

"Everything was going just fine until you started lusting after that woman."

"*That woman?* How dare you? Claire is going to be my wife. I—"

Elliot squares off against him. The two are nose to nose, hissing like feral cats.

"I am not talking about Claire. I'm talking about that bitch of a woman you married ten years ago."

"How dare you bring *her* into this," Jack spits through clenched teeth.

"*You* brought her into it. You exposed all of us to danger. The reverberations are still lingering, even now. You were always blind to her, Jack. Blind to her faults. Blind to her actions. Even after she died, you kept the blinders on. You've never wanted to see what's been right in front of you."

Jack's fist connects with Elliot's nose and blood spurts. Elliot stumbles backward, both hands to his face, blood pooling through his fingers.

"You fucking asshole." He flings the droplets to the ground, wipes his hands on his trousers, and lunges toward Jack.

Jack steps forward, too, happy to brawl this out like they used to as kids, but Brice reacts lightning fast. He grabs Jack's arm and hauls him out of Elliot's space.

"Stop it, both of you. Fighting isn't going to solve anything."

"He started it."

"Elliot, don't be a child," Brice says, and Elliot rolls his eyes but sits down, a snowy white linen napkin held to his nose. It grows increasingly red, and Jack feels a terrible sense of satisfaction at bloodying his brother.

"I don't think the data has been wiped for good," Brice continues. "Someone's stolen it. Moved it to their own server and wiped ours clean. They're holding it until we respond to the threat."

"What's been accessed?" Elliot asks, gamely trying to gain control.

"All of it," Brice replies.

"Does someone want to clue me in on what we're supposed to be admitting to in the next twenty-four hours?" Jack asks wearily.

Elliot begins to speak but Brice holds up a hand. "It doesn't matter. We say nothing. We don't respond to blackmail. I've planned for this very situation. I have a self-destruct mechanism built into the personal servers. Within an hour, if a passcode isn't entered, the files will kill themselves. The passcode is generated from a keycoder that I carry on me at all times and is controlled with my personal biometrics. It's an automated process, the passcode resets every sixty minutes. So, it doesn't matter. This will all be over, and the joke's on whoever thought they could hold us hostage."

Elliot throws the bloodied linen to the floor. His nose has stopped bleeding, but his face is puce with anger, his nose swollen and bruised. *Won't he look charming in the photos*, Jack thinks.

"You never told me that. What if something happened to you? I need to have access to these files, too. I mean, God forbid, but what if one of our enemies decides to drop *you* off the cliffside? Without your active biometrics, the files are useless. Besides, whoever has them can still read the files right now."

"Thank you for the vote of confidence, El," Brice says drily, pouring himself an espresso. "I have contingency plans in place should something happen to me. But without the physical evidence, there will be no proof. And someone smart enough to crack our encryptions and break through our firewalls will know that without proof, they have nothing. This will all go away."

"Who's done it, though? Who managed to get into our system in the first place?" Jack asks.

"That's what we'll need to figure out. Karmen will get to the bottom of this."

"Karmen is a bit overwhelmed, don't you think?" Elliot says. "She's already dealing with the *situation* in Nashville."

"Fuck off, Elliot. They're tied together, obviously," Jack says. "The break-in, the servers, finding Morgan's body... It's all tied together. The question is, what are we going to do?"

"We're going to sleep on it," Brice says. "There's nothing you can do right now anyway. The SOC and Karmen are handling things. We don't respond to threats. We'll figure this out tomorrow."

Jack has always been astounded by his father's calm in a crisis. Brice claps his eldest son on the shoulder.

"It will all be okay."

"Doubt it," Elliot says.

"Stow it, Elliot," Brice snaps. "Go tend to your wife. I have this under control."

Elliot storms from the room, passing Ana and Claire as they return. Ana watches him go, then looks at Brice. "Everything okay?"

"We're fine. Just a misunderstanding. I'll fill you in upstairs."

Ana hugs Claire, then Jack.

"Good night, my dears. We'll see you in the morning." She leaves with Brice, and Jack blows out a huge breath. They are finally alone. Claire breaks a breadstick in half and nibbles on it.

"Everything okay?"

"Yeah. Dad has things in hand, of course."

"Elliot looked pissed."

Jack laughed, sharp and short. "Elliot is being a dick."

"They're getting divorced. He and Amelia."

"Mom told you that?" She nods. "I suspected as much. He's been on edge for weeks. And Amelia looked terrible."

"Are we going to be okay?" Claire asks. "I mean, the servers, surely there's something important... Are you still okay with everything? I know——"

He cuts her off with a kiss. "Hey, bride. Wanna get drunk under the stars? It might be our last chance to be alone for a while."

The way she smiles at him makes his entire body light up. "Yes, please."

"Good. Follow me."

22

Making Love Out of Nothing at All

We go down the hall to the library again. I hadn't noticed the French doors on the near wall. The curtains are drawn, huge, thick sheaves of oyster Dupioni silk draped in front of the doors. He pulls them back with a *schwing* and I can't help myself—a gasp flies from my lips.

"Oh my God, the view is incredible from here. Why would you ever close these?"

"Light can damage the books. We're on the edge of the island. Doesn't it feel like we're dropping off in the sea?"

"Is that the infinity terrace we saw from the boat?"

"Yep."

He leads me out, positions me at the stone's edge. The sun has slipped away now, and the sky is a few shades darker than the lavender of our bathroom ceiling. The clouds are ominous, but still holding themselves back. Jack pours champagne in our glasses, then tips his glass to mine. "To my bride."

"To my groom," I reply, taking a sip. I hadn't noticed the label, but it is excellent, of course. I expect nothing less.

"To your 30 percent. I hope you aren't *too* taken aback by our little arrangement," he says, voice now laced with amusement. He sounds himself again.

"Jack, you know I'm not interested in your money. But a little heads-up would have been nice. I felt foolish."

"I wanted to surprise you."

"Oh, you surprised me, all right."

A small smile quirks the edge of his lips. "I'm to take note that you don't like surprises, correct? Marriage lesson number one?"

"Yes. Marriage lesson number one. Marriage lesson number two… It's too much, Jack. A third of your estate? What am I supposed to do with it?"

"Buy a small country?"

"Ha-ha."

He brushes a piece of hair back from my cheek, tucks it behind my ear. "Claire. Listen to me. I love you. I want you to be taken care of, no matter what. As you might have just noticed, being a Compton can come with certain…constraints. This is your safety net. If something happens to me, I wanted you to be covered."

"If something happens to you?" The sentence ends on a shrill squeak. "What do you think might happen?"

He hesitates, and I have the strangest sense he is about to say something huge and important, but the moment passes.

"Darling. Monday should have been the first clue. Tonight, another. We are often targets. This is the world we live in. We have no idea what might happen from one day to the next. I have no intention of being parted from you willingly. But should the unexpected happen, I want you taken care of, no matter what. Yes, the terms of the settlement are generous, but the NDA is quite stringent and serious. You can't break it, Claire, or there will be nothing, and the family can prosecute you for breach of contract. I don't have any control over this. And I want you to have everything. You deserve everything. Okay?"

"Of course. I have no intention of mentioning anything private about the family. Like I told your parents, it's no one's business."

"Good. Are we friends again?"

"Yes. Good friends."

He kisses me, startling me again with his intensity. It's like we are never going to kiss again, and he needs to memorize every inch of me. I quickly realize he's doing more than kissing me. One hand is wound up in my hair, and the other has travelled to the button of my jeans.

"Jack, stop. Not here. Let's go to our room."

"Yes, here," he replies, silencing me with another soulful kiss. "No one can see. This is a very private terrace."

"No no no no. I'm not so much of an exhibitionist that I'm going to drop trou right here in front of God and your parents and the library door. But if there's someplace close by that affords a bit of privacy…"

I trail my fingers along the buttons of his jeans, and he groans.

"Come with me."

He marches purposefully down the stone stairs to a long, fragrant path. In the gloaming, it is so vividly green I can practically hear the breath of the trees, feel their heartbeats thudding, growing, soaking up the dripping wet from their leaves. Or maybe it's my own, thundering in my ears, a physical expression of the desire coursing through me.

"Where are we going?"

"You'll see."

We are moving fast—the path is well trod; one Jack clearly knows intimately. I see a corner ahead, and the grimacing face of a stone Medusa on a pedestal.

"Is this another entrance to the labyrinth? Your mom took

me through it earlier, but I didn't realize there was more than one way in or out."

"It's a safety thing. Four corners, four entrances. One day, we'll sit down with the layout and I will show you exactly how to navigate it from every angle. In the meantime, if you find yourself lost in here, turn left. Always turn left. For the moment, just follow close."

We speed through the turns, left, right, left again, then we're back out into the clean sea air and we're approaching the cottages. They sprout like mushrooms from the forest floor. They need work.

"Why haven't your parents done a restoration on the artists' colony?"

"We thought maybe you'd be interested in working on it."

"Me?"

"Who better to restore and recreate an artists' colony than the world's greatest artist herself?"

I think perhaps this is something I can do for the family. Clear the area, get the cottages restored—revive the artistic tradition of the island. I can hold retreats, bring in other artists—painters, writers, filmmakers—work with them, create with them. I've been here only a day and I'm already inspired—a week in the colony and I might come out with a new mission statement entirely.

"I would love to."

"Good. Mom will be thrilled." He stops walking at the first cottage. "Private enough for you? It better be."

He pulls me to him, kissing me intently. I'm weak with desire already, his kisses always turn me on, and our flight through the labyrinth has left me short of breath. Being here, with him, on the island, outside in the salty air and frangipani breeze, turns me on even more. He brushes a warm hand against the skin of my stomach, and this time I murmur my assent. He unbuttons my jeans and slides down the zipper roughly, his long fingers finding their way inside my panties. I collapse against him, rev-

eling in the sensations rippling through my body. It isn't long
before one leg is free, hooked around his hips, and he has my
back up against the cottage wall. I take advantage of the position
to reach between us to free him of his jeans, and he groans as
they slide down. He takes me there, against the stone. It doesn't
last long, for either of us.

"Love you, Claire. Love you so much."

He is talking into my hair, stroking me. My back is scraping
against the rock. He must have felt me flinch because he pulls
away and gently, so gently, lays me down in the grass.

"Open your eyes, Claire."

I do, and the naked fear on his face almost makes me cringe.
It shifts to sweetness and love the moment his eyes lock on mine.

"You're mine now," he said. "Forever."

We dress, straighten ourselves, giggling a little at the headi-
ness of being in love. Then we stand together, staring out at the
sea. I sense the dogs moving near us.

"Do they live outside?"

"No. Well, yes, technically, but their kennels are the size of
your sister's apartment in New York. Heated, cooled, cushy
beds. There's even a therapy pool in case one of them needs
work. You know these larger breeds often have hip dysplasia as
they get older."

"So they're not spoiled at all."

"Lord, no."

I take a deep breath, blow it out. I am suddenly exhausted.

"What's wrong, darling?" Jack asks, so solicitous, so warm.

"Just…worried about my parents and Harper getting here
okay."

"Ah. Don't worry. They'll all get here in time."

*Tell him your fears. Admit your obsession. It's time he knows ev-
erything about you.*

"It's a funny thing, Jack—"

"Wait. What is that? Hold on."

He dashes away, leaving me standing alone on the edge of the grove. I follow slowly, picking my way through the brambles and stones. While the labyrinth path is well tended, the cottages and the grounds surrounding them have been left to decay. I don't know why they would have let it go, unless it's something to do with Jack's grandfather, and his dementia.

I find Jack at the farthest cottage. He's gone inside—the door is propped open. A musty scent emanates from inside. I look closer at the eaves above the door. All of the wood has been left to rot, we'll have to restore them, too. Olive wood or Cyprus would be good, both are rot resistant.

"Damn it."

"Jack? What's wrong?"

He emerges from the darkness, turning off his cell phone's flashlight.

"Don't come in here."

"Why not?"

"Someone's been camping in here. It's disgusting. The cottages are closed—they're unsafe, as I'm sure you can see."

"Someone? Like who?"

"I don't know, but I'm going to have a conversation with Karmen. We can't have strangers wandering the grounds. She should have a tighter hold on things."

"Is she here?"

"Everyone's here, darling. But she's not a part of our wedding party. She's tucked away in her lair, handling security."

I wonder, just for a moment, how many of our thirty guests are Compton staff. Henna handled the list, as she handled most everything else.

Compton staff are family—long-term, well liked, privy to all the little secrets. I'm sure they've all signed the same nondisclosures I have.

Jack wipes his face with the bottom of his shirt. "We need

to go back to the Villa. I need to let them know. It's probably someone from the restoration team who didn't want to go back to the mainland over the weekend—there's food and trail clothes in there, plus a sleeping bag and blankets—but everyone who isn't family or staff are supposed to have left the grounds to give us our privacy. We don't want any media sneaking in—you know that."

Oh, boy, do I. The Comptons are notoriously private when it comes to family affairs.

I have to stop thinking about the family this way. I am about to be a Compton. I belong to this servant-laden, helicopter-flying, island-owning, yacht-sailing, computer-mogul-gazillionaire privacy-at-all-costs family.

"Jack?" A voice is calling from up the path, and I scramble to make sure I'm truly decent. Private, my ass. My God, anyone could have come out and seen us in flagrante delicto in the colony. I'm mortified at the thought. I'm no prude, but I'm not entirely comfortable around the Comptons yet. I always feel like I'm about to make a misstep. Boinking the heir in the shadow of the Villa counts.

"We should go," Jack says. I twist my hair back from my face in an effort to smooth it just as Fatima appears at the entrance to the labyrinth.

"There you are. Karmen needs to speak with you." She looks amused and I have the most horrible feeling she knows exactly what we've been doing.

Despite myself, I yawn, a jaw-cracking yawn, and Jack grabs my hand.

"Come on, sleepyhead. Let's get you back to the Villa."

23

Somebody's Watching Me

The library is clearly the staging area for the family. Fatima disappears discreetly after showing us to the door, which feels so damn weird. I mean, Jack knows the way around his house, he hardly needs to be escorted. Especially with Malcolm and Gideon lurking around.

Ugh… I'd forgotten myself outside. Bet they got an earful. How mortifying.

Karmen Harris waits for us. She has taken a seat by the fireplace. Two chairs sit opposite her. I look for Brice or Ana, but we're alone. Jack closes the doors behind us and we take our seats.

Up close, I'm surprised to see how small she is. She can't be more than five feet tall, but she commands the room. She has a large gun in a holster under her jacket. I suppose if I had that kind of firepower, I'd reek of confidence, too.

"Jackson," she says by way of greeting. "And this must be Claire. Lovely to meet you."

"You, too. I've heard good things."

She smiles but doesn't offer her hand, and I don't offer mine.

"Karmen, someone's been camping in the cottages. You need to look into it," Jack says.

"Camping?"

"Living, camping, spying. Who knows? There's a sleeping bag and other stuff out there."

Her eyes shutter, and she nods. "I'll deal with it. First, though, we have a bit of a situation. The Nashville police want to speak with Claire again." I must have leaned forward because she puts up a finger. "Don't worry, it's routine for them to follow up, especially when a suspect is killed. They're just looking for confirmation of your story."

Jack squeezes my hand in reassurance, or to warn me not to speak again, I'm not sure which. "Did they talk to Malcolm? He was the one who shot the intruder."

"They have. Like I said, this is routine, so long as everything shakes out the same."

It is hard for me to explain the flush of panic that surges through my body. It's as if I've grasped a live wire. Before she can explain further, Jack's phone rings, the 615 area code flashing on the screen.

"Put it on speaker," Karmen says with a reassuring nod. "It's all going to be fine. I'll explain what they don't afterward."

Jack gives me a sharp look, his brows furrowed, and presses the speaker button. "This is Jack Compton."

A sharp male voice speaks. "Mr. Compton. This is Lieutenant O'Donnell, Metro Nashville Police. I'm joined by Officer Cooper—you met him on Monday, he was the responding officer to the break-in."

We did? I don't remember.

"We wanted to follow up, and discuss our findings."

"I appreciate that. My fiancée is here with me, Claire Hunter, and our head of security, Karmen Harris. What can you tell us? Who is he?" Jack asks.

"We're having some trouble with a formal identification," O'Donnell says. "He didn't have any ID on him. We did find a car down the street from your house. It was rented in California by a man named Francis Wold. Does that name ring a bell?"

I shake my head. "No. Not at all. Jack?"

"I've never heard that name."

"We're running the prints, too. We're thinking that Wold ID may be fake. In the trunk, there was a duffle bag. The items inside were…disturbing. Rope, duct tape, entry tools, flashlight, another gun. All items that tell us the suspect was planning to hurt someone. We're not sure whether he was getting up his nerve, or casing your house, or stealing your underwear, ma'am—we just don't know. But there's more. There were also packages of wires and cameras."

"Cameras? What kind of cameras?" I ask, confused. Lightning quick, Jack's face shifts from concern to realization to outright terror.

"The kind used to watch you without you knowing," O'Donnell says. "Very small. Easily hidden."

"Where did you find these cameras, if I may ask?" Jack asks tightly. "Just in his car?"

"No, sir." This is Cooper, I think, his voice is rougher, meaner, than the lieutenant. "When we swept the house, looking for them, this time, we found multiple hidden cameras. Obviously, there are currently security cameras in your house, Mr. Compton, but these—they are very small. They were well hidden. We found drill marks in the rafters, empty shafts. Looks like they were installed in the mechanism of the fans, in the lights."

"How many cameras did you find?"

"At last count, there were at least twenty. They were spread through the house—the master, the living room, and the studio.

One of them seems to have shorted out, there were burn marks in the rafter in your studio, ma'am. Lucky we found them, it could have burned down the house."

Jack looks ready to explode. I put my hand on his. He needs to keep his composure.

"Why would someone want to spy on us?" My own voice is shaking, both with anger and fear. Someone's been watching me. Watching me with Jack. Watching us together. And whoever it is must have had a front row view to the events of Monday. This is bad. This is very, very bad.

"I have no idea, Ms. Hunter. Do you?" O'Donnell doesn't seem worried about assuaging me at all. I'm surprised Jack doesn't scold him for being so short with me.

"No. Of course not. This is terribly disturbing, Lieutenant."

"Understandable. It's quite an invasion of privacy. From what we can tell, the cameras aren't recording on site, they're transmitting to another location. Ms. Harris, I was hoping you could provide your footage from the security cameras that were supposed to be recording. Can you send that along?"

Jack leans forward, but Karmen shakes her head. "We have a problem there, Lieutenant. I've been working on this all day. It seems the tapes for the past week were written over. An internal review is underway. Trust me when I say this won't happen again."

Jack tenses, staring at Karmen in fury. She writes quickly on the notepad in her lap: *I'll explain later roll with it.*

O'Donnell's voice gets more curious now. Even I find this awfully convenient, though I am so, so grateful. I hope Karmen knows what she's doing.

"What do you mean, they were written over? Is this something that happens regularly?"

She answers smoothly. "As I'm sure you know, for most offsite security systems, it's typical to recycle the tapes on the first of the month. Assuming there's nothing suspicious on them, naturally. In this case, there was a screwup. It is my understanding that our regular technician was in a car accident and ended up in the hospital, and while he's been out this week, his replacement recycled all the tapes every night at midnight, as was done in his previous employ. I interrogated them both thoroughly, and am certain this was an oversight, not a nefarious act on the part of the substitute. Regardless, both have been fired with cause, as well as their immediate supervisor."

"A shame we don't have the video of the break-in from your side. Especially of your man shooting the suspect. It would have helped to have the whole picture, to see exactly what he was up to inside the house." O'Donnell is polite, courteous to a fault. "If you do find something, please let us know. In the meantime, we'll keep things running on this end."

Karmen spins a finger, signaling Jack to wrap it up.

"We're just grateful no one else was hurt," Jack says. "If you wouldn't mind sharing the information you get on the remote feed, that would be a great help. You're sure all of the cameras were retrieved?"

"We think so. And of course, we'll share what we find. Just one more question. Ms. Hunter, we're all assuming this break-in is related to Mr. Compton, but I would be remiss if I didn't ask you if anything strange has happened to you lately? Have you noticed anyone lurking around? Were you receiving threats?"

"No. I haven't. There's just…"

Jack turns his gaze on me, full of warning. His voice is solicitous, though. "Claire? Do you know something?"

Karmen is slashing her hand across her throat. Shit. Shit!

"No. There's nothing. I wanted to say thank you. I so appreciate everything you're doing to help, Lieutenant."

The lieutenant waits a moment, then says his goodbyes. Jack carefully ends the call, then turns off his phone completely. I sit up. He's about to lose his composure entirely—I can feel the wave coming.

"That went as well as can be expected," Karmen says.

"Cameras? There were cameras in the house? Fuck!" Jack screams the curse and is out of his chair and pacing. "Is it true? The security tapes were overwritten?"

"Yes. I'm still investigating what happened, but what I told the police was the truth. We have no footage of the incident. Obviously, that was an important factor in keeping this situation from getting out of hand."

"Who the fuck was able to put cameras in our house? My God, Karmen. Do you know what this means? How compromised we might be?"

I read between the lines. They erased the tapes so no one could see what I've done. That I, not Malcolm, killed the intruder. I feel a bit faint. Someone has been watching me. Watching us. They have violated my sanctum, my home, physically and emotionally. And what I've done is on camera somewhere.

What Karmen's done to hide my sins, it's risky. So risky. I suppose we're about to see just how much power the Comptons have.

"Jack, we should just tell the truth," I say. "I don't remember what happened, not exactly, but there's no way anyone would prosecute me. It was self-defense. If there are cameras out of the family's control, lying to the police will get us all in trouble. I think we should come clean, right now, before this gets out of hand. Self-defense is one thing. Perjury is something very different."

They both glance my way. I have the sudden urge to run from the room. I've never seen Jack this mad. He's almost scary. My fiancé has always been in turns funny, sweet, solicitous, passionate, and kind. But roaring with fury? Not a look I'm excited about.

Karmen raises a brow. "Is that what you were about to tell them, Claire? The 'truth?' After everything that's been done to protect you, you want to expose everyone as liars?"

Jack is by my side in an instant. "Hey. Go easy."

"It's okay, Jack. No, Karmen, I'm not stupid. I would hardly volunteer information that might hurt Jack, or the family. I would take full responsibility."

Karmen spits out a laugh, and even Jack sighs.

"You don't understand," he says. "What happens to you happens to us all. Malcolm is licensed to carry, he's responsible for our safety. His job is to protect us at all costs. That he wrestled the gun away from the intruder and shot him...it's the logical story. The police aren't going to push the narrative any further. Trust me. They don't want this hassle, either. A break-in occurred. Clearly the guy was up to no good. He had a murder kit in his car, for God's sake. We've done the world a favor. I'm sure when they figure out who he is, he will have had a long, bloody history with law enforcement. Stay the course with me, darling."

"Jack is right," Karmen says. "The family can easily weather the storm of our security doing their job."

"We will figure out who's behind this well before the police, Claire. Won't we, Karmen?"

The threat is implicit. Fix this, or else.

"Of course. My people are already on it." Karmen assesses me. "What *were* you going to tell them?"

"That something odd did happen, though I doubt that it's related."

"What is it, Claire?" Jack asks. He's gotten himself back under control, sounds calm and assured again, but I can tell he's at his wits end. How many times has he told me to be open and honest with him? But this...this I've kept secret for a reason. A good reason. I've screwed up, opened my big mouth, so now I have to ruin the surprise.

"A few weeks ago, a woman came to see me."

24

A Stranger in Our Midst

The muscle in Jack's square jaw is ticking. "A woman? Who?"

"It was supposed to be a surprise," I say, hoping to see something other than anger in Jack's eyes. "I've sold another painting. At least, I think I have. A client's representative came to the studio a few weeks ago. She was interested in *Jolina*."

This does get Jack's attention; he lights up.

"Who is Jolina?" Karmen asks.

"Not who. What. *Jolina* is the name of a painting I've been working on. It's a massive undertaking, a twenty-by-forty-foot canvas. A magazine asked me what I was working on and I mentioned a megalith, and apparently the woman's client read the piece and wanted a preview.

"It was strange because she walked in off the street. Normally, a buyer's agent would make arrangements, an appointment, but she was very casual about it all. She wouldn't tell me her client's name, but that's not unusual. The agent's name is Ami Eister.

But I'm not going to let *Jolina* go somewhere random. And no one knows about her. I'm not explaining this well. Jack?"

He covers my hand with his. He's relaxed now that he realizes I'm not offering up the family to the wolves.

"You know Claire is poised to break out massively on the art scene, so we've been very careful about who gets to see her work. It's part of growing her as an artist, as a brand, but also to keep her focused. We don't need her distracted by the business side of things."

"Yes, I do know," Karmen says. "It's very exciting. Was there something the woman said that made you feel uncomfortable, Claire?"

"She was very intense, asked me a number of questions about my work, and my inspirations. Normal stuff. But she knew the painting was called *Jolina*. That's what was so weird. When she came in, she introduced herself, gave me a card, and said her client was interested in a preview. I've never, ever said the painting's name to anyone but Jack. I have no idea how she would know. Except..."

"The cameras in the house," Jack and Karmen say at the same time.

"Well, this proves it," Jack says. "Someone *has* been spying on us. And whoever is behind it, they're related to this Ami Eister woman."

I'm feeling more secure that I've shared this news now. This wasn't supposed to be an awful surprise, but a wonderful one. I was going to tell him after the rehearsal dinner. Jack, the Comptons, have been so instrumental in my recent success that when Ami Eister came to visit, I felt like I'd conquered a hill of my own. Brought more to the table, an unseen, unqualified dowry of sorts. *Jolina* will go for six figures, easily, possibly even seven, to the right buyer. She is my best work.

Karmen has been making notes. "Claire, did you save the business card?"

"I did, it's in my studio in Nashville. She was based out of New York, that I do remember."

"We should have the studio swept immediately," Jack says. "If there were cameras in the house, chances are they're elsewhere. This is unbelievable." He mutters the last, and I can only imagine the shitstorm that's about to be unleashed inside the Compton Security division. It's an invasion of our privacy, absolutely, but clearly it's something more. I know exactly what Jack is thinking—how could they let this happen? Especially with the end result of the break-in. Everything I've just said is true, and he knows it. Despite his assurances, it can hurt us if our narrative is challenged. If someone has it on tape? We're screwed.

"You're sure you haven't mentioned the piece—*Jolina*—to anyone?" Karmen asks.

"I'm 100 percent sure. It's a superstition of mine. I've only told Jack."

"Okay. Other than an overly familiar interest in your art, any idea why someone would want to spy on *you*?"

"Goodness, no."

"This woman did come to see you though, Claire. The break-in was at your primary residence. We can't discount that this is about you."

"Stop it, Karmen. You're scaring her."

She's not scaring me, she's pissing me off, royally, but I keep my mouth shut. I am a good soldier. I'm going to follow Jack's lead, especially within the family.

"All right. I appreciate this information. I will follow up, have a conversation with Ami Eister, see how she came to know the name of your painting. I'll let you know if I find out anything more. Try to enjoy yourselves, though I know it might be hard. I have this under control. No one will hurt you. Not on my watch."

Karmen leaves, and Jack takes her seat opposite me.

Without the buffer of the strangers across the sea and the diminutive head of security, I wilt under his keen attention. Jack clears his throat. Here we go.

"Why didn't you tell me, Claire? *Jolina* is a big deal."

"I know. That's why I didn't say anything. I wanted to surprise you with a sale I'd brokered on my own."

"But that's why Mom hooked you up with Anton Bowmore. He's supposed to handle the business so you can focus exclusively on the creation. All of the press we've been doing lists him as the contact, and everyone knows he's representing you. Why didn't Eister go to him? And why didn't you tell her to speak with him immediately? Did you call him, let him know?"

"That's a lot of questions, Jack."

"I'm sorry. One at a time, then."

"I didn't think to send her to Anton right away. I guess I got caught up in the idea of handling it myself. I was flattered that she sought me out. You don't realize, Jack, that sometimes, all of this—" I wave my hand, gesturing vaguely toward the exquisite library and meaning so much more "—I'm not used to it. I'm not used to being the center of attention, and I'm not used to the press, the scrutiny. I'm certainly not used to my art being of worth to strangers. It's wonderful, and an ego stroke like nobody's business, but emotionally I'm still the struggling artist you met the night of the art crawl."

"You will never have to struggle again, Claire. Never."

I run my fingers along his hairline, from his forehead to ear, touched by his sincerity. "Struggle is good for art, Jack. It's part of the process. Just don't be mad at me, okay? I know I screwed up, but I wanted to surprise you. It won't happen again."

"I'm not mad, darling. And you've hardly caused a mess. But going forward you really do need to remember who you are. You're about to be Claire Compton, and that comes with certain responsibilities. Let Mom and Anton handle the business. You create. You are the most talented painter I've ever seen."

"You're just being nice now. Buttering me up isn't going to

fix this. If the police figure out who planted the cameras, and see the footage, they will know we're lying. With the servers being hacked, and the note Elliot received... Jack, we're vulnerable here. I know you see that."

"Not if we get to the truth first. And we will. Karmen is very good at her job. She will find the answers. Out of curiosity," he asks, "did you look her up? Ami Eister?"

"Well, yes, I did, but there wasn't much to see. She has a website, and an Instagram, though it's private. Check her out, you'll see."

He pulls out his phone and taps the screen a few times. I can see his eyes flying, processing. "Her LinkedIn profile is pretty bare bones. The website is as well. But that's not unusual for these dealers. I don't know the name, maybe Anton will. I'll ask him."

"Jack? Are we going to talk about what happened at the house? And why? Someone's been spying on us. That man was *spying* on us. He broke into our home, and now he's dead. And I—I still don't remember everything, but really, I think—"

Jack's brow furrows but he smooths his thumb across my mouth in a startlingly intimate gesture, considering the topic at hand. "Darling. You let me worry about this, all right? My parents and Elliot need to know what's happened, both with the house and with this mysterious art buyer, and though Karmen's on it, I want to mention the squatter in the cottages. Karmen will get to the bottom of things. She will handle the police going forward. Don't worry yourself anymore."

"But—"

He cuts me off with a kiss.

"Trust me. It will all be okay. Do you want to wander around the house while I talk to my parents?"

"I could come with you?"

He smiles, but I can already see the answer is no. And to be honest, I'm relieved. I need some headspace. I need to process.

"Never mind. I'll just…go back to the room. I'm exhausted. Tomorrow is a new day. Everyone will be here, we can get back to normal. Right?"

"That's right, darling. I'll be up in a few minutes. Do you know how to get back upstairs?"

"I do."

I trust Jack with my heart, with my life, and with my art. I need to trust him all the way, to give him every piece of me. I need to be alone. I need to arrange my thoughts.

A break-in. Cameras. Strangers. Cover-ups.

A little voice that has been screaming in the back of my mind since we sat down with Karmen is finally barging in, wanting to know why, exactly, the Comptons made me sign so many forms saying I won't reveal anything I know about them, under risk of being prosecuted?

What else might the family be so intent on hiding?

And what was the predator who put cameras in my house trying to learn?

25

The Dying of the Light

Jack always was naive.

From the moment we met, I knew how easily he could be led. Of course, I underestimated him in the end, but while I knew him, he was as malleable as a child.

For the longest time, outside of my habit of spying on strangers through virtual peepholes, he was the most exciting thing that ever happened to me. In the moments I wasn't trying to get him to fall in love with me, when I could step aside and observe him, I thought that he was a good match for me in so many ways. Smart. Elegant. Moneyed. Cultured. We had fun. Spoke the same business language. But soon enough, I was bored. So, I pushed him. Accused him of keeping secrets.

When his real personality emerged, showing him as a devious, sly man who lied about everything, pathologically so, I admit, I found him twice as attractive. We had more in common than I thought. For a while, things got better between us.

I liked walking the draglines of the spiderweb he wove for me, knowing if I made only one misstep, I'd be consumed.

Our short life together was intense. There were explosive fights. There were frenzied makeups. No apologies, ever, from either of us, just physical collisions and exquisite release.

I will say this, fucking him was like driving a really good car a hundred miles an hour. Once you got going, you wanted to go faster and faster, give yourself over to the experience, ignoring the speedometer, the very real threat of death a specter over your head. There was an edge of fear involved to bedding him; he was volatile, and unpredictable. And I liked taking chances.

And then, for reasons I had yet to ascertain, he proposed. I accepted. It was…anticlimactic.

Without the grand pursuit to love and be loved, it was boring. *He* was boring. Our *life* was boring. The fights felt prosaic. The sex, too. He spoke about wanting children. How maybe we could start trying now, before the wedding, since we both wanted a family of our own so badly.

I have no idea what made him think I wanted a family. I wanted a fucking race car and miles of open road, not a loud, messy, disgusting passel of leeches sucking at me and dragging me down.

He had no idea it was never, ever going to happen.

Therein lies the power of the female prerogative. We can hold off motherhood through any number of means, physical, chemical, or otherwise. So, I smiled and cooed at the thought of imminent stretch marks and cribs and nurseries and chapped nipples and said of course, darling, we should start trying immediately, how about right now? And I took down his fly.

Like I said, naive.

Then I died, and he pretended to mourn, and he went on living his life, and the family went on being the unethical creeps they are, and then he met Claire.

Of course, I had to add her to my repertoire.

Watching him with Claire was like watching my own life replayed without me at its center. Hearing the same words, the same sack of lies, the same pressures applied—we're engaged now, let's forgo the birth control, I can't wait to make babies with you—enraged me. I'd made sure nothing like that was going to come about for me. I'd had my tubes tied before I met Jackson. But for her... How to stop her from getting pregnant kept me up at night. Lace her daily pots of tea with contraceptive pills, or Plan B? Bump into her in a crowd and inject her with Depo-Provera?

No option I came up with was feasible.

In the end, I needn't have bothered. When I followed her to her annual exam, moved up the moment Jack started talking about his baby fever, I learned her lovely little secret. My God, the nurses and doctors talk so loudly, it hardly takes ten seconds to ascertain exactly what's happening in the room next door.

Despite agreeing to start trying right away, Claire was there to get the implant, and there was no way she was removing it until she was good and ready. That would buy her three years at least.

Score one in my column for Claire. At least she wasn't as easily seduced by his begging as she'd played to be. Perhaps she was more of a worthy opponent than I thought.

26

La Familia

Jack walks the familiar halls of the Villa to his parents' rooms. Though it's late, he barges in without knocking. The suite on this side of the Villa is similar to the bridal suite though the terrace faces the other direction. It is a sunrise catcher, not a sunset.

Jack had fought against his parents giving up their rooms for him and Claire, but Ana was adamant. It was tradition that the eldest son took the Venus suite as a newlywed. Period.

Elliot had groused that they hadn't given it up for him and Amelia, but Ana simply cast her gimlet eye on her second son and shook her head. Tradition was tradition, and she preferred the sunrise view anyway. Better for sun salutations on the terrace.

Brice sits at the desk by the French doors to their terrace, his computer out, Elliot by his side. Both have earpieces in, both are nodding at the same time. They are absorbed enough not to notice Jack's grand entrance. The server issue is being handled, and Jack feels some tension leave him. Whoever is trying to break them won't succeed. He won't let them.

Ana is lying on the chaise, long legs crossed at the ankle, the latest issue of *Endless Journey* in her lap, a book of poetry by her side, and a glass of champagne at her elbow. The very picture of relaxation.

Rattlesnakes relax, too. They curl up in the sun to warm their skin, completely harmless to passersby. If left alone. If they are not threatened.

The champagne bottle is half empty. Ana and Brice have been indulging more than usual lately. He's tried not to notice, but it's been hard to miss. Not that Jack is one to talk—he's been drinking too much, too. A bottle of wine in the evening instead of a glass. Double scotches instead of singles. He's blamed it on the stress of the wedding, of not telling Claire everything, convincing himself that's what is getting to him.

Keep lying to yourself, Jack. Keep pretending. That always works.

"Any word on the servers?"

Ana puts a finger to her lips and gestures toward his father and brother, then crooks her finger in a *come with me* gesture, swinging her legs off the chaise. Jack follows her toward the terrace. Ana pats Brice on the shoulder as they pass. He twitches at the intrusion and keeps on talking. Jack hears "More trouble in Tanzania?" as he follows his mom outside.

That is not good news. The Tanzania project was one of Jack's babies—one he's stepped away from for the wedding. If everything goes south...

Not your problem today, Jack. Let them handle it.

The terrace is sheltered but misty; the rain has died down to a gentle patter from the night sky. Soon enough, the patter will be a roar again. The island's early summer storms are impressive.

Ana closes the door gently and lights a cigarette.

"When are you going to quit that nasty habit?"

Ana smiles languorously and blows a stream of smoke over his head.

"We all have to die of something, Jacky. I might as well enjoy myself until I go."

"One day, you might come to your senses and realize you'll live a bit longer if you stop now. What's gone wrong in Tanzania? Is it related to the server issue?"

Ana waves a hand. "Nothing we can't handle. Elliot's working on it. You're off the clock, remember?"

"I remember. It doesn't mean I need to be cut out of the loop."

"Elliot has this," she repeats, taking another drag. "Besides, you said you wanted out of the main business after the wedding to spend more time on the Foundation. Let your brother step up. It's time. Now, what's the problem?"

She has left no room for argument, so he changes tack.

"We have another problem," he says. "It seems someone's been spying on us."

Now he has his mother's full attention. Her dark eyes flash with suppressed anger, but she nods. "Explain."

Amazing, that tone. She can turn him from thirty-eight-year-old accomplished man into five-year-old quivering child with a single command.

"Claire was approached by an art dealer's agent a few weeks ago. She asked to see a painting for subsequent purchase. By name. You know how Claire is about her work. She hasn't shared the name of the painting with anyone but me. We have to assume the two are connected. And whoever is driving this server issue probably planted the cameras, and sent the man to the house to hurt Claire and me."

Ana isn't easily rattled. She is always strongest in a crisis. But at the last sentence, Jack sees the blood drain from her face.

"You think he was sent to kill you?"

"It's a strong possibility. The police found his car, and a murder kit in the trunk. I don't believe he was there to rob us."

"Was he after Claire? Or you? And how the hell did he get past our security to plant cameras?"

"I don't know the answer to any of that. Somehow, our security footage was conveniently overwritten. Karmen's working it. She can fill you in on her thoughts."

Ana is silent for a moment. "All right. How compromised are we?"

"I haven't shared anything about our business dealings with Claire yet, if that's what you're asking, so the *family* is not compromised. I was waiting for her to sign the prenup before discussing our situation. And I don't do business from home. I'm not reckless, Mother."

"I know you're not. When were you planning to reveal your true position to her?"

He laughs. "If I'm stepping away…never?"

"That's not an option and you know it. Claire isn't stupid, nor is she a frivolous girl. She will understand business is business. Don't start your lives together on a lie, Jackson."

"Irony alert, Mother. I've had such an excellent track record in that regard. You want me to tell the truth about our business, but lie about Morgan?"

Ana softens. "Honey. Stop. You can't undo the past. The door on your first marriage is closed, especially now. You should be relieved, actually. You're moving forward and that's the smart, healthy choice. Claire is a wonderful girl, and she will support you. Will support us. There's no reason for her to hear about Morgan, but the family business, that, she must be told. It's already been agreed to."

Against his will, but yes, it had. Jack wanted to keep Claire out of the family business. He'd been overruled. Now that she's signed the prenup, Jack is expected to sit down with his fiancée and explain the family's longstanding relationships with the governments of the US and the UK. Explain how Compton Computers had been designed with one end goal in mind: use their technology to spy on enemies of the governments they worked for.

Claire is his safe harbor. Jack knows she will never expose him, nor the family, and the paperwork demands her privacy as well. But he'd been against bringing her in, instead offering to leave the business entirely and take the Foundation straight. The family made a compromise: the first year of his marriage, he will step back and let Elliot take the lead on his projects. After that, he is expected to be back to full force.

Jack is their best asset, after all.

Claire will have to be a part of the deception, too. Her art, and the connections she makes through her sales, will get the family into places they've never been before. Allow them access to the homes, offices, private lives of Claire's buyers. Slipping a mic or camera into a picture frame? Easy as pie.

Claire isn't simply getting married. She is being conscripted.

He feels ill at the very idea of telling her how complicit she will be, how she won't have a choice but to work alongside them. How she will be used. All the ways they practice to deceive.

Will she feel he targeted her because of the possibilities she presented? And when she wraps her head around her new role, will she ever forgive him? He doubts it. Claire isn't the manipulative type. She doesn't have dark, dirty secrets. She doesn't exist on lies.

"I should get back—" Ana begins, but Jack, internally roiling at the situation, catches her hand.

"Wait." There is a sharp crack of lightning followed by an intense drumming of thunder, and at the same moment, the lights go out. The island stands alone and quiet in the darkness.

He rakes a hand through his hair. "This weekend isn't going as planned."

"It's just the electricity, darling. Give it thirty. It will come back on once the generators are engaged. And the storms will end, as they always do. Try not to worry too much."

"It's not the lights I'm worried about. Claire's freaked out by what happened in Nashville. The remains. And now her dress is ruined."

Ana nods. "Poor girl. It's been quite a disturbing week."

"Oh, that reminds me—has Karmen found out who's camping in the cottages?"

Ana sighs. "No, but no doubt it's one of the restoration people. We're handling it. I have a meeting with Karmen shortly, we'll discuss everything." She stubs out the cigarette. "You, my darling boy, are the groom, and you need to enjoy your weekend with your adorable bride. Go to Claire, Jack. She needs you. Get some rest. Everything will be fine. I swear it."

27

Foundational Aspects

Allow me to explain how the Compton's pet project really works.

What William Compton hath wrought in the forties with his friends in DC who were determined not to let another despot ruin the world was carried on in a variety of aspects as the family grew in both power, influence, and money. William developed the initial infrastructure, Eliza right there at his side with the international component, bringing in informants from Europe and beyond during the war. Their son Will took it through the artistic community. Their brilliant, quirky grandson Brice expanded the family fortunes into IT, developing software that lived on pretty much every computer in the free world, which gave them access to everything and everybody, and by marrying Ana, was able to continue within the artistic community through the magazine, *Endless Journeys*.

Jack and the youngest Compton brother, Tyler, were the ground invasion, working to further the family business and disguise it as altruism. On the surface, the Foundation was their own version of Doctors Without Borders, addressing both medical needs and technological innovations for impoverished nations. The Computer and Band-Aid Brigade, Jack called it, when he was in a self-deprecating mood. Though he rarely joked about it, because running the legitimate side of the Foundation was serious work, lifesaving work, backbreaking and heartfelt, terrifying at times and gloriously fulfilling in others. Jack and Tyler took it to the streets, hitting the deepest cesspools and elegant ballrooms of the world.

Below the surface, it allowed the Comptons access to an infinite number of sources.

Elliot, the middle child, stayed closer to home, working with Brice Compton in the IT business, running the AI branch—artificial intelligence—that serviced government facial recognition and biometrics. Though Compton had a massive consumer branch, their most lucrative contracts were all top-secret government work, just like all the major firms.

And there you have it. Four generations, reporting for duty, sir.

Oh, was I not supposed to say that?

Fuck their NDA. I'm dead, remember?

I can't be forced to keep their nasty little secrets.

But Claire, eager, people-pleasing free-spirit likes-it-from-behind Claire, has now agreed to be their bitch. And in so doing, has started a cataclysmic shift in her universe.

That's how it always happens with the Comptons. The stroke of a pen, the stroke of a clit, and boom, they have you wrapped in spider silk, ready to be sucked dry.

Will she survive it? Will her precious chrysalis crack open and free the raging butterfly trapped within? Or will it wither and die?

I really don't care. So long as the family is stopped, nothing else matters.

28

I Know What You've Done

Jack uses the light on his phone to see the contents of the drawer in the closest of the omnipresent hall tables outside his parents' suite. He pulls out a flashlight, flips the switch, and starts toward his old rooms, playing the beam along the floor. He doesn't really need the light, he knows the Villa so intimately he can easily maneuver in the darkness, but he's feeling unsettled, so welcomes the extra illumination.

He needs to think, damn it. None of this makes sense. An assassin sent to Nashville, someone spying on them, and Morgan's body showing up two days before his wedding? Add in the hijacked servers... It doesn't matter that his mother thinks things are under control, Jack fears something truly sinister might be afoot.

Someone is trying to stop his future with Claire.

Too late. He smiles internally. Too fucking late. They are here now, on the island, where he can keep her safe. There is nothing he won't do to protect Claire. He doesn't understand why anyone would want to test him. He will trample anyone who dares try to hurt her.

From the moment he met her he knew, deep in his soul, this was his person, the one he was supposed to be with, raise a family with, grow old with. He'd never felt that with Morgan. Not like this, at least.

Maybe it was the way the light hit Claire's eyes as they walked through the streets of Nashville. Maybe it was the way she moved, graceful, like a dancer, the strides long and confident. Maybe it was her art, her abandon when she held the paintbrush, how she was so wholly in the moment he could tell she was on another plane entirely.

Maybe it was the smudge of paint on her cheek, when she showed him the big bloody painting she was working on, the monstrosity of a canvas that he, having grown up around the great masters, recognized immediately as important but had no real idea exactly what it *meant*. Unlike Ana, who was a tastemaker, art to him was simple; he knew what he liked and what he didn't. As to the rest, well, that was part of what he found so fascinating about Claire, how she saw the world, how her mind's eye took the mundane, synthesized it, and made it into a masterpiece.

Maybe it was her humility. She didn't think she was the greatest artist, though he tended to disagree. With time to focus on her work, and the right patron, he thought she could be a household name.

Maybe it was the way she looked at him, like he was the most handsome man in the world. Maybe it was because when she looked at him, she didn't see what he could do for her. She didn't see his money, his family, his destiny. She saw him. All of him.

Claire had no idea who he was when they met, and he'd kept the illusion in place long enough to be sure she was in love with him. Just him. Just Jack.

There is no other woman like her, and he knows this first-hand, having sown his oats across four continents. No, he won't let anything happen to her. He fears, though, more people will die before this attack is over.

Who is behind it? The family has plenty of enemies. They've been exerting their unique brand of pressure discreetly for decades. The list of people who would be happy to see the Comptons fall is long and varied.

So why now? Claire is the only common denominator.

He wants to head to the bridal suite, to see her, be near her, but, recognizing his overprotective mood and knowing she has to be asleep by now, he detours to his own childhood rooms to catch his breath. Ascertain where the threats are actually coming from.

He plays the flashlight over the main room fondly. Eventually, his children will take over this old space of his. It is still relatively unchanged from his childhood. The twin beds pushed against the walls on either side of the window with their soft hand-loomed quilts, the cracked leather club chair, the bookcase with its multihued spines, calms him. He chooses a book at random and takes it to the chair, opens it, unseeing, listens to the raindrops patter on the courtyard below. When he glances at the title, he realizes he's chosen his well-thumbed copy of *Where the Red Fern Grows*, and has to fight back the wave of emotion that courses through him. Those damn dogs. Old Dan and Little Ann.

Will used to read him stories before bed, and this was Jack's favorite. Every summer, when the family came to stay, Will would read it to him. This is one of Jack's dearest memories, being snuggled under the covers, in thrall to the great man. That Will wanted to spend time with him, with a kid, instead of the famous people mingling downstairs, was intoxicating. He'd bring the dogs—there were always Italian wolf dogs around the Villa when he was growing up—and allow them to sleep in Jack's room overnight.

Will's savage declaration earlier: *You know what's going to happen. It happens every time.*

It doesn't happen every time, but it happens too often for comfort.

Compton men lose their wives too soon. William, Will, and Jack, all three lost their wives to early death. Elliot is losing his to divorce. Brice is the exception, but Ana is an anomaly in so many ways. Her strength, her courage, her innate sense of familial preservation, is impossible to conquer. She is kept safe, safer than the others.

With everything that's happened, Jack hasn't allowed himself to think about the incident with Will. He touches his cheek gingerly. Nothing broken, but it's still sore. By God, the old man still has some strength in him.

Seeing his grandfather so confused, so violent, was a shock. Will Compton had always been so much fun. He'd lived a great life here at the Villa, with movie stars and artists and writers flocking to the island to spend time at the colony. They'd create during the day, and in the evenings, would be invited to the Villa for parties. Legendary parties. There was nary a biography of any major name in the arts that didn't mention at least one wild weekend on Isle Isola, with Will Compton at the center of the gaiety.

It was only in the past ten years that the parties had started slowing down, when Will started seeing old friends as strangers, and the artists' colony had begun its decline. Heartbreaking.

Jack shoves away the ghosts of his grandfather's issues and focuses back on the present. What is he missing? Who is trying to derail his life?

He's done everything in his power to shelter Claire from his own violence. He wanted her to get used to the idea of the family business before she was forced to participate in it firsthand.

And then they'd surprised this creep in Nashville, and she'd managed to pick up the gun and shoot the fucker.

No. Malcolm shot the intruder.

God, she's going to be so pissed he hasn't told her everything. About himself. About the family. About their history.

His mother is right, Claire is safe now. Here, on the island, no one can touch her. She has all the protections he can give her and will bear his name soon enough. There is nothing else he can do but hold her in his arms and shield her with his body.

And he will. If anyone comes for his family, he will protect Claire first.

He stretches out his long legs, crossing them at the ankle, wincing at the tiny *pop* the right one makes as it settles over the left. Thirty-eight and falling apart at the seams. That's what happens when you lived rough half the time. Lap of luxury or a field tent in the bush—his two extremes.

He flips through the pages of the book, but the words swim. He is exhausted. He can't read, can't focus. He puts the book back on the shelf in its proper spot and starts for the door. He will slip into their room quietly, get into the bed, and hold her. It will make him feel better to have her soft breath on his collarbone, her body solid and safe in his arms. She has saved him, and she didn't even know it. Before he met her, he feared he was becoming numb to emotion, numb to the world. An automaton with a gun, controlled by Ana and Brice and their vision for the company, the world.

With Claire by his side, he can finally live again.

His phone chirps from his pocket with a new secure text. Elliot or Karmen with news, he expects. He opens his family-designed app, end-to-end encrypted and utterly unbreakable, developed by his father in the early days of the SMS that now lives on hundreds of thousands of security professionals' phones.

He doesn't recognize the number. There is a video attached,

with an encryption key. He taps on it, and the video opens and auto plays.

The video quality isn't remarkable, but it's clear enough. A small snippet of the events from Monday night, it shows the body of the intruder, the man the police tentatively identified as Francis Wold, bleeding out on the landing. There is no audio, but there's no need for it to sink them all… Claire is holding the man's gun. God, her eyes, her eyes, wide and frightened and shocked.

A plain text message comes in.

I know what she did. Soon, the whole world will, too. Repent, Jackson. Repent.

"Son of a bitch!"

He needs Elliot to trace the encryption key. Karmen needs to find out where the planted cameras broadcast to. A wireless signal, hell, who knows if it was secure or not. The neighbor across the street could have hacked the Wi-Fi.

Who the hell is threatening them? It's not just Francis Wold, not anymore. He hadn't acted alone. Who is he working with? Who is close enough to the family to peer inside their lives this way?

His mind offers him a solution.

Morgan.

Good grief, Jack. That's impossible. Ghosts can't send texts. No, Morgan is dead and gone—this he knows in his heart. And he can prove it to himself now.

He clatters down the main stairs, down yet another flight to the kitchens, straight back into the darkness by the wine cellar. He knows the way through the maze of halls and storage rooms, but uses the flashlight so he can move quickly. Claire must be wondering where he is. Once he's satisfied himself here, he will go to her.

The heavy iron door to the crypt is usually barred by a massive padlock on its handle; it is now cracked open several inches.

He halts, catching his breath. Who is here? Who would be so careless as to leave the door to the crypt open? Especially with the life-changing evidence lying within?

The scent of must and mossy dirt wafts out from the black beyond. It is cool, so cool he shivers. Darkness bleeds before him. This isn't a movie set, with a burning fire and ready-made torches to be dipped and lit. This is emptiness. Vast nothingness. This is the personification of death—the unknown blackness beyond.

He listens intently for the tiniest whisper, for a footfall, a breath, the scratch of claws through the dirt, the struggle of a minute life in a sticky web, but there is nothing.

With a deep breath, he steps into the darkness.

29

The Crypt Keeper

The flashlight is bright in the still air, illuminating the path, but Jack moves slowly. The crypt is only accessible by traversing a long dark downward-sloping tunnel of dirt, framed out overhead with thick wooden trusses that date back to the fortress's inception, well before the Villa was built. There are several tunnels and levels excavated below the fortress; typical to the islands in the area, some of the tunnels lead down to the grottos, coves, and beaches.

The sea caves were used for many things over the centuries. Some were practical—escape hatches, boat storage, a way to ferry supplies up to the fortress. In some cases, they were more metaphysical. As lore had it, several of Isle Isola's grottos were used as nymphaeums, shrines dedicated to the Roman nymphs and sea goddesses. And of course, on Isola in particular, Venus. They were even rumored to be places for witches to gather and hold rites.

Jack always believed the grottos were designed for practical, not supernatural, purposes, but as a child, he wasn't comfortable alone in the dark with the specter of witches holding rites down the darkened tunnels or sea goddesses rising from the depths. The fortress held a dungeon at one point, too, rumored to be somewhere down here, but he and his brothers never found it. Not that it mattered—his grandfather had gated off all the grotto tunnels with heavy iron driven into the rock as a security measure. The Comptons couldn't risk enemies trying to enter the Villa through the ancient tunnels, nor curious little boys slinking through the darkness.

The crypt though—this is someplace they've all been, semi-regularly. His great-grandparents William and Eliza are buried here, as is his grandmother May, plus a number of previous inhabitants of the fortress, monks and kings alike. The crypt is actually a series of rooms, and Jack, as a child, explored them all. It stopped being a fun place to visit after they laid his grandmother to rest, though. When they lost May, he was old enough to conceptualize what was happening behind the square doors on the wall. For months after her interment, he woke at night screaming, besieged by images of her moldering body waking in the darkness several floors below him, clawing her way out of her hole in the wall, wandering the hallways to his room. He'd insisted on a chair beneath his bedroom door handle for months.

He supposes some families would be happy to have their dead so close. Because of his childhood nightmares, he still finds it deeply disturbing.

The island itself is a mausoleum to the past. There are cemeteries and graveyards scattered about as well, including one attached to the church where he and Claire will be married, but that houses the inhabitants of the island, not the landowners themselves.

He hears something, a sound, deep in the darkness ahead, and pulls up so hard he stumbles into the wall and drops his flashlight. It lands hard, extinguishing the beam. He is plunged into darkness, heart thudding in his ears.

What is that?

Crying. He can hear crying.

The sound is eerie, but entirely human.

He takes a deep, shuddery breath. *God, Jack. Are you eight or thirty-eight? Still scared of the dark?* Blowing out one more quick breath, feeling silly at his reaction, he picks up the flashlight, thumbs it back on, and starts forward again. He arrives at the interior doors to the crypt to find them open, and his grandfather, a lit candle in his hand, standing by May's resting place, wiping his eyes. Wax drips down the gnarled joints, but he doesn't seem to notice.

"Gran?" Jack calls softly, not wanting to scare the old man.

"Eh? Who's that? Brice? What are you doing here?"

"No, Gran. It's me, Jackson. Are you okay?"

Jack angles his flashlight so he can see Will's face but isn't shining the beam into his grandfather's eyes. He's afraid Will won't remember him, but there is recognition. Recognition, and resignation.

"Hello, son. I'm just visiting my May. It's been a while since I came down here." Though it's clear he's been crying, his voice is hearty, and not at all confrontational.

"Me, too." Jack puts a hand on the plate that marks his grandmother's dates. *Beloved May. Born April 7, 1945. Died June 29, 1989.*

The anniversary of her death is coming soon. No wonder his grandfather is here, mourning.

She was only forty-four when she died. His great-grandmother Eliza was only thirty-three. They both saw a great deal in their short lives, but it still hurts that he didn't get to meet Eliza, or see May grow old.

Compton women die young.

Morgan was only twenty-five when she died…

"Do you remember her at all, Jacky? She loved you to pieces. I've never seen a woman so proud to have a grandchild before. She thought you hung the moon, and though you couldn't even crawl yet, the moment Ana put you in May's arms, you stopped crying and looked up at her with such wonder. She fell in love in an instant, and you did, as well. You used to toddle after her everywhere she went. You couldn't stay away. Like magnets, you were."

Jack smiled. "I do remember her, Gran. I remember her hair, and her smile, and the way she always smelled like pine needles, so fresh and clean. She wore red lipstick, all the time. And great-grandmother's pearls, of course."

"That she did. She wouldn't leave our rooms without Eliza's pearls. Ah, I do miss her. Do you remember the time May went swimming with the dogs?"

Jack isn't about to ruin the old man's moment, so he stands with him and listens to a few of the stories. He knows them all by heart—Will has told them all a hundred times before—but he listens, and laughs, and wipes his eyes a few times. Finally, when Will slows down and yawns, Jack suggests the two find their way upstairs to their respective beds.

With a sigh and a good-natured pat of the plaque on the door to May's tomb, Will agrees, and Jack thumbs on his flashlight again and blows out the candle. He is careful to secure the padlock to the crypt, vowing to return later to see Morgan's body and lay her ghost to rest in his mind.

He leads his grandfather toward the kitchens, careful not to show worry, or scold, just grateful they've had a moment together to revisit some of the old stories.

At the door, Will grabs Jack's arm with surprising strength. "Be careful, Jacky."

"Careful? Of what?"

"The dead don't like to stay that way."

"Signore Compton, there you are. We've been looking for you everywhere."

Fatima stands at the edge of the root cellar, a scowl on her face, hands folded in front of her. She is half in shadow and Jack is reminded of a bleached skull. Her hair is a wiry gray mass, and her face is lined. She has always been slightly warped in his mind. He would think her an unhappy woman if she weren't so devoted to his mother, and so excellent at her job.

Will moves past her gruffly. "Well, you've found me. And I'm thirsty. Let's have a nightcap."

Moments later Will's nurse, Petra, bursts into the kitchen. She is out of breath and overflowing with apologies.

Fatima looks at her coldly, and barks in Italian, "It is not safe for him to be wandering around alone."

The nurse bows her head. "I know. I fell asleep. It will not happen again."

"See that it doesn't," Fatima says, and stalks off.

Jack hands his grandfather over to the nurse, who looks relieved to have found her charge in good hands.

"Va bene?" Petra asks Jack warily, and he nods and replies in English, "Just fine. We had a nice chat."

"I'm glad." She nods once, then scuttles after Will, scolding him lightly. "You scared me, you can't wander off like that."

Will says over his shoulder, voice fading as he strides off, "G'night, Jacky. Petra, get me two fingers of Oban. And quit hovering. I'm not a child."

Jack sags back against the wall. As heartbreaking as that had been, it was good to connect with Will.

Jack knows he should go back to the crypt, satisfy his curiosity, but the idea is suddenly distasteful. What purpose will it serve? Dragging up the horrible memories of the night Morgan died, what good will that do? It is a way to cling to the past, to continue accepting the blame for her death.

He resolves to stop looking back. He wants to look forward.

To carve out his love story. His childhood nightmares seem far, far away. Seeing Will talking to May's spirit was comforting. There was such peace between them. Such love, and such peace.

One day, he wants Claire to weep over his body, or he, hers. He doesn't want his life with her to start sullied by the vision of the blanched bones of his first wife. He knows himself well enough. That vision is something he will never, ever be able to erase. It's time to let the ghosts of his past rest, and focus on stopping whoever is trying to hurt him now.

30

Love Is Blind

Don't let him fool you. This is simple. An unassailable truth.

We met. We fell in love. We were perfect together. Everyone said so.

So, we married.

And then he killed me.

And he's going to kill her, too.

I'm going to make sure of it.

THURSDAY

"Though she be but little, she is fierce."
—William Shakespeare, *A Midsummer Night's Dream*

31

Hide and Seek

Karmen rubs her eyes and leans back in her chair. She's been up all night chasing down the identity of the man who broke into Claire and Jack's house in Nashville. The fake ID—for it was a fake ID, of that she's now certain—wasn't well backstopped. Amateur hour. A case of identity theft and good papers, good enough to get a credit card, a driver's license, and a rental car, but that was about it. The Nashville police will be responsible for investigating further, though this sort of identity theft, alongside personal property crimes, aren't exactly lighting fires under the boys and girls in blue these days.

The deceased's fingerprints, though, are something else entirely. The Nashville police finally made their match official and sent along the files at three in the morning. The man cooling in the Forensic Medical morgue drawer in Nashville is named Shane McGowan.

And Claire Hunter knows him. Intimately.

McGowan came up in Karmen's exceedingly thorough background check of Claire, the first thing she'd done when Jackson made it clear he was seriously considering marrying the girl. In her report, the family had been warned—Claire dated a boy in high school who went on to land himself in jail on several occasions, finally taking up residence in San Quentin. Though it could be an embarrassing media story should it get out the wrong way, it was deemed a nonissue. Claire couldn't be held accountable for bad judgment as a fifteen-year-old, and McGowan wasn't set for parole for another ten years. A crisis management plan was attached to the file in case of problems surfacing down the road, and the file archived. They'd cross the bridge of Shane McGowan when—if—he got parole, or the media found the connection and chose to make something of it. Karmen was good at her job, though. She could usually make these sorts of spurious stories go away.

But... McGowan got bumped up the ladder when the state of California early released a bevy of nonviolent drug offenders, and Karmen had missed it.

That wasn't a firing offense. That he'd made his way to Nashville, somehow managed to bypass Compton Security, enter the home of a family member, and nearly kill them?

Karmen might as well prepare her resignation, because when she tells Ana and Brice Compton about her little fuckup, she's going to be kicked out the door without a second thought. Unless she can find the truth, and fast.

They're lucky McGowan is dead, lucky Malcolm is willingly taking the fall. This is Malcolm and Gideon's purview, after all, personal protection of Jackson Compton. The Nashville police have been handled—the ex-lover getting out of jail and making a visit to right old wrongs theory held water for them. There was a threat, it was neutralized in standard operating procedure, and the police won't dig any deeper into who pulled the trigger.

Assuming video doesn't surface. The cameras planted in the

house create their own problem. Who is behind this? McGowan? Someone else? Does video or still shots exist of Monday night? And if the answer is yes, what do they show? Are they damaging?

Karmen doesn't know how she's going to manage that part yet. She still has to talk with Claire, tell her the identity of the intruder.

Tell the girl who she killed.

Karmen's office in the Villa is equipped with a small kitchen. She slices an apple, gets a glass of water. The big brunch for the wedding guests is today; she will not be there. Which is fine. She doesn't expect to be a part of the family. She's responsible for protecting them. Protecting Brice, primarily, though her personal protection days are over. Now she runs everything security related, and it will be her head on a spike if this isn't handled perfectly.

Sustenance onboarded, she sits back at the desktop and starts pulling the video files of the people she interviewed when she did Claire's background check.

She clicks on the files, one after another, looking for the interview that mentions Claire's troubled past. The file she's looking for is labeled K_Elderfield. She'd hit the mother lode with Claire's best friend, Katie Elderfield. None of the other interviewees revealed much, but Katie was a treasure trove.

Karmen pulls the transcript of the interview, too. She reads along as she listens, highlighting the relevant sections. She speeds through the interview to the spot she wants and hits play.

Elderfield: Her dad, Dr. Hunter, was a pediatrician, a nice guy, too. We all went to him as kids. I used to love doctor's appointments, no matter how wretched I felt. He had superhero Band-Aids and lollipop rings and his sweet nurses called me honey and darlin'. When I had a sore throat, he sanctioned ice cream in bed, and when I needed a shot, he'd put an ice cube against my skin first so I wouldn't feel the needle.

When it was clear I wasn't going to be the tallest girl in my class, he tweaked my nose and told me all the best things come in little packages. And then he insisted my parents enroll me in martial arts so I could always defend myself. He thought it was too easy for smaller women to become victims of violent crimes. He convinced them I needed to be able to fight off an attacker.

Harris: That comes in handy. I took martial arts, too.

Elderfield: And you're even shorter than me. [Laughs] I assume you already know about the scandal?

Harris: Why don't we pretend I don't know anything.

Elderfield: This is all private, right?

Harris: Absolutely. For my eyes and ears only, assuming there's nothing we need to explore further. I can't imagine there is. Claire seems like a very nice girl.

Elderfield: She is. She's a good girl. Always has been. Well, except for that little while… Claire's mother— she drank a lot, by the way—was having an affair with one of the English teachers, Mr. Henry. I don't know how it got out, but it did, and the Hunters got into a messy, nasty custody case. It felt like everyone in Nashville knew about it. It was so public, like, in *the Tennessean* public. I always felt so bad for them.

Harris: Sounds hard.

Elderfield: Totally. Before the divorce, Claire was larger than life. She was a smart girl, and a damn good artist, too. She could draw, paint, sculpt, the works. It was a no-brainer that she'd end up a professional artist of some kind. She had that tortured creative streak running through her, carried around Camus like he was a god, quoted Nietzsche and Kierkegaard, dragged everyone who would go to a Virginia Woolf play at the Belcourt Theater one year, and to the Frist for the modern art exhibits. She liked all that stuff. She painted this massive, throw-paint-at-the-canvas Jackson Pollock-esque piece for the talent show one year—live, on stage, in front of the whole school. She was a rising star, the darling of all the teachers.

Harris: That's pretty cool. She sounds like a fun friend.

Elderfield: Mmm, at times. Sometimes, too fun. You know the legend of Icarus. Claire flew too close to the sun and it nearly killed her. After the scandal broke, she acted out. Started seeing this older guy from Hillsboro High School. Stopped painting, her grades dropped. Something was wrong, clearly, but we were kids, we didn't have the same sort of overdeveloped radar we have on these things now. Looking back, I'd bet cash money he was abusing her, but I never saw any bruises, and she never said a word. I know he was providing her with drugs. He got her into all sorts of trouble.

Harris: You were a kid. No one expects you to know bad things are happening. She never confided in you?

Elderfield: No. Anyway, he was trouble on a stick, just that kind of kid who you know is going to end up in jail, at the very least, or the penitentiary. Claire went wild for a while. Drinking, drugs, tattoos, piercings. I helped with some of that.

Harris: Your tattoos are beautiful. Artwork.

Elderfield: Thanks. I planned everything, both sleeves. Claire drew a few of them for me. Anyway, she'd always had a nihilist streak, which was fun for me, but it really messed her up. She got expelled from Harpeth Hall for cheating our junior year, and that was the summer of the accident.

Harris: The accident?

Elderfield: You know about that, surely. She and Dr. Hunter were in a terrible car accident. He died, she was badly injured. Broke a vertebra in her back. They thought for a while she might be paralyzed. They did all kinds of surgeries and she got the use of her legs back. After that, she was a totally different person. The fire was…dimmed. Not gone, but she wasn't the same girl. It was like the accident stripped her of all her defiance, and she turned into an obedient child again. She got back into her art, started teaching classes at an art studio downtown. The Before Claire was so dynamic, so alive, so intense and vivacious. The After, she really fell apart. She kind of turned into this seething bag of hatred. She and I weren't really close for a while. She pushed everyone away.

Harris: You knew the boyfriend, right? What was his name?

Elderfield: Ugh, yes. Shane McGowan. He was such an asshole. I don't know what she ever saw in him, outside of what drugs he could get. He wasn't even that cute.

Karmen hits Stop. She pulls McGowan's sheet from the FBI's NCIC database. As a security professional, she is granted access.

She's seen this before, but goes through it again, just in case, flicking through page after page. McGowan was a frequent flier, with arrests in multiple states. Property crimes, possession, a gas station stop and rob. No sexual stuff, but plenty of bookings for assault. He was pled down on a manslaughter charge three years ago, then immediately picked up for possession with intent. Third strike.

Then the jails got overcrowded, and the laws changed, and Mr. McGowan was spit out into the world again.

So what happened between his release from SQ and his arrival at the house in Nashville? Was he plotting the break-in all along? Was he watching from afar? Was he smart enough, talented enough, and creepy enough to evade Karmen's own security protocols and install over twenty micro cameras in Claire and Jack's home?

She puts a pin in that question for the moment. Karmen is an excellent compartmentalizer. She's not going to deal with the cameras, not yet. First, she needs to figure out something else. Something that's been bothering her, that makes her senses come alive whenever her mind lands on the name for a moment.

Who is Ami Eister, the phantom art dealer who visited Claire's studio?

Because it's always her first step when investigating people, she plugs that name into the NCIC database. Might as well see if the woman is legit or not.

The computer whirs for a moment, and a file appears on the screen. Sure enough, Eister is a criminal. What luck.

Karmen congratulates herself for her smarts—she knew something was wrong with that story—then settles in to read.

Ami Rebecca Eister. Thirty-one, Caucasian female, black on blue, five nine, one-twenty. Several trespass violations, felonies, pled down to misdemeanors...ah, Eister was a member of PETA over a decade ago, the trespass charges were group things, trying to get animals out of labs. Nothing violent, just the actions of a young conscience.

She types the name into Google, and within moments, several entries come up. The first is an obituary notice.

This Ami Rebecca Eister is deceased. She died six months earlier, while on vacation in the Bahamas.

Karmen finishes off the last of the water and stands, stretching her back.

She's missing something. She searches again. The name is common enough, but there is only one Ami Eister with ties to the arts scene. Perhaps Claire got the name wrong.

Karmen glances at her watch, it's nearly 9:00 a.m. Surely the bride and groom are up. She grabs her notebook and her blazer, straps her Glock into its holster under her arm. She needs to run this down, now.

32

Rules for Life

Harper Hunter's photography rule number one: never shoot family. She'd fought against it, albeit halfheartedly, when her sister called to break the news.

"Guess what? We're getting married. In Italy! His family has a small island off the western coast of Italy. I've seen photos. It's very romantic. There are ruins."

"Nothing like the evidence of the decline of Western civilization to add a little ambiance."

"Don't grumble. I thought you'd be thrilled. You love to travel. Italy will give you tons of opportunities for sponsorships."

Oh, the exasperation of a sister making sense. *"I do love to travel. And yes, I will be able to make hay with it. When is this blessed event occurring?"*

"June. Naturally. I need a favor."

"Oh, no. No way."

"You're the world's most famous Instagram photographer. Your work

has appeared on the cover of every travel magazine known to mankind. You are practically a household name, a revered online icon."

"Claire. Reciting my CV won't change my mind. I am hardly the world's most famous anything. I only have a million followers."

"You're the best photographer I know."

"Flattery… Is the dad going to be there?"

A pause.

"Brice? Of course. His son is getting married."

"I wonder…"

"I'm not asking for you to document the whole thing, Jack's family will hire a photographer and videographer. But a few shots of us, done with your eye, in your style? I would really appreciate it. I'll pay you."

"Get me a gig with Brice Compton, and I'll do it. And you're not paying me. I'm your sister."

"I don't know, Harper. Brice is notoriously private. He may not want to be photographed, even by you."

"Not a session. An interview. You know I'm branching out, writing freelance for some of the magazines. And you're about to be his daughter-in-law. At the very least, ask. It would be good for both of us."

Claire, shockingly, *had* asked. Brice, shockingly, had agreed. So not only was Harper going to take a few pictures of the wedding of the decade, she had landed an interview with one of the richest men in the world. She'd pitched the story to *Flair,* and they said yes. Goodbye Instagram, hello real journalism.

The hydrofoil ferry leaps through the waves, bringing Isle Isola closer and closer. Rain drums on the roof and decks, splashing water onto her arms. Harper has her phone up, doing an Instagram Live of the channel crossing to the island.

"It's raining pretty hard now, so I'm going to sign off. And just so you know, I'll have to be offline for a few days, friends, because there's a—" she turns the camera back on herself "—media blackout. I'll try to sneak a few photos into the feed for you, though. Have a lovely weekend, and remember, always shoot for the stars. This is Harper Hunter, signing off."

She waves and grins at the camera, then stops the video.

Her mother sits in one of the hard plastic seats nearby, clutch-ing her purse to her chest. She's looking green, and Harper thinks the rocking ferry has nothing to do with it. Trisha seemed very loose this morning, and smelled minty fresh, so minty and so loose Harper wonders if perhaps Trisha got into the minibar last night. She has no idea when her mom started drinking again. Harper has adopted a don't ask, don't tell policy. They've been in Italy for a week, sightseeing, wandering ruins, shopping, and of course, eating tons, and so far it's just been a glass of wine or two at dinner, but who knows what's happening when Trisha and Brian are behind closed doors. This isn't good, Trisha has a long history of problems with alcohol, but if they can just get through the weekend, Harper will have a talk with her as they head home. Get her back into rehab, or at least going to meet-ings again. That's where she met Brian in the first place. Harper hasn't seen him drinking at all, though he wouldn't meet her eyes when Trisha ordered that first bottle at dinner.

Trisha looks up as if she can hear Harper thinking about her. "Question?"

"Yeah, Mom?"

"Do you ever find yourself feeling exposed, doing all that communicating with strangers?"

Here we go.

"They aren't strangers, they're my fans. I know many of them personally, and others through years of chatting. I don't feel ex-posed at all. It's fun. I like it."

She likes it so much all she wants to do is close the account, but she can't do that because when you've spent ten years build-ing a following that's now in the seven figures, and people pay seriously good money for you to wear their clothes and use their bags and send you on trips with other "influencers," you'd be crazy to want out.

Plus, things have kicked into high gear since Claire and Jack got engaged. Once her fandom realized Claire Hunter was Harper's sister? Her numbers have gone off the charts.

She supposes she should really thank Claire instead of being upset with her. But Harper is perpetually upset with her big sister. Claire, the whirling dervish of chaos that had permeated their teen years. Claire, with her drugs and alcohol and tattoos and suspensions, sneaking out at night, making Harper cover for her. Claire, whose self-destruction killed their father. Claire, Claire, Claire.

Embarrassing, infuriating, a murderer. It was not fun being Claire Hunter's little sister in the small enclave of Harpeth Hall. No, Harper wasn't Claire's biggest fan.

Harper's therapist raised a point a few years earlier—Claire had broken her back in the accident and needed rods inserted, and maybe her pain was punishment enough. Harper stewed on that for exactly one minute and had shaken her head. No. It wasn't fair, it wasn't right, and there was no way to balance the scales. Claire had taken their father away. The accident that hurt her, took their father's life.

Losing their dad created a gulf between them so wide and deep that they were out of touch for years.

Lately, though, Claire has been trying to make things better between them. Getting engaged to Jack Compton only increased these overtures. The new Claire buys small presents, sends flowers, little notes. She is generous and understanding, complimentary and contemplative. She likes every post and shares them widely. She pretends things are fine between them, that she didn't cause the worst years of her sister's life.

Adulthood hasn't softened Harper's stance. She's tolerated Claire's attempts at friendship. The constant apologies, asking her to be in and shoot the wedding, getting her the interview of a lifetime, are all just markers, adding up, though always falling short. Not that Harper isn't going to take advantage. She is owed that much, at least.

Maybe, when this sham of a wedding is over, when the most powerful family in the country is on their knees, beholden to her, maybe then she'll feel like the scales are tipping back toward even.

But appearances must be kept until she is ready to lower the boom.

Claire doesn't deserve the path she's tripped onto. After all she's done, and Jack Compton still wants her? Used goods for a prince. Though maybe they deserve each other. Jack Compton is…what? Too rich? Too perfect? Too handsome? Too crooked?

Definitely too crooked.

Harper has been digging around in the Compton's world for months now, ever since Claire admitted she and Jack were getting serious. Harper just couldn't understand why a powerful, wealthy man like Jackson Compton would want a used-up mouse of a train wreck from Nashville.

She wanted to do an exposé of the family—this was her dream, after all, investigative journalism. Instagram was just a springboard. But Harper got nowhere of worth, just found a load of perpetual, simmering resentments without any teeth, until the email came.

She had no idea who it was from. She'd nearly deleted it as junk. But she didn't, reminding herself that if she wanted to be an actual journalist, tips could come in the oddest ways. She trusted her instincts and opened the note. Unsigned, with only one line.

You should look into the history of the island. It's cursed.

Attached was a photograph. When she saw it, her heart began to race.

It was Isle Isola.

Never one to look a gift horse in the mouth, she started researching. She found a story about a housekeeper named Elevana who went missing. There could be something there, but Harper had the feeling that wasn't what the email was suggesting. It just wasn't...big enough.

She kept digging. She pulled every conceivable article and interview of the Compton family, starting with Jack's grandfather. Will Compton was the one who was famous first, after all. His exploits were legend.

And she found out his wife died on the island, a drowning accident. Tragic, but hardly something that would break down the doors.

There was one line in a *Rolling Stone* interview that gave her pause. Will Compton mentioned his mother's untimely demise in a hunting accident. His great-grandfather William was some sort of government bigwig during the Second World War—he was the one who'd rebuilt the Villa. Eliza was shot by one of her own hunting party.

On the island.

Two wives, dead. One drowned. One shot. A missing, presumed dead housekeeper from the house. That was three women.

And then she found the story about Jack's dead ex-wife.

She found it in the comments section of a random personal blog from a kid who lived in Naples, talking about the history of the area around Pompeii. She was shocked the Comptons hadn't had it taken down, but then again, even the tightest ships leak at times.

Who else saw the searchlights over the sea toward Isola last night?

And in the threaded response, this:

I have a friend who works on Isola. He said there are rumors about an accident last night, that the new wife went over the cliff. Has anyone heard the same?

Nothing else. No one answered. No one commented.

It was the date that jumped out at her. According to all the online sources, Jackson Compton married Morgan Fraser on

July 7, 2011. She went missing and was presumed dead July 20, off the coast of Monterey. Harper double-checked it.

The blog comments were dated July 21, 2011.

The day after Morgan died.

And there it was. Not only was there a pattern, there was also a cover-up. A big cover-up.

Morgan didn't die in California. She died on Isola.

Four women dead, all tied to a single family, and a single familial location? That was compelling as hell.

She couldn't figure out why the Comptons would lie about Morgan Fraser Compton's death, though. Why would they stake their lives, their word? Why would they cover it up? Why would they even try? What difference did it make whether the woman died in California or Italy?

Harper could find nothing else to dispel the known narrative. All the reports, articles, news stories—everything about Morgan Compton said she died off the coast of California, a boating accident.

Every instinct Harper had screamed the Comptons weren't what they seemed. And now, with her exposé, Harper was positioned perfectly to pull back the curtain and reveal them as liars, and possibly even murderers.

When Claire called to say the Comptons were a go for the interview and photoshoot, things moved quickly. The editor Harper pitched at *Flair* squared away the details with the Comptons' PR folks. Harper sent in her bio, her headshot.

A few days after that, a new editor reached out, from the magazine's investigative editorial team. She asked if Harper was interested in making the story meatier, if at all possible. Not the usual fluff piece. She offered to bump the piece to a five-page spread and three thousand words, if Harper could provide anything internal to the family that might be of interest? The editor had heard that there was a history to be delved into.

Bingo.

Harper confided what she'd found. Pitched a slightly different angle to the story, the nobody marrying the prince, not knowing the prince's family had secrets. Deep, dark, secrets. The kind that see dead bodies washing ashore.

The editor took her seriously. Helped her shape the piece. Helped with the research. Helped Harper find the perfect voice. A perfectly clear and devastating voice.

And the decision was made, the story was going to print with or without the photos, with or without the quote from Brice Compton. If Claire's life got upended in the process, well, maybe then they'd really be even.

The horn sounds, and the ferry captain gives them instructions on where to go as they disembark, first in Italian, then English. Harper gathers her bags, helps her mom, finds her stepfather, Brian, who is wet and grinning after watching the approach from the outer deck.

They dock, and make their way off the hydrofoil. The island Villa is easily spotted above, looming over the beach. They are met with umbrellas, hustled into the funicular, and are rising up the hillside moments later.

Harper texts her editor that she is on the island, and to stand by for the quote to finish out the story.

Three dots greet her, then a wide smiley face emoji pops onto her screen.

33

Did You Even Know Her?

Jack types quietly so he doesn't wake Claire. When he'd gotten back to the room earlier she'd been totally sacked out, so asleep she didn't even notice him climb into bed. She's still asleep now, an arm flung up over her face defensively, as if blocking the morning from finding her. It makes him laugh, and feel tender things, when he sees her like this.

He does not feel tender things toward the text message he received. In fact, fury is a better emotion. The audacity of whoever is trying to ruin his wedding weekend is off the charts, and he is not going to put up with it any longer. His phone dings with a text, from Elliot. As angry as he is with his little brother, he was forced to ask for his help. He'd sent the text and all the details. Elliot is unparalleled at tracking. In a past life, he would have been the village's best hunter. Now he's not searching for wolves in person, but online. Hunt. Trap. Kill. Elliot's specialty.

I need to talk to you. I'm in the library. Let's take a walk.

Great.

Jack logs out and grabs his phone. He casts a last glance toward the bedroom, decides not to wake her. He writes a note instead, props it on the pillow.

One more day, soon-to-be Mrs. Compton. I'll see you before the brunch. Love, J

Elliot is waiting for him in the library. His nose is swollen and his eye slightly blackened, but he seems otherwise unharmed, and no longer pissed off. A fire roars in the grate, and the room is warm and cozy.

"Sure you want to go out? It's pouring," Jack says.

"Better to be outside. What, afraid you're going to melt? Such a delicate flower you are."

Elliot grins, and Jack knows all is forgiven. This is how brothers work.

The door to the back patio is latched tight against the rain. They pull on Wellies and grab umbrellas, lumber off onto the grounds. Mud squelches under their boots, and the air crackles with static electricity. Thunder rolls in the distance. The dogs come tearing around the corner, their coats glistening, running in happy circles around them. They like rain, the fools. Thunder dogs, Will calls them.

"Maybe we shouldn't linger out here," Jack says. "I don't want to get struck by lightning."

"You're such a pussy."

Jack shrugs and starts walking again. "Whatever, El."

"The server was breached from inside the system. Someone coded a back door. We're running checks on every employee who left the company in the past three years."

"Does Dad know it was an inside job?"

"Yes, and he's not very happy."

"I'll bet."

"Jack, knowing this breach is internal, I want to talk to you about that night. I think you should come clean. I think you should tell the authorities what really happened."

Jack doesn't answer. They're at the cottages now, and duck inside one, shaking the umbrellas and wiping rain off their shoulders. The roof needs fixing, rain drips through in spots. Romulus stops at the door and sits on his haunches, watching, guarding. Remus comes inside, makes a circuit around the room, whining softly, then goes to join his brother.

"Why in the world would I do that? Why would I implicate Claire in this?"

"I don't mean Monday night. I mean the night Morgan died. I think that's what the threat's about. Whoever sent that text, whoever hacked the servers, knows what really happened with Morgan."

"Impossible. The only people who know are on this island, and there's no one here I don't trust with my life. You included, asshole."

Elliot gives him a half smile. "Jack, think about this. Someone knows. The texts to you and me prove it."

"They prove nothing. I agree, the threats are serious, but there's nothing that ties back to Morgan. And whoever did this didn't really hack the servers. They're holding the data hostage. Big difference. No one can read that data, and it will self-destruct before they can decrypt anything."

"You don't know that. This is a warning shot. Whoever sent this knows how to cover their tracks, just as well as we do. I have a really bad feeling about all of this. There's more to come. So you might think about calling it off. That's all I wanted to say."

"What, call off the wedding?" Jack's tone is so incredulous Elliot flushes, a deep red that Jack knows is a warning sign he'd better back off. Elliot never has done well moderating his emotions. But Jack is tired of being careful with his little brother.

"Why do you not want me to marry Claire, Elliot?"

"Oh, please. Don't be so dramatic. I couldn't give two shits if you marry her or not. She's a nice girl, but she's hardly your equal. But that's your problem, not mine." He moves closer, and his voice drops menacingly. "What is my problem is this family, and our company. Dad isn't taking this seriously enough, and neither are you. We're all going to go down if this doesn't get handled immediately."

"What's on the server that you're trying to hide, Elliot? Is there something you know that I don't?"

"It's not my back I'm trying to cover, Jackson," he fires back. "It's yours."

"You let me worry about my life, and my choices. I want to know what's driving this sudden altruism on my behalf. You don't need to bribe me. I've already offered to step aside and let you take my place in the company. What more do you need from me?"

"You just don't get it. This is about what's good for the family. All of our leverage is gone. We'll have to start over."

"I disagree, and Dad does as well, clearly, or you wouldn't be out here trying to convince me to disobey him. He knows what he's doing. I trust him. You should, too."

Elliot throws up his hands. "Fine. Don't say I didn't warn you." He starts away but Jack grabs his arm.

"Who sent me the text? Did you find out?"

"Why do you think I'm trying to talk some sense into you? It came from a New York number. It belongs to the woman who visited Claire in her studio, Ami Eister. All roads lead to a brick wall."

"That's impossible. Everything is traceable."

"Normally, yes. But whoever is behind this knows how to cover their tracks. Karmen's working on it."

"Karmen has a lot on her plate."

"The SOC is working on it, too. God, Jack. Hover much? I don't know how Claire can stand all your mothering."

"Elliot, what the hell is really going on here?"

"I've told you. Your negligence is about to bring the world crashing down around our ears."

He stalks out, grumbling at the dogs to get out of his way, leaving Jack to stare at his retreating figure.

What the hell was that?

34

Auld Lang Syne

In the darkness of my mind, a woman with black hair stands atop the cliff. The sky is slate gray with the impending storm, and she is screaming a warning to me, but I can't hear, can't understand—

I'm dreaming. I know I'm dreaming.

Wake up, Claire.

The words are a whisper, and I come fully awake to a murky gloom. The candle has guttered out, and the sense of someone standing over me, soft breath tickling my cheek, is overwhelming.

I sit up, looking around the room wildly, but I am alone.

The rain is coming down in sheets. It's weirdly dark; there is no light in the sky, though I can tell it's daylight.

There is a gentle knocking. I go to the living room, but it grows fainter. It's not coming from our door.

I hear the knock again. Hollow and light, this time it seems to be coming from the bedroom. It stops as soon as I get to the doorway.

I know the Villa is supposed to be haunted, there's a Gray Lady in the history I read. Still, I don't believe in ghosts. Someone must be knocking on another room's door. Maybe a floor below, or above. Or it's the pipes. The Villa is old, and I've been here only a day. I'm sure I'll get used to all the house sounds soon enough.

Still, weirdness, on top of that creepy dream, does not settle my nerves.

I startle when my phone rings, a very real, normal sound. I don't recognize the number, but it has a 212 area code. New York.

"Hello?"

"Claire? It's Karmen Harris. Are you alone?"

I spy the note on the pillow. Jack must have gotten up and slipped out without waking me. He always has been an early riser. I am not. If given the opportunity, I will skip breakfast and lounge in bed instead.

No time for that today. The brunch is in a few hours, I have to figure out my dress, and Henna will be all over me with a hundred last second things that need to be done. Now Karmen needs a heart to heart? This can't be good.

"Jack isn't here."

"Good. We need to talk. I'm outside." There is a sharp knock on the door.

Uh-oh. Why do I immediately feel like I've done something wrong? *Guilty conscience*, my mother says from that weird, spectral place that all mothers live in their daughters' consciousness.

I've done nothing to feel guilty about, I snap back at her. *Malcolm shot the intruder.*

"Give me a moment, I need to put on some clothes. I slept in."

I dress quickly, throwing on yesterday's jeans and a Simple Minds T-shirt from the closet. It's Jack's, it's too big, and I love wearing it. It makes me feel safe. I scan the bathroom floor for leftover glass, just in case, but there's nothing. The rug is back in its proper place and looks freshly vacuumed.

I brush my teeth, fluff my hair, though there's no point, it's still raining and the humidity and rain and salt air triumvirate is making it curl riotously around my head.

I open the door and the diminutive security agent enters the room as if she owns the place. I remember that up until yesterday, this was Ana and Brice's suite, so yes, she's probably spent a lot of time here. It's makes me uneasy, how close the security needs to be to the family. I've never thought about it like this, but there's a lot of Compton business done in private places.

Karmen looks like she hasn't slept, and is all business. She parks herself in one of the matching armchairs in the living room. I sit opposite her, pulling my legs up onto the chair and wrapping my arms around them. She has no paperwork, no briefcase. A social call, perhaps?

"I've identified the man who broke into the house. By now, I'm sure the Nashville police have, too."

"I thought his name was Francis Wold."

"A false identity. The intruder's name was Shane McGowan."

My heart stops, then starts again with a pump that is so intense I can't see for a few moments for all the adrenaline pulsing through my veins.

This isn't happening. This isn't possible.

My mind is laughing at me, mocking. *You knew it was him. You knew. When Malcolm took off his mask, you saw him and you knew.*

He was older. He'd gained a lot of weight and a lot of muscle. He looked hard, and dirty, and that half smile etched on his dead face was just as terrifying now as it was a decade ago.

The last time I saw it was in the courtroom before he was sent to prison. He smiled at me as I sat on the stand, testifying against him, more a sneer than a smile, though it somehow still held some promise of love in it. The wrong kind of love. The kind that hurts and tears, not comforts and hugs.

"Claire? Did you know it was him? Did you recognize him? It's okay if you did, we are not deviating from the narrative. Malcolm shot him, and that's the end of it. But I have to ask, because the police will, too. Did you know it was him?"

My voice sounds strangled. "No. Not before…not until Malcolm took off his mask. Even then, I wasn't sure."

"Has he been in touch? Has he reached out? When did you speak to him last?"

"At the trial. Before. No, he hasn't been in touch."

All the strange incidents over the past few months that I've shrugged off to my being clumsy, accident prone, having bad luck, line themselves up in my brain. Everything comes into startling, terrifying clarity.

I'm wrong. Shane has been in touch, in his own insidious, awful way. He wasn't just trying to intimidate me. Or watch me. He was getting back at me. He was trying to kill me.

I should get Jack. Right now. I shouldn't be telling anything to Karmen Harris before I tell my fiancé. But this feels very big, and very scary, and the urge to confess is overwhelming. Karmen is staring at me as if every thought I've just had was spoken aloud.

I sit up straight, cross my legs.

"He hasn't been in direct contact, no. But a lot of weird stuff has been going on."

I tell her about the odd happenings over the past several weeks. The feeling of being watched. The window in my bedroom left open when I knew it had been closed. The near misses by cars as I walked to the coffee shop down the street. The horrid food poisoning that sent me to the hospital; Jack had shared the same meal and had been totally fine. And here at the Villa, the French doors being open, then closed, the knocking from inside the walls, the broken glass on the rug. That creepy ass note.

The blood on my dress.

WHORE

Kamren isn't taking notes, thank God, just committing my words to memory. When I finish, she asks the obvious question.

"Have you told Jack?"

"No. I didn't want to seem like an idiot." I didn't want to seem weak.

She must understand what I'm saying, and what I'm not, because she gives me a sympathetic smile. "Thank you for trusting me with this information, Claire. It helps. It helps tremendously. I'd like to pivot for a moment. Let's talk about the art dealer who came to see you. Ami Eister."

"Were you able to speak with her?"

"Not exactly. She's dead."

I'm sure my jaw has dropped unbecomingly. Dead? Shit. Am I going to get blamed for this, too? I don't know if *Malcolm killed the art dealer* is going to fly.

"What? When did that happen?"

"Six months ago. She died on vacation, out of the country."

So I can't be blamed. Is it ungracious of me to feel utter, complete relief at this? I never said I was a good person.

"I don't understand. She was just at my studio three weeks ago. How could she have died six months ago?"

"I think it's clear whoever was at the studio, it wasn't the art dealer Ami Eister. It's entirely possible someone was using her identity to get to you."

She breaks off, watching me closely, allowing me to catch up.

"They were working together. Shane and this imposter."

"There's a solid chance that's true. Until we ascertain her identity, we won't know for sure. What exactly did she say to you? What did she ask you?"

I go through the Ami Eister story again, step by step, moment by moment.

"You never mentioned the painting by name to her?"

"No. No way. I just assumed... I've been so distracted lately, with the wedding and all the work I'm doing, I figured maybe I slipped. In an interview, or something."

"I think we've established you didn't slip. There were cameras in your studio, too. Whoever this women is, I think it's safe to say she and Shane had a plan for you, and for Jack."

"Can you identify her?"

"I can. Facial recognition technology is very advanced. Our security system didn't capture her when she visited your studio, but there are other cameras in the area. We'll find her on one of those and get an ID as quickly as possible."

"What was wrong with the security system in the studio? How could it miss her?"

"An excellent question. It seems someone's been interfering with our protection of you and Jackson. I intend to find out who."

35

Unforgettable

I wonder, if, in another life, Claire and I might have been friends.

In the beginning, I found her incessantly fascinating because of Jack's obsession with her, yes. But if I'd met her on the street, or at a party, on my own terms, would she and I have chatted? Complimented each other's outfits? Gone for coffee? Would I have connected with her the way I do now?

The way she observes the world around her and puts it into her art, the way the colors swirl and images emerge, not portraits, nothing so specific, just the barely controlled chaos of the modern aesthetic, how even a full canvas of icy white slashes with a sole dot of black in the center—an eye to the universe—can evoke the impulsivity of human nature to leave their mark, to prove they exist in this vacuum we call life… She does an excellent job of that. It's in her mission statement on her website, this ethos of commonality she planned to explore through her work.

I know you would have a hard time seeing the sublime in a black dot on a white background, but trust me, seeing it in person is overwhelming. *Allesandra* hangs in the lobby of Comptons' Manhattan offices.

It is brilliant.

And from what I'd heard, *Jolina* was a masterpiece beyond anything Claire had ever done.

The only reason I went to the studio at all was to witness *Jolina* for myself. That's all. It wasn't to see Claire face-to-face. It wasn't.

Her musings about the composition, how she couldn't capture the scale of it without making the canvas a monstrosity, what she was planning, the vision she saw in her head, how it might have taken years but something, something, had been driving her. It was frightening, her attachment to the piece, but she was so excited, I could see it in her face when she talked to Jackson about it...yes, I had to see this for myself. The cameras installed in the studio should have worked perfectly, but because of the size of the piece, Claire had been forced to turn the damn thing around, so all I could see was the canvas tacked to the skeleton of two-by-fours that held it stable, and every once in a while, the halo of blond curls as she danced around the edges.

I needed to see it. I desperately needed to see it. I wanted to touch it, to run a finger along the drying edge, to leave behind my own mark. It would be covered by a frame eventually, only to be discovered decades later, a stranger's thumbprint, who could it be? (Me, me, me.)

To see her, paintbrush in hand, with her creation.

To smell her.

To touch her.

To have one moment together to remember her by when she was gone.

We all want to be remembered for something. We have children, we paint, we write, we fight, we conquer. We leave behind marks on the fabric of humanity, and while some are content to stay in the background, some of us want to make those marks as vivid and overwhelming as possible.

We don't just want to be remembered. We want to be unforgettable.

She was so surprised by my visit. I sometimes forget how young she is, how easily manipulated. All I had to do was say I was an art dealer from New York, I had an offer from a client, could I see the work? She blushed and fumbled and tried to hide her excitement, but I could see it there, suffusing her skin, turning her from accomplished artist to insecure little girl, and the words rose from her mind in an almost outrageous clamor.

What if she doesn't like it what if she goes to the client and says it's trash what if I'm not good enough what if my work is a joke what if this is a setup what if she wants to buy it anyway?

What if, what if, what if.

With every internal question she grew smaller and quieter and more aloof.

But as I said, she is young. It didn't take much persuading to open her up again. How impressed I was by *Allesandra*. How unique is Claire's esthetic. How no one's seen anything like this since the sixties, how this new style will influence a generation.

Lies, all of it, but all artists are simply walking bags of ego and insecurities and succumb to flattery with such ease.

When she was pink with pleasure, believing in herself again, I suggested she take me around to the back of the studio, so I could see *Jolina* for myself.

She was about to do it. I could feel her deciding, and knew she was going to say yes. With a flick of my finger in just the right spot, I was going to tip her over the edge and make her mine.

And then she declined.

The bitch said no.

She took my card and promised to let my client have first

rights of refusal, but unfortunately the piece wasn't ready. Thank you so much for your interest. I look forward to talking to you again soon. I'm getting married—I'm afraid I haven't been able to stay as focused on my work as I would like these past few months. But soon. The moment I'm back from my honeymoon, I'll finish, and then I'll call.

I nearly killed her on the spot.

How dare she refuse me? After all I'd given her? Without me she would be nothing.

I was forced to break in and see it in the darkness, in pieces, shining my light across its edges, making circles into its heart. It was a piece of shit. Without her near it, it was just a huge, clunky wall of chaotic nothing.

I still pressed my thumb in the edge, but the paint there was already dry.

36

Do You Remember When?

After Karmen leaves, I get myself together and dressed for the brunch. I wonder if this is how I'm going to live my life going forward, acting as if everything is normal while inside my very being screams in agony.

I'm supposed to be happy right now, damn it. This is the weekend of my dreams. I'm marrying the man I love on a gorgeous Italian island, and instead, my past is haunting me and my present has gone insane.

Who the hell is the woman who came to my studio?

I shot Shane.

The hydrofoil ferry horn echoes into my room, and I can hear the dogs barking. God, I hope Harper and my parents are on the boat. I wonder if Ana was able to get in touch with Harper about bringing me a new dress?

"Claire? You in there?"

Sanity, in the form of an extremely excited and tattooed

bridesmaid. Katie doesn't notice anything is wrong, not yet. She stares over my shoulder at the terrace doors, then shakes her head with a grin.

"This place is bonkers. Thank God the generators kicked in, I'd have never found you otherwise. What are you doing sitting here in the dark? Let's go outside."

It's not quite as dark as she claims, but it is gloomy. I hadn't bothered to turn on any lights when Karmen came to talk.

Katie grabs my hand and pulls me across the bridal suite to the French doors that lead out onto the sizable terrace. The pergola shields us from the rain, though I can feel the mist curling around my body.

"Have you ever seen anything like this? Even in the rain it's so gorgeous. You're going to have a whole new series of paintings after spending any time here. Your Italian period." She affects a terrible accent and spins around, making me giggle.

"We'll see about that."

"I passed out when I got here. I feel like I slept for a week. I'm raring to go. Did I miss anything?"

I don't often lie to Katie, because she can see right through me. The ferry horn shrieks again, and I take the opportunity to change the subject.

"Hopefully my parents and Harper are on the ferry. I think this is the last run. The storms are going to get worse later."

"Joy. Harper Hunts Life is coming to document every moment of our existence…"

"Come on. Instagram has been good to her. She's making oodles of money. She has over a million followers now. A real reputation."

"I know, I know. At what cost, though? She's living it as out loud as you can. It's not like she's doing it for the art. She's not the artist you are, Claire."

My heart swells a bit, and that nasty little voice that lives inside me says—see, even Katie says you're better than Harper—but I shove her away and demur.

"That's very sweet, but she's good, great even, and you know it."

The daggers she shoots at Harper are nothing new. Katie is horribly jealous of my little sister's following, not that I can't sympathize. Until Jack came along, I was, too. Everything comes easy to Harper.

For Katie? Not so much. Katie's an aspiring songwriter by day, but that vocation isn't paying the rent, so she bartends downtown on the vampire shift, as she calls it. She'd kill to have Harper's following. It would make her. And it will come, eventually, if she sticks with her songwriting and performing. That Harper went viral on a random, unplanned post—a beautiful photo taken of her standing on a beach at sunset, her shadow stretching behind her, with the caption *Never be afraid of what scares you the most*—was admittedly a fluke, but that's life, right? You never know what might connect with someone, or infuriate them, or both. Either way, you've gotten an emotional response.

I guess I shouldn't be too surprised that my sister can evoke emotions in millions of people at once. She's been doing it to me all my life.

Katie is peering at me worriedly. "Are you okay, Claire? You're pale."

Am I okay? Nope. Not even close. But I can't tell her everything, and the reality of what that NDA really means crashes into me in a wave of regret. With the stroke of a pen, I am cut off from everyone. My friends. My family. I have only Jack and the rest of the Comptons in my confidence now. The thought is positively frightening.

"Claire?" Katie asks again.

"I'm okay. I got a little seasick yesterday—I've been lying low since I got here. Haven't even had the full tour yet."

I'm saved by a familiar voice calling from the hallway.

"Hellooooo? Claire? Are you in there?"

"Harper," we say in unison, with varying degrees of happiness, and turn to welcome my sister.

Harper, loaded down with packages, barrels into the room, talking a mile a minute in broken Italian to a man I've not seen before who is hidden beneath a mound of bags, both suitcases and shopping.

"*Si, grazie*, put it *ecco. Per favore*. Thanks. You're the best! *Buongiorno.*"

I bite back my first reaction—do you have to dump all your crap in my room?—instead wave my sister out to the terrace. Harper gives me a thumbs-up, pulling her wallet out of her purse to offer a tip, which is immediately declined. She rewards the man with a smile instead, and he leaves her belongings on the floor by the door, looking utterly lovestruck.

Harper can make anyone feel special. When that smile lands on you, it's like the sun has paraded out from behind a cloud for the first time in weeks.

We couldn't be more opposite if we tried. I'm relatively quiet, studious, shy; I let my art speak for me. Harper is larger than life, and rarely at a loss for words. Even our coloring is in contrast—Harper is a stunning brunette with perfectly balayaged extensions and the curves to match. What I wouldn't do for some of that bust and ass. Her hair is bought, yes, but the rest of Harper is 100 percent good old-fashioned Hunter DNA. And the extroversion…everyone knows when Harper is in the building. She lives life with gusto, throwing herself at everything, heedless of embarrassment, upsetting people, or otherwise making waves.

Not to mention she's a seriously talented photographer and writer on top of it all. And a successful social media influencer. Whose brother-in-law is about to be Jack Compton.

The sky is the limit for @HarperHuntsLife.

Harper and I haven't always gotten along, but lately, things have been on a good, even keel. Both of us are happy. Both are having a measure of success. Being adults has helped. Without the triple-barrel carpet bombs of teenage hormones, our father's death, and our mother's alcoholism, it's easier for her to put her fury at me aside, and easier for me to forgive her eternal anger.

Harper joins us on the terrace, chattering like a jaybird. "Jack's brother was on the ferry with us. Tyler? He's totally hot, and there was another equally hot guy with him. How are you? You look pale. I brought all my makeup—I can get some color in your cheeks before the rehearsal if you want me to. And when are we doing the last fitting for the dress? You know you need to have it nipped once more, you just keep losing weight, lucky girl. I don't know how—"

"Harper. Take a breath," I say, amused. "Look around. Enjoy the moment. Listen to the rain. Exist. Isn't that your brand strategy, existing in the moment?"

"Sorry, sorry, I've had about forty espressos today."

"We can tell," Katie replies with an eye roll.

"Where's Mom and Brian?"

Harper's face falls a bit. "Mom went straight to her room, she is still super jet-lagged. She…"

She breaks off, looking at Katie.

"She what?"

Harper sighs. "She had a few glasses of wine this week."

My heart sinks. This I don't need right now.

"She's fine—she's totally fine. Like, literally had two glasses and stopped."

"Two glasses total? Or two a meal?"

"Really, Claire, I shouldn't have even said anything. Forget I mentioned it. She's fine. Wow, it's beautiful here." Harper stalks to the edge of the terrace, and I realize she is wearing studded Louboutin high-heeled boots. Good to see New York is treating her well.

"That yacht is incredible. We're having the rehearsal dinner on the boat, right?"

"Right. Brunch today, rehearsal tonight. There's supposed to be a break in the weather."

"The wedding is moved up, too?"

"Yes. It's not such a big deal, especially since now, everyone's here." I smile, injecting some extra sweet into it to cover my dark thoughts. If my mother is drinking again, that is bad news.

"I swear, Claire, if you were any more agreeable…"

"Hush, Harper. No sense fighting it. Henna knows what she's doing. So does Ana. I'm just along for the ride. Besides, I'm down with being married sooner. I'm going mad with all the waiting."

"Speaking of the wedding, Harper, you can't wear heels that high for the ceremony. You're going to tower over everyone," Katie gripes.

"I know. Don't worry, I have flats. Like, ten pairs or something. I couldn't decide which matched the dress best, so I brought them all. I can take pictures and let my peeps decide."

"You know, if you weren't such a savvy businesswoman, Harper, I'd think you were a vacuous twit."

"Fuck off, Katie."

Well, this is a lovely start. "Truce, ladies. Please? For me? Hey, if it stops raining for a while, maybe we can spend some time exploring. We can hike up to the big cliff. Did you know Caesar once hid here? The history is incredible."

"Sounds like fun. Though we don't need you tripping and breaking an ankle before the wedding." Harper's camera is in her hand, she is already snapping away. She stops, looks at me over her shoulder. "I'm looking forward to…you know," she says quietly.

"I know. Jack will come get you later. I'm not sure of the timing."

"For what?" Katie demands.

"The photoshoot," Harper says, the sense of pride in her voice obvious.

At Katie's confused look, I provide the rest. "Brice and Ana thought it would be nice for Harper to do some candid family shots," I say.

"And *Flair* is going to run the spread. I'm going to interview Brice and Ana for them."

"Because this wedding is all about Brice Compton," Katie grumbles. "Figures."

"It's a legitimate business opportunity, and of course the story will discuss Jack and Claire."

"Yeah, right."

I'm so used to their fussing that I've already tuned out their squabble. Always the same. It's why I don't normally try to get them together like this. Harper and Katie snipe at each other, incessantly.

Then again, Katie snipes at everyone these days. My transition away from her best friend to Jack Compton's wife is going to be a difficult one, and we both know it.

We need a distraction, and I'm hot with the urge to confess. To purge myself. To be washed clean by the benediction of the women in my life. They will understand. They will.

But I have to censor myself. I can't get them in trouble.

Katie sees me trying to find the words. "What's wrong, Claire?"

I blow out a long breath. "I guess the most pressing thing is someone ruined my dress."

Harper whirls around. "What do you mean, someone ruined your dress?"

"Someone painted the word *WHORE* on it in what looked like blood. It's ruined. Ana was going to reach out to you, Harper, to see if you could find a replacement on the mainland. I take it she didn't get you?"

"She may have, but my phone hasn't been working well. I must have missed her call. Oh, Claire. I am so sorry."

Katie puts an arm around my shoulder. "Are you okay? You're in love with that dress."

"I'm a little numb, to be honest. I mean…" My voice quavers, and I clear my throat. I am not going to cry. I refuse to break again. That's what this has been designed to do, a long-term, steady campaign to get me to break. Fuck whoever is screwing with me.

"Where is your dress now?" Harper asks.

"The seamstress took it away yesterday."

"Oh, I wish Ana had gotten through, our hotel was right by an adorable shop that I could have gone into before we left."

Twist that knife, sister. Yes, it would have been nice if you'd bothered answering your phone. I don't for a second believe that it wasn't working well, how else were you uploading all your photos online this week?

I must have sighed, because she catches my hand. "Claire. Do you want me to see if it can be fixed?"

"Henna was going to try to cut a panel out of it, but it's trashed. Past recovery, I'm afraid."

"You let me make that call. I bet I can find a length of satin and we can replace it."

"We're on an island in the middle of nowhere, Harper. Where are you going to find fabric that matches?"

She smiles, the radiant sunbeam that knocks people down in its glory. My sister is a pretty, pretty girl. "We're in Italy, Claire. This is the fashion capital of the world. Let me try, at least. The dress is so beautiful, I'd hate for you not to be able to wear it."

Breathe, Claire. Let her help.

"Okay. Thank you, Harper. I would appreciate that."

Harper gives me a swift hug, disappears into my rooms like a shot. I hear her rustling around, she must be grabbing her bags on the way out.

Katie looks impressed, which is saying something. "Maybe little sister will save the day. Though if I get my hands on whoever messed with your dress, I'll kill them," she says, still watching me. "There's more. What is it, Claire? What's going on?"

I blow out a breath. "You can't tell anyone about this, okay?"

"Cross my heart and hope to die."

"An intruder broke into the house Monday night. Malcolm, Jack's security guard, shot him."

"Dead? Shot him dead?"

"Yes."

"Who the hell was it?"

I stumble on my answer. I am not quite ready to pull back the curtain on the mess that is going to ensue when I admit to my fiancé that I do know the intruder. I know him very well. I'd prefer to have this part of things private, at least until Jack and I can have a talk.

But this is my best friend. She knows my secrets. My lies. Maybe she can help me find the path.

The uneasy sense of newfound knowledge—how could I have missed it before?—assails me. How had my mind tricked me? How had it thrown up the barrier to let me look right at him and still not see it?

"Who was it, Claire?" she asks again.

"It was Shane. Shane McGowan. He—"

My words are cut off by Jack, calling from inside the room. "Where's my bride-to-be? It's time for our brunch!"

I whisper, "Do not say anything, Katie. Please."

"He doesn't know about Shane?"

"No. He doesn't. Just stay quiet, for me. I will handle this."

"You'll handle what, darling?" Jack asks, stepping onto the terrace.

37

The Great Confession

Jack is soaking wet.

"Where have you been?" I ask.

"Oh, Elliot needed to talk about the server issue."

"In the pool?"

He swipes a hand through his hair, slicking it back into place. "We walked to the cottages. Hey, Katie. You all settled in?"

"I am, Jack. Thank you. Your family's hospitality is wonderful."

I shoot her a look—she's laying it on pretty thick.

"What are you going to handle?" Jack asks me.

I don't answer. My head is still reeling, my mind is screaming not to tell him anything, that he's going to hate me, that he's going to leave me.

This is my greatest fear. I can put voice to it, now that I'm faced with its imminent prospect. If he finds out about my past, he's going to walk away. Why would he want to be saddled with me? His family, his parents, they aren't going to want me as a part of the Compton clan when they find out the horrors I've been through. The horrors I've caused.

"I texted, but you didn't answer."

He glances at his phone. "It didn't come through. The signal is pretty bad today, with the weather. What's up?"

"Oh, it's nothing. Just checking to see where you were."

"Missed me already?"

"I always miss you when you're not here."

He beams at me. Katie clears her throat. "God, get a room."

We laugh, then silence envelops us.

"Well, that's my cue. Brunch is in fifteen minutes. I better get moving. I'll see you down there."

Katie gives me a stare that says *tell him or I will.*

Once the door is shut, he rubs his face and sighs. "God, what a morning. Elliot is being a first-class asshole. Just a heads-up, in case he's rude to you. He's in a mood."

"Got it. Everything okay with the servers? Any news?"

"Nothing yet. Seriously, you don't need to worry about it. Dad's got it handled."

Jack pulls me in for a hug and the move strikes me in a way it never has before. Unlike my previous lovers, he is a gentle, tactile man, never worried about PDA. He's always holding my hand, draping an arm across my shoulders, playing with my hair. Lots of kisses and private touches. I've never had anyone so openly affectionate before.

Normally it makes me feel cherished, treasured.

But at this moment, with the specter of Shane drifting about, I don't want to be touched. I certainly don't want to be hugged. I'm feeling claustrophobic. I want to get out of here. To run away. It's what I do best, run. I do not want to have to tell my soon-to-be husband about my ties to Shane McGowan.

I have no choice, though. I must, before someone else does.

I extricate myself from his arms, ignore the spike of guilt. He doesn't seem to notice me pulling away, just smiles benevolently. But there is something sharp beneath his look.

"Katie was being weirder than normal."

"I told her about the break-in."

"Ah." Jack crosses his arms. "You told her what, exactly?"

"Don't worry. You know me better than that."

He goes in motion, such a classic Jack response to a difficult question that I know something is coming. He strolls around the room, touching things. The flowers, the marble-inlay table, the handle to the French doors. Such expensive trinkets and furnishings. So decadent. He stares out at the rain for a few moments.

"I know it's been rough going, darling, but it's going to be all right. I promise."

"I'm not so sure."

"What do you mean?"

I join him at the terrace doors, look out over the turbulent sea. The water has gone from blue to gray, small whitecaps forming. The winds are picking up; a fresh wave of storms are coming in. Clouds are scudding hard across the sky, and thunder rolls across the bay.

"I know who it is. Who...Malcolm shot."

"What?"

"I haven't been entirely honest with you, Jack."

There's genuine confusion on his face, and when I say the words I've been dreading for so long, watch the ticking of the muscle in his jaw that indicates he is furious, I decide I better go all in.

"Can we sit down?"

"Yes, I think we should," he says, the words clipped and tight. We face off—him on the sofa, me in the wing chair next to it. He keeps hold of my hand, trying to reassure both himself and me, I think.

"The man who broke into the house, the man who was shot, his name is Shane McGowan. He was my boyfriend for a while.

Back before my father died. He was bad news, and I stopped seeing him after the accident. Because he went to jail. I had to testify against him. I—"

Jack has dropped my hand. I feel suddenly cold, and small. Jack's face is turning red. I expect an explosion, but his voice is as quiet and deadly as I have ever heard.

"That bastard got out of jail and was trying to intimidate you? I'd fucking kill him if he wasn't already dead. How did Karmen let this happen?"

I'm completely confused. "You knew? You knew about Shane?"

"I don't know the details. But yes, I know of him. He came up in your background check. I was assured he was nothing to be concerned about. Of course, now we know that assessment was wrong. That's Karmen's problem, not yours."

"Well, it is mine."

"No. Stick with the plan, Claire. We've got this covered. But I'm curious. Why you didn't tell me about this Shane character?"

"Because he was a bad decision, and I thought he was out of my life forever."

"Fair enough. I admit I hadn't given him a thought, either. But we're a team, Claire. You have to share everything with me. I will never hold your past against you, and I would hope you'd offer me the same courtesy."

"You aren't mad at me?"

"Because you dated a jerk in high school? Why would I be?"

"If it gets out, it will embarrass the family. Embarrass you. He is—he was—trouble."

"Oh, Claire." He hugs me again, and this time, I let him. "If Karmen, or my parents, for that matter, thought this was a problem, they would have made more than a casual mention to me. This situation isn't on you. Karmen is the one who has to redeem herself in the eyes of the family. This situation is of her own making."

"I… I don't know. I was just… I can't believe you're not mad."

"I'm relieved, to be perfectly honest."

"Relieved?"

He pulls me to the sofa next to him, and I lean into him. This time, instead of being claustrophobic, it's comforting.

"Listen to me. Even if your past association with this asshole was embarrassing, don't you see? It's all over. I'll bet the cameras in the house were meant to capture something that he could use to try and humiliate you, to blackmail you. To blackmail us. It wouldn't be the first time someone's tried to blackmail a Compton. With him dead, this is all over."

"You think so?"

"Yes. I hate that you've been upset, and Claire, you have to promise me if something happens in the future you will tell me immediately. But there's nothing more to be concerned about. We can move forward with the rehearsal tonight, and with the wedding tomorrow. We'll work out something with your dress, and it's all going to be fine, darling. I promise. All the craziness is over. Are you feeling up to the brunch?"

"Of course. But I almost forgot. What happened with the cottages, and the remains they found? Is that why you went out there with Elliot?"

I pretend not to notice his body stiffen beside me.

"The remains…" He sighs, looking at the ceiling. I sense he's struggling with something. "It looks like it might be a former member of our staff. Her name is Elevana. Fatima's mother. She went missing…gosh, it must be twenty years ago? Her family thought she'd left to go to the mainland, and something happened to her there, but now it looks like she never made it off the island. She must have fallen down the cliffside path. I heard them say her skull was cracked. I know it's awful, but at least her family has answers now."

Will Compton's bulging eyes and high-pitched cries invade my mind.

He killed her. He killed her. You know that he killed her.

"You don't think this had something to do with your grandfather's reaction to seeing me yesterday, do you?"

"No. Absolutely not. I talked to Mom about his mental state. She says he's been confusing some of his movies with reality. He did a number of thrillers back in the day." His voice thickens. "I hate that you might not get to know him as I do. He's a great guy. I bumped into him last night after you'd gone to bed, and he seemed to be back to normal. The disease is stealing him away, a bit at a time."

My stomach growls. What an inappropriate response to this terrible news. "I really am so sorry, Jack. Maybe tomorrow will be better."

"I certainly hope so."

"We better get going. They'll be waiting for us."

"Yes. Let me change really quick, and we can go down."

He stands with me, and touches my cheek gently. His voice is soft and rumbling.

"Did he hurt you, Claire? McGowan?"

Did Shane hurt me? Yes, he did. In too many ways to count.

"Shhh," I say, wrapping my arms around him. "It's over now."

38

The Watcher

Well, that was stirring.

Did you enjoy watching them confess and cuddle? I did.

Oh, don't be such a prude. I did mention that I like to watch.

Jack and Claire are my favorite highlight reel, my number one streaming show, my elegant night out at the theater, my furtive glimpse of porn. Everything they do, everything they say. The fights and the fucking, the little kindnesses and the grand gestures. The fear, the joy, the rage.

What would they do if they knew they were on display for me? Would they be outwardly horrified but inwardly excited at the attention? All the world's a stage, and all the men and women merely players, yes, yes. Jack, I know would hate it. But Claire...hasn't she been begging for attention all these years?

No, for me, the invasion of their private world, that's the best part. I think ultimately, they would be horrified to know what I know, and that makes me...happy.

Have I always been this way? A voyeur? Possibly. I'm sure you imagine me as a delinquent child peeping through keyholes and lingering outside of cracked doors. I was never so obvious, so crass. There was a fabulous store down the street from the protective services offices that catered to the private eye Hollywood set. The owner took a liking to me, allowed me to test out his wares so he could have firsthand samples to show his clientele. I had a deft hand, and my mentor explained things well. It wasn't long before said clientele wanted to know how he got such excellent compromising shots. So, he pimped me out. Not in the sexual sense, but for my skills at getting in, placing the cameras, and getting out unnoticed. No one pays attention to a child playing happily while waiting for their mother to finish with whatever shopkeeper or home visit they are on. Oh, you think they do, you hear stories all the time of people being taken to court for negligence, but trust me, so long as nothing seems amiss, no one gives a second glance. They're all too busy wrapped up in their own world.

As I got older, I started researching on my own. And then tinkering. Taking the cameras apart, putting them back together. Stripping out the unnecessary components, so they were smaller and smaller. Easier to place. Easier to hide.

My mentor was my first client, naturally. He spread the word.

I got my first round of VC money when I was in college. I got the second round right before I met Jackson.

I didn't need anything else after that. I had the man, the ring, the education, the career, the reputation.

But I liked to watch.

It was dirty, and it was wrong. But nothing could cure me of that desire. It lived deep within me. Nothing else could fill me, not food, not drink, not love. Nothing could stop me.

Not even death.

39

Ching Ching

We head down to the breakfast room. Though smaller than the expansive dining room we ate in last night, it is straight out of Downton Abby—a long, graceful space with a double tray ceiling, crisp white wainscoting and crown molding, and an antique sideboard covered in silver chafing dishes. Bottles of Dom Perignon and jugs of freshly squeezed orange juice are chilling in a massive silver tub. A veritable display of meats and cheeses line the sideboard: bacon, prosciutto, salami, mortadella, ham, slices of Swiss and cheddar and mozzarella. The chafing dishes hold more treats, these of the eggish variety: cheesy scrambled eggs, eggs Benedict, hardboiled, spinach frittata; fragrant, crumbly quiches. The usual European selections of tomato, yogurts, muesli, and Nutella finish out the choices.

Jack has a grin for everyone, and I feel my own shoulders drop a notch. Jack will know what to say, what to do. He always does.

"Good morning, good morning," he says heartily. There is

a babble of conversation—teasing jokes about our late arrival, comments about the house and the weather. More people are filtering into the room, and Jack is consumed with greetings, hugs, handshakes, slaps on the back. I see the Crows standing at each entrance, unsmiling. Malcolm catches my eye for a moment then glances away. Do I look guilty of my sin? Does he look guilty enough for me?

I am presented to a few new-to-me friends, and a few I've met before. The lawyers, Maggie and Henry, are there, plates already full, with special smiles for me. Elliot glides in, and Amelia follows, slower, still looking out of sorts. Poor girl. Jack gives Elliot some serious side-eye. They aren't getting along, and I'm not entirely sure what's happening.

Tyler, the youngest of the Compton boys, enters the room from the courtyard doors, his dark blond hair damp from the rain. When he hugs me, I swear I can smell the sea.

"Sis. How's tricks?"

"Tricks are…good. I'm a little overwhelmed, but good."

"You'll get used to it. Mom and Dad like things to look grand for guests but when no one's around, we're all just piled together in our pajamas, drinking coffee out of paper cups and fighting about who has to go fetch the *cornetti* from the baker by the beach."

"That sounds idyllic. What the hell is a corn…thingy?"

Tyler smiles. "It's like a croissant, basically. Hey, I brought my boyfriend, I hope you don't mind a plus one. Claire, this is Peter Mayfair."

Peter Mayfair also has floppy dark blond hair that's wet from the rain, and though they are the same height, nearly as tall as Jack, Peter has broader shoulders and a more chiseled jawline, complete with a deep dimple in his chin. He is devastatingly handsome.

"Good to meet you. Any friend of Tyler's is a friend of mine."

"Thanks for letting me crash the party." Peter loops an arm

across Tyler's shoulders, gives his new boyfriend a smile. Tyler beams back.

I know Peter is a new addition because we talked to Tyler on FaceTime three weeks ago and he was very single and bemoaning the fact that he'd be flying solo at the wedding. It's good to see him with someone. He's pushing thirty and has been alone too long, in my opinion. He works insane hours in difficult conditions, and he deserves some peace and happiness. And boy, does he look happy now.

Jack joins our conversation. "Ty. And Peter! How wonderful to see you. I didn't think you were going to be able to get away. Claire, Peter's one of our doctors in the Brigade."

"Well, at least I know if anything happens there are two doctors in the house."

There is a small commotion in the hall and my mother and Brian enter. Mom's looking rough, slightly green around the gills, eyes red and puffy. When I hug her, I can smell the must in her breath, leftovers from the night before, even though she's brushed her teeth. Great. She's sporting a hangover. What's happened to get her started drinking again?

Brian hugs me, and he smells like soap. I don't catch the scent of alcohol coming from his pores.

"I was getting worried that you weren't going to make it. How are you guys? How was Rome?"

"Amazing," Brian gushes. "Harper took us all over the city, to all her photoshoots. We saw the Colosseum, and the Vatican. A special tour, just for us. It was incredible. And the food… I'm already thinking about the next time we can come visit."

"You're welcome anytime. Mom, did you have fun?"

"I did. I've developed a fondness for pistachio gelato. Harper told me about your dress. I'm so sorry, Claire."

"Yeah. Totally sucks." She's distracted; despite her condolences, she's not even making eye contact with me. "You sure you're okay?"

"I'm fine, I'm fine. The ferry ride was very rough, the waves got us all damp. I hear you've had to move up the schedule?" she looks queasily at the dishes of food, and even more so at the champagne. Brian pours her a cup of coffee. He's pretending nothing is wrong, so I go along with it. I'll talk to him about it later. Or tomorrow. Or never. I resolve not to let my worry for my mom interfere with things. I have enough on my plate.

"Yes, you're going to be eating all day. Rehearsal is tonight. It should be a fun party—it's down on *The Hebrides*. I've heard there's a big surprise."

"Sounds like fun, honey. This place..." She smiles, an actual, genuine smile, one I don't get to see very often. "I'm proud of you. You certainly landed yourself a catch. Hold on to him."

She takes a seat two down from me, a leg curled beneath her on the chair. Those daily yoga classes have paid off, she's limber as a teenager. Harper drops down next to her.

"Any news on the dress?"

She shakes her head. "I wasn't able to find Henna to talk to her. I'll deal with it after brunch. Promise."

Speaking of Henna... I don't see her anywhere. Granted, she's running this show, but she should at least be able to enjoy the fruits of her labor.

Ana arrives, looking severely elegant in a black wrap dress, Brice in ironed jeans and a black turtleneck at her side. They mix and mingle and are delightful hosts, taking special pains to include my family in the conversation.

This is perfect. The room is so happy, with the clinking of silverware and glasses, the laughter and general conversation. The bottles never seem to disappear or get empty, the dishes on the sideboard stay full. I finally see some of the kitchen staff, who have been coming in and out silently, unobtrusively. They've managed all this without the main power on, running entirely off the generators. They know how to manage a roomful of people, and a tiny part of me relaxes. Under Henna's guidance, the dinner tonight will be flawless.

Fatima is the only one who isn't smiling. She stands at the far end of the room by the door to the kitchen watching over everything with a sharp eye. She is dignified, remote, with her hair screwed back into a bun and her chin high. She has not had time to grieve her mother, not at all, but I recognize the stance of a woman who is content to wait her turn.

I realize Harper is talking to Ana about the interview. They've scheduled the shoot for after brunch. I'm glad. Harper's been on me about this for months—now that it's happening, I hope she'll get off my back and we can resume our benign neglect of one another.

Satisfied, I lift my mimosa, and hit my glass gently with my fork. Everyone settles. There are a few whistles. Jack looks at me, surprised but clearly delighted. I stand. I've been preparing this speech for days, wanting to surprise Jack with a bit of extroversion. I don't normally get talkative unless I've had a few drinks. I've had to modify it a bit, but the gist is the same.

"I'd like to make a toast."

"Toast this," someone shouts, and Jack throws a piece of bacon at the offending someone.

"I'd like to make a toast to all of you. For being so flexible—" more wolf whistles, and now I'm blushing, and Jack is openly laughing "—for agreeing to join us in Italy for our wedding, halfway around the world for many of you. We adore you all and are so grateful you're here with us. Jack and I prepared a whole weekend of activities for you, but as you can see—" lightning flashes, and thunder booms, right on cue "—we're going to be stuck inside more than we'd planned."

"And we know what you and Compton will be doing," a tall blond-haired man at the second to the last seat of the table calls out, followed by more wolf whistles. I obligingly roll my eyes; this is clearly the horniest group of merrymakers. Maybe Katie and Harper will find themselves partnered off. After all, they are the bridesmaids.

"I want to thank Jack and his family as well, for offering the hospitality of their delightful home." Another crack of thunder, and we all laugh. "Thank you for helping us start our lives together." I raise my glass. "Ching Ching."

"Ching Ching!" they shout.

Jack hops up to clink glasses with me, a smile on his face. My toast is the Italian way of saying cheers, or bottoms up, and I know he likes that I took the time to figure it out.

Jack holds up his glass. "And if I may say thank you as well, to my bride, the love of my life, who has opened her heart to this grizzled old man. May this be the first of many happy breakfasts together."

There's another smattering of applause, then all the guests start hitting their glasses with their cutlery. Jack obligingly sweeps me into his arms and kisses me, and the room explodes into shouts of happiness.

Their joy burns away the clouds that have shrouded me. I finally feel like a bride. I finally feel like things are going to be okay.

40

Wake Up, Wake Up

Don't think I've gotten attached to this woman. Not for a moment. Oh, I know what you're thinking—she's not obsessed, she's not out for revenge.

She's in love.

And you'd be wrong, on so many levels. Do you understand what love really is? Do you?

Love is simply a word we use to explain the biochemical nature of species propagation. It's something we use to justify the base desire to experience pleasure with another person when in fact it's just about making procreation more palatable. We say we're in love, but what we really mean is we want to connect so we don't feel so alone, and in so doing, create stronger familial constructs that allow us to fend off other familial constructs who want to take what we have.

Love is code for the powerful urge to survive among predators.

No, I'm not in love with her.

I'm in hate with her.

I'm in hate with him.

It is intoxicating, this hatred. It has taken all my time, all of my ferocious attention. All of my abilities to stay hidden, the spider in the corner no one notices. It feeds me, this hatred, and I bloat on it; I grow, and I grow, and I grow.

They've blithely gone on living while I was forced to be dead. I've lived this way against my will for a decade and I will not do it any longer.

I will not.

My God, are you not listening?

Wake the fuck up.

41

And Then She Dies

When brunch finally ends, we are decidedly tipsy. Our guests peel off for an afternoon on their own, which, for most of them, considering the rain, will probably mean hanging out playing billiards or drinking some more. It's such a shame they've come all this way to have a fun Italian vacation and it's pouring.

Harper goes with the Comptons to do the interview. Katie says she's feeling inspired and wants to write some lyrics and will come help me get ready for the rehearsal later. Mom and Brian head off on a tour of the house. Jack suggests a siesta back in our rooms, which sounds like fun to me. I'm ready for some time alone after all the interaction. A natural extrovert I am not.

It's raining hard, and the hallways are dark. He has to use the flashlight on his phone so I don't trip. When we get to our rooms, they are dark, too.

"Have the generators stopped working?"

"The majority of their power is for the common areas and

the kitchens, to keep the food and stuff cold. It won't light up the private spaces unless it's necessary. There have been plenty of dark days and nights in this place since it was built. Let's find a candle. There should be some in the drawer, here."

He digs around in the night table and pulls out a thick white candle and a pack of matches.

"That almost sounds like you enjoy this, Mr. Compton."

"Being alone in the dark with my bride? I do. It's even more romantic with candlelight."

The match strikes with a sulfurous *whssst*, and he sets the flame to the wick. The shadows in the room begin to dance, strobed every few minutes by flashes from outside.

He fits his mouth to mine, and things are progressing quite nicely when banging starts on the door, a hand rattling the knob.

"So much for alone time," Jack grumbles. "Who is it?"

"Jack? Is Claire with you? And Harper? We can't find anyone, and the lights are still out in our room."

It is my mother.

With a small vocal groan that matches my internal sigh, Jack slides off the bed and makes his way to the door.

Framed by the bleeding black silence of the dark hallway, her face pale and ghostly in the storm light, it's clear something is off. My mom's coppery hair is in disarray, her white shirt smudged with black on the left shoulder. Her eyes are bright and hectic, not entirely focused.

I don't know how long we've been apart, less than an hour, but in that time, she's managed to get very, very drunk.

"Well hey, you two." The words run together in a slurred Southern drawl: *wallhayewetew.* "Goodness, Jack, this storm is terrible. Such a beautiful house. A little dark and creepy without the lights. Claire, where have you been? Have you seen Harper? I can't find her anywhere. I've been looking and looking—"

I put a hand on her arm. "She's interviewing Jack's parents."

"Yes, Mrs. Reed—"

"Jack, I've told you a hundred times, it's Trisha. You can call me Mom if you want."

The coy smile, the slow blink, damn it, she is completely toasted. Drunk Trisha equals chatty, flirty, overflowing with Southern charm Trisha, at least until she tips over the edge into misery and anguish. Even when she drank regularly, she was only a good drunk if she stopped at three or four. Anything more and she devolved rapidly. This feels like much more.

It's my fault. We shouldn't have served champagne at the brunch. I should have known better than to put temptation at her right hand.

"Trisha," Jack amends. "Let me call Fatima and have her show you the way back to your room."

"Oh, I think Claire can do that, can't you, dear? Surely you've discovered this old place's secrets."

I am already pulling on my shoes, relived to have a chance to scoot my mother away before she says something truly mortifying. "Sure, Mom. Let me grab a flashlight and I'll get you back there. Brian's probably missing you."

Jack puts a hand on my arm. "Claire—"

"No, really Jack, it's fine. I think I know where their rooms are."

I hope he can tell by my tone that I need to be alone with my mother. Sure enough, he takes the hint.

"Yes, darling. Down the hall, turn left, and you'll find the entrance to the guest wing. I'll wait here for you, all right?"

I blow out a grateful breath. "I'll be right back. Come on, Mom. Where's Brian? I thought you two were taking a tour?" I maneuver my mother down the hall, a hand on her elbow, tugging her along like she used to do to me when I was a child and she had to pull me away from the candy display at the grocery. Trisha seems not to notice my urgency, prattling on in her drunken sing-song voice.

"Oh, Brian's in bed, the lazy bones. He made his excuses

and went to the room, left me to do the tour by myself." Lord knows how much of this is true.

She prattles on. "I can't believe the lights went out. Such a bad storm, so glad we got here. When's this rehearsal dinner now? Tonight? I can't believe that woman changed the schedule on us, I mean, it's just not done—this is a wedding. Have you decided what to wear? If you want me to, I could do your hair in a French braid. Though Jack probably has servants who are hairdressers. Oops!"

We turn the corner by the staircase and Mom goes down, a flurry of curses streaming from her mouth. I shut my eyes and count to ten. I remember this version of my mother all too well, and it is in turns heartbreaking and frustrating. Trisha is suffering from a disease. I know this. I know my mom doesn't *like* being an alcoholic. But why, in the name of God, has she chosen *now,* of all times, to start drinking again? What will Ana and Brice think?

Something's happened, I remind myself. *Something's wrong. You know she hates this.*

"She didn't drink like this until after dad died. You caused her to be like this."

I don't blame Harper for those harsh words. They're true, after all.

"Come on, Mom, up you go." I put a hand under her arm, feel something ominously sticky. I flash the light on my hand and gasp. Blood.

"Mom? Are you okay? Did you cut yourself when you fell?"

"No. I just…can't…what *is* this?"

Trisha is still tangled up on the floor. I shine the flashlight and see a lump of spotted fabric on the floor beneath her. My heart kicks up a notch.

"Mom, stop moving. Give me your hand."

She complies and I yank her upright.

"You don't need to be so rough," she starts, but I cut her off.

"Mom, stop. Now. Jack? Jack! We need you!"

My voice is shrill in the dark. Moments later, Jack comes running.

"What's wrong? I heard you calling—"

I point to the floor, hit the spot with the light.

The body is crumpled and so bloody, and I don't know what's happening, not really. I've been operating on instinct, the sense that something is terribly awry, since I realized my hand is covered in blood. It isn't until I hear Jack's gasp of horror that my mind allows me to put it together. To identify the sleek spill of hair and the gray silk blouse, stained dark and wet.

"Henna!" Jack cries, dropping to his knees. "Oh no, Henna!"

42

Tumble Tumble Fall

I'm frozen in place, whether from terror or a morbid curiosity, I'm not sure, watching this awful scene unfold. With the lights out, the chaos in the hall is amplified. My mother sobbing, Jack shouting into his phone for help. The empty husk of the woman who's assisted me with everything from finding a dress to the seating charts to the vows and all in between, the travel arrangements, the hassles, the concerns, the tiny meltdowns—everything I worried about: being good enough for Jack, marrying into the Compton family, finding time to paint while stressed about the wedding—Henna has assured, assuaged, comforted. From day one, Henna welcomed me with open arms, and now she is dead, twisted and broken on the thick wool runner.

The light from the windows on the landing is a cloudy green, like looking through emeralds, and the beam of the flashlight tells the tale: Henna's neck is broken; the blood on her beautiful silk shirt from a massive gash on her forehead. It's looks like she fell down the stairs, she must have hit her head somewhere along the banister.

Jack has put away his phone and is attempting to interrogate my mother, who in turn is answering incoherently between hiccups and sobs.

"Did you hear anything? Any cries or calls? God, Trisha, stop trying to touch her. Quit...moving..."

Mom is squirming and reeling, her hands covered in blood, disturbing the scene. She manages to get her feet crossed and immediately trips. One bloody hand hits the wall, leaving behind a perfect, gory handprint, black in the dim flashlight-lit corridor.

So much blood.

It is that handprint that makes me swing the flashlight in arcs around the scene. There, on the floor, opposite the melee, is a thick pewter candlestick. It has rolled against the baseboard. I can't tell if there is blood on it or not. It could have fallen when Henna went down, it could have been knocked off by my mother's gyrations. Or...

No, she couldn't have killed Henna. Could she have? Could she have been drunk and surprised in the darkness and reacted? No. No way. Henna fell down the stairs. One perfectly polished Jimmy Choo is canted sideways on the steps, next to the spilled-open notebook she used to keep all the details of our wedding intact.

Finally shocked into action, I grab my mother by the shoulders.

"Mom. Stop, right now. Come with me." And to Jack: "Honey, she's drunk. She's useless like this. Let me get her out of here. We can talk to her when she sobers up."

"How dare you!" Mom cries. "I am not drunk. I haven't had a drink of alcohol in five years." She yanks her arm out of my hand and promptly falls face-first into the wall with a mighty *thump*.

I sigh deeply, forcing back my own sobs. I have to get her out of here. She will be mortified when she sobers up, if she even remembers. I pray for a blackout to save her the embarrassment of this. I get a hand on her belt and tug. "It's okay, Mom. Let's go to your room. Right now."

Jack is on his cell phone again, this time talking to Tyler. "Ty? I need you. Henna's fallen down the stairs. It's bad."

His voice breaks, and I take a step toward him by instinct, but he waves me away. The pale wash of his face is disturbing. It doesn't take any sort of intimacy to see he is rocked to the core.

It's bad. Henna won't be vertical ever again, but maybe Jack isn't used to death, doesn't recognize it when he sees it. Maybe it took someone who's caused it before to know Henna's soul has long since left her body.

The hallway is long, the flashes of lightning and the bobbing yellow beam of my flashlight the only breaks in the oppressive darkness. Why does this place not have more windows? It is strangely musty; the heavy rain brought out the wet in the stone. A centuries-old fortress, the stone cliff of the island itself, areas of the Villa not always occupied, the staff not getting the rugs clean, who knows? I have the strange sense that if Ana was aware of the smell, she would be furious. Maybe Fatima isn't as good at her job as we are led to believe.

My mother has sagged against my shoulder and is crying quietly. Wrestling her down the long hall is like walking the gauntlet with a large sack of potatoes strapped to my side.

"What did you drink, Mom?" I ask. "I didn't see you have anything at brunch."

"I told you, I didn't drink anything other than a cup of tea that pinched-face housekeeper brought me. Why are you being such a bitch, Claire? Oh my God, I smell disgusting."

She's right, she does. The mustiness isn't only the rain. I flash the light over her body and see why—she is covered in Henna's blood. I gag convulsively, cover my mouth as if stifling a cough.

My mother doesn't notice. She puts on the fake little girl voice she uses to mock Harper and me when she is especially angry. "'She's drunk, Jack.' I didn't drink anything. How could you accuse me of something like that, after all I've been through? I swear, Claire, you always have to make a scene. Make it all about you."

"As it happens, it *is* about me, Mom. This is my wedding. You decided to get bombed and a woman is dead. So yeah, accuse *me* of making a scene."

"You never have understood how things work. How the world works. It's not here to bend to your will. We aren't your servants to order about as you like. Just because you're marrying a man who has money, that doesn't make you a princess."

Ah, here we go. We've tipped over into the nasty stage of the buzz. First sweet, then flirty, then just plain hateful and mean, that's Mom's trajectory when she drinks.

I don't bother arguing anymore. We've had variations on this fight for a decade. There is no winning. There is no rationalizing with Trisha when she is deep in the bottle.

My nose is overwhelmed by the dank vegetal scent of blood. I have to get out of here, get a shower. "Do you have your key, Mom?"

"Brian," she says, mumbling now. "Money. So much money. This place…it's…it's…ostentatious. Gaudy. So tacky, all just to show off…"

We're close to her room now; the huge Palladian window is at the far end of the hall. Using my light, I see the hand-lettered names tacked to the doors atop the room's usual definers—Bell Tolls, Blue Danube, Starry Night. The rooms in the guest wing are named for famous figures or the room's creative inspiration. Supposedly, it started when an artist stayed in the room and declared it their own, but there's no way to know if that's verifiable. The truth of their pasts died with them; we're only left with the legends.

I feel a spike of sadness. Henna hand-lettered the personalized signs for the guest wing herself, the calligraphy elegant and precise. My flashlight turns the signs ivory as we walk down the hall. Katie Elderfield, Harper Hunter, ah, here it is—Trisha and Brian Reed.

I prop my mother between the door jamb and my left shoulder and pound on the door. *Oh please, Brian, don't you be drunk, too.* "Brian? It's Claire. Are you in there?"

"Brian, you in there?" my mother echoes with a tiny giggle, losing her balance as she reaches for the knob. "Briiiiiannnn… Mommy's home."

Oh, ew. There are just some things you aren't ever supposed to know about your parents.

Brian opens the door, red hair standing on end as if he's been buried face-down in a pillow. The light lilt of his Irish accent heavier than I'm used to. "What in the world?"

I shove my mother into his arms. "She's drunk."

"She's covered in… Is that blood? Trisha? Honey? Where are you hurt? What happened?" To me: "I had no idea. I was beat after brunch, came up for a nap. She stayed downstairs, chatting. I am so sorry, Claire. I'll get her straightened out. But where is she bleeding from?"

"It's not her blood. Get her cleaned up and keep her in here, okay?"

Without waiting for an answer, I take off back toward my wing of the Villa.

I stop briefly at Harper's door, listening. I hear nothing, so I knock. She doesn't answer. She must still be with Ana and Brice.

Someone will need to tell Ana. Please let that not be me.

As I hurry back, I realize something. Brian didn't seem too shocked that Mom was wasted. Which means Harper's insistence that it's just been a couple of glasses here and there while they've been visiting Italy is probably not true.

Mom's drunk. Henna's dead. What a mess. My God, what else can go wrong?

I mentally smack myself as soon as the thought forms. *Don't curse yourself, you idiot.* But now it's too late; the thought is out there in the universe, ripe for the picking.

I don't realize I've taken the wrong hallway until I come to a staircase that is not the main route up into the Villa. Damn it. I turn and head back, but within minutes it's clear that in my distraction, I've managed to get myself lost.

I go to the closest window to get my bearings. The rain is hammering the house, the grounds, coming down so intensely I can hardly make out what's below me.

The sea. That's all I can see, the whitecaps frothing against the rocks.

"Shit."

The stairwell down is my only course. It must lead to the kitchens, must be the servants' access to these floors.

Should I try to go back, or should I try to go down? Surely this will lead somewhere I'm more familiar with. If I can find the foyer, or the kitchen, I'm golden.

Decision made, I shine the flashlight on the steps and start down.

43

Surmising, Surprising, Sizing Things Up

Henna's body is on the floor between the bridal suite and the guest wing, just at the turn toward the staircase, the staircase that leads to the lower floors between the two halls. Malcolm and Gideon stand guard to make sure no one accidentally comes up or down the stairs, allowing Tyler to do an assessment without being interrupted.

"I think she tripped down the stairs and cracked her head against the marble table," Tyler says. "Broke her neck. God. Henna. Mom's going to be devastated."

Considering the series of events over the past few days, Jack tries to look at this with altitude. He doubts Trisha is anything but an inconvenient scapegoat. No, if Henna's been killed, this attack is personal. What stronger message could their unseen tormenter send? Taking out Henna, beloved, innocent Henna, means all bets are off.

But if she hadn't fallen, had been pushed, who could be capable of such a thing? The very thought makes him squirm. The pool of possible suspects can only be drawn from two groups: the staff, or the wedding guests.

Where is Claire now? Damn it, what was he thinking, letting her go off alone?

"I have to ask, Ty. Could Henna have been killed?"

"What, like someone pushed her? Who would do that?"

"I don't know. The damn candlestick is covered in blood. Claire's mom was clearly intoxicated. She could have been surprised by Henna coming down the stairs and, not thinking clearly, feeling threatened, reached out for the closest thing to keep herself safe."

"It is entirely possible, though not probable. These stairs are steep, and without the lights, and Henna wearing those damn heels… It's not your fault, Jack. I'm sure this is just a terrible accident."

"God, I hope you're right. I'm being paranoid, but with everything that's been happening, it feels too coincidental for my liking."

"One of us needs to go tell Mom."

"You do it. I can't bear to."

Tyler nods sympathetically, puts a hand on Jack's arm. "Hang in there, okay? We'll figure this out."

When he's alone again, Jack looks at the area with fresh eyes. This part of the house is built in compass-driven architectural wings—east, north, and south. The west wing, two floors up, meanders back into the cliffside, meeting up with the original fortress, and is blocked off from the main areas of the house. It is accessible from the north wing through a back staircase originally built for servants, but no one ever goes there except the Italian restorers his father has hired to make the fortress rooms livable. With three sons, Brice hoped his brood would eventually expand, and wanted room for all the families to visit at once, and their families in the future.

The three main spokes—east, south, and north—are all accessible through the grand staircase. None of these hallways have access to one another. They are full of furniture and the accumulated bric-a-brac of the Comptons' life well-lived: framed movie posters from the thirties and forties Italian cinema compete with trophies from early hunts, moth-eaten fur and threadbare animal heads with fuzz covered antlers, soulless brown eyes staring reproachfully; marble tables with family heirlooms; wing chairs; shallow armoires—the original design of the Villa didn't include closets, so the linens for each room are stored in the hallway armoires.

Perhaps someone could have been hiding in the shadows, or inside one of the heavy walnut pieces, lying in wait for Henna.

The thought of someone lingering, watching, chills him, and he shines his light up and down the carpeted hall. Ready for mayhem, braced for someone to spring from the nearest dark wood cupboard, Jack checks them, one after another, only to discover nothing more threatening than fresh sheets and towels, redolent of the cedar blocks stashed in the corners.

He glances at Henna's body, situated in the middle of the corridor, so close to the staircase. Trisha would have had to step over Henna to knock on the door of the bridal suite.

It still appears Trisha had been the only one in the hall.

Except for Jack and Claire themselves, when they came up from the brunch earlier. But they hadn't seen Henna. Had someone managed to kill her—silently and quickly—in the intervening moments between Trisha stumbling down the hall and Claire taking her drunk mother back to her room?

The thunder is booming still—that could easily have masked a cry of surprise. A stranger strikes, the body drops, and the killer has easy egress up or down the stairs.

Unless, it was someone Henna knew. Someone who wouldn't cause her alarm.

He hates his next thought.

Will.

After his earlier run-ins, it's clear that Will slips his nurse's steady gaze on occasion. Fatima's reaction was easy testament to that. So where is his grandfather now? Could he be responsible? Will's rooms are down the north hall, so if he sneaked away from his minder again, it is possible.

But stealth isn't a hallmark of the dementia-addled Will Compton. He is a bull in a china shop. When he was younger, it was a different story. He was a shark though water, sleek and silent. Deadly. Will had deftness and stealth that Jack still tries to emulate.

Lightning flashes, and in the brief illumination from the window at the end of the hall, Jack can swear Henna's body twitches, though that is impossible. He tries not to look at her eyes, her beautiful eyes, already starting to cloud. No, it is a trick of the light, the strange flashes of lightning doubly reflected on water and glass, warped in the dark. She is definitely deceased. He bites down on his lip in frustration. Damn it, Claire should be back by now. He's going to have to go find her.

Perhaps Tyler is right. Maybe Henna simply tripped in the darkness and hit her head on the corner of the table. They won't know for sure until an autopsy can be done, evidence collected, things Jack isn't sure will happen, now or ever. That is up to his parents. But to be able to put the specter of doubt onto the situation is a help. A reach, yes, but a help. Even though he knows, deep in his heart, with everything that's been happening, he's grasping at straws. That candlestick covered in blood tells the story, one he can't deny.

Henna has been murdered.

44

Twist Again

The Villa has so many rooms and suites and hidden nooks to choose from to set up the photo shoot, Harper was thrilled to find this one on the third floor, which overlooked the labyrinth and the sea beyond. It seemed perfect.

Now, alone with the Comptons, it feels too small, too close. Ana Compton is intimidating. So still, so self-contained. A wolf, wary, watchful. Harper has a hard time meeting her eye, is fumbling around with the camera and the screens.

Get it together, Hunter.

"Okay. I'm nearly ready. This is a beautiful room," Harper says.

"I'm glad you chose it. It's always been one of my favorites," Brice says. "It was my mother May's sitting room at one point."

Brice glances once more at his phone, a reminder of how important he is, how many more pressing matters he has to handle, before shoving it into the pocket of his jeans. Going along. He is easier than his wife today, more mellow. Jovial, almost.

On the way up here he'd been downright chatty, pointing out paintings and tchotchkes. He is proud of his things, proud of his life, proud of his unique history. Harper sees her opportunity, butters him up.

"Your home truly is outstanding. Thank you so much for having us. And I really appreciate you doing this."

"We're happy to have a chat, Harper. It was kind of you to think of us," Ana replies, smooth as silk, and Brice nods, smiles. "We ready to go?"

"Almost. One more second."

"What's the agenda here?" he asks.

Harper finishes straightening the screen. "If you're okay with it, I'd like to shoot some photos as we do the interview. It allows me to talk with you instead of just firing questions at you. In my experience, it ends up being a more natural interview. Are you willing to let me do that? Tape this, so we can have a conversation?"

"Certainly," Ana replies. "Just so you're aware, we'll need to wrap by 4:00 p.m. There are still things that need to be dealt with for the rehearsal dinner."

"Right. We'll be done well before that. This won't take long."

No. Not long at all.

Harper gets them set in the chairs she's picked out—dark wood frames with deep red velvet coverings, so regal—and takes a few last test shots. She adjusts the lights. Picks up her phone. Clears her throat. Tries not to wither under Ana's impenetrable gaze.

"Excellent. Let's do this."

Snap. Snap. She checks the result in the screen.

"Chin up, please," she murmurs, and Brice squares off to the camera. She checks again.

"There it is. Perfect. I'd like to talk a bit about your family history. Is it true your grandmother Eliza was friends with Gellhorn and Hemingway?"

Brice's smile shows his dimples. "She was. An amazing woman, Eliza. Started as a Parisian model, but when the war began, she stepped to the other side of the camera and turned war photographer. Before that nasty incident with Franco's Guarda, she was on the lines with Hemingway and Gellhorn. We have letters, notes, a few discreet photos of the three of them she mailed to my grandfather. Of course, in the end, the Guarda took her cameras and ruined the remainder of the footage. She fought them all the way. She was a rare woman."

"She sounds like it. And her husband, your grandfather William Compton, he's the one who bought the Villa and restored it?"

"Yes. They fell in love with the views, the people, and decided to buy the Villa and fortress. He started the restoration in 1938, and we've been slowly improving it to modern standards since. My dad, Will Compton—"

"The cinematographer."

"Yes. You'll want to talk to him this weekend—he's a fascinating man. He ran with an exceptional crowd and continued the artists' colony so his friends could enjoy the island as well. It became quite an exclusive invitation."

"I would like to talk to him. What happened to his wife? Your mother?"

Harper feels the tension bubble off them. Don't lose them yet…

"Sorry, none of my business."

Ana replies instead of Brice. "May died, tragically. An accident in one of the grottos. The tide rose quickly and she wasn't able to get out."

"That's so sad. I'm sorry to hear it. And you took over the magazine from her, Mrs. Compton?"

"I did. May started *Endless Journey* with Eliza's photographs. It had grown, obviously, but I wanted it to be a household name. I tried to continue their legacy in the only way I knew how, by sharing their vision with the world."

"It's a great magazine. We always had copies growing up. My dad had a subscription for his doctor's office, but he had to have five copies at a time because people walked off with them."

There, a rare, sweet smile from Ana. Harper depresses the shutter before it flees.

Snap. Got you. You're human after all.

"And Eliza Compton, she died here on the island as well, didn't she? A hunting accident?"

No answer, but a glance between the two of them. Damn it. Has she gone too far?

"I'm sorry. We'll stay with the present family, if you're more comfortable. You went into computers instead of following your father to Hollywood, right, Mr. Compton?"

"Yes. I was fascinated by the advances in technology. And I was better at math than he was."

Harper laughs obediently. "That's awesome. Could you look over at Mrs. Compton for a moment, please? Thank you, that's great. You're both household names. What is that like? I mean, you seem so…normal. But your lives, your histories, are extraordinary."

"We've been very blessed," Ana says, practically stretching under the praise. The wolf is gone, the wariness fled. Harper can practically hear the thoughts: *This is a puff piece. This girl is just an Instagram phenom who might or might not be able to write— isn't she sweet with her "new method" for interviewing. She's being nosy, who can blame her.* "It's our mission, our calling, to give back to as many people as we can. The Foundation is the perfect example of this."

"True altruism."

"You're too kind. We're not doing this for ourselves. We're trying to make a real difference in the lives of the world's less fortunate. It's the least we can do. With Jack at the helm, the Foundation has grown exponentially. We're saving lives, changing the course of humanity."

Harper stands upright, camera down. "You *have* made a difference in so many lives. It's amazing. And that's something I'm confused about. Why would you risk four generations of genuine legacy over one woman's death?"

The wolf is back. "Excuse me?"

"Morgan. Jack's first wife. She didn't die in California. She died here. On Isola. Why would you want to cover that up? If it was an accident…like May was an accident. Like Elevana was an accident. Like Eliza was an accident. Morgan died falling off the cliff here. If it was an accident, like all the others, why would you pretend it happened in California?"

Ana's face is stone and she is out of the chair like a shot. "I have no idea what you're talking about. We're done here, Harper."

Brice, too, is in motion, though he's headed toward Harper's phone, which is on the table.

She scoops it up before he can get there. "I'm still taping. Don't come any closer."

Brice continues advancing.

"I'll scream."

He sighs. "They always do. Give me that. You've abused our hospitality, and it's time for you to go."

"Why did Jack kill Morgan?" she says into the phone, praying, praying it's still live, still working. "Why did you cover up her death?"

Brice has her backed up against the wall now. He wrenches the phone from her hand.

"Stop that. You're hurting me."

He ignores her, goes to turn off the audio. She watches his face fall when he realizes that it's a phone call, an open line. He clicks it off, carefully. Turns off her phone completely.

"Who did you call, Harper?" His voice is quiet, but the intensity makes her squirm. Shit.

"My editor. She was listening." This is said with no small

amount of pride—they can't do anything to her, there was a third party. A witness. Thank God Ami suggested it—it worked perfectly.

"And who is your editor, pray tell?"

"Her name is Ami Eister. And she is transcribing the conversation as we speak. She heard everything." *God, I hope she did.* Between the words and the video, because Harper was recording the last few minutes on her camera, too, and thank God Brice doesn't seem to know this, because he hasn't even glanced at the camera on the table.

This will be a smash. Even if they deny it, the look of fear on both of their faces when she mentioned Morgan's death is enough to lodge doubt. The way they swung into action confirmed it. They clearly covered it up. My God, Ami was right.

"Ami Eister?" Ana asks sharply. "Your editor's name is Ami Eister?"

"Answer the question," Harper tries again, forcing herself to stay with the story, stay engaged with exposing their deception, just like Ami taught her. "Why would you lie about Morgan's death?"

Brice is making a call now. He taps a nail against his front teeth as he waits for it to connect. "Yes. I need Karmen, please. Thank you."

He doesn't seem fazed. Neither does Ana. Their entire demeanors have changed.

What the hell? They should be freaking out. "I'd like my phone, please."

"Karmen, I need you to trace a number for me." He reads it off. "Yes, it belongs to this Ami Eister woman. She's now posing as an editor for *Flair*."

"Posing? Ami isn't a real editor?" Harper is confused, but she's not stupid. Everything is about to go south, she can feel it. "What the hell is going on?"

Ana smiles, and there is nothing friendly about it. "You've

been taken for a ride, Harper. Ami Eister is an imposter. She's not an editor with *Flair*. I assume she gave you all of this salacious information? Made this ridiculous claim for you to run with?"

"No...no. I found it on my own."

"That's a lie, and we both know it." Ana is almost pleasant now. "Even you had to know we have no reason to lie about where Morgan died. Now, you're going to have to give us everything. The photos. The video. And every detail on this situation, how you were contacted, how she tricked you. You've been used, Harper. And you've also insulted Mr. Compton and myself. Our family. We can't allow this to continue, do you understand?"

"What are you going to do to me? I wasn't kidding, I'll scream. I won't let you hurt me or make me disappear." Harper starts toward the door, but Ana gets a hand on her, clamps her fingers around Harper's wrist.

"Don't be ridiculous. We will sit down like grown-ups and discuss what's the best course of action here." The smile is now motherly, and Harper recoils from it, trying and failing to yank her hand away.

"I don't understand."

Ana situates herself between Harper and the door, glances at her husband, then releases her wrist.

"Ami Eister is playing a cruel joke on us all, I'm afraid. She approached your sister a few weeks ago as well, posing as an art dealer who was there to buy a painting. She seems to have planted cameras in Claire's home with the help of an associate. And she's clearly gotten to you as well. How did she reach you?"

"Wait, she knows Claire?"

"Please, just answer me. How did she reach you?"

"Email, then by phone. This is bullshit. She's legit. She sent me all her information."

"I'm afraid she's not. The real Ami Eister died six months ago. Whoever you've been dealing with is an imposter."

Harper tries to wrap her head around this news. God, she's been taken for a fool.

There's a knock on the door, and Tyler, the hot younger brother, comes into the room, looking flustered.

"Mom, I've been looking for you. There's been an accident. Henna's dead."

45

Sabotage

When the power went out on the island, they didn't panic. Jack's family knew the storm was coming; they'd brought everyone in early to be safe and laid in supplies. Plenty of gas for the generators to keep the overly stocked refrigerators and water running, mounds of candles and cute little matchboxes with C&J printed on them in embossed gold foil, flashlights with baggies of batteries in each room.

They were ready. Prepared. They'd done this a hundred times over the years.

What they didn't count on was the sabotage.

What they didn't count on was me.

46

The Dark Beyond

The stairs lead me directly down three stories to the kitchens, as I suspected. The kitchen itself is gleaming, and empty. They must have already moved everything to *The Hebrides* for the dinner tonight. Now I just have to find my way back up. The halls in both directions are pitch black, as if it's the dead of night instead of afternoon. What the hell is the deal with these magic generators that are supposed to keep the Villa lit and safe?

Choices are limited; I have a 50 percent chance of getting it right. I look both ways like I'm about to cross a busy street. Left. Right. Left again.

Oh, hell. I don't know. It's dark down here, smells slightly spicy, garlic and basil and something darker, something off. Maybe the trash needs to be taken out. That makes sense—with the rain, the staff couldn't clear out the waste.

Deep breaths. Through the mouth, not the nose. You went left before.

I wind into the darkness, glad for the powerful flashlight.

Jack said the generators would kick in and the lights to the common areas would come back on automatically, but the private areas would stay in darkness to conserve energy. And he said the kitchens would be considered necessary. I stop again. Things are too quiet. The refrigerators aren't running, which means the generators aren't on. I have a spike of practical concern—if they haven't moved everything to the yacht, what are we going to feed the wedding guests if the food spoils?

But rational thought reigns supreme. What is actually going on here? Henna is dead, the power is out, the storm is raging, my dress is ruined, and my mother is hammered. Someone has been spying on me, is clearly trying to derail my wedding, and I'm getting pissed off. Whoever Shane was working with, because he's not smart enough to figure this out himself, that's for sure, has to be behind this. It's not just bad luck. And whoever it is, they will underestimate me. Everyone does. *Oh, she's such a lovely painter. Oh, she's so sweet and kind. Claire Hunter? She wouldn't hurt a fly. Lost her nerve after her father died.*

Wanna bet? Bring it, bitch. I am fed the fuck up with this nonsense. I'm wearing as many disguises as you are.

Determined now, I head off again. The temperature in the hall is getting cooler, so I did go the wrong way. I should have turned right, instead of left. Okay then. I've eliminated this path. If I retrace my steps, I'll be back at the kitchens.

I start to turn but see a wood and iron door ahead that is cracked open. I shine the light around the edges, then inside. There is a slate floor that looks like it leads downhill. What's down there? I swear I hear water. I listen intently, yes, there's the small roar of the sea against the rocks. I take a few steps inside, shining my flashlight. Indentations in the walls hold iron sconces, and wooden braces with iron fittings creep overhead. It feels very old. What would this look like if the lights were on? Illumination in the past would come from candles or oil lamps, but the Villa has been completely modernized. I flash my light on the wall to the door's interior—there it is. A light switch.

No keypads, though. This area is controlled by a padlock only. It's off the grid.

Where does this tunnel lead? To the water, most likely, with the downward slope and cool air. Is it a wine cellar? That makes sense, it being so quiet and cool, and close enough to the kitchens.

Okay, Nancy Drew. Time to get back to Jack, face the music.

I hear voices, and they're coming from down the tunnel. My heart starts to kettledrum and my breath catches in my throat. I am not alone. Who is down here in the dark?

"Signorina?"

I jump and scream, dropping the flashlight to the ground. The voices stop.

A gray-haired head bends in front of me and picks up the flashlight.

"Signorina Claire? What's happened? Why are you covered in blood?"

"Oh, Fatima." I blow out a huge, shuddery breath. "You scared me. It's Henna. She fell down the stairs. Then I—I got lost. I couldn't find my way back to the stairwell after I took my mom to her room. I ended up here. I think someone's down there." I point down the tunnel. "I heard voices."

In my shock, I'm babbling. Fatima's face is ghoulishly pale in the flashlight's xenon beam. She doesn't seem alarmed.

"That is the path to the crypt, Signorina Claire. There are no voices there except those of the dead. Come, I'll take you back to Signore Jack. Henna has been hurt?"

I nod. I'm not breaking the news that Henna's dead.

"Then we must go help." With a deft hand, she reaches for my arm and gently pulls me out of the tunnel, pushing the thick wooden door closed behind me. She resets the huge iron padlock, locks it with a snap.

"See? No one there to worry about. The dead can't leave. Come with me."

We begin walking, and soon the air grows warmer.

"Jack didn't tell me there was a crypt."

"This is quite typical of these old island Villas."

"Is the…are there Compton family members buried there?"

"Not buried, interred. In the walls. Yes, there are Comptons, and there are previous owners' families as well. I believe the oldest tomb in the crypt dates to the 1300s. That's been found, that is. There was a cave-in many years ago and there are tunnels that have been blocked off. Of course, the paths to the grottos were closed as well. Signore Will wanted to keep the boys safe, so he had a number of areas blocked off many years ago."

"I see."

I am thoroughly freaked out at this point by the idea of the voices I heard belonging to the Villa's previous residents who live in the walls of the crypt, but before I can quietly collapse into fits of hysterics, we are back on the main floor and at the staircase.

"Up the stairs and right at the landing. That will get you back to your rooms. I'm sure Signore Jack is missing you. And you need to shower and change—we must be getting ready for the rehearsal dinner. I'll be along in a moment. I need to check why the generators have turned off."

Because someone is screwing with us, I want to say, but I bite my tongue. Though I know I'm hardly being paranoid, I need Jack to take the lead with his family on the situation. And I do need to change. I'm covered in blood and I'm shaking with cold and anger.

I march up the stairs, trying to put the voices I heard in the crypt out of my mind. I can't help it, though, the shadowy whispers consume me. Fatima brushed them off as my imagination, but I still don't believe in ghosts. The voices I heard were entirely human.

I stop at the huge window overlooking the labyrinth. The rain sheets down, but it seems lighter. I suppose that means the first wave of storms is over, and we'll have some peace for the evening's events.

I jog the rest of the way up the stairs and head to our rooms. Jack will be worried by now.

47

The Cavalry Returns

Jack is prone to paranoia, he has to be, considering the side work of his family, but on the island, he's always felt safe. It is the ultimate controlled environment. Barring a torpedo or drone strike, naturally, which their enemies aren't exactly capable of. Yet.

Until Henna's death, all of the terrors of the past few days could be chalked up to the twisted desires of Shane McGowan. Jack had thought his death meant things would quickly return to normal.

Now he has to believe McGowan was simply a symptom. A hired gun with a convenient backstory tied to Claire. Someone else is pulling the strings. He's willing to bet the farm it's the woman who came to visit Claire at the studio. Ami Eister by name, but not in truth. Who the hell is she? How does she tie into their lives? Who sent her, and why? Well, that's a silly question. Her goal is the destruction of the family, clearly. Starting with the one they hold most dear.

He just can't fathom someone he knows killing Henna. A stranger is the only explanation.

So who the hell is this imposter?

Could she somehow have gotten to the island?

Into the house?

He hears someone coming fast up the hall and acts on instinct, tensing for battle. One hand goes to the back of his waistband out of habit, though there is nothing there to use for defense. The other brings the flashlight up in a grip that assures it is as much a weapon as a deterrent—in the gloom, the intense beam of the Maglite will blind whoever is rushing toward him, and he can easily use it as a club if needed. The butterfly knife he always carries in his pocket comes out, whips open, and with a few deft flicks of his wrist, the blade snaps into place. He'd gotten in the habit of carrying the knife years ago, though he's rarely had to use it.

He waits until the last moment to thumb the switch on the Maglite. Does he recognize that breath? He hesitates and is relieved to see Claire turn the corner and run toward him. He blows out a breath, drops the knife into his pocket, and opens his arms. Claire throws herself at him, burying her face in his chest.

"Oh, Jack. I am so sorry. I don't know what's happened. My mom was hammered, she'd been drinking without a doubt, I could smell it on her breath. Brian claims he wasn't aware, that he'd gone to take a nap after brunch, left her touring the house. And then I got lost, downstairs, and Fatima found me, and—"

"Shhh. It's okay now."

She peeks up at him, her beautiful eyes swimming with tears. It breaks him, seeing her so unhappy.

"Will the cameras capture anything, do you think? Will they be able to see what happened?"

"No. Without the power on, the cameras are conveniently offline here."

She must hear something in his tone. "What do you think happened? Do you think she fell? Or—"

"Shhh," he says. "Let's not jump to any conclusions." He'd so love to be screaming, raging, *she was murdered, and it might have been your mother.* But he knows this can't be the truth. Knows it in his bones. Whoever killed Henna is working to destabilize the family entirely, and Trisha doesn't care enough for that.

He realizes Claire is quietly fuming. He can feel anger shimmering off her in waves.

"What's wrong? Did something happen?"

"Other than Henna dying and my mom getting bombed? Something else is going on. Something bigger. Jack, when I was downstairs—"

There is a clunk and a whine he recognizes as the generators kicking in again, and the lights in the hallway flash on. It feels almost garish after the velvet-dark intimacy of the hallway. The scene is more horrible in the light—blood everywhere, Henna twisted, Claire a calamitous wreck. But the light will help to discern what's happened. And to cover it up, as quickly as possible. They don't need the guests wandering into the crime scene.

Gideon and Malcolm, burly in their gray suits and red ties, come back into the hall, followed by Fatima. When she sees the body, she utters a tiny little scream, the *meep* of a kitten stepped on by her mother, then collects herself, raises her chin and marches to Claire's side, taking her by the arm.

"Come with me. Let's get you cleaned up."

Jack gives Fatima a grateful nod, and squeezes Claire's shoulder. "Go on. I'll handle things here. You're a mess. Hold on to her clothes, though, Fatima. In case the police need them."

Claire looks down at her bloodstained shirt in distress. "I have to throw it out, I need—"

"Darling, it's evidence. Just for now."

She pales but nods, and Jack is relieved when she allows Fatima to walk her back into their rooms. The ruse is necessary. There will be no police. Jack intends to hunt down whoever is responsible, and kill them himself.

When the door closes, Jack turns to his security team. They are eyeing Henna's body, but neither have spoken a word. Extremely well trained, they can handle pretty much anything. Even a dead body in the middle of a raging storm on an isolated island.

"What took so long?"

"Generator was out of gas, though hell if I know how that happened. We were down working on it."

"All right. Gideon," Jack says to the slightly taller of the two men, "I see no need to inform the Italian authorities, since there's no chance of them reaching us in this storm. I can't see that it would be wise to raise the alarm bells right now. For our own knowledge, we must document every inch of this crime scene, and then move the body and clean the scene. We can't have her lying on the floor out here."

"Yes, sir," Gideon says.

"Is there any chance the cameras were online?"

Malcolm shakes his head. "Since the generators went down, we've all been in the dark. Something's wrong with the generators, other than being low on fuel. I'm not sure how much light we have, and the cameras are still offline."

"Convenient."

Gideon is assessing the scene with a practiced eye. "You think it's murder?"

"You don't?"

"I hoped it was an accident."

"I did, too. See the edge of the table?"

Gideon gets close. "Could be," he says. A few seconds pass, and he nods again. "Yes, I can see it. She tripped down the stairs—the momentum took her headfirst into the table, smashing her temple, and she went down. Knocked the candlestick down the hallway. I bet the only prints on that thing are from the staff, the most recent cleaning. Fatima, maybe, arranging things."

Malcolm nods his agreement. Jack exhales, hard.

"That's the party line, do you understand? Until we can figure out who might be behind this, who might be trying to hurt me, or Claire, or the family, the rest of the guests will only be told that Henna's death is a tragic accident."

"Understood."

"And get rid of that fucking candlestick."

"Yes, sir," Malcolm says, retrieving it.

Jack wipes a sleeve over his forehead; he's started to sweat. "We have to figure out what the hell actually happened. I didn't hear anything like an attack. Claire and I were in our rooms when Claire's mother, Trisha, knocked on the door. She and Claire tripped over Henna on their way back to Trisha's room. Perhaps we say she was going to handle the problem with the generators."

Gideon nods again, brushes his hands together as if washing them of the subject. "Yeah, that's a small window, there can't be too many other people around. I think it's safe to say Ms. Shaikh slipped and hit her head. Poor woman. What a shame. I liked her, very much. We'll figure it out, Mr. Compton. Go talk to your parents. Your mother is waiting."

"Don't let anyone down this hall until you're finished. And when you're done, Malcolm, I want you on Claire exclusively. Just in case. She's not to be left alone out of my presence, do you hear me?"

Malcolm doesn't seem surprised. He nods. "Yes, sir. I'll keep her safe."

"And I need a weapon."

Malcolm lifts a pant leg and pulls a Beretta Nano from his ankle hostler, hands it to Jack. Jack gestures, and Malcolm gives him the holster, too. Jack racks the slide, clearing the chamber, snaps out the magazine, then reseats it and chambers a bullet.

He straps the holster to his ankle, tight, so it won't slide—his leg is smaller than Malcolm's—but keeps the Beretta itself in his right hand. Regardless of the situation, accident or otherwise, he is not about to get caught flat-footed with just a knife and a flashlight to defend himself.

His bodyguards immediately get to work.

Jack watches for a moment, then, satisfied, sets off to his parents' suite.

His phone dings and he glances at the screen as he walks. The unidentified number, with the same message as before, only the video this time is slightly altered. This time, it shows Jack with the gun, rubbing it down.

Rubbing off Claire's fingerprints.

Repent, Jackson. Repent.

If this video is released, they all go down.

48

Playing Dress-up

I walk woodenly to the suite, trying not to think about the crypt, or the sticky blood on my hands, my clothes. I must have touched my face, too; I feel something slick on my cheek. I swipe it away with the hem of my shirt, see the crimson smear, and my head swims. I fight against the urge to faint—being unconscious won't help anything.

Until Monday, I hadn't been close to a corpse since my father died. In the past three days not only have I've killed my former boyfriend, a lost body has shown up, Henna's fallen down the stairs, and I've found out the whole Villa is perched over hundreds of dead. Was it too much to ask that Jack warn me we'd be living in a graveyard?

Henna's blank eyes. I glance at my hand, at my cuticles rimed in blood, and shudder.

Do I really want to go through with this?

It is a mutinous thought, and I try to wrestle it back into its lidded box, but once I've thought it… I've had the sense that something is wrong for days now. Maybe the universe is trying to tell me something. Maybe I shouldn't marry Jack. Maybe this is the wrong path.

The door to the suite opens with a discreet *beep*, and Fatima bustles me inside.

"Where will they take Henna? Will they put her in the crypt?"

"I do not know, Signorina. It is best for you not to worry about such things. You need a shower," she says softly, leading me through to the big marble bathroom. She starts the water and gestures for me to strip and get in.

When I hesitate, Fatima gives me a knowing, reassuring smile. She seems kind, now, not scary or bossy. Solicitous. "I'll be right outside. You're safe. Go on, now."

The bathroom door closes and I am alone.

I slip inside the shower, have a moment's shame that I am the one standing here, not Henna, then push the thought away. I've been fighting the battle against survivor's guilt since my father's accident, I'm not going to go down that destructive wormhole again.

The hot water feels good, clean. I let it wash away the physical evidence, and the emotional aftermath.

I hear a knock on the bathroom door, and though I'm hidden in the shower by the wall, I reflexively clutch the washcloth to my chest.

"Yes?"

"Fresh towels for you, Signorina. I'll leave them on the chair."

"Thank you, Fatima."

The door closes again, and I try to breathe and relax. Once I'm feeling more in control, I scrub myself clean, wash my hair carefully, trying not to catch my fingers along the edge of the stitches, then, recognizing I can't waste any more time, dry off with a warm, fluffy towel, wrap another around my hair. I pull open the drawer to grab my comb and remember the freaky note I found in Jack's drawer earlier.

Don't you miss me, darling?

Just in case, I open his top drawer, but there's nothing unusual. I resolve to ask Jack about it when he gets back.

I drop the towel, pull the comb through my hair, and walk to the dressing room. Fatima has hung my dress for the rehearsal and dinner. I found it in a shop on 12th South in Nashville, and it is one of the most beautiful creations I've ever seen, next to my wedding gown, of course. It's Laura Blake couture, pale crushed satin cut on the bias, the barely-there pink of a delicate shell, gathered at the bust and shoulders, with a long skirt that clings to my body. When I move, the satin slips against my legs in sensual swishes. I made sure it pulled up to my hips easily, without ripping, when I tried it on. Jack is going to go mad for it.

I call out the door. "Fatima? My dress is out. Are we really going forward with everything?"

"Of course we are. The weekend has not been cancelled, Signorina Claire. It goes on as planned."

"But Henna—"

"Your guests expect the rehearsal party tonight. We shouldn't disappoint them."

"We should cancel."

Fatima comes in without waiting for my approval. I scramble into the robe that's hanging on the dressing room door. I've never been the kind of girl who can strut around naked in front of strangers. Even with Jack, if it's not dark, I still sometimes hesitate before dropping my towel.

Fatima ignores my discomfort, picks up the damp towels and opens a small door in the wall—a laundry chute, I realize. The towels disappear with a *whoosh*.

"Signora Compton has indicated all is moving forward as planned."

"But...I thought...and with your mother, too..."

Oh, well done, Claire. Toss that in her face.

But Fatima's expression doesn't change. She is staring at my Medusa curls with something close to distaste. "Do you need help with your hair? I am quite good with hair. It has been a long time since I had the chance to dress a lady for her wedding. If you like what I do, perhaps you would consider allowing me to help for the wedding tomorrow."

I want to say no. Harper has already said she'd manage my hair for the wedding, and who knows what sort of skills Fatima has. But she is peering at me, her eyes the shiny ebony of a crow's wing, expecting me to say yes. I don't want to offend her, and truth be told, I don't want to be alone. Plus, Fatima is going to be a major part of my life. Jack would want me to be polite.

"That would be lovely, Fatima. Thank you. Please be careful, though, I hit my head and have a cut that they stitched up."

I pull the robe tight and sit at the dressing table. Fatima wastes no time. She assembles the blow dryer with the diffuser and a curling iron. I shut my eyes and allow myself to enjoy the ministrations. She is gentle, so very gentle. Before long, my curls have been tamed into smooth, stylish, beachy twists that I've never been able to master on my own. She pins the unruly shorter pieces around my face and declares herself done.

"Your hair is like silk, Signorina. So soft."

"Thank you. There must be something in the water here. It won't normally do this." I admire the back of my hair in the hand mirror, fluff the front a touch. "Wow. It looks great."

She seems pleased with my reaction. "I agree. Signore Jackson will approve. Do you want me to do your makeup as well?"

"I don't normally wear much."

"You do not need much. You have such a glow of youth about you. I will make it look very natural." She opens the vanity door and pulls out a large quilted leather case stocked with brand-new high-end cosmetics.

She's true to her word. With creamy eyeshadows and a touch

of mascara, a berry-stain lip gloss that makes my lips feel buzzy and plump, I look fresh, not made up. Damn. I could get used to this kind of pampering. I'm starting to understand exactly why Ana would want someone like Fatima on staff. She seems quite versatile, and quite dedicated. Without Henna at Ana's side, I wonder if Fatima might get the job.

"Were you a hairdresser before you came to work for the Comptons, Fatima?"

"Ah, no. I've worked for the family most of my life. My mother did as well."

She finally looks down, and I see a tick in her jaw.

"I am so sorry for your loss. It must be hard to continue working when…well, when she's just been found."

"I prefer to work than to grieve. My family have been caretakers of the Villa since the Comptons bought it. We have been treated very well by the Comptons, for many years."

"So, you've been with them since before Jack was born?"

"Yes. Though it is only me now, my family has been on Isola for many generations." She begins putting away the makeup. "My mother was housekeeper here before me. For a time, I thought I wanted a different life, a bigger life. I went away to school, in Milano. I loved fashion. I worked at Prada, and Ferragamo. With the models, for the shoots. But it was not meant to be. When my mother disappeared, I was needed. So, I left Milano and came back to Isola."

"When did she disappear?"

"It's been twenty years now."

I do the math. Jack would have been eighteen. Which means Fatima is younger than I thought. Midfifties, maybe. The years have not been kind. And I doubt I could be as calm talking about my history if it was my mom, lost for years, then found.

God, Claire, what a horrible thing to think. Why are you transferring your emotions to her? And what exactly happened to her mother? "I am so sorry, Fatima. This must be hard for you."

"*Si, grazie*. We grieved my mother's death long ago. Now... yes, it is good to have closure. I'm sure my father is looking down in joy at the resolution of the mystery."

"When did you lose him?"

"He passed two years ago."

"I'm sorry," I say again, reflexively. I know how hard it is, losing a father.

"You are very kind, Signorina. I love working here, though. It is a beautiful place, and as I said, the Comptons, they have been so kind to us, always. It was good to see the boys grow into men."

"I would love to hear more about young Jack. Was he terrible?"

Her face is briefly suffused with something akin to love. "He was always a sweet boy. I will tell you more later. Now, would you like to see how your hair looks with your dress for the dinner tonight? In case you'd like to make changes?"

I resist glancing at my watch. I get it; Fatima has been instructed to distract me. And I am more than happy to be distracted. Playing dress up is as good a way as any.

"Sure."

"Good, because now, I have a surprise for you. Since your beautiful dress was ruined."

Fatima disappears into the capacious closet and comes out with a yellowed garment bag. She hangs this on the hook and unzips it with a flourish.

Organza and silk spills out of the bag. The heady scent of camphor follows.

"Phew, that's strong."

"I can air it out. I believe it will fit."

She shakes the fabric free and I realize this is a wedding gown.

An elegant, beautiful wedding gown.

49

Mermaids in the Closet

"I—I don't know what to say."

"Why don't you try it on? If it fits, I thought it might do for the wedding," Fatima says, and she smiles. It completely transforms her. She seems young again, shy. Girlish.

"Whose dress is this?"

"It belonged to my mother. When I heard about what happened to your dress, I went immediately and took it out of storage. Mrs. Compton loved the idea. Try it on. Let's see if it will do."

A dead woman's dress? Great.

But I have to admit, I am touched. And Fatima watches me so hopefully, how can I say no?

"That's awfully kind of you, Fatima."

I let her pull the dress over my head and feel the heavy fabric glide down my body and settle. I slip my feet into my ivory heels and go to the full-length mirror.

The dress truly is beautiful, a modified mermaid with a delicate crystal and lace embroidered bodice and plunging pearl neckline. The close-fitting skirt has a layer of sheer organza that makes it feel more like an evening ball gown. It really isn't my style, and the shape of the underskirt emphasizes my hips, but it fits like a dream. There would be no need to alter it. Amazing.

The woman I'm staring at looks elegant, grown-up. No more messy little girl. No more tattoos. No more piercings. I am a lady in satin and pearls now. I am ready to face the world as a Compton.

Oddly, though my hair is light instead of dark, I look a bit like Ana. I've never seen it before.

It's the makeup, the dress. Spit and a polish. But still.

I turn to see the view from the rear. The backline sweeps down nearly to my waist.

"Can you see my scar?"

Fatima looks at me, concerned. "You have a scar? From what?"

"Yes, on my lower back. I was in an accident when I was younger." I leave out the dreadful words, *the accident that killed my father.* Though Fatima confided her family's deaths, something makes me hold back on the whole truth. It isn't that I don't trust Fatima, of course I do. I just don't know her well enough to bring her into my confidences.

Fatima stares at my back, where the gown cuts low. "No, Signorina. Nothing shows. You are perfect. So young, and so sweet."

Feeling suddenly vulnerable and nervous, I catch the older woman's hand.

"Do you have any advice for me, Fatima? Marrying into the Comptons, I mean."

Fatima's face closes. "No. They are a lovely family, Signorina. You will fit in very nicely."

I feel absurdly pleased by this benediction.

"That's kind of you to say, but I fear I'm in over my head."

"Oh, no. Signore Jackson would never bring home another woman who wasn't perfect."

What? What did she say?

"Another woman? He's brought women here before?"

Fatima pales, then her face flushes bright red. "I did not mean that."

Oh, yes, she did. Though she's blushing and looking away, there is a small smile on her face, something quick and cruel. I feel slightly better that I haven't confided too much in her.

"You can tell me. I hardly think Jack was a monk before we met. He is ten years older, after all. And I know he was married before. It's not a secret. Was it his first wedding? I thought that was in California."

But Fatima is done with true confession girl time. "I will check on things now. Let me unzip you. Hang the dress and I will be back soon to air it out. *Mi scusi.*"

She yanks the zipper down roughly, practically knocks me out of the dress, then leaves me standing alone in front of the floor-length mirror.

I hang the loaned gown carefully. The dressing room closet is dark and smells of cedar and the mustiness of the mothballs this dress was stored with.

My mind whirls while I slip on my jeans and a button-down, pour a cup of tea from the pot Fatima has brought. I take a sip, careful not to mess up the lipstick Fatima put on me. It is too strong; I abandon the cup on the table.

Who else did Jack bring home to Isle Isola? Is there someone else in his life Jack hasn't told me about?

That note: *Don't you miss me, darling?*

Damn it, I am missing something. Something major. Something important.

Stop it, Claire. You're borrowing trouble. Just wait for Jack to come back, and you can talk to him about all of this.

But I can't help myself. I start to obsess. The dark whirlpool of emotions that seized me earlier swirls into my mind, and I feel my breath coming short again.

Everything, the trip, the storm, the break-in, the fear in Will Compton's voice, the horror of finding Henna in the hall—God, what are they going to do with her body? Oh yeah, the crypt, I bet they put her down there in that cold, cruel darkness. And now there is the specter of another faceless woman who once captured Jack's heart enough that he brought her home to his parents.

A chill flows through my body, and tears begin to prick at the edges of my vision. My heart rate starts to climb, and I see spots. The strange nausea from earlier surges; I put a hand to my mouth and swallow hard, again, and again, choking back my sobs. I'm torn between hurt and fury. Jack never mentioned another serious girlfriend. Something like that would have been all over the news; Katie would have laid it at my feet like a Labrador with a tennis ball. But the way Fatima shut down so abruptly was troubling. She had overshared, and she knew it. So, there is something to her claims.

The Comptons and their damnable secrets. Do they not understand how impossible it is to lie to people in this world? To keep a life private? How am I supposed to live inside this gilded cage?

Come on, stop it. You can't keep having panic attacks for no reason. And quit whining. Women would kill to be in your shoes. Quit it.

I breathe deeply, trying to hold on, trying so hard to keep it together.

Don't think about this now, Claire. Don't ruin everything. It's all going to be okay.

Jack will handle things.

I catch my breath and start to calm. What a cop-out *that* thought is. It disrespects Henna's memory and my own nature to step aside and let the big strong man take care of everything. But what am I supposed to do? Jack does make me strong. I have to be strong for him now. I have to be strong for the family I am joining.

I cross the room to the French doors, unsteady on my feet, my steps oddly loose. The rain is lashing the panes, coming down in opaque sheets. There will be no sun today, but the view has lightened as an unseen orb mounts the sky. The fragrance of the lemons is subdued by the sharp scent of ozone. The worst of the severe weather is past for now; it's just heavy rain with some occasional flashes of lightning. The thunder is distant. Watching is meditative, calming. After a few moments, I'm surprised by how warm and snug I feel inside. *That's it, Claire. Warm and snug. You're safe. You're safe, and nothing will happen to you. Or to Jack. Everything's going to be okay.*

As pretty as it is, I don't want to wear a stranger's dress. I want my own gorgeous gown. I want my glorious, fun-filled wedding weekend, not this drizzly, murderous mess.

My thoughts are jagged, disrupted, kaleidoscoping through my head. I can't focus on anything for more than a second at a time. I think briefly about Henna again but shake the vision of her broken body away. The blood. The blood, everywhere. My mom. She's going to have one hell of a hangover.

All I had was a cup of tea with that pinch-faced woman.

I cross the room unsteadily to the teapot. Fatima made me the tea, did she? Or did I make it?

I can't remember. I lift the lid and sniff. It smells like English Breakfast with a hint of something floral.

Claire. Your mother lies. You know this. There were plenty of opportunities for her to drink some champagne, or something stronger. There is nothing in your tea. You have a concussion—they told you the side effects: dizziness, nausea, blurred vision, headaches, fatigue. Don't be an idiot.

I toss the tea anyway, pour myself a tall, cool glass of water and gulp it down. The dizziness is passing. They said I could take ibuprofen, and I do. I breathe through it, feeling better, steadier, with each inhalation.

See? You aren't being poisoned. Way to get all paranoid there, Claire.

Still a little lightheaded, I take a seat in the dressing room, and assess.

My rehearsal dinner dress hangs inert, waiting for me to slide into it and practice my vows. I suppose if my wedding gown is truly ruined, and I don't want to accept Fatima's gift, I can swap it out with my Laura Blake. It is more appealing to me than wearing the loaner from Fatima, but maybe that's me being stubborn.

I pull it from its hook and hold it in front of me, thanking whatever ironic elves decided to have Fatima do my hair and makeup. I'm basically ready to go for tonight already.

Yes, the Blake is lovely, though a bit sexy for a church wedding. The world won't end if I have to pivot. And I won't have to bedeck myself in someone else's dream.

There. Better. Logic brings calm.

I'm tired of making compromises. I'm tired of not feeling 100 percent. I'm sick and tired of the rain. And as bad as it sounds, I'm ready to just get this weekend over with. Say our vows and go home. I've had enough of the Comptons for the time being.

I've answered my earlier traitorous thought. I do want Jack. I want him badly. And I'm willing to fight for him.

My phone squawks, and I grab it, relieved to be drawn away from my dark thoughts. I recognize the New York number this time. Karmen, again.

"Karmen?"

"Hello, Claire." She sounds rushed, harried. "I'm sending you some screenshots, just to confirm this is the same woman who came to see you. The picture isn't the best."

My phone dings. "Hold on."

She's sent a series of grainy shots; I recognize the intersection near my studio. And I recognize the woman who stands so stiffly, waiting for the light to change.

"That's Ami Eister. Absolutely."

"Okay. I'm going to load her into our facial recognition system and see what pops. You hang in there, Claire. I'll be in touch."

Seconds after I hang up, I get another text, this time from Harper.

I think I have a solution for your dress. Come see!

Finally. *Finally.* Something good.

I text her back with a lightness in my heart I haven't felt in days.

On my way!

50

The Deepest Betrayals Start at Home

Jack finds his parents sitting together quietly in their bedroom. Brice has an arm around Ana's back. Her shoulders move delicately as she cries. Henna was more than her right hand, she was her best friend, her confidant. Ana ruled the family with an iron fist; Henna was the velvet inside that glove.

"Mom. I'm so sorry."

Her back stiffens. "Thank you, Jackson."

"Tell me what I can do."

She tosses a tissue into the trash and faces him. He hates this, her tear-streaked face, her nose red, her eyes swollen. He's never seen his mother so distressed before. He doesn't remember ever seeing her cry, outside of May's funeral. Ana is the strong one. She is their backbone.

"There's nothing that can be done, my darling. Nothing will bring her back. Accidents happen."

"Mom. It wasn't an accident. Henna was murdered."

"By who?" she snaps. "Who in this house could possibly be

a killer? It's a ridiculous thought and I won't have it, do you hear me?"

Brice waves him off, jerks his head toward the terrace. Jack follows his father outside.

"I disagree with your mother," Brice says. "Ami Eister is the common denominator. Karmen is working on an identification now. We find her, and we take her out, before she can do any more damage to the family."

"Agreed," Jack said. "She sent me another text on my way up here. More footage from Monday night. If this gets out… But why hurt Henna?"

"Why do people ever get killed, Jackson? She knew something, or she saw something."

Jack blows out a breath, hard.

"Henna's death. The break-in, the cameras. Finding Morgan's body… It's all tied together. It's coming from within the house, Dad."

"I know. Come. Let's go comfort your mother. Security is on high alert, everyone is being watched. We're safe, for now."

Inside, Brice's phone is ringing.

"Oh, for God's sake, now what?" Ana grumbles.

"It's Cay."

"Put her on speaker," Ana says.

"What is it, Cay?" Brice asks.

"Mr. Compton, oh my God, I'm so glad I caught you." Cay Evans, the firm's chief legal counsel, sounds breathless, and Jack stops his pacing to listen. He's never heard Cay so rattled before.

"What's wrong?"

"*Flair* is about to drop an article online. It's a damning piece, claiming that Jackson killed Morgan Fraser and the family covered it up."

"Fuck," Jack says under his breath.

"Sir, they want a comment and they claim they're going live with the piece in five minutes. I told them you are in Italy and they have to give us the appropriate amount of time to respond, but they're insisting. Apparently, they've been working on the piece for several weeks, and they claim they have a quote of denial from the family."

"I am going to kill that girl," Brice growls just as Ana says, "What's the quote?"

"Hold on, I have it here. 'When asked about the series of deaths on Isla Isola, the Compton family home, Brice Compton dismissed the claims out of hand. Quote: "The idea that my family was involved in any deaths, much less covered them up, is preposterous." End quote.'"

Ana and Brice shoot knowing glances at one another. First rule of crisis management—don't talk to the press. The quote is a fake.

"Who is the byline?" Jack asks.

"It doesn't matter," Brice says. "We know exactly where that quote came from. Harper Hunter. Because she asked us about it an hour ago."

Jack drops into a chair. "What the hell is happening?"

Brice holds up a calming hand. "Cay, you have to get it stopped. I don't care what you have to do. Threaten them with everything we've got. We're being set up. Claire, and Hunter, were approached by a woman calling herself Ami Eister. She's an imposter, and I believe behind all this nonsense."

"Sir, I don't know that it matters. They're running it with or without the comment. I'm sorry. If I'd had any idea... I was blindsided. We all were. It's horribly unethical of them not to give us time to craft an appropriate response. I've told them we'll take immediate action if they don't drop the story, but they don't seem to care."

"They think they have the better angle. Regardless of the publication, word gets out and we'll be tried in the court of public opinion. That's the game here."

"Cay? It's Ana. You tell them Ami Eister impersonated an

editor at *Flair* to gain access to our family and drum up spurious charges against us. We will sue them into oblivion if they don't drop this inquiry immediately."

"Ma'am, they claim they're passing the information along to the feds. If there's any whisper of truth to this, the FBI could get involved."

Jack can hear exactly what Cay is really saying. *If you did this, I'm not going to jail for lying for you.*

"If law enforcement wants to get involved, we will be happy to cooperate." Brice says. "Whoever this Ami Eister woman is, she's trying to blackmail us into action on something that is patently false. It was a mistake, that's all. A huge misunderstanding. Handle it. Fix this, right now. That's what I pay you for. Get the story pulled. If they insist on running it, slap an injunction on them immediately. And you get me in touch with Florio Cedar. He owns *Flair*. If his people balk in the slightest, I'll pull the plug from higher up."

Jack casts a glance at his father, pacing, roaring in frustration, and knows this is a mistake. In the face of such a massive breach, putting their kind of pressure on someone they've been spying on isn't a good idea.

Cay's voice is sharp. "Yes, sir. I'll…do what I can."

While Brice gets on the phone with the owner of the magazine to ensure the story is spiked, Jack listens to Ana's description of the interview with Harper with incredulity.

"She got an anonymous tip, an email, suggesting there have been deaths on the island. I'll give her some credit, she did her research, put together a whole story that is as unlikely as it is salacious. When we set up the *Flair* piece, it was all legit, and then Harper was approached by an 'editor'—" his mother makes little quotes in the air "—by the name Ami Eister."

"Ami Eister, again. Who the hell is this woman?"

"I don't know, Jackson, but she—or the people she works for—is clearly out to get us."

"I want to talk to Harper. I want to hear this for myself. I want to be sure she's not the one behind this. She and Claire have a long history. They haven't always gotten along."

Ana shakes her head. "Harper is busy. She's talking to Karmen, detailing everything that's happened, all the contact she's had. She's being very cooperative. Once she understood the situation…that she'd been duped… No, she's not behind the plot, I'm certain of it. She's being used."

"Yet someone went ahead with this story, and the damn media has it now."

"Cay will shut it down. Don't worry. This is bigger than Harper. Bigger than Claire, too. They're pawns. Karmen found the imposter on a traffic cam, and is running facial recognition. We'll know the identity of this woman soon. Once we know who she is, we'll go from there."

Jack watches the waves crashing against the rocks below the cliff. Relentless, again, and again, and again. They're missing something. They are all missing something.

"We need legal protection here," he says finally. "Counsel. With Henna's death, with this imposter playing with Claire and Harper, these allegations can get blown out of proportion. We can't—"

"I think we need to pull the plug on the wedding," Elliot interrupts, striding into the room. "This is just out of control. These texts, the threats, and now Henna's dead? Mother. Please."

"How dare you? This is my wedding. It's my call."

Ana holds up a hand to stop their argument.

"Perhaps he's right, Jackson. Claire seems to be the center of the storm, and the catalyst here. It's only prudent for us to question the situation. Do you want to marry her, Jack? With all that's happening, are you certain this is the right course of action?"

The thought of bailing on Claire, on his life, his happiness, is impossible. "Yes, I'm sure. I love her, and I want her protected. But we're under attack. We've already had one death in the family, and threats that will take all our efforts to combat. An imposter is using Claire and Harper to take us down. I won't fight if you feel we should cancel. The family comes first. Always. I won't make the same mistake twice."

"So you think," Elliot mutters, but Ana nods once. Jack has said the right thing. The decision is made. The marriage will go on, come hell or high water. And maybe even then.

"If you're set on this course, I suggest we consolidate. Let's leave off the rehearsal and jump straight to the ceremony. We were scheduled to be on *The Hebrides* for the rehearsal dinner, we'll simply make that the wedding reception. We'll stay there, and the moment the weather clears, we sail. It's a controlled environment. We will see every person who walks on board. That way, we can keep everyone safe until this Ami Eister character is unmasked. And we can decide how to approach Harper Hunter's egregious breach of trust. I already have an idea."

Not to mention being on *The Hebrides* in international waters will put the family out of reach of the FBI, just in case Brice can't apply the appropriate pressure and they come calling. God, his mother is a force to be reckoned with. Ana always was five steps ahead of everyone else in the room.

"Agreed. It has to be someone close, Mom," Jack says quietly. "It has to be someone here."

"Perhaps. But we're on alert now. No one will be able to take advantage."

If you're set on this course. If anything, he is more set than ever. Marriage will provide Claire with a significant amount of protection, both financially and otherwise. Someone is after him, and he wants her completely protected. Especially if whoever is targeting the family succeeds in taking him out. Though she's already signed the NDA, until the marriage license is signed and witnessed, she won't get anything. Not that he thinks he's about to die. But still...

"Should we really wait? Should we not focus on getting the family off the island? Claire and Jack can get married on the mainland, we don't have to do it today," Elliot says.

Thunder answers his query. Their gazes move to the windows, to the billowing clouds, another storm surging over the mainland and headed their way.

"We do it today," Jack says, brooking no argument.

"I agree," Ana says. "There's no reason not to do it now. I don't think *The Hebrides* can handle the channel crossing in these storms. Besides, we have safety in numbers, right? No sense panicking our guests, but we can up our local security. Tie the cameras into the generators. Shift house personnel to security."

"Henna wasn't safe," Elliot snaps. "You're risking everyone's lives to satisfy his whim."

Ana flinches again but stays stoic. "You're out of line, Elliot. We're clear about the danger now. We can keep everyone safe, and we can fix this."

"We'd better," Elliot says.

Ana ignores the crack, stays focused on Jack. "You let Claire know. She'll need time to get ready. I'll handle everything else." She touches Jack's cheek. "We'll get through this together, Jackson. Let's get you married, and we can work from there."

Elliot huffs, peels off from the conversation. Jack can hear him inside with Brice, still arguing. But Brice won't give way. When Ana makes a decision, it is sacrosanct.

"Do you need to go help Dad?"

"I do. But first, I need to tell you something. Come with me."

He follows her into the suite, into her bedroom. She closes the door behind them.

"What do you have to tell me?"

"I'm afraid I wasn't entirely honest with you, Jackson. I'll beg your forgiveness now, though I don't know if you'll be able to…" She takes a deep breath.

"The body they found yesterday was not Morgan's after all."

51

The Plot's Afoot

Jack shakes his head, ready to throttle his mother. "What are you talking about, the body isn't Morgan's? You said it was her. You said the bones in her hands confirmed it. How could you make a mistake that big? What have you learned?"

"I didn't… Oh, Jackson, I was trying to protect you. I wanted you to have some peace of mind. I wanted you to be able to face the future with a clear heart and clear mind."

"She's not been found?"

"No."

Jack doesn't think he's ever heard a "no" in his life that resonates so deeply.

"I can't believe this. You lied to me? About finding my wife's body? I don't even know who you are anymore."

She reaches for him, trying to draw him in for a hug, but he whirls away. "No. You don't get to comfort me right now. What were you thinking?"

"It was a mistake. A terrible misunderstanding."

"I can't believe you."

He goes to the window, watches the rain lash the panes. Normally it would be soothing, knowing he is safe inside against the elements, but now, all he can think of is that night, how the rain pounded down on his skin until he was convinced he would never feel dry and warm again. Of her scream as she went over the ledge. How she shrieked his name, the sound fading as she fell to her death. That cry would echo in his brain through eternity, sending chills through his body whenever he allowed his mind to touch upon the memory.

"Jack, I am so, so sorry."

"If it wasn't Morgan's body, then who the hell was it?"

"We don't know. Not for sure, anyway."

"Who do you suspect?" Jack spits out the words. This isn't happening.

Ana lights another cigarette. Jack wants to slap it from her mouth.

"If pressed, I suspect it actually is Elevana, but without DNA or dental, there's no way to know for sure."

"And if it's not? How many young women will we dig up? How many more will wash up upon our shores?"

"I don't know the answer to that, Jackson. But if you want to protect your Claire, I suggest we stop arguing and move forward. I will get in touch with the priest and get the staff moving. Tell Claire. She'll understand."

Jack collapses back against the wall, running a hand through his hair.

This is insanity.

And yet…he needs to let Claire know they're moving up the wedding. Pray that she goes along.

Jack stalks the halls of the Villa, looking for anything else amiss. He is more comfortable now with the weight of the gun in his hand. Henna was murdered by someone in the house. Possibly someone he's invited to his wedding. Someone he knows.

The question is, who?

Fatima is with Claire, and Fatima can take care of the two of them with no problem. Malcolm is standing guard as well.

He hesitates at the split, then decides. Might as well rule his grandfather in or out. He walks the quiet hall to his grandfather's rooms. He stashes the gun in the waistband of his jeans and knocks on the door. Will's nurse answers.

"*Buon pomeriggio.* Signore Compton is napping."

"Has he left the room today?"

"We had breakfast in the kitchens, like normal, and took a walk earlier, with the dogs. Since then, he's been here with me. We didn't come to the brunch. Your mother thought it would be best, with so many strangers, that we stick to his routine. You know he was upset yesterday."

"Are you sure he's in his room? You need to go check. It's very important."

"I'm happy to check, Signore, but he—"

A deep voice comes from inside. "Who are you talking to, Petra?"

"It is—"

"Jackson! Good to see you, boy. Come in here and give an old man a hug."

Petra opens the door wide and Jack steps in. Will looks calm and rested. And, like last night, completely himself.

Will grabs Jack and pulls him into a bear hug. His hand brushes the gun at Jack's waistband, and he grunts. "Hardly need to come here armed, Jacky."

"We can let it be our little secret. How are you, Gran?"

"Fine, fine. A bit bored. This one—" he jerks a thumb toward Petra "—doesn't let me out of her sight. Ah, the trouble we used to get up to, you and I, eh Jacky? Maybe we can take a stroll through the labyrinth when the storm passes, like old times. You would let me if Jack was escorting me, wouldn't you, dear?"

Petra only raises a brow. "I wouldn't dream of stopping you from taking a walk with your grandson, Signore Compton."

"Excellent. Now, when do I get to meet the bride to-be? She looks like a sweet girl in the photos I've seen. Much too sweet for a dog like you." Will laughs and elbows Jack in the ribs, making him grin. This, this is the man he knows, the jokester, the ribald center of attention at every party, the man with the keen eye and even sharper business sense, a man full of life's experiences and the stories to go with them. He is so very different than the man who punched him. And he doesn't remember a thing about yesterday's incident, clearly.

He sees Petra shake her head slightly and touches two fingers to his sore cheek.

"The rehearsal dinner is this evening, Gran. You can meet her then."

"You should bring her by before, let me get a look at her. I thought I saw her earlier, actually." Will gets a faraway look in his eyes. "Yes, I'm sure of it. She was walking down the hall toward the staircase. She smiled and said hello but disappeared down the stairs before I could say hello back. You'll have to teach her not to be so shy, Jack. She's part of the family now."

"I will, Gran. Promise. I need to run. I just wanted to check on you, say hello, before things got busy with the wedding."

"Ah, don't go. Have a whisky with me. Let's toast the end of your bachelorhood, just you and me."

"While a whisky sounds delightful, Gran, I shouldn't. But I'll stop by later and bring Claire, so you can meet her properly."

"All right, all right. I yield." He hugs Jack close again, then breaks away. "What do you say, Petra, how shall we while away the time? Gin rummy or a film?"

"Cards sound good, Signore Compton. Let me see your grandson to the door. You shuffle, okay?"

Will obediently sits at his dining table and pulls the deck of cards toward him.

Jack stops by the door. "How long has he been this way Petra? Sometimes good, sometimes bad?"

"It's gotten worse over the past six months. The more we keep things at an even keel, the better he is. His medication works well, most of the time. I'll give him some extra this afternoon, so he doesn't feel unwell tonight. He is getting worse, though, I'm afraid. You saw him yesterday. He is…how do you say it? All over the place."

"I'm sorry to hear it."

"But this was nice, yes? Like last night, downstairs, he knew you, knew what was going on. He's been so excited for the wedding."

Jack tears up, thinking of his strong grandfather being felled by the insidious disease.

"You're sure he was here all afternoon?"

"*Si*. Especially after he slipped away from me last night. I stayed right out here. I would have seen him pass by me. I was relieved he slept at all, sometimes the medicine doesn't knock him out, just makes him drowsy and cranky."

"Thank you, Petra. I'll be back by in a while, try introducing him to Claire again. Keep the door locked, all right? Don't let him wander alone. If he wants to go for a walk, you go with him."

Without asking why, she nods and shuts the door behind him. He hears the deadbolt snap into place and blows out a breath, heading toward the second floor.

And then it hits him. If Will has been in his rooms since breakfast, how did he see Claire by the stairs this morning?

52

Tansy and Rue

Silly people, thinking they're safe. That they got away with it.

I will show them.

I will not be forgotten, erased, made insignificant.

I will not be conquered.

All it takes is the click of a button and their dirty little secrets will see the light of day.

What do you think they'll do to keep it quiet?

I know the lengths they'll go to. They have no idea how far I'm willing to take this.

Clearly I haven't dosed the tea enough. I will fix this, now.

They will rue the day they hurt me.

They will rue the day they created me.

53

When a Door Closes, a Window Opens

Harper sits on the edge of the Chinoiserie chair by her terrace door, staring out at the murky sea. She has been here, mortified, since the fiasco upstairs and her conversation with the head of security, an acerbic woman who'd clearly thought Harper was a first-class idiot. She's waiting for someone to come and take her bags and throw her on a boat. She can imagine Ana Compton up there in her tower giving orders. *"Never mind the storm, if it sinks, all the better."*

To think, she'd been taken in by a hoax. By an imposter. Ami fucking Eister, whoever the hell that was. Harper's own ambition got in the way of her common sense. She'd never stopped to wonder why a magazine like *Flair* would trust an untested rookie reporter with such a huge story. When Claire finds out, she is going to be livid. And she'll be well within her rights to be.

There is a soft knocking against the door, which swings open a moment later.

"Harper? May I come in?"

Ana Compton stands in the doorway to Harper's room. Time to be escorted to the guillotine.

Harper jumps to her feet. "Of course."

Ana moves through the room like a gentle wave, takes the chair opposite Harper. She has Harper's camera, which she sets on the table between them. She sits with her legs crossed, her look appraising. Calm.

"I suspect you want to know what's happening?"

"Do you know what's happening? If so, yes, I would."

"We don't know everything. Not yet. Brice's people are still working on the injunction, for starters. I thought you and I could talk a bit while they're getting the story quashed."

"But it's true, isn't it? About the women who've died here?"

"Accidents happen, Harper."

"Henna fell down the stairs. Fatima's mother went missing. Will's wife drowned in the grotto. Eliza was shot. And Morgan—"

"Died when she went over the cliff wall. But she fell off the ledge, Harper. She wasn't killed."

"How do you know?"

"I was there."

Harper feels the jerk of the live wire inside her. There is a story, after all. "What?"

"I was there the night Morgan went over the wall."

"But Jack—"

"Arrived after she'd already fallen. They had a terrible fight—Morgan was quite unstable, as we came to find out—and she rushed out of the house into the storm. We all went looking for her. Jack and Fatima went down to the cottages, Elliot and I went up toward the cliff, Will and Brice went to the landing. We searched the whole island, and finally came across her, ranting, walking atop the cliffside rock boundary. The rain was so heavy; the rocks were slick. She slipped, and went over the edge, before we could catch her."

Harper can see the cliff out the window. Imagining a body plunging from its apex into the sea is all too easy.

"By the time the storm abated, and we were able to send a boat around the promontory, the body had washed away."

"Why would you lie? You said she died in California? That makes no sense."

"Doesn't it?" Ana sits back, hands atop her knees. "We are very private people. The last thing a family like us needs is extra scrutiny. Things were...well, that's neither here nor there. Brice's business dealings were especially fraught at the time, and we didn't need anyone poking around in the island's history. This is one of the few places we can escape to that is remote enough to keep the press away. It is a sacred place for us, in many ways. A quiet retreat. Our sanctuary."

Harper shakes her head. "But her hand... Her hand washed up on a beach in California."

Ana nods. "A well-placed fabrication. We needed the chapter closed. And we didn't want any more publicity around Jack. He took Morgan's death hard. We needed to protect him. Protecting my family is paramount, Harper. There is nothing I won't do to keep my boys safe, and happy. One day you may even understand that."

"Then who is Ami Eister?"

Ana sits straighter. "That we don't know. But whoever she is, she is a danger, and she must be stopped."

"I'm just...so confused. I looked her up. She's totally legit. She's on the masthead at *Flair*. I read some articles she wrote."

"We think you probably saw a mocked-up and cached version of the website. Easy to do. It's basically a well-executed phishing scam. An overlay. Her phone number would look like she was from *Flair*, same extensions, just spoofed to go to the phone she possessed. Her email as well. She sent you links, right? For you to check her out?"

"Yes."

"I'm sure, once we examine your computer, we'll find the software that was planted. Keystroke analysis wouldn't surprise me, she's been keeping close tabs on things. It's a ruse. All a ruse. We don't kill people, Harper. We aren't that kind of family. That's for books and movies."

"But you do broker in information."

"Yes. That we do."

Harper feels a tiny bit of vindication. "Then not everything she told me was a lie. You truly don't know who it is?"

"We're tracing her right now. She's been texting my sons. Karmen has visuals of her visiting Claire in Nashville. We'll have her identity soon enough. And then..." Ana's face changes, goes completely feral, and Harper shivers. "And then, we will stop her. This...disruption...isn't seemly."

Harper has to make this right. This woman holds her future in her perfectly manicured hands. "Mrs. Compton, I'm so embarrassed. I have abused your trust, and your kindness. Will you be able to forgive me?"

Those cold eyes bore right through her. "I admit, I'm not thrilled by your lack of faith in us, that you wouldn't at least have the courtesy to talk to us before you tried to land the scoop of the century."

Harper nods, chagrined. "It wasn't very classy."

"No, it wasn't. But I admire your ambition. I admire the guts it took to try and go up against us. You were trying to right a wrong. A wrong that didn't happen, a malicious prank, but a wrong, nonetheless. And that's something I can understand."

"I'm grateful to hear that, Mrs. Compton."

"Please. Call me Ana."

"I... Okay. Ana."

"Which brings me to why we're having this little chat. Here's what I'd like to talk to you about, Harper. You're smart. You're stylish. You have guts, and determination, and independence. We've already established that you are ambitious, to a fault. You're also an excellent photographer and have quite a following. I've just lost my right hand. Henna was the most dynamic woman I've ever worked with. She too had style, and determination, and ambition. You remind me of her, in many ways. I know this is a sudden offer, but I wonder if you'd be interested in working for me. Taking over Henna's position."

Harper's head snaps up.

"I just tried to blow up your family, and you're offering me a job?"

"I'm offering you an opportunity."

Harper laughs, mirthlessly. "Claire won't like it."

Ana smiles. "From what I can tell, you don't particularly worry about your sister's opinion, do you? We'll make it work. We aren't all together like this very often. You wouldn't have to see her if you didn't want to—we could work the schedules so you're elsewhere. But I think, perhaps, you've had your revenge? A sister is an important part of a woman's life. I wish I had one. I always have. Good, bad, indifferent. It's a blood tie that can't be broken."

"Some things aren't forgivable." Harper hears the bitterness in her tone. She can't help it. Forgiving Claire is impossible.

"I understand. Well, you think about it. If you decide you'd like to work with me, you let me know."

Harper makes the decision without another thought. If this woman is magnanimous enough to offer her a position after she'd tried to screw her to the wall? It feels right, and she can always leave if it doesn't work out.

"I would like to, actually. Yes."

Ana's face breaks into a wide smile, and Harper is struck by her beauty.

"Excellent. I took the liberty of having an NDA drafted. As

you can imagine, what I've just told you is quite personal to the family. This will cover our current and future conversations. Will you sign it?"

Ana sets the blue-backed paper on the table between them, and hands Harper a pen. She barely glances at the document before signing. Is it her imagination, or do Ana Compton's shoulders relax a fraction when Harper sets down the pen?

"Wonderful. Let's get through the wedding this evening, and tomorrow we'll sit down and discuss your salary, your duties, and what I feel you can bring to the table. And you can think about how you'd like to work with me. And with your sister, of course."

"That sounds great, Mrs. Compton."

"Ana. Please."

"Ana. The wedding is this evening?"

"In light of everything that's happening, we're going to move up the ceremony. I assume you'll want to take some photographs of your sister?" She nods at Harper's camera. "It has a fresh SD card. I'm sure you understand."

Harper sighs. "I do. It's a shame. The photographs I took of you were wonderful."

"We'll do it again. Thank you, Harper. This is a burden lifted."

"No, Ana. Thank you."

"Before you do anything else, you need to talk to Karmen again, so she can get the process moving for your background check. Just give her your basic information, social, address, and we'll get the ball rolling. That won't be a problem, will it?"

"No. Absolutely no problem at all."

"Good. When you're finished with Karmen, get dressed. Help your sister. Check in with your mother. I trust you can handle her this evening?"

There is no question what Ana is implying. "I can. I will."

"Good. I look forward to working with you, Harper."

Ana gives her a little wave and disappears into the hallway.

Holy shit.

Holy shit!

She's going to work for Ana Compton.

Of all the ways today was supposed to shake out, this had never entered her mind.

Brice is waiting for Ana when she gets back to their suite.

"So?"

"She's in."

"That was quite a gamble, telling her what happened. You knew she'd go for it?"

"I hoped she would. Keeping her close is the best way to keep the family safe. Besides, she does have excellent style. She'll do. We better get ready."

Ana moves toward the closet, but Brice reaches out a hand and stops her.

"We've made a mistake."

"I know. I'm going to fix it. Don't worry."

At his look, she says it again.

"Don't worry, Brice. I have a feeling I know what's going on. Let's just get the kids married, and we'll deal with it. Jack is right, he wants to protect Claire, and giving her our name is the best thing we can do."

54

An Epic Failure of Imagination

Now that she's out from under the spyglass of suspicion, Harper Hunter answers Karmen's questions enthusiastically. She is young. So young. Karmen hopes Ana knows what she's doing. She'd called down moments before Harper practically skipped into Karmen's office. "Get her in the system, and make sure there aren't going to be any more surprises, do you understand me? I am finished with this nonsense."

Fifteen minutes later, Karmen tosses her reading glasses onto the desk.

"We'll need to do a full interview once the wedding is over, but that should do for now. I look forward to getting to know you better, Harper. Ana is a brilliant woman. You're going to enjoy working with her."

"Do you? Enjoy working with her?"

"Most of the time," Karmen says with a smile. "I understand we're to have the wedding this evening. You'd best go get ready."

Harper looks like she wants to ask more questions, but reads Karmen's impatience and simply says, "Thanks. See you later, I hope."

Already polite. Already deferent. Already intuitive. She seems smart, has an undeniable presence. She is so very different from her sister. Claire's strength simmers inside her, only exposing itself when needed; Harper's explodes from every smile, every step, every wave of her hand. Maybe Ana knows what she's doing after all.

Karmen opens an employment file, loads in the information, then goes back to her more pressing issue, trying to identify Ami Eister.

The traffic cameras in Nashville proved to be most helpful. She's found a good angle of the impostor standing on the corner by the Turnip Truck grocery store. She is wearing black, head to toe, from her sunglasses to her knee-high boots. Her hair is done up in a French twist. She crosses the street without looking left or right, moving swiftly, turns left, and walks directly to the door to Claire's studio.

"Gotcha."

Karmen marks the time and date, swaps to the camera on the traffic light to see if she can do a better face capture.

She gets another angle. Then another.

Three points. That's more than enough. Karmen plugs the still shots into the database. She traces out a jawline, an ear, the distance between the temples.

The software will do the rest. She has to trust the technology. This could take hours. She could have let one of the team in New York do this work, but it's important that she, and she alone, discover this woman's identity.

She should get some rest; she's totally burned out. Instead, she turns to the internet, and does some more searching on Ami Eister.

Clearly, someone is playing an angle against the Comptons, and against Claire. The two situations—the break-in, the visitation—are linked, no doubt. Maybe this woman is dating, or married to, Shane McGowan, and he's talked her into doing things for him.

She lets the thought sit for a moment. It's possible.

Flip it. The woman talks a thug into doing some work for her. And to twist the knife a bit, chooses a someone designed to truly hurt the victim. Revenge is an excellent motivator.

Karmen has read the court transcripts; she knows Shane McGowan covered for his young girlfriend. His lies meant Claire didn't go to jail for the robbery of the Mapco. But McGowan did.

Claire cost him five years of his life. His own stupidity landed him in jail for the rest of the decade since that first arrest. After ten years behind bars, it wouldn't take much to convince him to screw over the girl who sent him there in the first place, right?

People's pasts are interesting places. Even the most upstanding citizen has something to hide. Most unpaid parking tickets don't lead to the capture of a serial killer, but sometimes, they become a catalyst of another sort.

She turns back to the computer, does a quick search.

Morgan Fraser, twenty-three, flame-red hair and a bod to match. Now, this woman looks like she belongs to the Comptons. Not a sweet, gilded butterfly like Claire, or lush like Harper; Morgan was a raging lioness. Karmen can practically feel the power coming off the woman through the screen. She was dynamic in photos. In person? She was mesmerizing. Mesmerizing enough to capture the eyes and heart of a rich young playboy.

Though Karmen knows the details from the inside, she reads more. About how the two met. How Morgan Fraser, the hot young engineer sweeping through Silicon Valley, had landed 120 million in venture capital funds to produce high-resolution microcameras for laptops. She'd approached Brice at the Allen and Company conference in Sun Valley. How she'd scored an invite was still up for discussion—the conference was one of the most private, most elite in the world. Brice couldn't help himself—he bought out her nascent company over lunch. She'd already gotten her hooks into Jack at that point.

Microcameras. Morgan developed microcameras. Like what they'd pulled out of Claire Hunter's house? Over twenty miniature wireless encrypted cameras had been stashed throughout the house, and Karmen still had no idea where they'd been transmitting to.

The computer dings. The facial recognition has a hit.

The program has two photographs side by side. One is the profile shot of the woman who visited Claire. The other...

No.

That's impossible. They don't even look alike.

There are things that you can't change about yourself with traditional plastic surgery. The distance between your eyes. The depth of your eye sockets. The length of your jawline. The shape and set of your ears. It's why facial recognition software is so accurate.

Though the two women don't look at all the same, the program has found a match. And that means...

Karmen's senses have come alive. Everything crashes together, and she grabs her phone. She has to warn the family, now.

The knife slams between her ribs and she falls forward onto the keyboard. The shock of the attack freezes her senses just long enough for the knife to be pulled out and slammed in again, and once more, so deep she knows this is it. She is done.

She tries to twist, tries to fight, but the knife has penetrated her lung, she can't breathe. She collapses on the floor, facedown, the knife sticking from her ribs like a flagpole. Blood leaks from her mouth and back, puddling on the floor under her desk. She can feel it, taste it, sticky and iron sweet. It takes three minutes for her to die, the knowledge burning through her veins.

Karmen has failed in her most basic duty. She hasn't protected the family.

When the woman is dead, the computer is wiped, the match declined, the request for identification rescinded. The files are deleted, the hard drive wiped. The text is sent.

The words, spoken with a snarl.

"Good fucking riddance."

55

Bonny Lass Gone

Malcolm trails me through the halls silently. I suppose that makes me feel better, but I have to admit, of the two crows, I like Gideon much better. Malcolm just plain gives me the creeps. I don't know why. Some men set off your interior alarm bells. Maybe after Jack and I are properly married, and the police close the case, Malcolm will want a transfer. It's not fair of me to even think it, he's done so much for me, for Jack, for the family. But I don't want to spend my life with him looking over my shoulder.

"Harper?"

I knock on the door, but there's no answer. I turn the knob and the door swings open.

"Harper? Where are you?"

Nothing. The room is empty, but my wedding dress hangs on the open wardrobe door. It looks so lost, so lonely, drooping and empty. I approach it carefully, heart banging in my chest. I touch the fabric as if it might disappear at the lightest breath like a dandelion in the wind, using two fingers to pull apart the panels where the horrible word was scrawled.

The word is missing, cut free. But so is the entire back of my dress.

It's still ruined.

I feel a pain start, deep in my chest. So much for the glorious wedding dress of my dreams. There's no way Harper can recreate the look I've designed without this panel.

I swipe at my eyes and blow out a breath. Hey, they all tried to make this better. Ana, Henna, Harper, even Fatima. I should be grateful. Instead I want to burn it all down.

"Claire?" Katie slips her hand into mine. I hadn't even heard her come in. "Harper's not here. Ana came to talk to her, and then she left."

"She texted me she had the dress issue resolved. Obviously, that wasn't true."

"It's okay. You have that pretty back-up dress. It's all about the ceremony anyway. Don't let this break your heart. Maybe y'all could renew your vows next year and you can fix it and wear it then. We can have a huge party back in Nashville. It will give you time to put it back the way you want it."

"I know. It's just…" I collapse onto the edge of Harper's bed. I can smell the Philosophy perfume she loves so much, the same scent she's worn since I gave her a bottle for Christmas when she was in seventh grade, and it brings tears to my eyes. "Everything is so screwed up. Maybe this isn't the right thing to do."

"Marrying Jack, you mean?" Katie asks softly.

"Yes. God, I feel so disloyal saying that aloud. Maybe we've rushed into things. Maybe I need to listen to what I'm being told."

Katie narrows her eyes. "What, exactly, are you being told?"

"The universe conspires against me, friend. Henna's dead."

"What?"

"She took a header down the stairs. Mom and I found her."

Katie sits down cross-legged on the floor, the thick rug cushioning her. "That's tragic. I kind of liked her. She had style."

"That she did. It's only…what if it wasn't an accident, Katie? What if she was killed?"

"Then this is getting too weird, and you should bail. You don't have to do this, Claire. There's no rush, especially if you're getting cold feet. You don't need Jack and his family to promote your work anymore, everyone knows your name now. We can go back to Nashville, leave as soon as the storm breaks. I can move in, help you with the mortgage. You can paint, I'll write. It will be like old days."

Katie looks so hopeful. I fear there is no going back, though.

"First, we have to find Harper."

"Yoo-hoo! Harper Lee, where are you, sweet bird?"

My mother knocks on the open door, starts when she sees the two of us. She doesn't seem as intoxicated, her eyes are clear and she's not weaving.

"Where is your sister?"

"I don't know, Mom. She texted about my dress, but she's not here. We don't know where she is."

"What's happened to your dress?"

Wow, she really was checked out. Surely we mentioned this to her earlier.

"Someone painted the word *WHORE* on it. In blood."

"Oh. Your poor dress. I'm sorry, Claire. I know you must be disappointed."

"That's an understatement," Katie says.

Mom actually looks stricken, and approaches me as if she's going to give me a hug, like any normal mother would do in this situation. I don't fight the embrace, allow myself to be wrapped in her arms. I can't remember the last time my mother hugged me of her own accord.

I wonder if I've been too hard on her. On Katie. On everyone. I've been so blinded by my love for Jack, so romanced by the idea of our perfect lives together, of all the things I can have, all the things I can do, I've been pushing everyone else away. Pushing away their worries, their concerns.

Mom ends the hug. "I'm so terribly jet-lagged. I took a Unisom last night and it hasn't worn off. I'm going to rest some more before the rehearsal. If you need me, Claire—" She stares at me as if challenging me to contradict her. When I don't, she relaxes a little. "I'll be right here."

She sweeps out of the room like a queen.

"Wow. Is she still drunk?" Katie asks.

"Possibly. That's the nicest she's been since I took out my nose ring. We should go look for Harper, shouldn't we?"

"Where are we going to look? This place is massive. Call her first. See if she's just off doing something and not back here yet."

I glance at my signal, see the Wi-Fi is back up and running just fine. That's a relief. But Harper's phone rings and rings, with no answer. I leave a voicemail. I text. We wait a few minutes. Crickets.

"Have you checked her Instagram?" Katie asks.

"Well, duh. No."

I open the Instagram app and scroll to my sister's feed. Amazing, after this weekend, she's pushing toward the two-million-follower mark. Good for her.

The most recent post is shot from someplace I don't recognize. It's dark. There is water. I can see the glint of silvery light that indicates ripples. It doesn't have the usual artistic composition of Harper's shots—though it is beautiful in its starkness—and there is no caption. No platitude, no inspiration, no celebration of life, no words of wisdom. No carefully chosen hashtags. Nothing except 53,567 likes and 3,254 comments. None of which appear to be from Harper, who I know spends five minutes per post responding to as many people as she can. That is her secret to success.

Alarm creeps up my spine.

"What sort of picture is that? It looks like a cave." Katie twists the phone in my hand, and when the screen turns, I look closer. It does look a bit like a cave. And the shot has been taken landscape, but not rotated, so it's off. Like it was taken and uploaded from the side. What in the world?

I quickly scroll back through the rest of Harper's feed. Shot after shot from Rome, Naples, the boat, the island—I recognize the cliff face from my own journey in. Shots of the Villa's exterior, the labyrinth. My room. The three of us in a selfie on my terrace, the rain pouring down.

A few of the art inside the Villa—I bet Ana will be thrilled with that—a shot from one of the Villa's many terraces with the caption: *It was a dark and stormy night*. Then, the weird, unlabeled shot from the darkness.

"Check her stories. See if she went live at all," Katie says. There is concern in her voice, which almost surprises me. Almost. Katie might be jealous of Harper, might fight with her like a rabid cat, but she certainly doesn't wish her genuine ill.

Her stories are more shots of the island, the labyrinth, the cottages—gosh, Harper was a busy bee—a silly shot of her and my mother sticking out their tongues; that must have been from the brunch. Yes, my mom is clearly tipsy, her nose is red and eyes glassy.

The photo is in her stories, too, but this time, there is a caption, written across it in bland courier type. Not at all what Harper usually uses.

Three words.

Big News Coming…

Katie turns the phone around, trying to get the photo to straighten. "Okay, this seems…weird."

"I agree. Something's off. She is never coy, or vague."

Katie starts taking apart Harper's room, quickly, systematically. Drawers, the wardrobe, under the bed, under the mattress. She finds Harper's tote, pulls out her passport and wallet, her laptop, notebook, and camera. No phone.

"If she was in trouble, why wouldn't she just call?" Katie asks.

"I don't know. We're making a big leap that she's in trouble. Maybe she's just playing a joke."

"With everything that's going on…"

"You're right," I sigh. "I'll take Malcolm and go look for her."

"I'm going to help."

"No, it's okay. I'll find her."

"I want to help, Claire."

There's no arguing with her when she's like this.

"Fine. You take the upper floors of the house, I'll go down to the main levels. I will tell you this. Pay attention to where you are. I got turned around earlier and ended up down by the crypt. It's spooky as hell. Just…lay yourself some breadcrumbs so you don't get lost. This place has a way of turning you around."

"Don't worry," Katie says. "She's around here somewhere. She's just playing with you."

"I hope so. I'll text you if I find out anything."

Malcolm peels himself off the wall and treads silently behind me as I head back to the central staircase.

"You haven't seen my sister, have you?"

He shakes his head. "Last I heard, she was talking to Mr. and Mrs. Compton."

"Yes, me too. She sent me a text. Oh, here's another."

A new text has come in from Harper's number.

I have to talk to you. Meet me in the cottages. You don't know him at all, Claire.

I write back: WTF, Harper?

A flurry of texts come now, each angrier than the last. One after the other after the other, a steady stream of viciousness from my only sister.

You don't know him at all.

You don't know what he's capable of.

He doesn't really love you.

He's dangerous. You need to get out of here.

And then, one that makes me stop dead in my tracks.

Why don't you ask him how she really died?

56

The Gray Lady

Disturbed, I rush downstairs. I will set Harper straight. She has been against Jack and me from the beginning, I've always sensed her displeasure at my choice of husband. It's time we resolve this.

Footsteps behind me. My ever-present watcher follows at a respectful distance.

I've just turned the corner by the main stairwell to head into the west wing when a small strobe of lightning flashes, and I glance out the window to see a woman hurrying across the courtyard below. She is dressed in white, has long, dark hair. She disappears behind the trees. Darkness plunges around her, and then, the next flash of lightning, she is gone.

Was that Harper? It looks like her from behind, but what would she be doing rushing around in the rain with her hair wet and a weird white dress on? My sister loves her hair—I can't imagine her out in this muck without an umbrella. Was it someone else? There are plenty of servants I haven't met yet, this could be one coming late to work, or being sent on an errand.

Another thought strikes. The fort is supposedly haunted. Have I just seen the famed Gray Lady from the island's history, rushing about in the rain, forever trying to escape her terrible fate?

The idea chills me to the bone and I shiver. Historically, young women really didn't stand a chance, did they? They were so often treated as nothing more than chattel with a womb. Procreative property.

No. It has to be Harper. She said she needed to talk to me. She said she would meet me in the cottages. My imagination is on overdrive, that's all. And the rain distorts everything.

The air is laden with floral notes. The heady scent of the gardens and the rain wafts through the air. This part of the Villa is eerily quiet. I don't know if that's because we're being kept from our guests by the largeness of the manor house, or if it's just a function of so few people being here, or jet lag and mimosas are keeping people in their rooms, but I make it to the back terrace doors unmolested. There are umbrellas in a stand—a couple of them wet, which tells me people have been going in and out— and Wellies lined up in a rubber rainbow. I select a red pair that look close to my size and slip my feet into them. Perfect. I grab a windbreaker too—hooded and waterproof—from the array on the hooks above the boots. I have no idea where Jack is, text him I'm going outside to look for Harper, then stick the phone in my back pocket.

"Ma'am?"

I jump and whirl. I've forgotten Malcolm.

"Yes?"

"Jack asked that I keep a close watch on you. You aren't planning to go out there, are you? It's pissing rain."

"Malcolm, I had no idea you were British. You never talk."

He grins at me, probably the first time I've ever seen him smile, showing surprisingly white teeth. "I moved to America when I was young, so I lost most of my accent. You can't go out in this, you'll catch your death."

"Well, yes, I am going out there. I saw someone on the other side of the labyrinth. I'm hoping it's my sister, I need to talk to her about my dress."

He grabs an umbrella. "I'll have to go with you. Jack insisted."

"You don't have to—" At his look, I break off. I'm going to have company whether I want it or not. "Okay. Let's go now, though, before she gets too far from the house." And before he has a chance to stop me, I scurry outside into the pouring rain.

Within moments of leaving the terrace, I'm soaked through, despite the windbreaker and umbrella. I ignore Malcolm's call to slow down and run, pell-mell, into the labyrinth. It's not terribly complicated when you know to turn left, not designed to confuse or control, and I'm quickly on to the last turn when I see a flash of white.

I slow, not wanting to run into trouble, make the turn carefully. But it's not a person. Caught in the evergreen branches is a length of fabric. I retrieve it, unwind it gently, already knowing what I'm going to find. It is the desecrated panel from my dress, now cut away from the bustle, the word written on it melted into a brown stain.

Was it Harper I saw from the window?

Remembrance is a tricky thing. Was the hair black, or brown?

But wet brown hair is darker than dry brown hair. With the rising mist…it is possible.

There's no way my sister could possibly be behind this. She couldn't be. Ruining my wedding dress? We aren't bosom buddies, but she's never wished me genuine ill. I'm being paranoid.

Besides, she was trying to find a way to fix the dress.

Wasn't she?

Malcolm catches up to me. "Ma'am, please, don't do that. I can't protect you if you won't stay in sight."

"Well hurry, then. We're going to the cottages."

"Jack wouldn't want—"

I whirl on him. "I don't give a damn what Jack wants right now. Either get with the program or bugger off."

I start moving again, not waiting for an answer. Malcolm grabs my arm and pulls me back toward the house. His grip is tight, and I immediately start to struggle.

"Stop it, right now, or you'll regret it." He mutters something under his breath that sounds an awful lot like "Stupid bitch."

"What did you just call me?"

"You heard me." No longer trying to cover himself, he is sneering now, and I'm so shocked I forget to fight back. He manages to drag me back into the heart of the labyrinth before my brain kicks back into gear. This is Jack's security. His protectors. No, my security. My protectors.

Malcolm is part of this.

"Are you the one texting me?"

He grunts, no answer.

"Where are you taking me?"

"Someplace where you'll be safe."

"Bullshit. Let me go. Now."

His hand is clamped around my bicep so tightly I know I'll have a horrible bruise. I'm fighting back the panic. I can't let him take me away from the house, away from Jack. Getting every last ounce of breath in my lungs, I shriek, a full-on scream, right in his ear. "Romulus! Remus! Here, boys!"

He jerks my arm, pulling me close, and slams a beefy hand over my mouth.

"None of that. Try it again, and I'll toss you off the edge, and those fucking dogs, too."

I realize we are dangerously close to the cliff. Perhaps that can work in my favor.

The dogs come barreling through the labyrinth. They see the struggle and growl.

"Help me!" I shout at the dogs and as they leap, I bite at Malcolm's hand and start struggling in earnest. He's much bigger than I am, but I have the element of surprise, and he's trying to fight off the dogs now, too. Remus gets him in the arm and is shaking his dark head back and forth intently. Romulus latches onto his leg and Malcolm howls in pain. I knee Malcolm in the groin and shove, hard, pushing my body away from his. I don't catch him square in the nuts, but it's enough of a blow to make him stumble. The path here is rocky, and he's unbalanced and reacts accordingly, throwing out his free hand to stop his fall.

The moment the pressure on my arm is released, I shove against him again and he's forced to let go of me entirely. He lands hard on his back, unmoving, and the dogs swarm him. A warm spray catches me in the face. I wipe a hand across my cheek, and it comes away red, the blood pale, watered down by the soaking rain, and that's when I see the huge, gaping tear in Malcolm's throat.

An edging stake protrudes grotesquely from his neck. His mouth is opening and closing like a fish gasping for air, both arms are raised as if he wants to pull me into a lover's embrace. The dogs are still growling, their sharp teeth lodged in Malcolm's skin.

"Stop. Heel. Quit it," I say sharply, and the dogs release leg and arm and come to my side. I don't know how they knew I was the good guy in this fight, but thankfully, they've taken my side, or else Malcolm would have hurt me, badly.

The three of us stare at Malcolm. His mouth is moving still. He manages to wheeze out the words, "You. Are. So. Dead," before his eyes roll back in his head and his body goes limp.

Fuck. Fuck!

Malcolm shot the intruder.

Malcolm is trying to hurt me.

Malcolm is in on it.

Malcolm is dead, dead, dead.

I am off like a greyhound, running back along the edge of

the labyrinth to the house, screaming for Jack at the top of my lungs, trying to force the image of Malcolm jerking spasmodically on the ground, the rain washing his blood onto the slate, out of my mind.

The halls are still empty, unnervingly empty, when I burst inside, showering the marble with rain and mud. The dogs are glued to my side; they are a better deterrent than any human security might be. It's eerie enough that I slow, willing my heart to stop pounding out of my chest. It's not like Malcolm is coming after me. I move quietly now, watching, listening. The dogs' nails click on the floor. Where is everyone? Where is Jack?

Malcolm's body...spasming in death throes.

Oh God, what have I done?

57

WTF

Jack's phone dings with a text.

Looking for Harper outside. I'll be back in a few.

Outside?

Why in the world would Claire go out in the storm?

He diverts from the hallway to their rooms and heads down
the stairs instead. Something tells him to hurry. Everything is
spinning away from him.

He meets Claire, the dogs inside and at her side, by the library
door. The dogs' muzzles are covered in streaks of red. Claire
is wet through, shaking, and white as a ghost. Remus wags his
tail at the sight of Jack, and wiggles himself sideways to Jack's
leg. But Romulus growls at him. The bond the dog has formed
with Claire is incredible. He will protect her at all cost.

"It's okay, boy. I won't hurt her. Claire? What happened. Are you okay? Will you call off Romulus?"

"Malcolm's dead," she says flatly.

"Malcolm?"

"He attacked me. In the labyrinth. I was looking for Harper, I think she's gone missing. She posted a weird photo on her Instagram and sent me strange texts, wanting me to meet her. But Malcolm..."

"Harper's not missing. She's upstairs, with my parents. What do you mean, Malcolm attacked you?"

She shows him the pale underside of her arm, already marked with a livid bruise. "He tried to take me to the cottages. Called me a stupid bitch. We fought. The dogs attacked him. I pushed him away, and he tripped. What do you mean, she's upstairs?" Romulus is still growling, lips pulled back from his teeth. "It's okay," she says quietly, touching his head. "Jack's on our side." The dog stops, but sits at attention.

"Harper is safe, Claire. I promise." His mind is roaring. "Was Gideon with Malcolm? Or were the two of you alone?"

"Just us. Why would he try to hurt me, Jack?"

"I don't know. I need to go...see. Can you stay here? Will you be okay for a few minutes?"

She nods, and he takes her into the library. Jack grabs a chenille throw from the back of the nearest sofa and wraps her in it. He moves her toward the fireplace, pulls a chair closer, gets her gently settled. He puts another throw over her legs, and Romulus lays at her feet, still on alert.

"Good boy. Claire, I'll be right back. Promise. Just stay here."

He hears someone speaking in the hall, and Will Compton comes into the library.

"What's going on here?" he says with a wink. "Hello, Claire." Will takes Claire's frozen hand and plants a chivalrous kiss on her knuckles. Jack relaxes a fraction. Will seems to be himself, even going so far as to remember Claire from their first meeting. What a damn relief.

"Jackson. How fortuitous that I've found you. Your mother just told me we're moving up the wedding."

Claire stirs from her nest. "What's this? What did he say?"

"Mom thought, in light of everything, we should go ahead with the ceremony instead of the rehearsal."

"Jack, no. We can't. Not now."

"Why not?" Will asks.

"Because people are dying around us! We need to get the hell off this island, that's what we need to do."

Jack can hear the anger building in her voice. So can Will. He drops to the sofa next to her and reaches for her hand again.

"Jackson, you go do what you need to do. Claire and I will chat a little." When he hesitates, Will says softly, "Go. We'll be fine. Petra is bringing up some tea. I wanted to spend some time by the fire—these rains make my bones hurt. Go on. We're fine."

Claire nods her assent. Her face is blank with shock. Jack has to take the risk that she will be safe with Will; he seems completely lucid, and Romulus is parked next to her, worshiping at her feet.

"Okay. It's all going to be okay, darling. I'll be right back."

Jack calls Gideon as he leaves the library. No answer. Where the hell is the man?

Gideon must still be handling the situation with Henna. The guards had been split up when Jack assigned Malcolm to guard Claire's every move.

Malcolm. The bastard. How dare he hurt Claire? He deserves to be dead.

The wind is whipping hard when he steps outside. Rain lashes his face. He puts an arm back inside and grabs an umbrella, but the wind is so intense it makes the rain blow sideways, so there's no point. Instead, he uses his arm to shelter his face and heads into the labyrinth.

He finds the gory scene after only a minute. The rain has washed away much of the blood, but Malcolm's sightless eyes are already clouded. The stake emerges from his throat like a pike.

Why would Malcolm turn on him like this? Why would he try to hurt Claire? And how many more have to die until Jack gets the message?

He's gotten it now. His life is fucking cursed. He thought, prayed, that he was going to be allowed the grace to start over. To be happy. But the universe clearly doesn't want that for him.

He tries Gideon again. And this time, he answers.

"Where the hell are you?"

"I just finished in the crypt."

"Malcolm is dead. He attacked Claire."

"What?"

"Just get up here. I'm in the labyrinth, near the cottages' entrance."

"Jack?"

Elliot stands at the edge of the path, sheltering under a black golf umbrella. Jack stashes his phone in his pocket, wary of the timing of Elliot's intrusion.

"Elliot. What are you doing?"

"Getting away from Amelia, who is moping around the Villa like her cat died. God, I cannot wait to be rid of that woman. Why, what—" He spies Malcolm's feet. "Jesus, Jack. What have you done?"

"It wasn't me, asshole. He went after Claire. She pushed him, he fell. She's inside with Gran freaking out. I needed to come see."

"Damn." Elliot taps his toe on the edge of the stake. Malcolm's head wiggles in agreement.

"You didn't hear anything, did you? A struggle?"

"No. I was down the hill."

They stand in silence, staring at the body.

"Well, Jack, unless you've changed your mind and want to call it all off, I suggest you get a move on. Let Gideon and Karmen clean up this mess."

"I will never understand what you have against Claire. What has she done to upset you?"

"God, Jack, give it a rest. I'm just soured on marriage in general right now."

Possibly true. "For what it's worth, I'm sorry I punched you."

A flash of teeth—his brother is amused. "Naw, don't worry about it. I deserved it. I shouldn't have said anything about Morgan. I know she's a sore subject for you. And I know it's been hard on you. But trust me, you're so much better off without her. She was a wreck. You deserved better. We all did."

There's something in Elliot's voice that makes Jack's radar go off. He sounds almost…hurt.

You deserved better. We all did.

A low vibration starts in Jack's gut.

"Elliot. Is there something you need to tell me?"

Elliot tips back the umbrella and looks to the sea. "Nothing that matters, Jackson. There's no undoing the past."

"Elliot, what happened the night Morgan died?"

"Oh, God, are we really doing this now? You were there. You know. Bitch deserved it, anyway, after what she did."

Elliot starts away, and Jack grabs his arm.

"What the fuck, El? 'Bitch deserved it?' Morgan deserved to fall off the cliff?"

Elliot shakes his head. "You still don't know, do you? My God, Jack. I had no idea you were so naive. She was screwing anything that moved."

Jack stills, his hand dropping from his brother's arm.

"What did you just say?"

"Oh, don't get all choir boy on me. You heard me."

"And you know this, how?"

Elliot doesn't answer.

"No. No way. You didn't. Tell me you didn't."

Elliot shrugs, finally looking faintly ashamed. "We were drunk. After the Foundation party in San Marino. You had to leave for a meeting. We were bored. One thing led to another."

"Oh, and that makes it okay? I had to go run our company, so you slept with my fiancée? You're full of shit. Morgan didn't touch alcohol or drugs. She didn't like being out of control. She didn't even have champagne at our wedding."

Elliot laughs uncomfortably. "Jack. Did you know the woman at all?"

"I did, unfortunately. You might have been drunk, but she was not. If this is remotely true, she used the hell out of you. So according to you, she cheated on me, that's why she deserved to die?"

"You're taking this well," Elliot says.

"Answer the fucking question, Elliot."

"Fine. Is this what you want to hear? Morgan was manipulative and dangerous. She had eyes for me, had eyes for Dad, had eyes for Gran. She would have screwed Tyler if he'd been into it. She would screw Gideon if he was into it. She would have screwed the dogs if they could get her what she wanted. Are you understanding me yet? She wasn't who you thought. Not by a long shot."

Oh, Jack knew Morgan. He knew her inside and out. In his darkest moments, he'll even admit to himself that he's happy she's dead.

"You didn't think you should warn me? Hell, you claim she was screwing around on me, yet you stood by my side as I married her?"

"Mom thought I should stay quiet."

"Mom? Mom knows?"

Elliot shakes his head. "Do you think I'm a total idiot? Not about that. I just told her I thought Morgan might have been playing it fast and loose. I would have said something if I thought it was important. I figured you'd get bored and divorce her soon enough."

"Well, you took care of that for me, didn't you? Your actions that night helped her right on over the wall. You son of a bitch."

"You have your version of the truth, Jack. Why do you need another?"

Jack lunges toward Elliot. Gideon chooses this moment to burst onto the scene, coming around the edge of the boxwoods at speed. He nimbly avoids Jack, but gets between the two brothers. Spying his partner's body, he grimaces.

Elliot laughs bitterly. "Your savior arrives. And your guests await, brother. Go play the doting bridegroom. I won't tell a soul what's happened here. But be warned. Someone else might."

Jack holds up a finger to Gideon, speaks low to his brother. "Elliot. We are not finished."

"We were finished a long time ago, Jack. Time for you to step aside and let me take care of business."

Elliot laughs as he walks away, the black umbrella spinning in the rain.

"What the ever-loving fuck happened?" Gideon asks.

"Help me carry him. I'll tell you inside."

"Elliot—"

"Let him go. We need to get Malcolm's body to the crypt. I left Claire with Will in the library and I don't want things to go south there, too."

"Forgive me for saying this, boss, but your brother is a first-class dick."

"I'm starting to see that," Jack says, moving to heft Malcolm's inert body. "This one, too. When did he turn? Has he been acting strangely?"

Gideon nods. "He has, actually. He said he was considering quitting a couple of weeks ago. Said he couldn't take the pressure. I assumed he meant our work—we've been burning the midnight oil lately, just like you. I told him I could pick up the slack, but he should talk to you, STAT. If he was doing something wrong…"

"You should have told me. I trusted him with Claire. And he has to be the one who killed Henna. He must be working with this Eister woman."

"That's a safe bet. Boss, I am so sorry. I didn't see it, but I take full responsibility."

"We'll discuss this later. For now, let's get this mess cleaned up."

Malcolm's body is wrestled free of the stake, and Jack is thankful for the heavy rain, which washes the blood away, into the wet ground. They make it down the hill to the external entrance to the basements that hold the crypt. Jack puts a hand on the biometric pad. They maneuver Malcolm inside, and Jack drops the heavy inert legs to the dirt floor.

"We'll deal with this shithead later. Is there anything else I need to know about? Have you been approached by anyone?"

"No, sir."

"Would you tell me if you had?"

Gideon starts to sputter and Jack holds up a hand. "Okay. I had to ask. I don't know who's on my side anymore. Karmen's still with us, yes?"

"Absolutely. She's always been devoted to your dad, and the family. I'll tell her about Malcolm. She's not going to be happy."

Jack digs in Malcolm's pocket and brings out his phone. "Any idea what his passcode is?"

"Try 20210611. We rotate them daily based on the date. Secure but easy to remember."

Jack inputs the numbers into the keypad and the phone unlocks.

The phone casts a strange blue light in the dark space. Jack goes to Malcolm's text messages, which are empty. His email doesn't have anything weird, either. But the recent call list has a single number. It's a 212 area code—New York. Could it really be this easy?

Jack presses the number and puts the phone on speaker as it connects.

On the fifth ring, a female voice answers brusquely. "Is it done?"

"No," Jack says. "It's just beginning."

58

Leverage

For the record, Elliot was a terrible lay.

I only fucked him to get back at Jack, after he blew me off at the Foundation party, though of course I had no intention of Jack ever finding out. It was a little silent leverage I had. A girl always needs some leverage, right?

I didn't expect Elliot to develop feelings. I didn't expect him to fall in love.

Idiot.

He had to make things complicated. Panted after me like a puppy, calling, texting, when can I see you again, you're amazing, blah, blah, blah. He even tried to corner me in a bathroom at my wedding, tried to stick his tongue down my throat. I want you, I love you, you should have married me.

As if.

I had to push him away and he stumbled backward into the lounge sofa and went down, hard.

"Never, ever, touch me again, do you understand?"

No, Elliot didn't take rejection well.

He got his revenge.

Soon it will be time for mine.

59

Some Grandfatherly Advice

"Let me get you a drink," Will says, and I nod in agreement. There is a large globe near the window to my left, which he cracks opens to reveal a cleverly hidden drinks cart, replete with crystal decanters and thick-bottomed crystal glasses. He pours without asking my preference and returns with two whiskies, neat.

"Oban Little Bay. My favorite," he says.

I accept mine and take a deep sip, coughing and sputtering a bit at the intense liquor.

"Slow down, dear. It's meant to be savored. If you blow into it a bit, like this—" he puts the glass to his lips and puffs into it gently "—then take a sniff, then take some on your tongue and let it sit, then swallow and breathe out, you'll enjoy it more."

"Is it that obvious I don't drink Scotch?"

"Yet. You don't drink Scotch *yet*. After this, you will. It's all about knowing how to enjoy it."

I follow his lead and suddenly, instead of sharp spirits, I smell caramel and peat and salt and rain. I take another, more cautious sip, and he's right, it does taste good.

"Fascinating trick."

"I'm surprised Jackson hasn't taught you already."

"I've always been more of a wine girl."

We sit together, he and I, by the fire, with our drinks, with the storm screaming at the windows, my hair curling wildly from the soaking. My heart rate drops, and I draw my legs up onto the chair, cradling the drink between my knees and my body. Romulus whines once, in question, and I rub his ears. He is wet, too. Poor guy. Remus has wandered over to the fire, is toasting himself dry. "Go on. Go get dry."

I swear the dog understands me, he pads to the rug and joins his brother, shaking himself once to rid the exterior of his fur of water.

"Remarkable. I've never seen him be so protective of anyone before."

"They saved my life in the labyrinth."

"You were worth saving," Will says quietly, then cracks a grin that makes him seem much younger than his years. "Though Fatima is going to be livid when she sees the mud on these rugs. The dogs aren't allowed in the house, you know."

"They are now," I say.

Will watches me for a moment. "I daresay you're right."

The fire is hypnotic, dancing and crackling. It could be now, it could be a moment ago, ten years ago, a thousand years…the same grate, the same wood, the same fire has warmed the people of the Villa forever. I sink further into the chair, my body finally relaxing.

Safe. I am safe.

I'm so used to the silences of the Compton men that when Jack's grandfather asks, quite conversationally, "So Claire? What secrets are you hiding from my grandson?" I blurt out the truth and he doesn't blink an eye.

"I killed my father."

I've never spoken of the night my father died. I didn't tell my mother. My sister. My friends. I certainly haven't told Jack.

But Will Compton sits to my right in the dim light, ready to hear my confession.

"Tell me," he says softly. And I do.

The party was loud. Raucous. So much fun. Shane scored some Molly and gave me a double dose. I was crawling all over him soon enough, which made him happy. For a while. After an hour, he got tired of my frisky sloppiness and dumped me onto the couch next to a couple of his Hillsboro friends, who were more than happy to let me coo and pet them. Everything was perfect. Everything was right in the world. I was present, and they were present, and we were present together.

Someone gave me a beer. I didn't like the taste, even then, but I drank it. It mellowed me out, so I was able to sit on the couch and stare into space.

And then Shane decided it was time to go.

I didn't want to leave. I don't know that I could have walked, I was so fixated on the couch, but he grabbed my hand and dragged me upright.

I put my arms around his neck and kissed him, but he was in a bad mood and pushed me away. I don't know what had gone wrong with his evening, but mine was great, I was rolling hard, and had no desire to be put off.

I still remember the pain when he grabbed my ponytail and yanked. "We're leaving now. I want a fucking Coke and they don't have anything but this pansy diet shit."

I didn't have enough room, or energy, to fight. He dragged me to the car, and we got in.

There are parts of the night that I don't remember. But this part I do. Shane was in rare form, ranting, frantic. Someone had screwed him over, reneged on paying for their drugs, leaving him dangerously short. He had to pay it up the line that night, or he faced "consequences." Even I, in my stupor, knew what that meant. A broken leg, a broken arm. If he showed up short, his distributor was going to take it very badly. I'd met the guy once, and trust me, he was terrifying.

But Shane had a plan. "We'll take it from your parents. Your dad will have money at his office."

I recall the intense alarm at that idea. I may have been a fuckup, but I wasn't stupid enough to jeopardize my already-precarious relationship with my parents like that. I was perfectly happy getting high on Shane's dime, but I wasn't willing to steal from my family for him. Besides, my head still hurt from his mistreatment of my hair, and I had a massive bruise on my bicep. I wasn't feeling generous.

"He doesn't. It's Saturday. They would have taken everything to the bank last night."

"We'll go by your house, then."

"Shane, there's no money there, either."

"Then get your fucking ATM card out, bitch."

The bank haul was meager, two hundred measly dollars. He needed upward of two thousand.

He yelled at me then, how I was ruining his life, how I was responsible for…well, everything that was bad in his world. I tried to get out of the car, and he pulled me back in and took off, driving erratically. We made it all the way out Highway 70 to Bellevue when he remembered his vital need for a Coke. He pulled into the Mapco. Threatened to kill me if I got out of the car. He left it running. He always left the car running when he went into a store. I thought it was dangerous, but whatever. It was his thing.

He wasn't in his right mind that night, I testified to that.

Though the word of a screwed up fifteen-year-old was hardly enough to sway the jury in his favor.

He came out of the store at a run, shouting, "Drive, drive, drive!"

I remember his eyes, flared so wide I could see the blood-shot whites around his brown irises. He looked like one of the hounds of hell I'd seen in one of my mythology books. Slavering at the jaw and utterly enraged.

I scooted over to the driver seat and he dove inside.

"Go, for fuck's sake. Go to 40."

The interstate was a mile west of the Mapco. There was only one problem. I didn't know how to drive. I hadn't even gotten my learner's permit yet. Add in sheer panic, a beer, two doses of Molly, and an irate boyfriend?

I put it in Reverse, gunned it, and backed straight into the dumpster. He howled in fury at me and slammed it into Drive. "Drive, now." That's when I realized he had his gun out, and it was currently pointed at me.

"Did you rob the Mapco?"

"What do you think? Drive."

We didn't make it far. The police nailed us by the Taco Bell, and despite Shane's screams to gun it, I took my foot off the gas. We coasted to a stop against the curb, and they were on us moments later. Honestly, I was relieved. Shane was out of control; who knows where the night was taking us.

Shane wrestled with them like a prize fighter, but a quick jab with the Taser had him down on the pavement a heartbeat later.

I stood and shook, tears coursing down my face. The car was mangled. I was still high as fuck and terrified into silence. The policeman wasn't gentle when he slapped the cuffs on me and shoved me into the back of his cruiser. It was fear that made my adrenaline rush so hard it blotted out my memories. But I did hear the word *arrest* before I passed out in the back of the car, sitting awkwardly on my hands.

Then my dad was there.

They called him.

He came for me.

It was three in the morning and he came without a moment's hesitation. The policeman took the cuffs off me and I heard him talking quietly to my dad. I caught only a bit of it, but the gist was Shane told them he kidnapped me from the party.

I will never, ever understand why he lied for me.

My dad got me settled in the car, gentle as an egg, putting the safety belt across my body and latching it without a word. When he climbed in, he said, "Claire. What did you take?"

"Nothing."

"You want to try telling me the truth, for once?"

"Fine. Some Molly. It's no big deal. Everyone was doing it."

"Are you going to be sick in my car?"

"No."

Though I did feel sick, the remnants of the adrenaline rush ready to spill from my pores.

"Did that boy hurt you?"

He was looking at the livid red bruise on my arm, and I tucked it to my body and stared out the window. The patrol car bearing Shane was pulling out, and he didn't look my way, not even once. "It's fine. It's nothing."

My father didn't speak anymore, only started the car and put it carefully in gear. He didn't speak until we were nearly home.

"Your mother and I have decided you're going to rehab. It's the best thing for you to do."

"Since when do you and Mom talk?" I spit out, my fear abating in the face of anger and something else, a combination of hope and humiliation. Rehab meant I could get away from Shane and get straight, the former of which was appealing, but rehab also meant leaving all my friends and having the stigma of a recovery center forever in my past. No. No!

"I won't go. You can't make me."

"Claire. You've been acting out for months now. You've been expelled from school, you're covered in tattoos and piercings, you're doing drugs and God knows what else. Your mother and I don't recognize you anymore. You've been hurting yourself. No one else. But tonight…no, my little girl, you crossed the line. I don't know what really happened with you and that greasy jerk back there, but he robbed that Mapco, with a weapon, and you were driving the car. He has drugs on his person, and you're clearly messed up. You've given us no choice. The police are being rather generous, I think, not just hauling you downtown. It's rehab or jail, and I think you'll enjoy rehab much more."

"Fuck off."

He looked over at me, the shock and hurt rippling across his face, and I felt at once ashamed, so ashamed, and emboldened. If he had been stronger, Mom wouldn't have fucked some other guy. If he'd paid more attention to all of us instead of his precious patients, they wouldn't be getting divorced. If…if…if…

I screamed all of this at him, followed it up with "I hate you. I hate you. I hate you!" for good measure, reached for the wheel of the car, and—

I wipe the tears from my cheeks.

"And that's all I remember. When I woke up, in the hospital, he was dead, and I was broken."

"And you've never healed, have you," Will says, reaching over to pat my knee. "You've carried this for so long. You poor girl."

I get that ridiculous feeling of outrage and unease that accompanies any show of pity for my plight. I don't deserve pity. I never have. I killed my father. I deserve hell.

"I'll always carry it. It's my fault he's dead. I killed him. I think I was trying to kill myself. I never thought it would take him instead."

Will nods, slowly, sadly. "Ah, but look at you now. You learned a very hard lesson, and you changed. You altered the course of your life, by choice. Many, many young women would have plummeted, would have been dragged into the abyss. But you didn't. You showed great courage, my girl. It takes grit to change.

"And now you're a celebrated painter. About to be married. You know he's looking down on you, so happy that you're happy. It's all any father wants for his child. Trust me. Brice said some terrible things to me growing up. I knew he didn't mean it, not really. Something you need to remember, though. As a Compton, there will be extra scrutiny on you. Perhaps even judgment. But it's your heart that matters. Follow your heart, young Claire. It will never steer you wrong."

I swallow the last of the Scotch. It's strong, and I'm feeling lightheaded.

"You're kind to listen. I appreciate it. And the advice."

When Will Compton smiles, it's easy to see how he charmed half of Europe. "You're my granddaughter now, dear. You can talk to me about anything."

I don't know what makes me say it, but the words are out before I have a chance to think.

"Tell me about Morgan. Tell me how she died."

"I think that's my story to tell," Jack says, stepping into the library.

60

The Truth, at Last

"Jackson!"

Will seems so happy to see his grandson I can't help but smile, though it quickly flees when I see Jack's face. He looks as thunderous as the sky.

"Everything okay?" Will asks, clearly sensing the mood.

"No." Jack pours himself two fingers of Oban. He offers to top off mine, but I shake my head. I'm feeling quite warm enough, thank you. Warm, but…lighter. Alcohol always has loosened my tongue. Confessing, even to an old man who will probably forget all I've said or twist it around, has helped me. I've never spoken the words aloud: *I killed my father.* I feel shriven.

Eventually, I will be able to say the rest.

I killed Shane.

I killed Malcolm.

But for now, admitting to my first murder is enough.

Jack tosses back the Scotch. "No, things are not okay. But I hope we're at least on the path to normalcy. Did you two have a nice visit?"

"We did," Will says. "And now I sense it's time to leave you alone." He rises, slowly, with a small groan. "Don't get old, Jack my boy. It's a pain in the ass."

Will takes my hand. His blue eyes are sad, but he smiles. "My dear. It's well past time for you to stop punishing yourself. Let it go." He pats my hands sweetly, and takes his leave.

"What was that about?" Jack asks.

"I'm afraid your grandfather got me drunk and I confessed all my sins. It's a tragedy that he's suffering from dementia. He's a kind, dynamic man. I wish I'd gotten to know him sooner."

"I wish you had, too. He is a great guy." Jack settles into the chair his grandfather vacated. "Sins, is it?"

Oh, Jack. You have no idea.

"First, what happened out there? Did you... Is Malcolm's body gone?"

"Yes."

"Is that why you look so fearsome?"

"Actually no. I had a bit of a tiff with my dick of a brother. Elliot," he adds, unnecessarily. I know he doesn't mean Tyler, who is the sweetest and worships Jack's very being.

"Want to tell me about it?"

He sighs. "I think I have to. Because I'm starting to believe my brother killed Morgan."

I listen, incredulous at first, then with a general wariness, as Jack talks of his former wife for the first time.

"I hardly know where to begin."

Why did you love her? Why did you choose her? Was it her red hair, her sky eyes, her talent, her voice? The way she made you feel? Will I ever be enough?

Though I already know the answer, I settle for, "Start at the beginning. Tell me about your first meeting."

"We were at a cocktail party, in Tiburon. We were both on the back deck, staring over the bay. The wind was blowing, her hair was flying around in the breeze and she didn't move to capture it. It whipped around and she looked wild, and free, and lovely, and so alone, and I fell, hard. I found out later that she had just gotten a massive round of VC funding and was celebrating. We didn't talk much about the important things. We simply started hanging out, and she was beguiling.

"I found out after it was all a ploy. She knew I was going to be at this party. She positioned herself so I would notice her. She wanted an in to Compton. She wanted my father to buy her out. Which, for the record, he did. She could have taken that money and retired on the spot, but for some reason, she wanted to stay in the game. By that time, she decided she wanted me, too.

"I was flattered. She was stunningly gorgeous, and smart, and charming in the way only a true sociopath can be. But she was deeply, deeply disturbed. More so than I ever knew."

He stands and moves to the shelves behind me. I watch as he pulls out a thick old book. He opens the cover and out comes a slim notebook. "I found this after she died. I kept it... I don't know why I kept it. Maybe to remind myself. You know how the memory of terrible things tends to lessen over time? I didn't want to forget. I didn't want to make the same mistake twice."

He hands it to me. The notebook is worn, well used. I flip open the cover. The handwriting is tiny, cramped, so dark on the page that it seems impossible that the paper didn't rip under the weight of the pen scratching across it.

It doesn't take me long to ascertain that the writer is disturbed beyond reason. In the way of all genius, most of what I'm reading makes a certain kind of sense, but then it drops off the edge of reason into clear insanity.

J was out late again last night. He swears he was working, but I know he is lying. Surveillance to begin tomorrow.

Will use 4G Spark nano GPS tracker, adapt with extended battery—no reason to think this behavior will change anytime soon. If I find him under the moon, I will kill him. If I find him under the sun I will not.

Surveillance commenced. Laid in a bridge to his T1 line that allows for a wired keystroke analysis. He bears watching. He mustn't be trusted.

40,000 years ago, paintings in Chauvet Cave—did they know what was coming? Were they prepared for their extinction? Did they have one last party before they died, dancing around the fire naked and leering? Insert 6. They are watching again.

I watch him when he sleeps. Wonder what it would feel like to slip the edge of a dagger into that spot where his heartbeat pounds at the skin. To see the blood purl through the opening in his skin. What does he taste like inside?

J not cheating so far as I can tell. His nocturnal ramblings are simply running errands for B. GPS track shows straight lines between 500 and 1500 longitudinally aspect ratio. What happens on the jet stays on the jet. Flower agate is needed.

It goes on and on like this, page after page, some entries rational, some jumbled, convoluted remarks and observations that would make sense only to the writer. Threats of violence against Jack, his family, even herself.

"She doesn't seem to be in her right mind," I say, flipping the pages.

The book falls open. The spine is broken here, and an entry halfway through catches my eye. It has been circled, again and again and again, the swirls wild and fierce, and here the paper *has* been torn by the pressure of the pen.

> *Darling darling darling darling darling darling you will miss me when I'm gone fuck you DARLING.*

I finally look up, confused. "There was a note, earlier. I totally forgot to ask you about it. In the vanity, in the bath. It said 'Don't you miss me, darling?'"

"See? This is all too weird. I'm telling you, Claire, I think this might be Elliot's doing. Screwing with us. Trying to disrupt the wedding. Trying to chase you off."

"But why? I don't understand."

"I don't know. Because I'm trying to get out of the business? Because I'm finally happy? Because he's sick in the head? Because Amelia is divorcing him? Because he had a thing for Morgan, and he's upset she's dead? Because he killed her and it might be about to come out, so he's making it look like we're crazy? Damned if I know."

Because by marrying Jack, I will take a third of his estate? And that means less for Elliot in the long run? Surely, he's not that greedy. Though this kind of money is worth killing for.

"He hit on me, you know. At his wedding. He was bombed, and cornered me. I pushed him away."

Jack is looking at me as if I've just given him the scroll to decipher the Rosetta Stone.

"Wow. He's an even bigger asshole than I thought. He screwed around with Morgan, too. Though she took him up on it, apparently."

"Oh. That's…awkward." I close the notebook and set it on the table next to me. "Why would Elliot want to hurt you like that? You're his brother."

"God knows."

"Why would he want to hurt Henna? And what would he

have to do with Malcolm, who was *your* security? I mean, Malcolm was clearly trying to drag me off somewhere. Were they in league together, and he was taking me to Elliot? So he could do what to me?"

"I don't know. Before she died, Morgan was trying to blackmail the family. She'd been spying on me, on Elliot, and figured out how our business arrangements worked. When she signed the NDA, I thought that meant we were safe. But on our honeymoon, I found some correspondence. She'd been mapping everything out. You can see from the notebook she was surveilling me. I found her electronic footprints all over my computer, my phone, my car—she'd put a GPS tracker in my wheel well."

He takes a huge breath, spikes a hand through his hair. Little droplets of water splash on the hearth and rise as tiny fragments of fog, and the dogs watch him intently.

"I need to know it all. I need to know the truth of what happened to Morgan."

I feel his body tense beside me. "Claire, I'm not sure I know the whole truth."

"Then go back to California. The story is she fell off your boat, was swept away. She died at sea. That's not true, is it?"

"No. She didn't go off the boat in California. That's what we told the media. She disappeared from here. From the island. We came here for a family meeting. It didn't go well. She made her threats, and then she ran out into the night. There was a terrible storm, like now. We split up to look for her, and somehow, she went off the cliff."

Jack's face is tortured and he's babbling his confession now, talking so fast I can hardly follow.

"My mother and Elliot were there. Fatima and Will, too. They were all staring over the edge, and the rain was pouring down, and we couldn't see her. I can't even tell you the horror I felt. Claire, I heard her screaming as she fell. She was screaming my name. I got a boat and searched all night. I thought she'd been dragged out to sea. There was no way she could have survived. The storm was terrible, the waves were ten feet high. I barely made it back to land myself. And I grieved. I grieved for years."

"And you lied for years. Why? Why not tell the truth?"

He shoots the last of his Scotch, laughs mirthlessly. "I just wanted to protect the family. If Morgan died in California with me instead of Isola with all of us, I would be the only one at risk. With one small detail changed, the family was protected. I knew Morgan had no one who would question our story. That the police could be bought if necessary. And I was right. No one cared about the details. No one cared but me.

"And then I met you. And Claire, you have to believe me. If I could do it all over... I would have just let the truth come out and be damned with the consequences."

"How could you lie to me about this?"

"Darling, I have lied to everyone about this, for many, many years. I've had no choice."

A log in the fire rolls and bursts apart, shooting sparks onto the hearth. The dogs jump away from the hot embers, and Jack sweeps them back into the fire.

"Were you ever going to tell me the truth? Or is it with all these things, with Elliot perhaps trying to stop us marrying, you're being forced to tell me?"

"No. I have always wanted to tell you. I was just waiting for the appropriate moment." He breaks off, looks at his hands. "I understand if you don't want me anymore."

"I won't leave you because of it, if that's what you're worried about. I have a few deaths under my belt now, too."

I do. I've killed three men now. The first was the worst. By the third? Well, it wasn't easy, but it felt...familiar, in a hideous, awful way.

"But Jack, you have to swear to me, you will never lie to me, or omit, again. Will you give me your word?"

He gets down on one knee, like he did the night we were engaged, taking my hands in his. He looks me in the eye.

"I swear to you with my life, Claire, I will never lie to you. I didn't kill Morgan."

There is no doubt in my mind he's telling me the truth.

61

Liar

Liar.
    Liar, liar, liar, liar, liar.
    Don't let him fool you now.
    The last face I saw when I went over the wall was Jackson.
    And I take offense at his characterization. I am not disturbed.
    I am disruption.

62

The Blackmailer

I'm admittedly shocked. I really had wrapped my head around the idea that Jack was responsible for Morgan's death.

"I believe you."

"Thank you." He breathes out heavily in relief. The tension between us has dissipated, but I sense Jack isn't finished with his confessions.

"I wouldn't have had the patience to bring her here. I would have knocked her off the boat and let her drown."

Jack smiles ruefully at this. "Don't think I didn't want to. But I wasn't about to do something rash. I had no idea how much she actually knew at that point, nor what she'd done to secure her safety. I didn't know who she'd told. And I wasn't willing to go to jail over her."

This is a sentiment I understand fully.

"I believe you when you say you didn't kill her. But you have to admit, she died at a very convenient moment. What did she have on you?"

He takes the notebook gingerly, distaste on his face at even touching Morgan's madness again. "You need to know that once I tell you this, you're complicit. Our truth is the cost of marrying me."

"So why tell me, Jack? It is worth it? Am I worth it?"

"Yes. God, yes. I want to be happy, and I want you to be happy, and that means I need to share this with you, and if you decide to walk away, then I'll have to live with it. I'll let you go, though it will kill me to lose you."

I take his hand. "Jack. Just tell me. Trust me, at this point, there's not a lot that would be bad enough to chase me away."

He kisses me then, wild and unrestrained. "I love you, Claire."

"I love you, too. Now, for God's sake, tell me what the hell is going on?"

"All right. What Morgan was trying to blackmail us about— it's complicated. But in its purest form...we broker information. On the side. It's something that started well before me, or my dad. My great-grandfather was a spy in the war. Though he was an American, he had an allegiance to Churchill, and handed over as much information as he could that would help the Allies win the war. My grandmother Eliza worked with him, too. They had a good thing going, until she died. But William wasn't about to stop fighting, so he brought Will into the family business. That's how it happens, each son is brought in when the time is right. My grandfather was well positioned to gather information through the artistic community, and eventually, my dad saw ways to leverage technology to accomplish what couldn't be done by a person, face-to-face.

"There's essentially a back door written into all Compton software that can be opened if our partners need to see what's happening. It's clean, it's safe, and it's a very useful tool to stop powerful people from hurting innocents. I swear to you, that's all it's used for. None of our people are spying on your average Joe. It's only for international relations.

"But now, with the servers hacked—the servers where we hold this gathered information—we're vulnerable. Elliot is tied to this somehow. Someone might be trying to put pressure on him alone, and he's running scared. He won't tell us what he's done, but it will come out. Are you following?"

I follow. Prince Charming is a spy. This isn't the worst thing I could have heard, but I proceed with caution anyway, because now I'm starting to get it.

"What do I bring to the family table? I assume that's another reason why I signed the NDA?"

Jack nods, respect that I've grasped it so quickly mingling with dread on his face. "Your art. It opens doors into even more areas. Say we have a paranoid despot who has stopped communicating electronically. But he or she puts great stock in art. There are ways to rig up a painting with surveillance. It's not complicated. Only another avenue in."

This is insane. "Keep going. I'm still listening."

"Men with money have enemies. Enemies who will pay to gain an upper hand, to use leverage against them. It used to be different. It was more personal. Now, it's all driven by technology. Three minutes with a mark's cell phone and we have every keystroke we need to track his wrongdoings, gain access to his accounts, legal and otherwise.

"It's part of what I've been doing under the cover of the Foundation. I'm not proud of it, but if I can get close to someone who's taking advantage, who's going to harm people, I do. I know it sounds like I'm justifying breaking the law, but we are saving lives."

"But who decides who is the bad guy? If you're targeted because you don't go along with a government's decision, how do you know they're bad?"

"Trust me, I have a strong moral compass. I can tell who's bad. We only go after people who hurt people, darling."

I try to wrap my head around this.

"Claire? Say something."

"Is this why someone was spying on us in our own home? Could it be one of your enemies, trying to get back at you? Using me as leverage against you?"

"We don't know. I'd hoped Karmen would have a line into where the cameras were transmitting to by now. Malcolm was involved, obviously."

"He was willing to take the blame for me, though. For me shooting Shane."

"We will never know what he planned to do with that information, thank God."

"You hope. There's no way of knowing who has the video of that night, Jack."

"We'll figure it out. I swear it. It's all tied to Ami Eister. And Karmen is about to get an ID on her."

I finish the last bit of Scotch in my glass. I should be horrified. I should be storming out of the library. Instead, all I feel is…intrigued. This life with Jack won't be boring. And Ana…

"Your mom runs all of this, doesn't she?"

"She plays a large role. Yes."

I knew it. I knew Ana was more than she seemed. "How does it work, exactly? You get the information and you do what with it?"

"We turn the temperature up, we turn the temperature down. People respond. If they don't…"

"So, you're blackmailers."

"Not exactly."

"Yes, exactly."

"We are information brokers, Claire. That's all."

"Oh, so you need to carry a gun to broker information? Or to apply pressure when the 'temperature' isn't high enough. Admit it, Jack. You're no better than Shane, you just have more money."

"Claire." He winces at the insult, but I can't help it. Now that it's sinking in, I am so furious. How dare he not tell me this sooner? How dare he not trust me until now?

"How did you know I have a gun?"

"Jack. I'm not stupid. I can see the outline under your shirt. And the ankle holster is kind of a dead giveaway."

He takes the gun from the small of his back.

I hold out my hand. "May I?"

He frowns but racks the slide, popping the bullet from the chamber, then ejects the magazine and flips the gun around, handing it to me gingerly, butt first.

The metal is warm from his skin, the grip rough in my palm. I gesture toward the magazine. Curiosity crosses his face, but he hands it over. Brave of him, considering that once the gun is loaded, I could just pull the trigger.

Taking the magazine, I finger the open edge, feeling the hard brass of the bullets. Then I look up at Jack, meet his beautiful eyes, slam the magazine in place and rack the slide, chambering a bullet. I reverse the motions immediately, catch the bullet ejected from the slide in my hand.

All without looking away.

"Claire?"

I sigh and turn the weapon back over to him.

"Okay, Jack. You were honest with me. Now it's my turn to be honest with you."

It was Shane, of course. He forced me into it. I didn't want to have anything to do with his drug business, except to take them and disappear from the pain of my life for a while. But nothing comes free, does it?

He used me as a runner. Carrying drugs and money came with bona fide danger. When one of his less savory friends roughed me up one night, stealing both the stash and the cash, he decided I needed to carry a gun to ward off any more robberies.

This was before things turned south, before the night he robbed the Mapco and I killed my father. This was back when he was small-time, before he went full on gangster badass working for MS-13.

I was a terrible shot, but I loved the heft of the weapon he gave me. It made me feel strong, invincible. If I couldn't shoot someone with it, I could clock them across the nose, and that would work, too.

But the rules were the rules, and he wouldn't let me carry it until I knew how to use it. He made me practice. Over and over and over, until I could wake from a dead sleep and have a bullet chambered in seconds flat.

I was his backup, he used to say. He sweet little backup plan. The one no one would ever see coming. Until I became his biggest liability.

"You asked me if Shane ever hurt me. Of course he did. If I smiled wrong, he'd smack me. If I lost the stash, he'd kick me. If I upset him in any way…well, you get the idea."

"You got caught, though. Eventually."

"Yes. He had me driving the night he robbed the Mapco. He had a gun on me, there were drugs in his pocket, and more in the trunk. But I was a juvenile, and when we got pulled over, he said, 'Follow my lead.'

"The cops thought I'd been taken hostage. And that was the story we stuck with. Even when I sat across from him in the courtroom, testifying, looking him in the eye, he nodded and smirked at me to keep me going with the lie. So, I did. I told them he grabbed me from the party, forced me into the car, and they believed it."

"He loved you."

"Maybe. He treated me like shit on the bottom of his shoe, but in the end, he sacrificed himself for me. He went to jail, and I got my shit straight. He gave me a chance to turn my life around. I did."

"Oh, Claire. That breaks my heart. You were so young."

"But it made me who I am."

For some reason, I don't feel the need to tell him about my father right now. I will later. I will when I get to the bottom of things.

He's quiet for a few moments.

"Are you... I mean, do you...do you still want to marry me, Claire?"

I get up and move to him, sit in his lap, put my arms around his neck.

"Yes. I do. Even though I'm furious with you for not telling me sooner, I do believe you're trying to do the right thing, Jack. I do."

"That's a relief. Because I don't know what happens next. Whoever is behind this, whoever is posing as Ami Eister, knows everything and is trying to take the family down. She hired McGowan to plant the cameras. Hacked our servers and tried to release the information to the press through your sister. What's in those files—this story that was almost picked up—it would be the end of the family, do you understand? If Elliot is behind this, if he hired this woman to pretend to be Ami Eister... I can't wrap my head around it. I fear Henna realized what was happening and was killed before she could rat him out."

"That doesn't make sense though, Jack. Elliot already has access to all of the incriminating information. Why would he... oh. He's trying to make it look like you are responsible."

He nods. "That's exactly what I'm afraid of. He's trying to sell me out."

"What are you going to do about Elliot? If he is trying to hurt you..."

"I'm going to do the one thing that will piss him off the most. Marry you. If you'll still have me, that is."

"I will. But why do we have to do it here? Why don't you quit the family business, and we can elope? Run away. To hell with all of this, and all of them."

His smile is luminous.

"I couldn't agree more. But we don't have to elope. If you're still up for it, darling, then you need to get dressed. Put on whatever you'd like, and let's get married."

I feel a spark of anxiety. "Is that such a good idea? Considering what's happened?"

Considering I still have Malcolm's blood under my fingernails?

"Now. Mom's been putting everything in place to make it happen. Claire, I want you protected in case something goes wrong. In case Karmen can't trace this woman. In case Elliot does try to do something stupid."

My God. The aftermath of this woman is incredible. Ten years later, and Morgan is still poison to this family.

"Okay. Let's do it. It's never been about the big, crazy wedding for me anyway, Jack. I just want you."

"I know. I love you, Claire."

He kisses me, then walks me up the stairs to our room. He retrieves his tux, and says, "I'll see you downstairs, my love."

The door closes behind him with a gentle thunk, and I am alone.

63

Little Silences

Jack and I always have had little silences between us. Safe places where we can both retreat. We'd both been broken by our pasts and that's probably what brought us together so tightly. The commonality of it, the comfort in knowing we'd each had a great loss, suffered great pain.

I wonder if that's why Henna had insisted on a reading from Genesis for the ceremony: *Therefore, shall a man leave his father and his mother, and shall cleave unto his wife: and they shall be one flesh.* I wonder if she knew. Or at least suspected.

Our silences grew from two bent trees into a forest that provided shelter and safety.

I should have asked. He should have asked. But we spent so much time respecting each other's emotional limits that we never got to the heart of the things that mattered.

Jack didn't talk about his wife, so I didn't talk about my father, or Shane, or my former drug habit, nor why I got my tattoos.

Jack didn't talk about his wife, and I kept my simmering rage at being his second choice to myself.

Jack didn't talk about his wife, and I didn't question him about why.

I realize now that if Jack had told me he killed his wife, I would have told him I killed my father. We would have been murderers together. We would have cleaved together with our biggest secrets.

Instead, I will suffer alone. I guess that's marriage though, isn't it? You can only cleave together so much.

64

Only You

It was dumb of me to go out in the rain. Not only did I manage to kill someone, it ruined my beautifully done hair and now I'll have to do it myself.

But Harper and Katie are in my room, waiting for me, when I get out of the shower. They're both dressed in their elegant sea mist bridesmaid gowns, so beautiful a lump forms in my throat.

"Ana told us what's happened," Harper says. "Let's get you dressed. We can figure everything else out later."

I don't tell them what went down with Malcolm. I don't tell them what Jack has shared about Morgan. I will be locked in my own silence about the family forevermore, but I want Jack badly enough to make that trade.

It surprises me, this passion for someone who is clearly not what he seems. But I sense he's now told me the truth, at least all that he can, and that's enough for me.

Honestly, he could have told me he slaughtered Morgan with

a paring knife, and I would still love him. It's not like I'm an innocent in all of this. It's not like I'm perfect.

As they get started, I ask them, "Did anyone ever get in touch with either of you about me? A reporter, say, or a stranger?"

"What do you mean?" Katie asks.

"You said earlier that this was the wedding of the century. I just wondered if someone said that to you, or if you thought it yourself."

"You know there were articles written about the wedding, Claire. Remember the one in *Nashville Edit* that welcomed Jack to Nashville and gushed about how you two were going to be the society couple of the year? It's all anyone was talking about that week."

"Seriously?"

"Girl, you are so dense sometimes. How can you not see these things? Do you never Google yourself?"

The vision almost makes me laugh, almost, though it is not me I'm searching for online, it is my predecessor.

"God, no. I know plenty about myself, thank you very much. Why, have you Googled me?"

"Of course, I have." I must have looked aghast because Katie laughs. "I Google you, me, Harper, Jack, Taylor Swift, Chris Evans, the Kardashians. Like the rest of the free world. There were a ton of stories about your wedding. It was the hottest ticket in town. How can you not know this?"

"Because I knew we were only having the closest friends and family. It didn't seem important."

"Why are you asking all this, Claire?" Harper asks.

"I'm curious how much this Ami Eister imposter could have learned from what was in the public domain versus what she could get from spying directly. Don't worry, it's not important."

Harper looks radiant in her dress; the color is perfect for her. She seems chagrined, and I know she's got to be wildly embarrassed by her actions.

"Can I help?"

I am determined to let bygones be bygones. I smile, and hold out my hand, which she crosses the room and takes. "Could you fix my hair? It's kind of a disaster."

"Curls, or straight?"

"Curls are fine. Just sweep it up, out of my eyes."

I let them play with my hair, my makeup, until Harper steps back and nods.

"Perfect. You look lovely. Now. What about the dress?"

"I think I should just wear the one I brought for the rehearsal," I say, but I'm met with a chorus of "Noooooooos."

I look to Harper. She pulls out both dresses, has me hold the pink dress and Katie the wedding gown. "The pink is pretty, but it's very slinky, more of a cocktail dress for sure. If it were me, I'd wear the wedding dress. It is gorgeous. And much more bridal. I think Jack would be happy to have you in a wedding gown after all this, don't you? I know it's not yours, but it is very appropriate for a wedding."

"All right. I still feel weird wearing a stranger's dress. But if you think Jack would prefer it, I'll do it."

The pink dress is replaced in the wardrobe, and they get me into the mermaid dress. I really am indebted to Fatima for loaning it to me. Happily, the heady smell of camphor has lessened. She tucked sachets of lavender and rosemary into the bodice and now it smells like the gardens outside before the rain.

"And now for the piece de resistance," Harper says, and places the diaphanous veil on my headpiece, securing it. She lifts the edges and smooths them down the back of the dress. The veil is cathedral length and made of a soft silk tulle that draws around my body like a cloud. At least this part of my costume wasn't ruined. I loved it the moment I saw it, the blusher edged in thinnest satin that goes to my waist, the train that trails nine feet behind me. This is the only time in my life I'm going to wear something so outrageously romantic, and I'm planning to enjoy it to the hilt.

I feel a bit lightheaded. "Oof. I need to sit down for a second."

Harper pushes aside the train and I sit down carefully. The girls step away into the bedroom. They know me. They know I'm just feeling a bit overwhelmed. I stare at myself in the mirror for a few minutes. This is it. There's no turning back. I'm marrying into a gang of thieves, in a stranger's dress, and I'm okay with that.

"Everything all right, Claire?" Harper calls. "They're waiting."

"Yeah. Give me a second, okay? I went from zero to sixty with a glass of Scotch and I haven't had anything but tea since brunch."

Harper comes to the door with a roll of butterscotch lifesavers. "Here. Have two, your blood sugar is probably low."

I take the candy and suck on it, savoring the creamy sweetness.

"Yum. Butterscotch is my favorite."

"I know." Harper twists her hands in front of her. "Listen, I need to tell you something. I sort of blew it earlier. That Ami Eister asshole got to me, too, gave me all this terrible BS information about the family and tried to get me to give it to the press. It almost worked, too."

"I heard. Pretty awful."

"Yeah. But Ana was really nice about it and once I'd explained everything, she forgave me. And she offered me a position. Henna's position. I told her yes, but I wanted to ask you if you're okay with it. If you're not, I will go right now and tell her I can't take the job. I want you to be happy Claire. And if me being a part of this world with you makes you unhappy—"

I smother my little sister in a hug, knocking her back a few feet.

"Whoa." But she's grinning.

"If it makes you happy, Harper, you should do it. Ana is a

great lady, and you'll learn a lot. It would be wonderful to have you as a part of the family again."

And I'll have an ally if I ever need one, but I don't say that aloud.

"Well, I'm glad you approve, because I think it would be pretty awesome."

"My God, what are you two doing? Are you ready yet?" Katie is in the doorway now, too, crowding me in a sea of foamy organza. "I have your flowers. Fatima just dropped them off." She hands me the graceful bouquet—blush roses, ivory ranunculus, white hydrangeas nestle together with baby's breath and dusty miller the same color as the girls' dresses—so simple, yet beautiful, it takes my breath away. Henna knew me so well.

I swallow back the tears. *Oh, Henna. Thank you*, I think, hoping her spirit is somewhere near.

I smile at my sister. "Yes. Let's go get married."

"Hold on, just one second. Come here." Harper poses me by Venus and takes a few shots. "Just so we have a record... We'll do more, later. When the light's better."

Speaking of light, there seems to be a break in the rain, not actual sunshine, but a lightening of the sky, because the hallway outside my door doesn't seem nearly as dark.

The moment her camera comes out, Harper, in her element, takes charge, is now talking me through what's about to happen. "Everyone is waiting at the bottom off the stairs. Ana thought it would be great to go down to the church in one big party—it's a more typical Italian procession. So, this is your big entrance, Claire, coming down the stairs. They're all waiting, and I'll take shots of your descent. When the vows are done, we'll move onto *The Hebrides* for the reception. We'll do photos there, too. They've already set up the boat for the party. And there's a fun surprise, you're going to love it!"

"I might be a little over surprises," I say with a smile.

"No, trust me. It's cool."

We stop by the huge windows overlooking the labyrinth, just out of sight of the landing.

"Are you ready?" Harper asks.

I nod. We're moving so fast now I don't have any more time to be nervous. The flowers hold the gentlest scent, and I let it soothe me.

"Okay. We'll go first. Katie, I'll lead so I can get my camera out for you, then Claire goes." To me, she says, "When you see us at the bottom—" she points and I realize that if I crane my neck, I can see the overflowing urns that top the two pedestals of the base of the stairs "—that's your cue."

"Got it."

She snaps another photo. "You really do look beautiful, by the way. I'm glad you didn't let Jack do photos before. It's so much more romantic this way." She pulls the blusher over my face. "When I'm done with the photos, you will have an album to remember."

"Thanks, Harper."

The girls disappear, one by one, the heads sinking below the surface of my gaze as if they're slipping underwater. There is an appreciative murmur from the guests assembled below.

I watch for the floating sea to pass the urns.

One. Two. Three.

It's time.

65

A Mess of a Dress

The magnificent split staircase is perfectly situated for the dramatic arrival of a bride. Somehow, while I showered and dressed, they've been decorated top to bottom in flowers that match my bouquet. I remember the floating floral scent from earlier—they must have been in the breakfast room. Fatima and Ana certainly were busy overseeing things while Jack and I talked.

The wedding guests are arrayed at the base of the stairs. My mother, still a bit pale, and Brian, both smiling up at me tenderly. Katie, finally happy and excited. Harper, the shutter of her camera clicking away. The lawyers, Jack's friends, appreciative. Elliot, who is looking at me in utter wonder. I feel a stab of hatred toward him. *We will deal with you later, jerk.* Tyler, and his adorable boyfriend, Peter. Fatima, standing on the far edge of the room. She sees me, nods, and whips away with a satisfied smile on her face. She's headed toward the kitchens. I assume she's going to let everyone know we're on our way and I feel a rush of gratitude. I couldn't have done this without her.

I stand at the top of the glorious stairs and listen to the gasps.
I feel the grateful blush start running up my throat. All brides
look beautiful, this is a given, and this dress does look lovely
with my gossamer train.

I enjoy the sensation of being admired, letting all eyes find me.

Letting Jack's eyes find me.

My heart stutters as I realize the murmur that's started isn't
one of appreciation. It's the angry buzz of a disturbed hive. Shock
starts to register. Mouths drop open. I've done something wrong.
Something terribly, dreadfully wrong. The grins on Ana and
Brice's faces turn to horrified grimaces.

I look to Jack again. His face, blank for a moment, has drained
of all color. In a heartbeat that feels like it lasts an hour, his eyes
meet mine and the pain I see there is overwhelming, visceral.
He is angry with me, so angry that I recoil in shock.

He bursts into motion, bounds up the stairs, Ana right behind him. I flinch as he grabs my arm and pulls me away from
the stairs, down the hallway.

"Jack, what is it? What's wrong?" I stumble on the runner and
he hauls me upright. He doesn't speak until we get to our rooms.

He throws open the door and shoves me inside, then attacks.

"What are you playing at, Claire? Are you trying to get back
at me? Take it off. Take it off right now."

"What? What's wrong? What are you talking about?"

He stops and faces me, shouting, roaring at me: "That's *her*
dress."

Her dress.

Oh, my God. I search for words, at the same time trying to
find the zipper. I want it off as much as he does.

"Jack, I—"

Ana takes my hand, her voice steady. "Come with me."

She draws me away, and I glance over my shoulder to see
shock and fury in every line of Jack's body. He is close behind
me; I can hear his breath, harsh in my ear.

Ana gets me back into the dressing room and unceremoni-
ously strips me of the dress. She tosses it to the floor and kicks
it away. My skin prickles with cold, exposed as I am. I move for
the robe hanging on the door, feeling like I'm moving through
mud. I pull it over my shoulders. I'm exhausted.

"Where did you even find it, Claire?" Ana asks reproachfully.
"This is terrible. Terrible."

"Fatima—" I manage, before bursting into tears. Choking on
my sobs, I finally manage to get the words out. "Fatima gave
it to me."

"Fatima?" Ana is clearly shocked by this news, and Jack, still
growling and roaming the room like a caged tiger, draws to a
halt. "Fatima gave it to you? She told me she had found a dress
for you, but this...this is obscene."

"She brought it to me, said it belonged to her mother. She
had me try it on. That's why she did my hair, so I could see how
it would look. She thought it would be an option for me, since
my dress was ruined. She said you loved the idea."

"Fatima?" Ana says again, still in shock at the betrayal. "But
she—"

"Loved Morgan," Jack says, still wary, but starting to recover
now. "She doted on her. Every time we came here, Fatima did
everything she could to ingratiate herself. Morgan loved it. Having someone so close to the family who adored her? My God,
I didn't know she had it in her. What a terrible, awful prank.
Claire, come here, love." He folds me into his arms, and I nestle
there, safe, and sorrowful, hiccupping occasionally as the tears
wind down.

"I'm so sorry. I'm so embarrassed. I can't believe this is happening. Between Elliot and Fatima..." I swallow hard, trying
to keep myself in check. Inside I am a seething mass, I want to
kill them both. I want to wring that bitch's skinny little neck for
screwing with me. With us. I want to see Elliot off the cliffside.
I am so sick of impediments to our happiness.

Thunder rumbles, low and mean.

"God, not more rain," Ana says, moving to the windows. "I thought we had a break."

"She must have ruined my dress in a ploy to get me to wear this one. To embarrass me. To hurt you. God, Jack, I am so sorry. If I'd had any idea…"

Jack puts his hand under my chin. "Darling, this isn't your fault. Let Mom help you get changed. Let's keep going, all right? This is just another stupid obstruction, and it's not your fault, Claire, it's not. It was meant to hurt me, and it worked. I was shocked, but trust me, I am fine. Are you okay with Mom helping you, or I can send Katie and Harper back up, too?"

"No. That's okay. I can do it. I have my rehearsal dress. But our guests must be getting restless at this point. Should we tell them to wait downstairs? Or go ahead to the church?"

Jack is already halfway to the door. "Where are you going?"

"To find Fatima," he says. "And get the party moving to the church. There's no reason for everyone to be waiting below. We'll make our appearance there. Together, this time."

"No need. They're already going," Ana says, looking out the window. "The funicular is full of people. Harper must have gotten everyone moving. Smart girl."

"Good. Still, Fatima and I need to have a conversation." But before he can leave, my cell phone rings. I pull it out of the small beaded bag that is meant to hang at my elbow. I'd tossed it on the bed as we entered the room.

"It's Gideon," I say, confused, halting and putting the phone to my ear.

"Hello?"

"Claire! My God, I've been trying to reach you. Jack isn't answering his phone. I'm on my way up. Karmen is dead. She was murdered, stabbed, but she figured out who Ami Eister is. It's Morgan Compton. Claire, you have to tell Jack. Morgan is alive."

66

Revelations

One last gong of the bell and the seats are all filled. The lights go down, bleeding away from the glowing orbs until the theater is dark. There is murmuring and shifting, a few errant coughs, the turn of a page in the programs. The curtain is still drawn. The murmurs stop. The audience leans forward the tiniest bit, breath catching in their throats. They have waited for this moment, paid money to experience it.

An interminable moment ensues.

Then the curtain whips back, pulled on lead wires that fly through their metal rings, showing the stage, and a lone actor in a pool of light. A woman. Head down. Feet bare. She wears battered clothes as if she's survived a shipwreck. Her red hair hangs in stringy wet ropes. There is no music, only the heavy breathing of the woman and the gasps of surprise from the audience as she throws back her head, her eyes bright as glowing coals.

"Surprise!" I call.

67

She Is Risen

"What do you mean, Morgan is alive?" I say, and Jack and Ana both whirl to face me. "Gideon, hold on, I need to put you on speaker."

Ana's face has lost all color. "That's impossible. She can't be. She…she… I saw her…"

"Gideon, go. Say that again."

He's clearly running, his breathing is broken. His voice comes through the speaker, tinny and frantic. "Morgan Compton is alive. She has been posing as Ami Eister. Karmen found video of her coming to your studio, and got a facial recognition match. It's her. There's no doubt. I'm almost there. Lock the fucking door."

Ana has a hand around her throat, her beautiful features sharp in her delicate face. She is lost in memory, or agony, I'm not sure which.

I touch her arm. "The wedding…"

"If she's alive, Claire, there is no wedding."

I must have looked confused because Ana's face softens. "My dear, if she's actually alive, they're still married."

My heart sinks. My God, she's right. If Morgan is still alive…

It is impossible. If Morgan is alive, that means I've met her. I've talked to her. I spent months stalking her ghost and when she came to me, flesh and blood, I didn't recognize her? No, it can't be. It can't be!

Logic reasserts itself. "The woman posing as Ami Eister who came to my studio did not resemble Morgan. Her hair, her face…it wasn't the same person. I am…intimately familiar with Morgan."

Jack glances my way, an eyebrow cocked. "I'll tell you later," I say, and he nods, convinced.

"I agree," Jack says. "This must be a mistake. We know she's dead. There's no way."

Gideon bangs on our door. "Let me in."

Jack does. Gideon thrusts his phone at Jack. Gideon's pants and shirt are covered in blood.

Karmen. Oh, God, another death.

"Hit Play. She's had some work done. And her hair must be dyed. But the underlying bone structure can't be mistaken. Someone tried to delete the match, but Karmen had already sent it to me. Mrs. Compton, she's dead, ma'am. Karmen's dead. She was stabbed. I'm so sorry."

The video finally loads fully. The footage isn't great, and we crowd around the screen, watching. The tall black boots, a black chignon, black Jackie-O sunglasses. She strides across the street with a warrior's grace.

She looks like Ana.

I glance at Jack's mother, assessing. The similarities are overwhelming.

"The woman in this video is absolutely the woman who came to me and claimed she was Ami Eister. But that is not the Morgan I've become familiar with."

Jack is staring at the screen, mouth ajar. As I watch, he runs a finger across the blown-up chin of the woman. He glances back at his mother, then to Gideon, then the screen again. He sees it, too. Ana does, as well.

"She's dressed like me," Ana says. "But that's not me, obviously."

"There's more," Gideon says.

He takes the phone and opens a file. This shows the technical comparisons. Morgan leaps out from the screen, that wide brow, those piercing eyes, that strong, pugnacious jaw, the flaming hair.

The woman next to her is...less, somehow. Quieter. The jaw doesn't seem as strong, the eyes are hidden behind dark glasses.

"There's no chance this is a mistake?"

"No, Jack. No. The software is highly technical, we have a tactical identification system that merges with the FBI's NGI facial recognition database. But there are vector templates and surface texture measurements, you can see they all match... Look, it's not wrong. It's her."

There is a moment, a brief, quiet moment, before Jack speaks.

"Morgan." Jack's face makes it seem the word tastes of ash. "But how is that possible?"

He looks at his mother wildly, and Ana shakes her head once, sharp.

"Where is she now, Gideon?" Ana asks.

"Karmen had a note on her desk. A flight number and a date. JFK to Rome. Two weeks ago."

"She's here," I say, utterly aghast. "My God, she's here. On the island. That's who I saw in the labyrinth. That's who pushed Henna down the stairs. That's where Malcolm was taking me. To her. To Morgan."

"Fatima," Ana says, venom lacing her tone. "She must be involved with this. She knows. She has to. She could be behind Henna's death, too."

But Jack is still in shock, still holding out some sort of hope that we're going to be able to pull this off, that we're going to have a future together. He turns to me and softly, softly, with the finger that traced his wife's jaw on the computer screen a moment ago, traces mine.

"Claire. This means nothing. She means nothing. *You* are the love of my life."

"Oh, please. He told me that too, once upon a time."

The contralto voice is familiar and strange at the same time, and I whirl around in time to see the massive tapestry behind the statue of Venus slip back into place. The woman who is Morgan but is not Morgan stands before us, a gun in her hand.

"Surprise," she calls, then pulls the trigger.

68

Drifting Down the Seas

Gideon goes down first.

Ana is hit and crumples to the floor without a sound.

Jack dives for her with a shrill cry of "Mom!" just as a third shot rings out, and to my horror, Jack collapses on top of Ana.

Blood. There is so much blood. I can't see where she hit him, but he's not moving.

I can't breathe. I can't move. I am frozen, and she is here.

Morgan struts to Jack's body, stepping around Gideon with a small sneer of distaste.

"Tsk. Fatima will never get the stain out of this rug..."

She focuses her dark gaze on me.

"Hello, Claire. It's nice to see you."

She's going to kill you, too. Be brave, Claire. Don't let her win.

It takes every ounce of my being to look away from the black, empty cyclops eye of the gun, which is now pointed at my chest, and meet the eyes of the madwoman before me.

Her hair is a mass of tangles, and her clothes—what was once a white knee-length dress and thin sandles—are stained with mud, and blood. All hail the ghost of Isola. The haunter. Jack's Gray Lady.

"Hello, Morgan."

"Oh, I like hearing my name fall from your lips. Morgan, she says. Morgan. Such a strong name. A witch's name. For witch I am, sweet, darling, little Claire. A witch who rises from the dead to exact revenge on those who hurt her. My dress looked fabulous on you, by the way. I thought it might."

"How? How are you alive?"

"It seems remarkable, I know. But I didn't die when I went off the cliff. Not then. Not like he thought."

"Hard to make that mistake."

"Oh, I was dead. I've been dead ever since. Dead in my heart. Dead in my soul."

She's not kidding—her eyes are flat as rocks.

"When I went over the cliff, screaming until I landed, somehow, some way, I wasn't broken in two. I lay on the rocks, in that freezing cold water, twisted, in such pain. I couldn't move. I couldn't breathe. I lay there while they flashed their lights on me, while they decided what to do.

"And in the meantime, I let the water buoy my body. When I felt myself sinking and the sucking brine ran over my head, I moved my arms and legs, spread them out in the water. You know they call it the dead man's float? Well, eventually, I floated. Floated right out into the crashing waves, but the current brought me into the cove that led to the grotto. We used to swim there, all the time. Jack liked to make love in the grotto, under the watchful eye of the statuary. Has he taken you there yet?"

"No."

"Hmm. Pity. It's terribly romantic. Well, the storm was frantic, the wind whipping the waves onto the shore as if it was punishing the land for being solid. The boats had been lashed to the pier before the storm came in, but one had worked its way loose and was bobbing in the waves. I unmoored it and crawled inside. It was small, but I was so waterlogged, so pained, I wasn't thinking about the possibility of it capsizing. It was shelter. It was safety. I didn't care anymore.

"My little boat and I were swept up in the torrential waves. It floated out into the bay while I slept, while I was dead, while I was dying."

"Well, which is it, Morgan?" I feel a little hysterical pushing her, but I can't seem to help myself. She's mad. She even speaks like a crazy woman, sharing a story only she is experiencing.

"What difference does it make? Sleep is only a kind of death, one from which we usually awaken. I was resurrected. And now here I am. I have yet to awaken from this particular nightmare. But that's all about to change."

"That's quite a speech."

"Did you like it?" She smiles coyly. "I want you to like it, Claire. I know how much you like me. I know how much you enjoy thinking of me."

"Oh, please. Don't flatter yourself. I want you to explain yourself, Morgan. None of this mystical 'I floated away in a little boat' crap. You have been systematically trying to ruin my life."

"Not your life, Claire. His." She gestures with the gun toward Jack's prone body. "You, I find interesting. I'd prefer not to have to kill you."

This is utter bullshit. Her eyes are wild and mad. It's either her or me, and we both know it.

"All right. I'd rather not be killed. So, you floated away. Then what?"

"And then, my dear girl, I was transformed. I ran. I hid. And I became another woman. I bided my time. I worked from within. I recruited, and I planned, and I watched. Oh, I watched. Especially since you came into his life. I was there the night you met, did you know?"

Alarm fills me. What? "No. I didn't."

"You were so radiant. I wish I had it on video. You lit up like a candle the moment he looked at you. And of course, since he was so interested in you, I needed to be, too."

She walks in a tiny half circle, and now she's between me and the door. Fuck.

Where *is* everyone?

Assuming Jack and I are having a knockdown, drag-out fight, probably. Being discreet, a disease this whole family suffers from.

She's cut off my path to the door. But she came in elsewhere.

The tapestry. Jack told me they used to bring girls to the emperor through a tunnel. The boats came to the grotto. She came through the fucking wall.

If I can draw her down there, draw her away from Jack and Ana and Gideon, maybe someone will come find them, help them.

And then I can kill her. But I need to keep her talking.

"So, you watched me?"

"I did."

"And how did you meet Shane?"

"Research," she says simply, with a flip of her hand. "It wasn't hard to dig up your past. I am rather good with a computer, as you might have guessed. It was convenient, him getting parole when he did. I could have found any number of louts to do my bidding, but someone who wanted to take you down? Perfection. He couldn't wait to see you punished. We had a deal, he and I. I got my revenge on Jack, he got his revenge on you. His was less...elegant than mine, of course. Baser." She shivers delicately. "What you ever saw in him. Ah, the vagaries of youth.

"Of course, you must know already, that man is a first-class idiot. He broke with the plan. I guess he decided watching you wasn't enough anymore, he wanted to feel you again, taste you again. I didn't tell him to, and until that moment, he'd been quite good at doing what I told him."

"Maybe he decided he was tired of being your lackey."

"Perhaps." Morgan shrugs. "It doesn't matter. Money speaks louder than words with some people. Malcolm, for instance. Always second fiddle, always being bossed around. He was desperate for some power. He was supposed to bring you to me, to the cottage, so we could talk this out, like adults. And instead, you killed him. Such aggression from you. Did you know then, sweet Claire? Did you know I was waiting for you?"

"Of course not. And I didn't kill him. He fell."

"Oh, keep telling yourself that, darling. I have it all on tape." She continues as if I haven't said a word. "No, it doesn't matter. There won't be any reason to watch you anymore. Speaking of watching—" she tips the gun back and forth, back and forth, as if hypnotizing me "—you've done your fair share of watching *me*."

How could she…no, she's playing with me. "What do you mean?"

"Claire, Claire, Claire. Your search history is incredibly…focused. You seem to have a slight fixation on little old me." She smiles winningly, looking even crazier. Bat. Shit. Crazy.

"How could you—"

"Have you not figured this out yet? I've been inside your head, *darling*. I've been inside your body with him, and I've seen how you obsess about me. What was it like, falling in love with a ghost?"

"You really are a narcissist. I hardly call trying to find out who my fiancé was married to falling in love. Jack despised you so much he didn't bother uttering your name aloud. You were less than a ghost to him. You simply ceased to exist."

She flinches, her mouth thinning to a hard seam. She looks old, and tired, and wretched at that moment. This is how I win, I realize. I make sure she understands her insignificance.

"Jack spoke of you to me once. Only once. He said you'd

died. And that was it. He didn't even care enough to tell me how. And I didn't care enough to look until one of my friends pushed you on me. That was natural curiosity."

"Hundreds of photos stored in your little private website is more than natural curiosity."

"No. It wasn't. I wanted to be sure I was nothing like you so he would never hate me like he hated you."

She laughs, hard and sharp, and I can see I've wounded her. She wants me to love her. She wants me to be obsessed with her. Disdain for her cleverness is the key.

"I predict you—" she starts, but I cut her off.

"Hey, you can do the whole witch of Endor thing all you want. You don't scare me anymore. You're just a woman, and as clever as you are, as much as you think you know, you will never have him. He's mine. His heart belongs to me."

Lightning, and thunder close on its heels. Thunder so loud, so long, it takes me a moment to realize no, that wasn't thunder at all.

The sky outside my window is an orange ball, and Morgan is laughing behind me.

"What the hell was that?"

The percussion of the explosion hits the terrace doors and shatters them, spraying glass into the room. Venus topples, the tapestry blown aside, revealing the tunnel. The concussion is enough to fling open the door to the hallway. My ears pop painfully. Tiny slivers of glass rip through the sleeves of my robe, pinpricks of blood blooming like so many freckles.

It takes me a moment to realize what's happened. It's *The Hebrides. The Hebrides* is burning. The long whistle of a lone firework dies, and the sky lights up with brilliant colors.

"Aw, look at your surprise, all ruined," Morgan says, eyes alight with happiness. I can almost see the reflection of the flames in her pupils. "Now you have no way to get off the island. Now you're stuck with me."

The sky outside is popping and crackling as hundreds of fireworks go off at the same time. It is cacophonous, but I hear someone screaming my name.

"Claire? Claire, where are you?" Shit. Shit! It's Katie.

I scream as loudly as I can. "Don't come in here. Get help!"

Morgan glances over her shoulder and starts to turn toward the door.

"Don't you dare," I yell at her, taking advantage of her momentary distraction to leap toward her, shoving her to the ground.

Then I dive toward the remnants of the tapestry, fling it aside, and barrel into the darkness.

side, the insistent ebb and flow as old as life itself. This island, this sea, predates all of us.

How many women have felt terror in this darkness?

I burst into an opening, a good-sized sea cave. This is the grotto. The water is clearest cerulean, unlike the sea outside. There is a break in the rock that leads out to the sea, and I can see the orange fire of *The Hebrides* burning, smell the overwhelming, choking stench of fuel and the smoky scent of sulfur and gunpowder.

I realize this is where the photo on Harper's Instagram was taken.

Big News Coming...

Morgan sent it. And all those horrid texts. How easily she's hacked all of us.

She was trying to get me to come to her. If I had, would Jack and Ana still be alive?

Don't, Claire. Don't think about them yet.

"Claaaaire..."

The water is high, the tide must be in. There is no gentle slope, the basalt walls drop straight into the water. The light here is dim but I can see, across from me, indentations in the rock. Openings. Other paths. Escapes. One is lit up. If I can just get there, maybe I can circle back into the Villa...

But what if this is the only path that's not walled off?

No, the light leads somewhere. I drop the robe and dive into the water. It is freezing cold, so cold my breath leaves me. I stroke across the grotto quickly, then scramble out of the water and run toward the light.

I've gone only twenty feet or so before I run into an iron gate. I pull on it, but it is locked tight. Damn it.

Back down to the path. I have to get out of here—I have to find my way back to the Villa.

Bracing myself for the freezing temperature, I dive in and swim across the cavern again, haul myself into the nearest depression. This one goes nowhere, there are the remnants of a stone block. A statue once stood here. That makes sense; the smaller indentations are statuary niches. There's a metal bracket as well. They probably once held torches, a spot to leave offerings to the sea goddess or to Venus herself.

Back in again, to the next, and I can see from the water this one is no different. I feel the sea sucking at my legs, the current is pulling me hard, toward the small opening, toward the roiling sea. I have to get out of the water soon. Even if this one leads nowhere, I will be across the cavern from Morgan, and it's better to try and face her from afar than be swept out to sea and drowned.

What symmetry. Was this how she felt, sheer panic colliding with the urgent need to live as she slipped away from the rocks, the waves forcing her into the bay?

Stop thinking. Move.

The third impression has a dark seam. As I reach it, shivering, numb with cold, Morgan appears.

The watery light shows the anger on her face.

"Aren't you clever," she calls, the words echoing off the rock walls.

I have to get out of the water; I'm starting to lose feeling. She can shoot me if I expose myself. Hell, she could just shoot me in the head.

But she talks. It's as if she hasn't spoken to anyone for a very long time.

"Did you know the emperor's lovers were brought by boat for his pleasure? They would sneak them in, straight from the water up the tunnel to his bedchamber. They called them the Disciples of Venus, the women he used for pleasure. He fucked them, and then he killed them. Did you know that? It was like a roach motel—you go in, but you don't come out. They're all in the crypt, you know. All those women. All their dusty bones."

The crypt. Of course. It stands to reason the crypt has a path down to the grotto, too.

"Too bad you decided to take a swim. You could have just…" and Morgan disappears into the wall. Darkness bleeds into the grotto in her wake.

In my panic, I must have missed a passageway. I stupidly assumed the only way to the other side was through the water. There must be other paths around the cave.

I take advantage of her movement to jump from the water and run, full speed, into the crack in the wall. I have never been so cold. And this seam doesn't have the same ambient light as the one I traversed earlier. It's dark, and I stumble. When I get to my feet, I hear footsteps. She's coming.

I have to fight to keep my teeth clenched so they don't chatter. I surge ahead, not as fast as I'd like, a hand on the wall for guidance.

Please, please, please.

I don't know who I'm praying to. God? Venus? My dad?

All of them?

I burst through a doorway without realizing it's there, stubbing my toe against the wooden threshold. The door itself is standing open, and there is a path ahead.

I don't hesitate. I sprint again, upward this time. I'm heading back toward the Villa, but I have no idea where I'm going. I'm also half-naked, but that hardly matters, it's not like I'm going to burst into the foyer where the guests are milling about.

I hear someone calling my name and stop.

"Claire? Claire? Where are you?"

"Katie!"

"Claire!" She calls back. "Oh, thank God. We've been looking everywhere."

I stop, wait for a second, see the bobbing flashlight ahead. I take off toward it.

"Go back, go back," I call. "I'm coming. We have to shut her in here. We have to shut the doors."

But Katie stops, waiting for me.

And from behind me, Morgan appears.

70

Slow Motion

It happens like they say, in slow motion.

Morgan, stepping out from a side passageway behind me, the gun trained on my chest.

Katie, realizing Morgan has appeared, shoving me to the side and moving right in front of me.

The bullet, hitting her in the neck.

The ground, hard under my knees as I catch her and fall.

The echoing laughter.

The blood. The blood. The blood.

I try to staunch it, but it's gushing. I'm covered in my best friend's essence.

"Oh, God, Katie. Katie!"

"I love you, Claire. Be happy," Katie whispers, blood bubbling on her lips. And then she is gone, her head tipping back onto the stone floor.

It is that quick. She dies that fast, lying in my lap, her head trailing off my thighs, hair in the dirt.

She has just saved my life. Katie has sacrificed herself for me. I didn't get a chance to say goodbye. I didn't have time to say thank you. I didn't have time to tell her how much I love her. How grateful I am that she was my friend.

Another whistling explosion from down the tunnel. I don't have time to waste. I don't know why Morgan hasn't shot me, too, while I'm prone, but I have to move.

I kiss Katie's forehead, still warm, and lay her head gently on the packed earth floor and start back the way I've come. How dare Morgan try to take everything away from me? How dare she?

She knows I'm following her. She knows the tables have turned. She has nothing to lose—she is protected, she thinks, because the gun still has bullets. I've counted four shots, that revolver holds six bullets. She has two left; she doesn't want to waste them.

It doesn't take long to realize she's led me to the crypt.

To the forever silent witnesses to our game of cat and mouse.

I turn a corner and stop with a gasp.

The bodies are stacked up in the corner like cordwood. Henna. Malcolm. A gray head as well—Fatima. Morgan must have killed her because she is no longer of use, or she defied her in the end. Karmen's gone, too.

How many victims will she leave behind when this is over?

As distasteful as it seems, I run my hands along Malcolm's body, digging my hand into his front right pocket.

The knife is still there.

I've seen him clean his nails with it, I've seen him open letters with it.

And now, alone in the darkness surrounded by the dead, I'm going to use it to kill Morgan.

The rational part of my mind says *Run, run the other way, run to the safety of whoever's left out there.*

The irrational, furious, obsessed part says *Stop her, here and now, or you will never be free of her.*

I will never be free of her anyway. She is my nuclear winter; the fallout will last long after I am dead and gone. It doesn't matter if that's now or seventy years from now.

Standing tall, I flick the knife open and seat it carefully in my hand.

"Morgan," I call. "Morgan. Where are you? I want to talk."

And I start down the path toward the grotto.

It doesn't take long to find her. She is waiting by the door to the crypt. She is smiling, a pirate in the darkness. The revolver is at the ready, steady in her hand.

"What is it, Claire? Changed your mind? Now you want to talk to me?"

"Yes. What do you want from me?" I ask, still advancing.

"I want you to listen to reason. I've grown to care about you these past few months. Jack will lead you to ruin. He will break your heart. He will never love you the way he loved me."

"You killed him. What does it matter now?"

I took a self-defense class once, and one thing that stuck with me is this. Never hesitate. Don't draw back and let them realize you're going to swing. Plow ahead, even if you don't have all your power in the swing. The unexpected motion is as much a weapon as the weapon you hold. Your attacker naturally expects some sort of windup if you're trying to hit them. No pause. Just go straight in.

I walk closer, closer, closer, then, exactly when she would expect me to hesitate and stop, I lunge forward, knife out. She turns slightly, flinching away from me, and I catch her in the shoulder, feel the blade sink into her flesh. She screams and drops the gun. I try to yank the knife back out to stab her again, but the metal is sunk in too deep. I'd been going for her heart and ready to crack bone. Now I've just pinioned her against the wall between a door and a massive stone sarcophagus.

I don't know who is interred inside. I don't really care. Its edge is sharp, the stone as square as the day it was carved. It will do.

She wrenches herself free from my grip with a cry, eyes black with madness, and comes at me. She manages to punch me twice and I stumble back, blood slick down my face, mingling with Katie's. That gives me strength, and I launch at her again, forcing her back against the stone before I pin her good arm. She kicks my knee, and pain shoots up my thigh, but I don't let go. The edge of the crypt doorway is behind her, and I push hard against her body, forcing her back, back, back until she is wedged into the space. Slowly, my hand moves from her elbow, to her shoulder, to her throat.

"What are you doing?" she grinds out. "Don't be an idiot. We can work together, we can—"

"I will never let you hurt another person I love."

I shove, and the momentum of my body propels her into the stone. With a twist of my hand, I force her head against the edge. I push, hard, until I've levered her neck around the corner. She is whimpering and screaming and fighting, clawing. She scratches my face. I don't let up. She gets a finger under my pearls and pulls. The clasp, already damaged, breaks free. Pearls *ping* off the floor.

And now she's ruined my beautiful gift, too.

I am stronger than she is. I am enraged. I have the right angle to accomplish my goal. It's her, or it's me. There cannot be a world in which we both survive.

She says something I can barely hear, something pleading, *please*, and then the resounding crack of her neck snapping echoes in the chamber.

I hold on to her lithe body as it shudders and shakes with the last moments of her life. It doesn't take long. I release her, and she slumps to the floor.

I wipe my hand under my nose and fling droplets of my blood onto her lifeless body, blood mingling with the scattered pearls in the darkness.

"Goodbye, Morgan."

71

Finis

Will Compton finds me there, in the crypt, shivering with cold, lying next to Morgan's dead body.

"Claire. My God. We've been looking for you everywhere."

"It's over," I manage. "It's over. Is Jack?" I can't even finish the words. I've been down here all this time, afraid to find out the truth. Afraid to hear I've lost him forever.

Will pulls me to my feet, wraps me in a blanket.

"He's alive. They've taken him to Naples. He was badly hurt, but he will make it. Ana…"

He breaks off, and I know then my elegant mother-in-law is dead.

"She killed Katie, too. And Fatima. Before I…"

I collapse against Will, who shushes me. I allow him to walk me from the crypt.

There is fire.

There are lights.

There are questions.

All I can do is turn my face away. I am not capable of answering them.

72

Endings and Beginnings

Ten Years Earlier

I must get away, or I am going to die, I know it.

"Morgan? Mooorgan?"

He's calling for me, and the wind sweeps his voice away, making the last syllables so much lighter. Gentler.

The path is marked by towering cypress and laurel, verdant and lush. A gray stone waist-high wall is all that stands between me and the cliffside. It is cool inside this miniature forest; the sky blotted out by the purple-throated wisteria that drapes across and between the trees. Someone, years ago, built an archway along the arbor. The arch's skeleton has long since rotted away and the flowers droop into the path, clinging trails and vines that brush against my head and shoulders. It should be beautiful; instead feels oppressive, as if the vines might animate, twist and curl around my neck and strangle me to death.

The white dress, long and filmy, hampers my effort to run. The hem catches on a branch; a large rend in the fabric slashes open, exposing my leg. A deep cut blooms red along my thigh, and the blood runs down my calf. My hair has come loose from its braid, flies unbound behind me like gossamer wings.

In my panic, I barely notice the pain. I hurry along the path, trying not to look down to the frothing water roiling against the rocks at the cliff's base. I think the ruins are to my right. From what I remember, they are between the church and the artists' colony, the four cottages cowering on the hillside, empty and waiting. We've been here only one night. I am such an idiot to think he was bringing me here to do anything other than see me dead.

A horn shrieks, and I realize the ferry is pulling away. A crack of lightning, and I see the silhouette of the captain in the pilothouse, looking out to the turbulent seas ahead. A gamble that he makes it before the storm is upon us. It was my last chance of escape. Now I'm stuck here.

Don't panic. Don't panic.

Where is the church?

Yes, there it is, a flash of white through the trees. The stuccoed walls loom, the bell tower hidden behind the overgrown foliage. Now the path is moving upward, the grade increasing. I feel it in my calves and hope again I'm going the right way. The Villa is on the hill, on the northwest promontory of the island. If I can reach its doors, I will be safe.

It is too quiet. There are no birds, no creatures, no buzzing or cries, just my ragged, heavy breath and the scree shuffling underfoot as I climb. The furious roar of the water smashing its frustration against the rocks rises from my left, echoing against the cliffside.

Climb. Climb. Keep going.

I must get to the Villa. There I can call for help. Lock myself inside. Maybe find a weapon.

A branch snaps and I halt, breathless.

Someone is coming.

I startle like a deer, now heedless of the noise I'm making. Fighting back a whimper of fear, I break free of the cloistered path to see an old, decrepit staircase cut into the stone. *Careful,* I must be cautious, there are gaps where some steps are missing, and the rest are mossy with disuse, but *hurry, hurry. Get away.*

I wind up the steps, clinging to the rock face, until I burst free into a sea of scrubby pines. Two sculptures, Janus twins, flank a slate-dark path into a labyrinth of rhododendron and azalea.

This isn't right. Where am I?

A hard breeze disrupts the trees around me, and a rumble of thunder like a thousand drums rolls across my body. Lightning flashes and I sees the Villa in the distance. So far away. On the other side of the labyrinth. The other side of the hill.

I've gone the wrong way.

A droplet of water hits my arm, then my forehead. Dread bubbles through me.

I am too late. The storm is upon me.

The wind whistles hard and sharp, buffeting me against the stone wall. I can't move. Deep fear cements my feet. Rain makes the gauzy dress cling to the curves of my body, and the blood on my thigh washes to the ground. None of it matters. I cannot escape.

When Jack comes, at last, sauntering through the storm, I am crying, clinging to the stone, the lightning illuminating the ruins, the ancient stones, and stark, headless statues the only witness to my death.

I go over the wall with a thunder-drowned scream, the jagged rocks below my final companions.

His name echoes across the water, rising up the cliffside, the shriek audible across the island, dying off a little at the end, as I get closer to the water, to the rocks, to the ground.

"Jaaaaaaack!"

★ ★ ★

"Is she dead?" Jack asks.

"What have you done?" Elliot replies with horror.

"That doesn't matter now. Is she dead?"

A pause. They must be looking over the edge. Yes, the light, the flashing of a light as it sweeps across the rocks, looking for my body.

I know there is blood. I know I must look broken. I was able to move my mouth away from the water, yes, but that won't save me for long. I hold my breath, only taking tiny sips of air when it seems I will die if I do not.

The light finds me. It lingers.

Lingers.

Lingers.

"She's not moving," Elliot says.

"But is she dead?" Jack asks.

"How am I supposed to know? She's got a broken leg, it's twisted funny. And she's not moving. There's blood. A lot of blood."

I feel a deep, strange satisfaction by the fear and revulsion in Elliot's voice.

Good. I hope you drown, broken and bloodied, on these very rocks. If I get out of here, I will make sure you do.

"You shouldn't have chased her," Jack says.

"You shouldn't have pushed her," Elliot spits back.

The water, again the water, lapping, lapping. It's splashing over my face now, and I time my breaths to coincide with the recession of the small waves.

Splash.

Breath.

Splash.

Breath.

The light disappears.

Jack says, "If she's not dead, she will be shortly. The tide is coming in. It will wash her body away. When they find her—if they find her—we can say she disappeared and must have fallen off the cliff."

"Should we get help?" Elliot asks.

It is Ana who answers, her voice hard in the night. "No. Absolutely not. Come away. There's nothing to be done now. It's over."

JULY

Rough wind, that moanest loud
Grief too sad for song;
Wild wind, when sullen cloud
Knells all the night long;
Sad storm whose tears are vain,
Bare woods, whose branches strain,
Deep caves and dreary main—
Wail, for the world's wrong!

—Percy Bysshe Shelley, *A Dirge*

EPILOGUE

Second Deaths

It has long been known that sparrows flee disaster. I don't know if seabirds do the same, but as I watch from our terrace, there are flocks shooting south, ahead of what exact tragedy, I do not know. I thought we'd had all the tragedy we could handle.

Morgan's second death was only the beginning.

Brice reacted quickly. The carabinieri in Naples were alerted to the chaos and dispatched two teams who arrived at the island soon after *The Hebrides* exploded.

Morgan lied, thank God. It's what she did best. The whole wedding party was not on the boat—they were still in their procession from house to church. We lost a few of Jack's childhood friends who'd gone ahead to have a cocktail, and the crew, but we didn't lose the family.

Still, there were so many questions. Questions to which I didn't have the proper answers. I knew only what she told me, and what we found on the island.

She'd been living there, off and on, for several years. She had invaded a small shop down by the beach that had closed its doors, and she set up a massive surveillance network she'd tied into the Comptons' security system.

The shop itself was attached to the Villa through a tunnel, which led also to the cottages, and to the labyrinth, and to a side passage that had been cleared of rock and debris and allowed her to move into the crypt, too. All were former escape hatches for the emperors, or for the Disciples of Venus, or for the ancient witches who lived in the island's heart. Who knows how she discovered them all, but she did.

I'd almost found her nerve center myself when I ran into the huge iron gate. I saw it later, the next day, with Brice and the police. I had to walk them through the tunnels to find Katie's pale body, to try and explain what happened under the earth.

The back room of the shop was a dark rabbit warren of wires and screens, a jumbled jackdaw mess of a lair. I half expected to see the bones of small animals littering the floor.

From this vantage point, Morgan saw every move we made. The Villa was wired top to bottom with cameras and microphones. Our house in Nashville, my studio. She watched, and watched, and watched. Cameras, cameras, everywhere, for her to enjoy the show.

We would never know for sure if Fatima helped her plant them in the Villa, or if she did it herself, sneaking in when the family was gone and the Villa shuttered, with just Will and his nurse wandering the halls. She could easily have haunted him, helped drive his dementia with little games and tricks.

But it wasn't Jack, or the family, that she wanted.

It was me.

The material the police collected told the whole sordid story. Once I came into the picture, her obsessions with the family shifted. There were hundreds of hours of tape of me. Watching TV. Talking on the phone. Painting. Sleeping. Having sex with

Jack. Many of those she'd spliced together to play on repeat, so we writhed together in ingenious positions for hours.

And my obsession with her was well documented. We think she must have thought I had feelings for her, and that piqued her interest. With the software she had installed on my computer, she was able to see my private folders, all the photos and articles I'd clipped. Every letter I typed, every moment of my days. While I was looking at her, she was watching me. Always, always watching me.

I was only trying to understand why he'd loved her. But she wouldn't have seen it that way.

I spoke at length with the carabinieri about what transpired in the crypt. Granted, it was self-defense, but I still killed a woman. They don't know I killed Malcolm. That I killed Shane. And of course, only Will knows I killed my father and after the stress of the wedding, he's been more confused than usual.

The police decided it wasn't worth pursuing charges against me for killing Morgan. The Compton influence at work.

I have taken so many lives. The first time was the hardest. It gets easier after that.

Katie's absence is a hole that will never be filled. Harper handled all the arrangements for getting her body back to Nashville. We're going to have a memorial service once Jack and I come home. I don't know when that might be. Harper and I talked about it, and she thought it best that I stay in Italy for now. Too much attention on me in Nashville. The press has been speculating, as they do. Easier for me to be absent.

My parents have been sent home, and my mother, bless her heart, went straight to Cumberland Heights and is getting herself straightened out again.

I sent Harper to the editors of *Flair* to explain she'd been lied to. Told the FBI she'd been tricked. They had cause to believe her—Morgan resurrecting herself was enough to lay ample doubt. There may be consequences for the lies about the hand that washed up, but Brice has already been out spinning it. We discussed our options at length, and at my suggestion, he went back to New York with Harper to handle the FBI inquiry, which I've been told will be going away shortly. Nothing to charge any of the Comptons with.

Elliot had a bad few weeks. Morgan wasn't the forgiving type. With one last twist of her knife, she'd signed an affidavit, had it witnessed, too, that Elliot threw her over the cliff. The carabinieri, not being as easily swayed as the Compton-friendly US media, took him into custody while they did a thorough investigation. I admit, this didn't upset me.

But with Ana and Fatima dead, Will an unreliable narrator, Jack in and out of consciousness, and Brice vociferously denying the charge, they were forced to let Elliot go.

No one asked about the fresh bodies in the crypt. Henna was given a spot of honor. I have no idea what happened to Malcolm and Fatima, nor do I care.

The bones, though, were not Elevana's. I don't know whose they are, nor the story behind them. I fear... No. I will not think of that now.

I slept in Jack's hospital room the whole first week. It was touch and go for a couple of days. The bullet hit him in the stomach. He lost a lot of blood, so much that after an extensive surgery, he had to have three transfusions and they'd removed his spleen, but that finally stabilized him.

When Jack was discharged from the hospital, we took the chopper back to the Villa. Flying in was surreal. The pier where *The Hebrides* was docked was gone, the asphalt to the shops carved out as if a giant took a bite of a sandwich.

Otherwise, it all looked the same. As if the events of the past weeks were erased entirely.

Our rooms were resurrected. The terrace doors replaced, all

the shattered glass removed, though I will wear shoes inside for the foreseeable future, just in case. Venus Genetrix lost a shoulder, but a restoration team from Milan is working on her.

The tunnel to the grotto had been sealed, the door bolted and cemented into the wall. No one will be able to get in or out this way ever again.

I debated whether I wanted to stay here, considering how many rooms the Villa has, but in the end, decided I did. I like the view. Romulus and Remus love the terrace. Ana's cats are in mourning, and the dogs like to tease them into happiness in the sunshine.

There has been no more talk of a wedding, though once Jack is stronger, we'll have a quiet ceremony. It's warm and beautiful on Isola, now that the hellacious storms have passed. The terrace is the perfect place to do some sketching. I've spent a lot of time out here. Remembering. I hiked to the cliff top once. Looked over the edge. Imagined what it must have been like that night. The night Morgan died.

Will joins me. He and I have taken to having an afternoon walk. I like it. He's a fascinating man. He has good days, and bad. I've never asked him about our first meeting, when he snapped and punched Jack, crying out about the killer in our midst.

It is a long fall.

The blood test the Italian did to manage the legalities of our Italian wedding came back with a bit of a surprise. I wasn't seasick on *The Hebrides* after all. I haven't told Jack yet. I will, once I wrap my head around the situation. I should tell him now. I really should. But it needs to be my secret a little longer. Just until I decide what is to be done. The family's needs must come first now.

The library has become my refuge. I sit under the stained-glass window, wondering about what choices drove Eliza Compton to have Mephistopheles and Faust looking over her books.

These records are so hard to keep. But I write my thoughts anyway. One day, one of my children will find this notebook and perhaps they will hate me. Perhaps they will understand the choices I made.

Their mother is a murderer. I have taken life. I have done it through accident. I have done it on purpose.

The former was harder.

Our world slowly comes back to center. I'm surprised to realize we're moving into August now. Sunrises. Sunsets. Waves crash. Winds blow. Tired birds settle with relief in the branches of the trees. Flowers bloom and die. The island never seems to change. It is perpetually alone, in the midst of a roiling azure sea, a harbor for all our secrets.

I hear Jack stirring inside, he's been napping most of the afternoon. He still needs his rest. That's how he will heal.

He joins me on the terrace, all smiles. He has been so solicitous. Love is solicitude, is it not?

"What are you doing, darling?"

I slap closed the cover of the sketchbook. He doesn't need to see.

"You're awake. How are you feeling?"

"I feel good. Are you hungry? I thought we could ask Chef to make us some carbonara. Maybe a glass of wine?" His eyes twinkle. He is getting back to himself. He is happy. It is all over.

"No wine for you, mister. Not yet. Not until the doctor says you can."

"You're a tyrant, you know that? Drawing something?"

"The labyrinth," I lie. "I have a wonderful idea about incorporating the statuary into the view. I think we should transform the first cottage into my studio. I'll need at least forty feet for the canvas. I think I'll call her *Venus*."

"We can make that happen. Anything you want, darling. Sounds amazing. I can't wait to see her."

He kisses me and goes inside to make an order to the kitchens. I've come to realize living in the Villa is something like living in a five-star hotel. Anything you could possibly want or need is a call away. If we want to eat in our rooms, we do. If we want the dining room, we have it. If we want a picnic on the beach, it's ours for the taking.

The sun is starting to set, the cliff's shadows lumbering across the beach. I may go for a swim in the morning.

I turn to the page in my sketchbook where I've left off. My finger is holding the place.

I've been drawing Morgan's death again. That moment has become my dearest subject. There is something arresting about the combination of her old beauty mingled with her new at the moment of her death that is irresistible to me. It's terribly morbid, yes, but I can't seem to get her face out of my head.

The fall crushed her jaw and an occipital lobe. She had to have them reconstructed, and that's why she seemed so much softer, so less intense than what she was born with.

I'm sure you're wondering. It's only natural.

I had Morgan buried in the crypt. I wanted to keep her close. After all the Comptons put her through, it seemed only fitting. A gesture of respect for a valiant adversary. We loved the same man, and we handled that love differently. But the Comptons were hard on her.

Weren't they?

I can't get her last words out of my head.

I have replayed the moment of her death over, and over, and over, and I'm virtually positive what she said was "…killed me."

She could have said anything.

I love you.

Fuck you.

Forgive me.

But with her eyes bugging out of her head at the pressure

of my hand on her windpipe, she provided this narrative: "…
killed me."

I replay this moment again, and again.

It had to be "Elliot killed me." Had to be.

I suppose it could have been her begging for me to end it. A
declarative "Kill me."

But no, there was a word that came before, I saw her lips
move.

They touched together lightly before the harsh whisper came
out. I am probably imagining it. I mean, if you run through the
people who were there the night she went over the cliff, sound
them out, and then match them to how her lips touched…

I've done it in the mirror. So many times, now.

Elliot—lips open, tongue tapping the front teeth.

Will—lips pursed, then the tongue tap.

Brice—lips barely pursing before opening full.

Ana—lips fully open.

Jack.

J is a sound that must be done with the lips opened, mouth
open, tongue touching the palate like a small, hissing kiss. If I
were to play a mental video of her last moment and read Morgan's lips, if I were to apply this formula to the sound of her
whisper, it is very possible the missing word is…*Jack*.

Jack killed me.

I suppose we'll never know for sure, will we?

Because I will make sure of it.

However long the island allows me to be a Compton wife,
for we die before our time, I will stop at nothing to protect my
family.

★ ★ ★ ★ ★

ACKNOWLEDGMENTS

This book was an exceptional journey, full of mountains and valleys. It was born on my birthday, on a terrace in a little hotel on Lake Como. During dinner, a yacht sailed to the small island of Isola Comacina, and as the sky darkened, a fireworks display started across the water. I was quite impressed that my family had arranged for fireworks to usher me into my next half century, but quickly found out it was to celebrate a wedding, a tradition on the island. I knew immediately this was the basis for my next book. Many thanks to my family for taking me to Italy for my birthday and indulging me as I absconded from their company to write on the terrace.

Beginnings are one thing. Endings are quite another. Thanks and gratitude to the following:

Laura Benedict, who read too many versions of this to count, and was right in all of her suggestions.

My entire writing porch, Ari, Patti, Laura, Paige, Lisa and Helen, who keep me honest and on track with inspiration and commiseration. You are the wind beneath my wings.

The incredible author, actor, and narrator Julia Whelan for her pandemic inspired #500wordsaday Twitter challenge. Please bring it back!

Victoria Schwab, for perpetually good advice.

Lisa Unger, Heather Gudenkauf, Mary Kubica, and the whole #authortalks community. Love our Friday Twitter chats!

My best friend from childhood, Connie Gehrman, and her husband Chuck Martin for hosting me on tour and teaching me how oil paints work.

Scott Miller, who believed in this story from the beginning. Thank you for your many years of guidance and friendship.

Laura Blake Peterson, who took on a wreck of a writer, shepherded the book into being, hand held, bolstered, and cheered me along to the finish lines—both of them.

Holly Frederick, film agent extraordinaire, who continues to find wonderful Hollywood homes for my work. I know what season two is!

My longtime editor Nicole Brebner, for spitballing, pushing, challenging me to do better, and finally, laying the last puzzle piece into place. You always make my work come to life!

Those who both volunteered as tribute and claimed they were ready to die when I ran my Who Wants To Die In My Next Novel contest: Katie Elderfield, Henna Shaikh, Morgan Fraser—I hope your deaths were satisfying!

Karmen Harris, who won an auction to have her name included in the book. You were a cop, a security guard, a cop again, a couture dress label, and finally the head of Compton Security. You gave me a merry chase, but in the end, you were exactly who you were meant to be. Sorry about the knife in the back.

The YouTube AMSR ancient library videos were hugely instrumental in setting the tone for this novel. Highly recommended.

My intrepid assistant Leigh, who keeps the trains running on time and the social media feeds gorgeous!

Joan Huston, for the crash edit and honest opinions.

Andi Baynham, owner of Salt and Starlight, whose divine choice of crystals raised my vibrations and brought my voice to life when I needed it most.

The entire team at Harlequin and MIRA, who deserve every bit of thanks and gratitude I can muster.

The Literati, the greatest little Facebook group ever.

The incredible booksellers and librarians who have found myriad creative ways to connect readers with our books during the pandemic.

Authors are always inspired by other great artists, and I am no different. I want to thank the following great artists whose work helped me through a most difficult time while I was writing this book:

Emily St. John Mandel

Diana Gabaldon

Lisa Gardner

Lori Gottlieb

Shonda Rhimes

Rina Mimoun

And a few more who will remain nameless but to whom I owe a great deal of thanks.

My fabulous family—my parents: first readers, and constant sounding boards; who gave me the gifts and the space to grow them. Jeff, Jay and Lisa, Jason, Kendall, Dillon; my in-laws Jimmy and Jo; and my lovely goddaughter, Isla—I love you all more than life itself.

And finally, my darling Randy, my lifeblood, my heart, my Prince Charming. You soldiered through this with me, and I owe you one. Always.